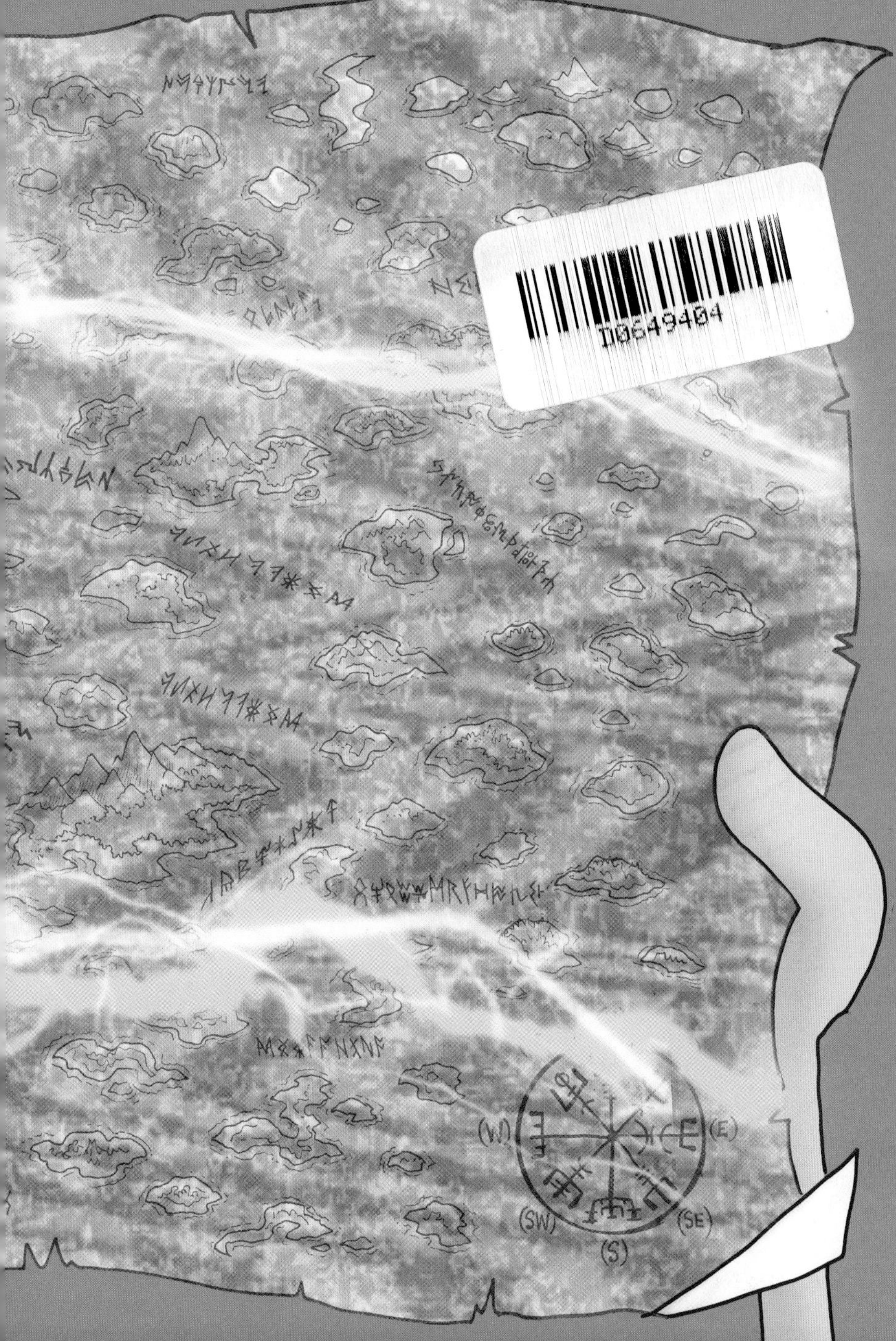
(W)
(E)
(SW)
(S)
(SE)

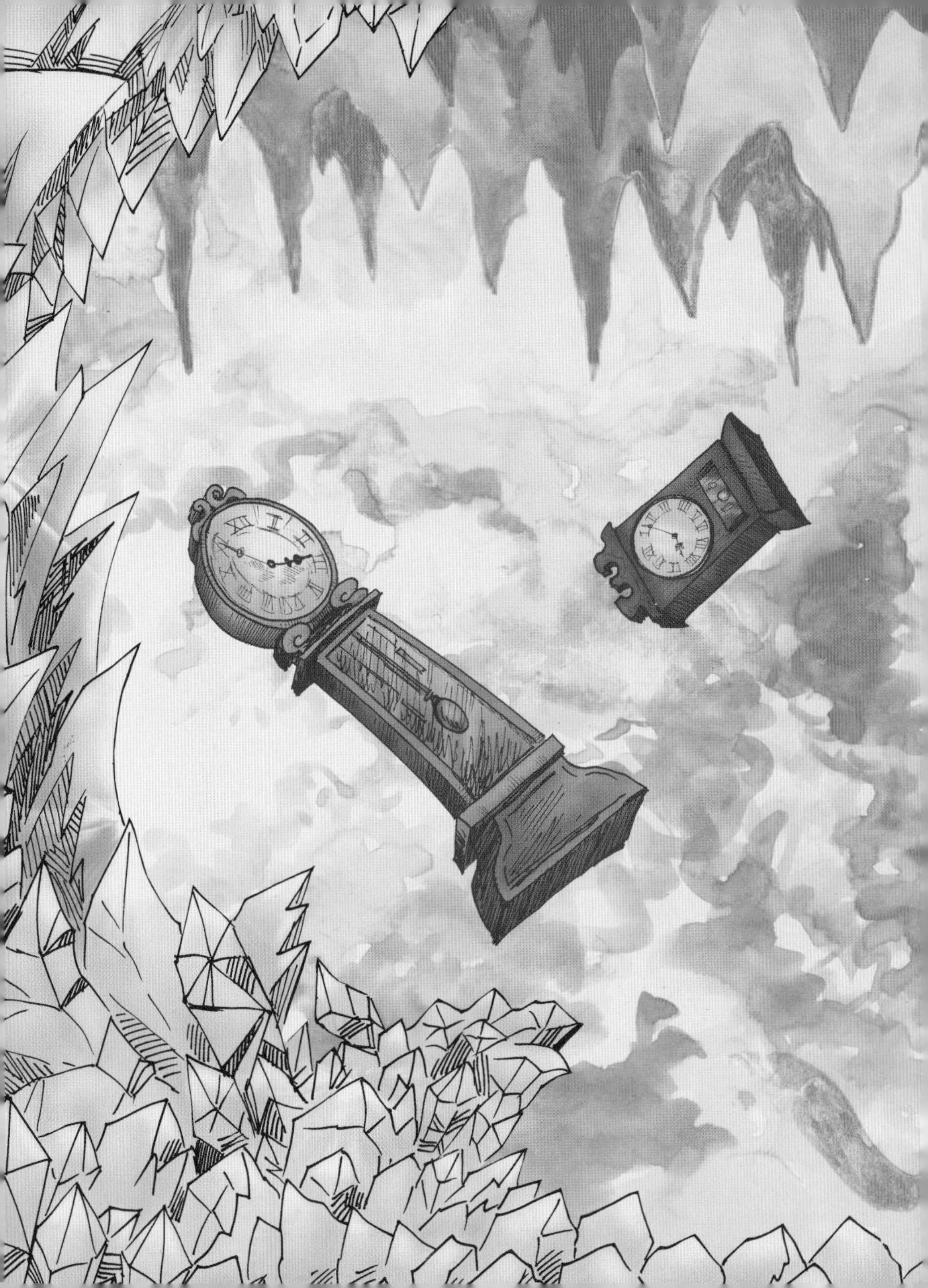

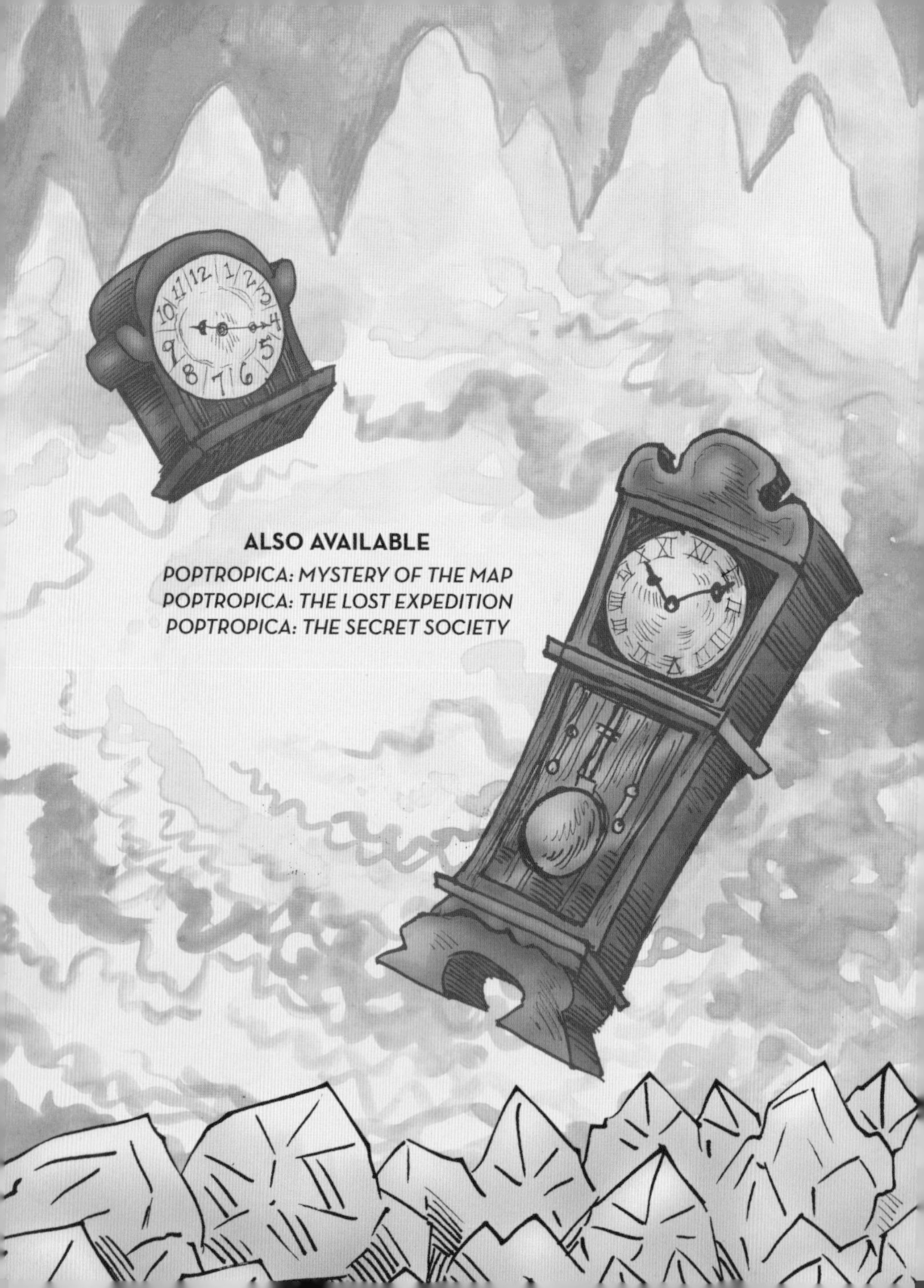

ALSO AVAILABLE

POPTROPICA: MYSTERY OF THE MAP
POPTROPICA: THE LOST EXPEDITION
POPTROPICA: THE SECRET SOCIETY

Poptropica 4

THE END OF TIME

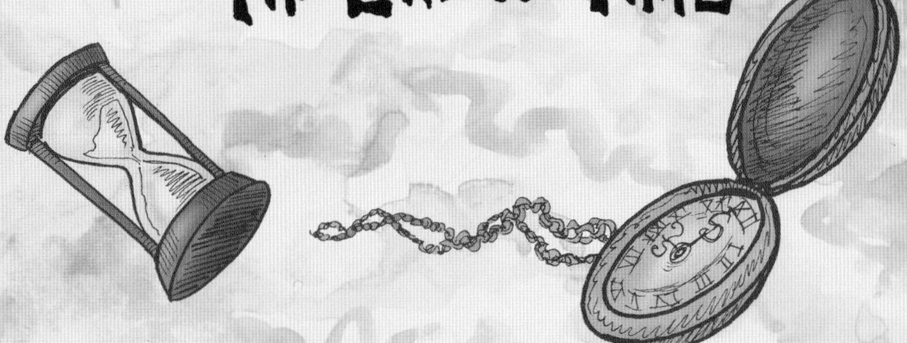

BY
MITCH KRPATA

ILLUSTRATED BY
KORY MERRITT

SERIES BASED ON
A CONCEPT
BY **JEFF KINNEY**

AMULET BOOKS
NEW YORK

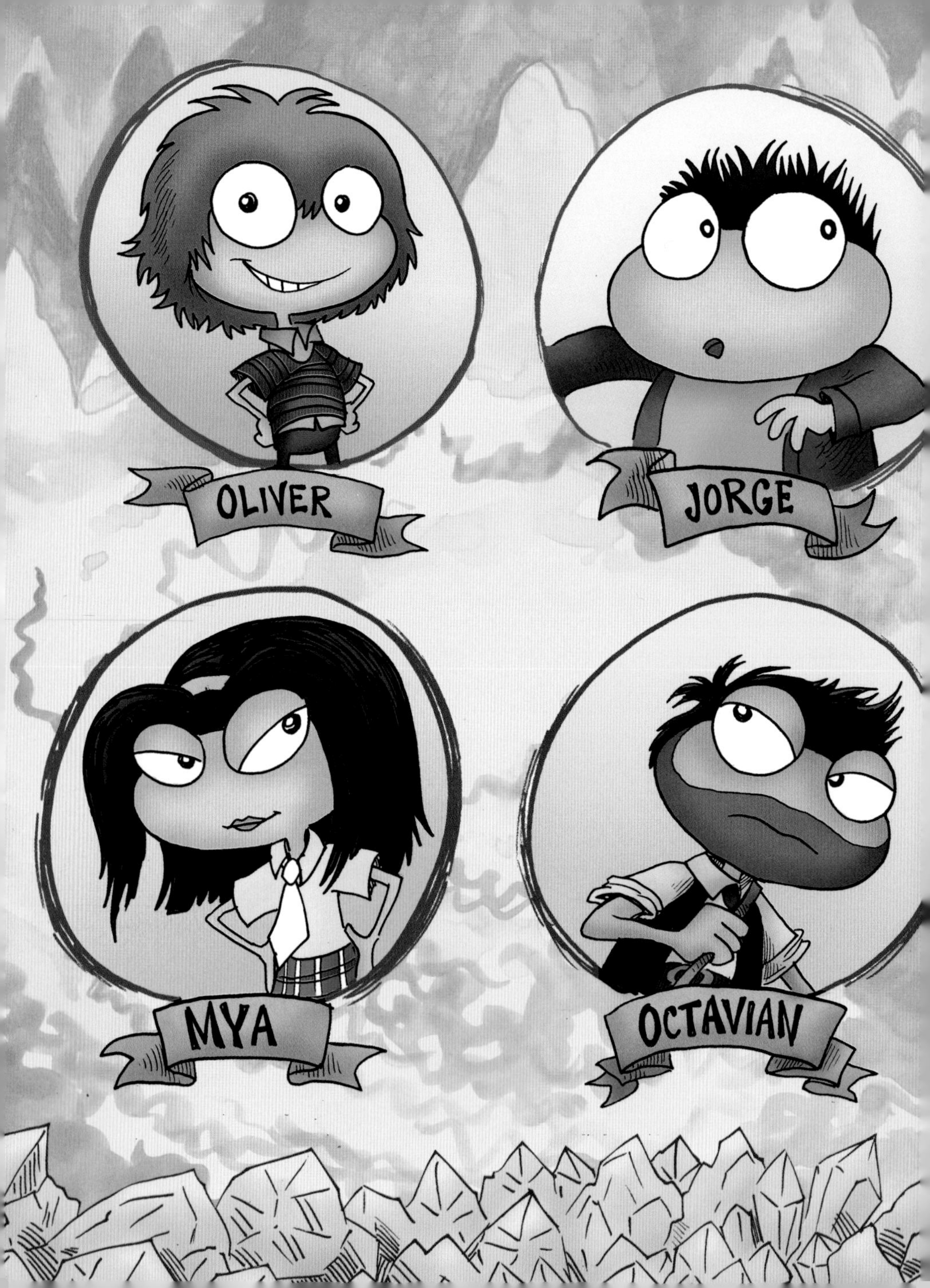
OLIVER
JORGE
MYA
OCTAVIAN

Previously on

Poptropica®

Mya, Oliver, and Jorge destroyed

the Aegis—a stone with the power to

alter time itself—and the Protectors fled the

island world. As Poptropica stands on

the brink of collapse, its fate lies

solely in the trio's hands . . .

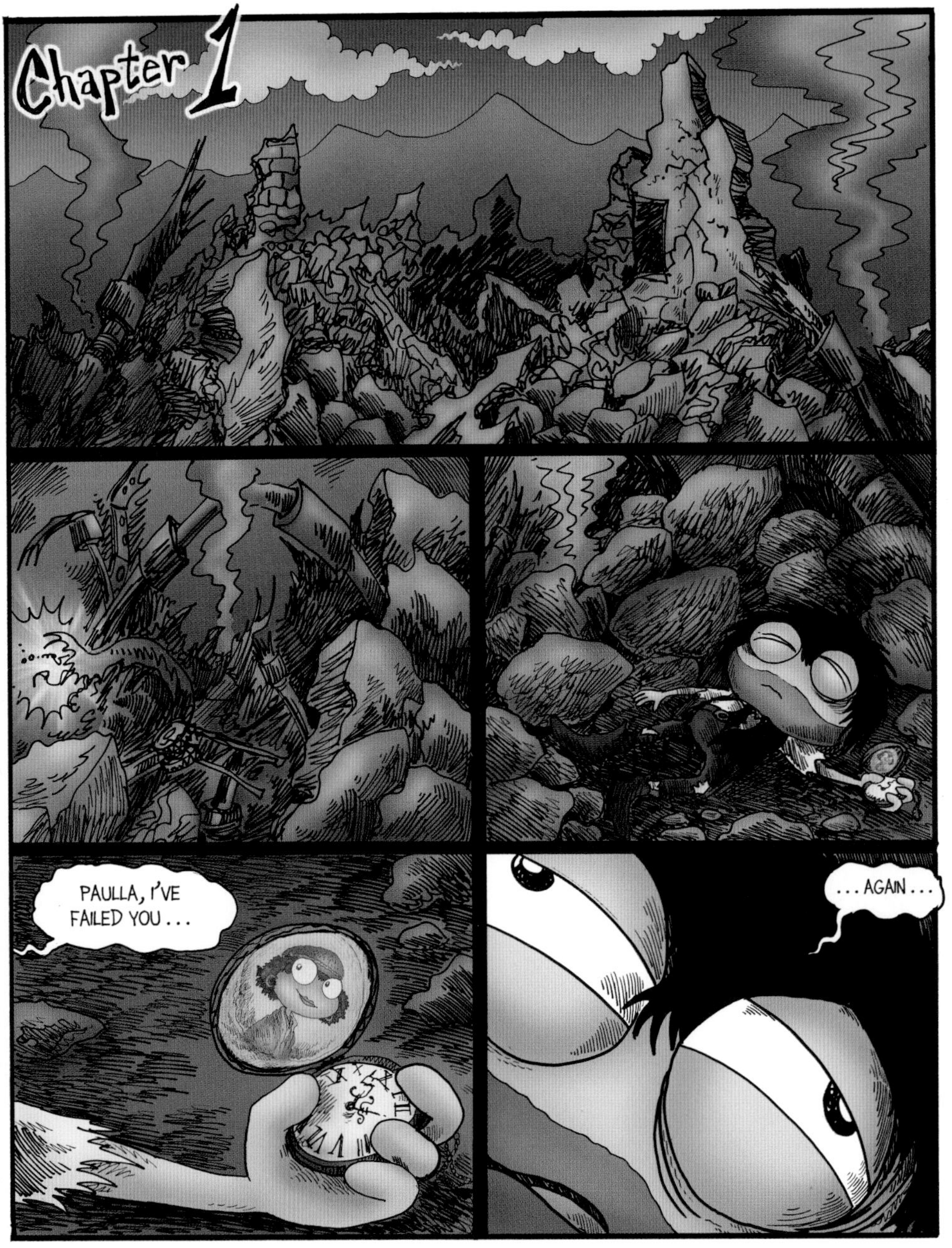
Chapter 1
PAULLA, I'VE FAILED YOU . . .
. . . AGAIN . . .

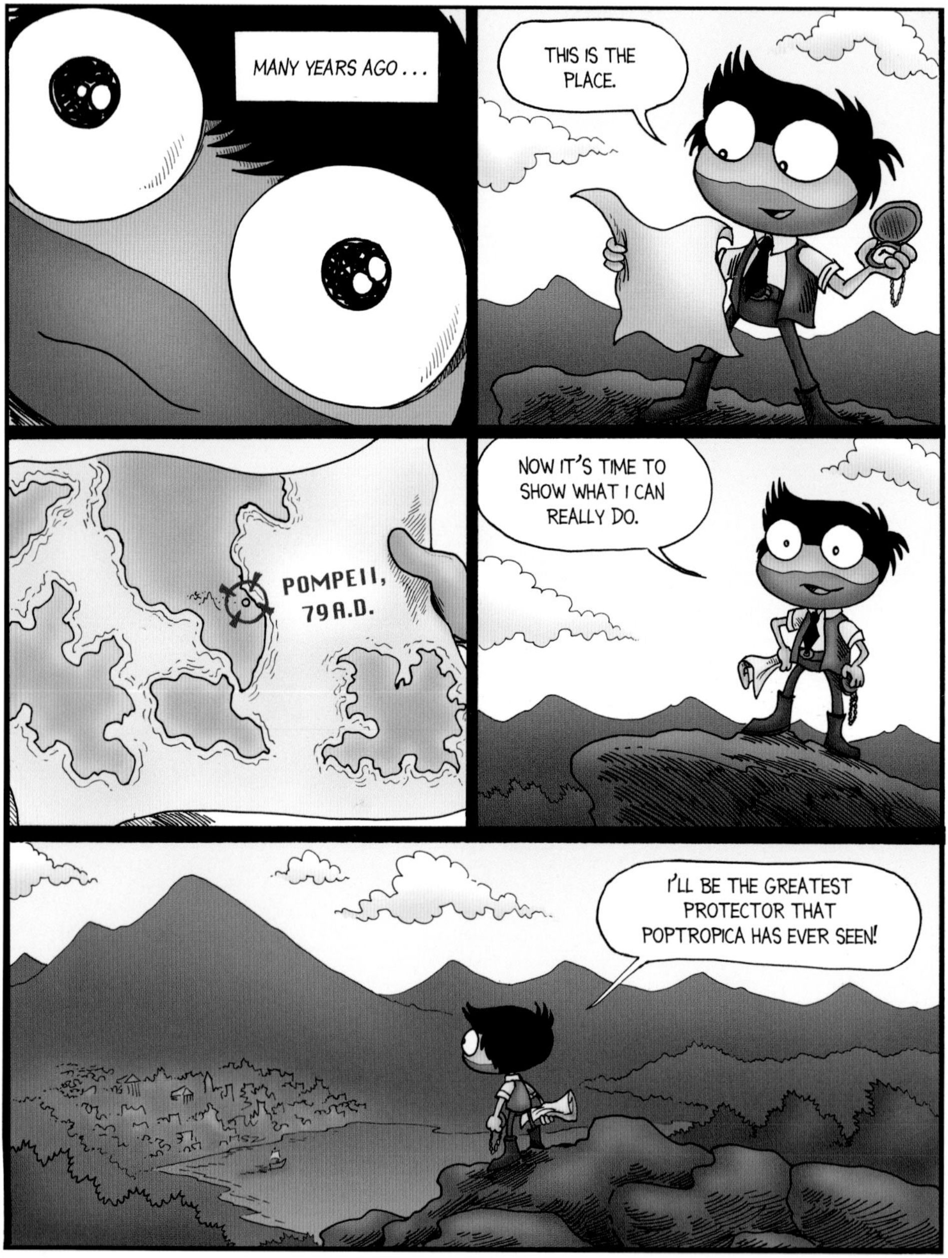
MANY YEARS AGO . . .
THIS IS THE PLACE.
POMPEII, 79 A.D.
NOW IT'S TIME TO SHOW WHAT I CAN REALLY DO.
I'LL BE THE GREATEST PROTECTOR THAT POPTROPICA HAS EVER SEEN!

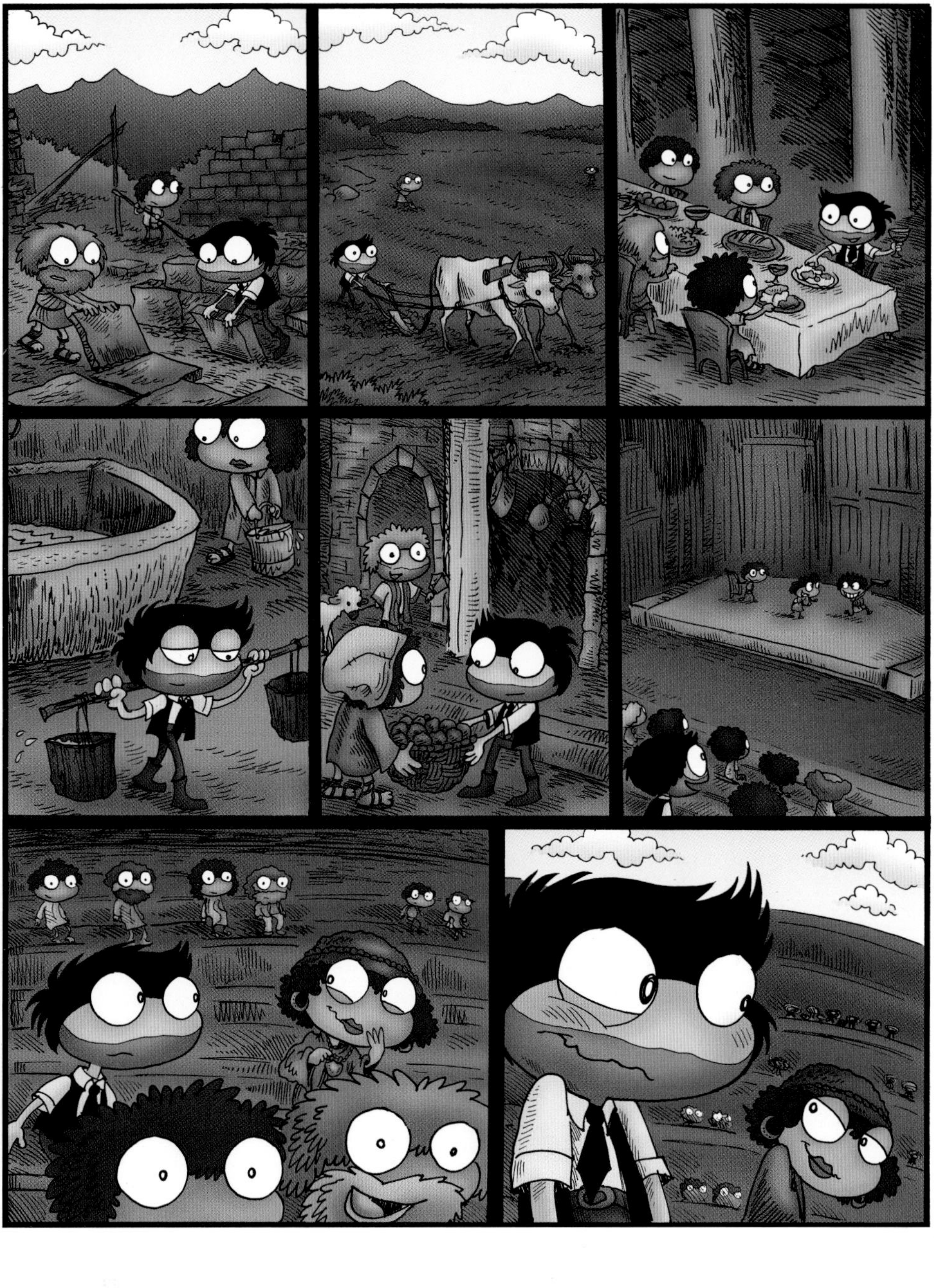

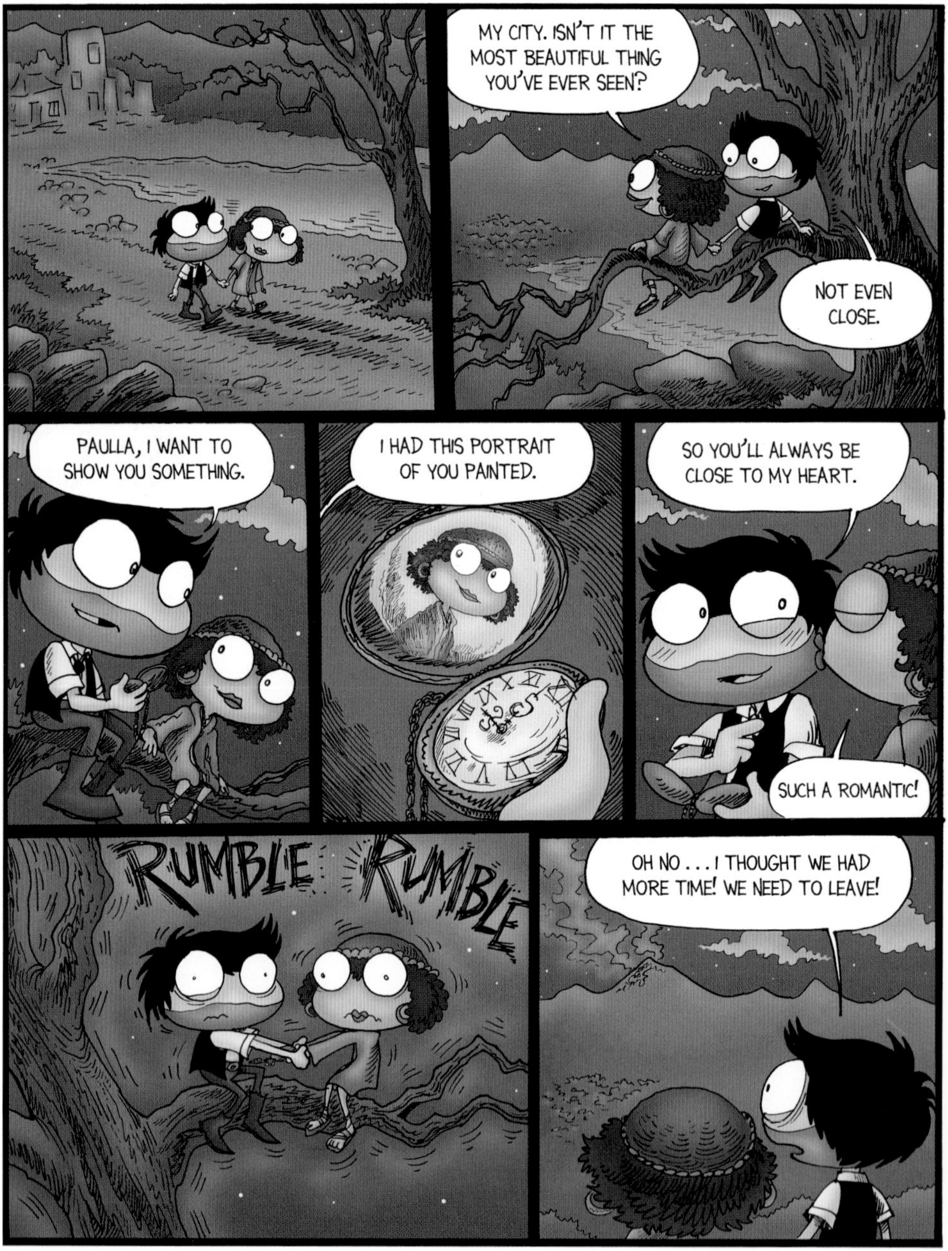
MY CITY. ISN'T IT THE MOST BEAUTIFUL THING YOU'VE EVER SEEN?
NOT EVEN CLOSE.
PAULLA, I WANT TO SHOW YOU SOMETHING.
I HAD THIS PORTRAIT OF YOU PAINTED.
SO YOU'LL ALWAYS BE CLOSE TO MY HEART.
SUCH A ROMANTIC!
RUMBLE RUMBLE
OH NO . . . I THOUGHT WE HAD MORE TIME! WE NEED TO LEAVE!

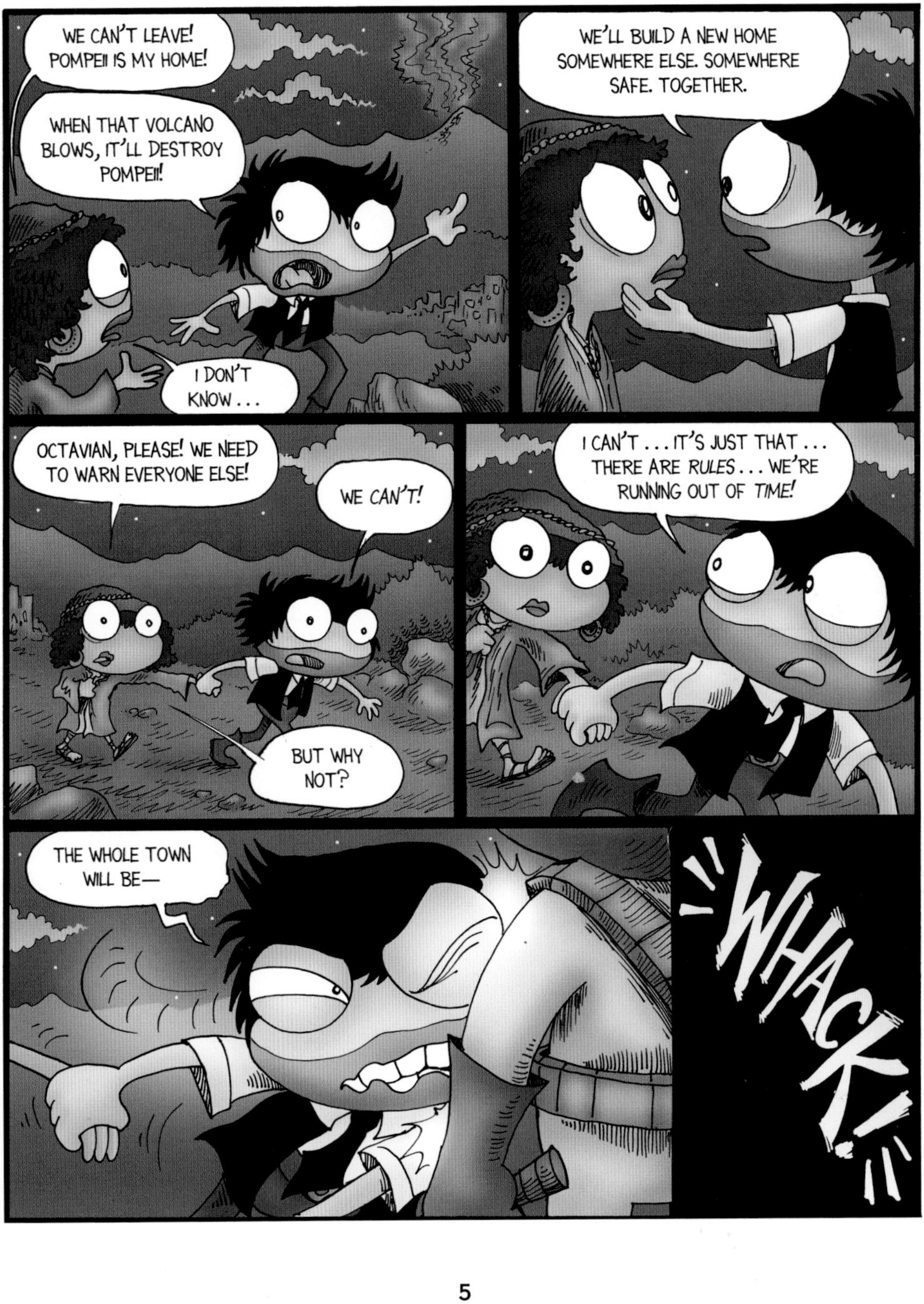
WE CAN'T LEAVE! POMPEII IS MY HOME!
WHEN THAT VOLCANO BLOWS, IT'LL DESTROY POMPEII!
I DON'T KNOW . . .
WE'LL BUILD A NEW HOME SOMEWHERE ELSE. SOMEWHERE SAFE. TOGETHER.
OCTAVIAN, PLEASE! WE NEED TO WARN EVERYONE ELSE!
WE CAN'T!
BUT WHY NOT?
I CAN'T . . . IT'S JUST THAT . . . THERE ARE RULES . . . WE'RE RUNNING OUT OF TIME!
THE WHOLE TOWN WILL BE—
WHACK!

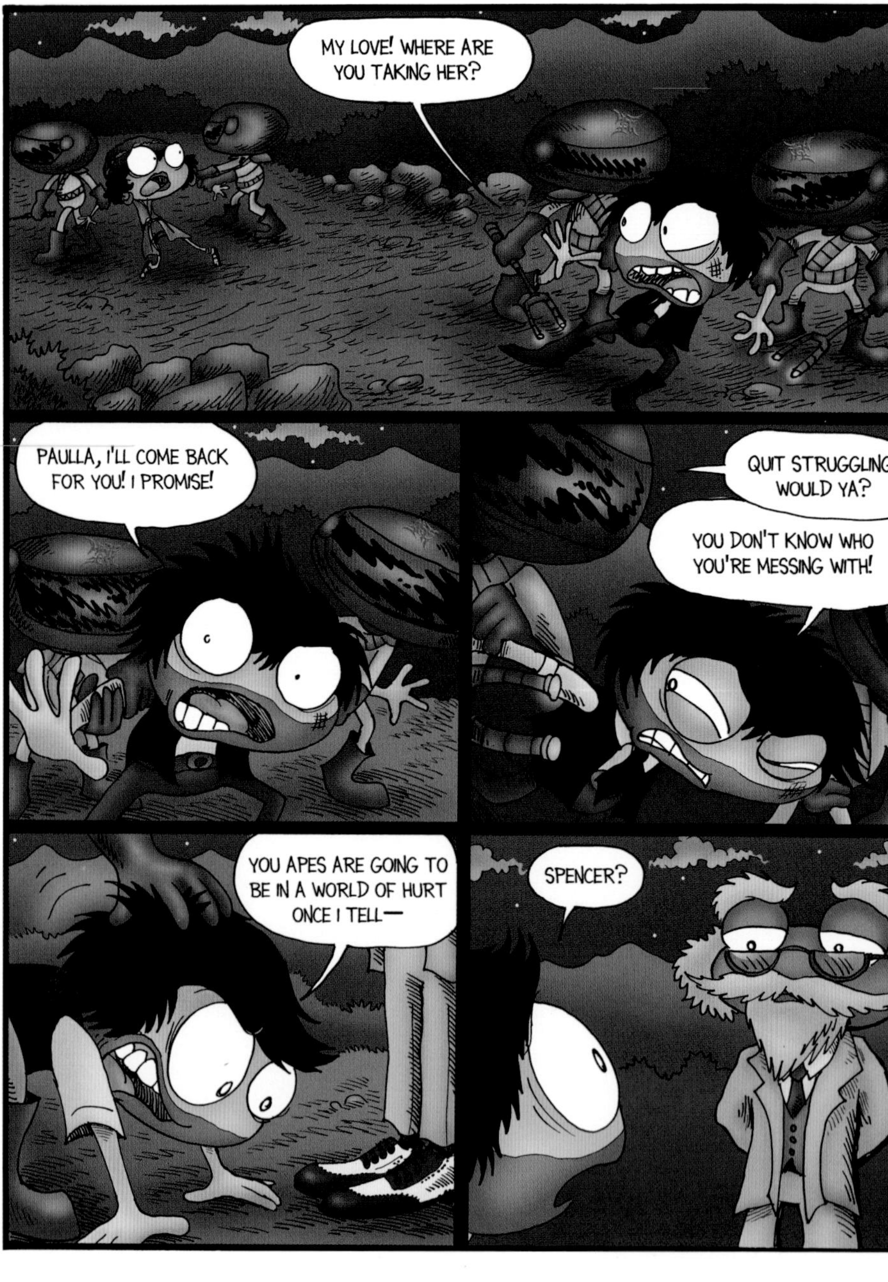
MY LOVE! WHERE ARE YOU TAKING HER?
PAULLA, I'LL COME BACK FOR YOU! I PROMISE!
QUIT STRUGGLING, WOULD YA?
YOU DON'T KNOW WHO YOU'RE MESSING WITH!
YOU APES ARE GOING TO BE IN A WORLD OF HURT ONCE I TELL—
SPENCER?

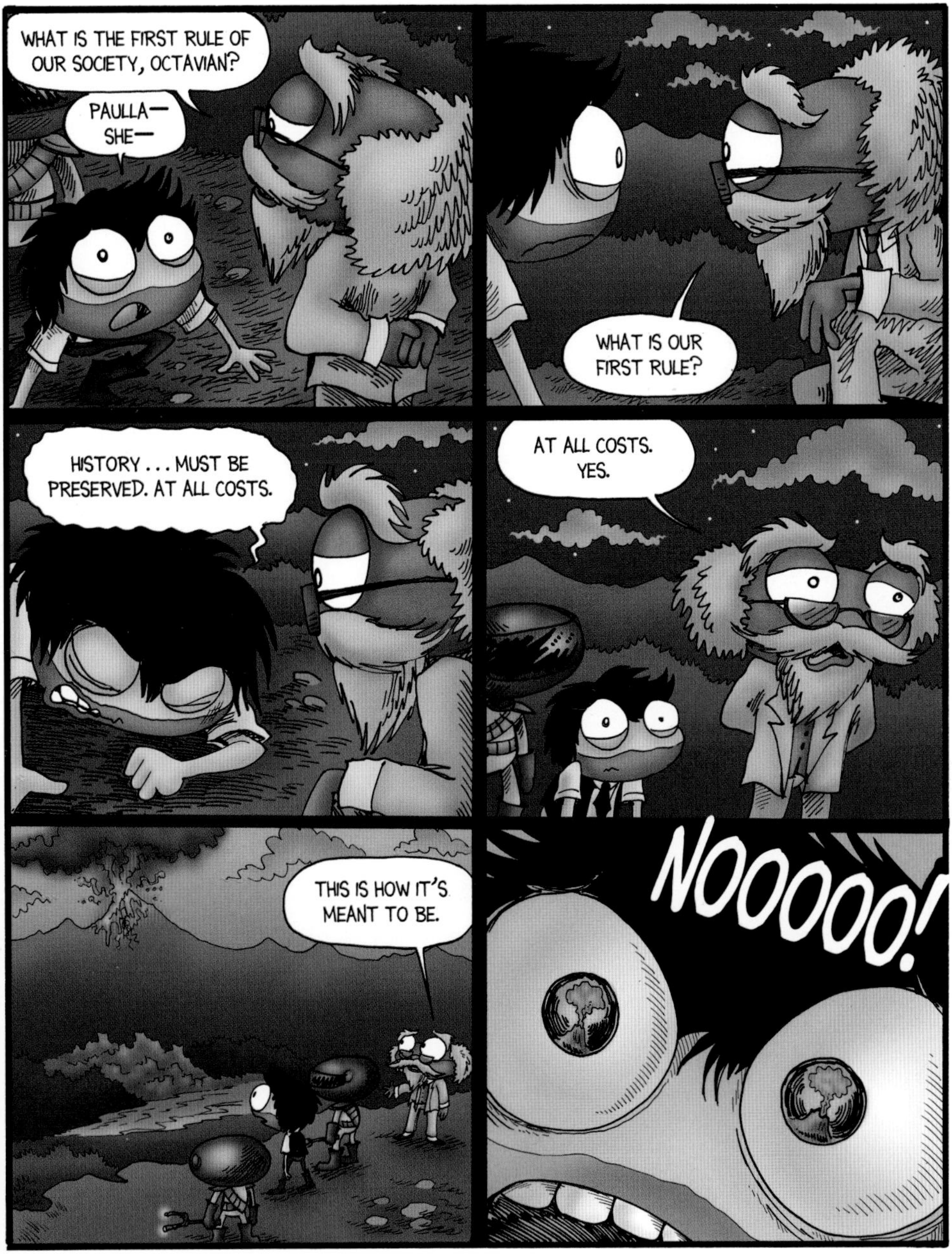
WHAT IS THE FIRST RULE OF OUR SOCIETY, OCTAVIAN?
PAULLA— SHE—
WHAT IS OUR FIRST RULE?
HISTORY . . . MUST BE PRESERVED. AT ALL COSTS.
AT ALL COSTS. YES.
THIS IS HOW IT'S MEANT TO BE.
NOOOOO!

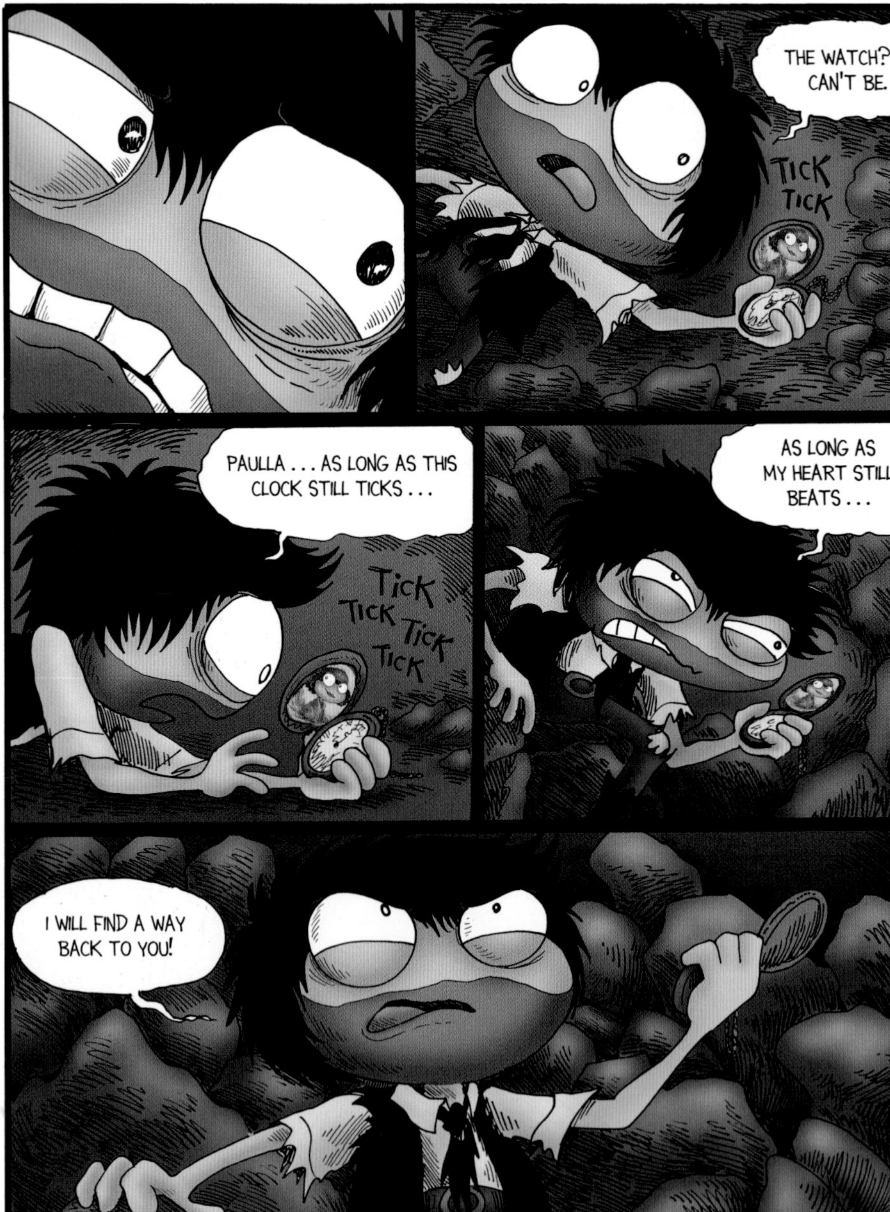
THE WATCH? IT CAN'T BE.
TICK TICK
PAULLA . . . AS LONG AS THIS CLOCK STILL TICKS . . .
TICK TICK TICK TICK
AS LONG AS MY HEART STILL BEATS . . .
I WILL FIND A WAY BACK TO YOU!

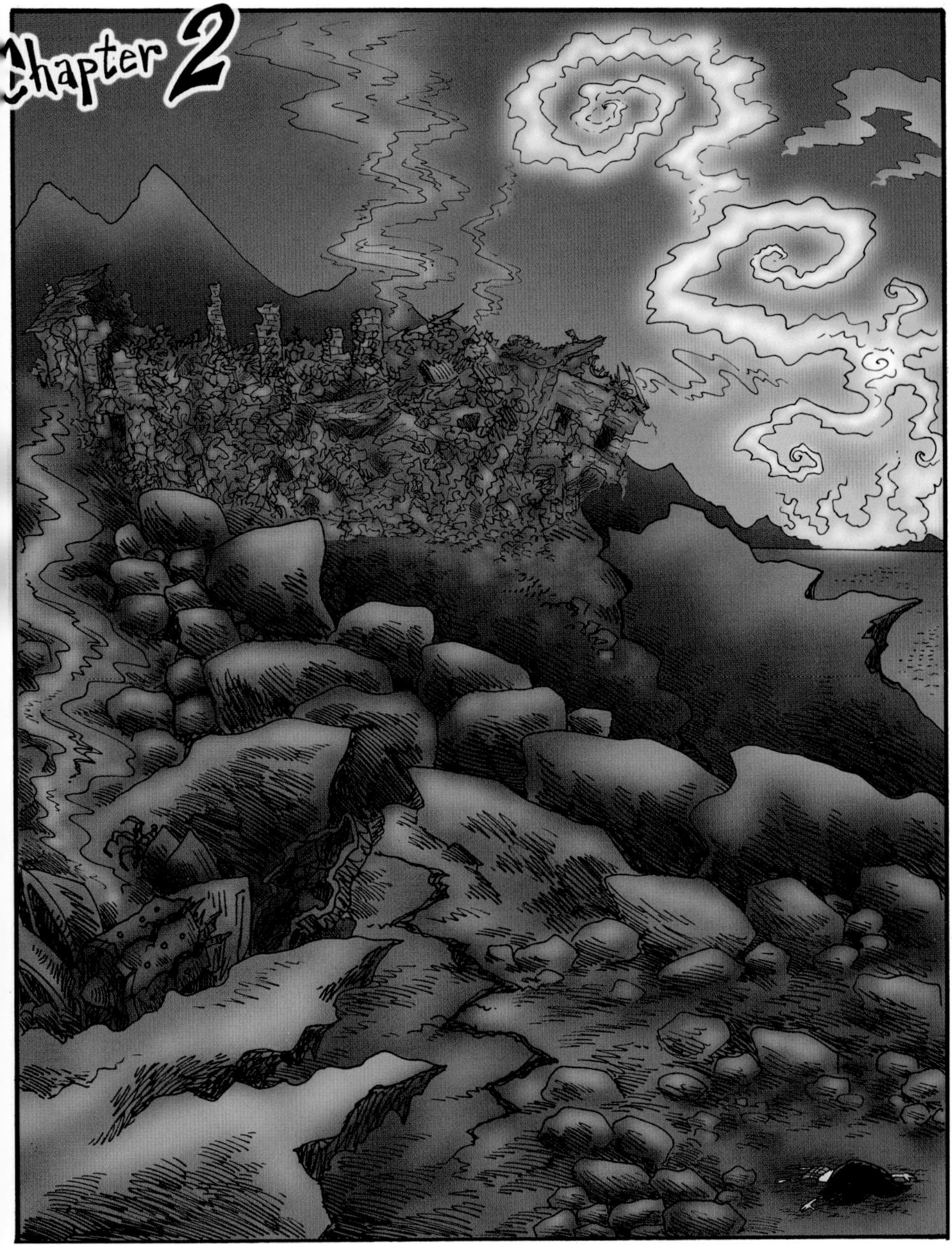
Chapter 2

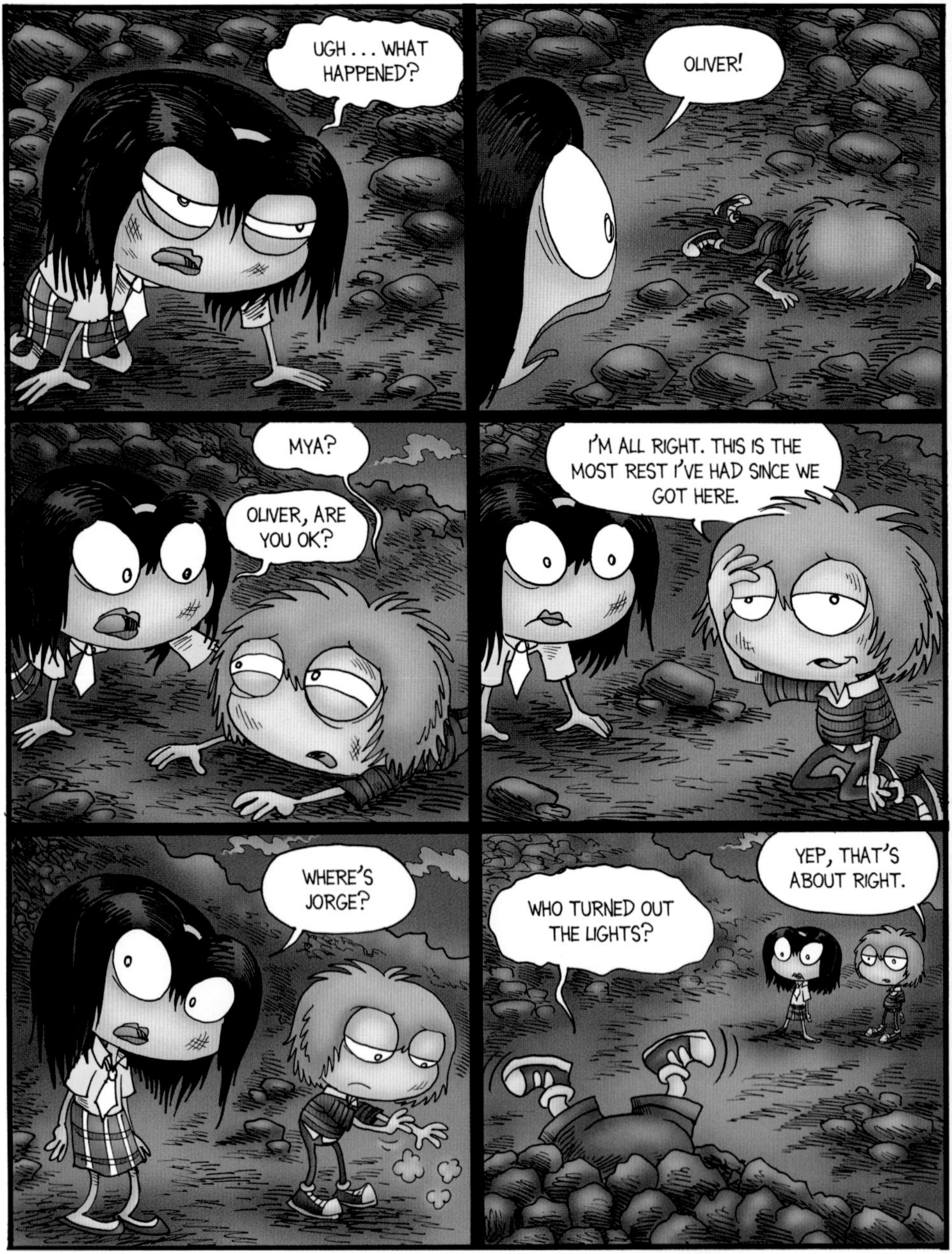
UGH . . . WHAT HAPPENED?
OLIVER!
MYA?
OLIVER, ARE YOU OK?
I'M ALL RIGHT. THIS IS THE MOST REST I'VE HAD SINCE WE GOT HERE.
WHERE'S JORGE?
WHO TURNED OUT THE LIGHTS?
YEP, THAT'S ABOUT RIGHT.

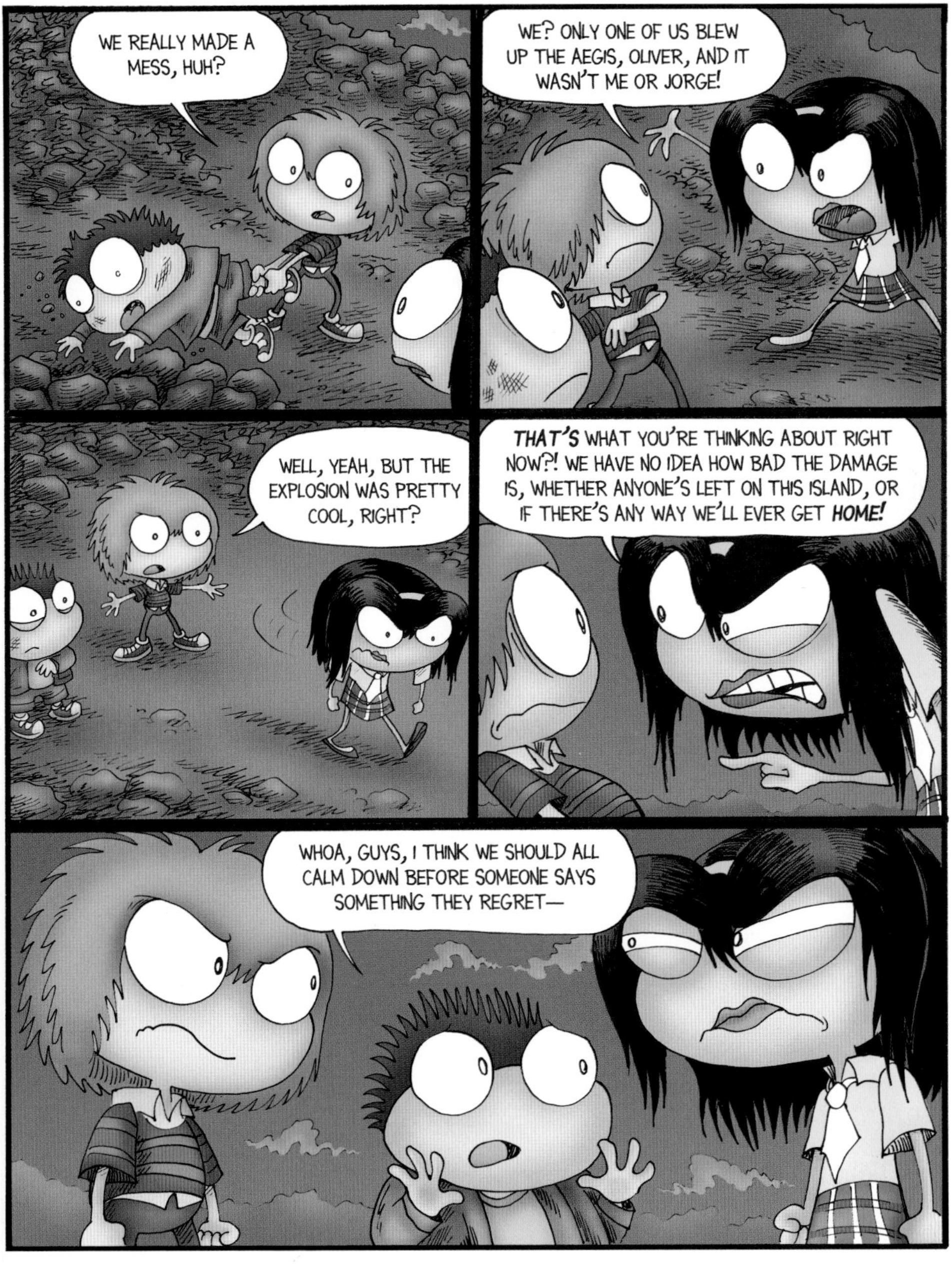
WE REALLY MADE A MESS, HUH?
WE? ONLY ONE OF US BLEW UP THE AEGIS, OLIVER, AND IT WASN'T ME OR JORGE!
WELL, YEAH, BUT THE EXPLOSION WAS PRETTY COOL, RIGHT?
THAT'S WHAT YOU'RE THINKING ABOUT RIGHT NOW?! WE HAVE NO IDEA HOW BAD THE DAMAGE IS, WHETHER ANYONE'S LEFT ON THIS ISLAND, OR IF THERE'S ANY WAY WE'LL EVER GET HOME!
WHOA, GUYS, I THINK WE SHOULD ALL CALM DOWN BEFORE SOMEONE SAYS SOMETHING THEY REGRET—

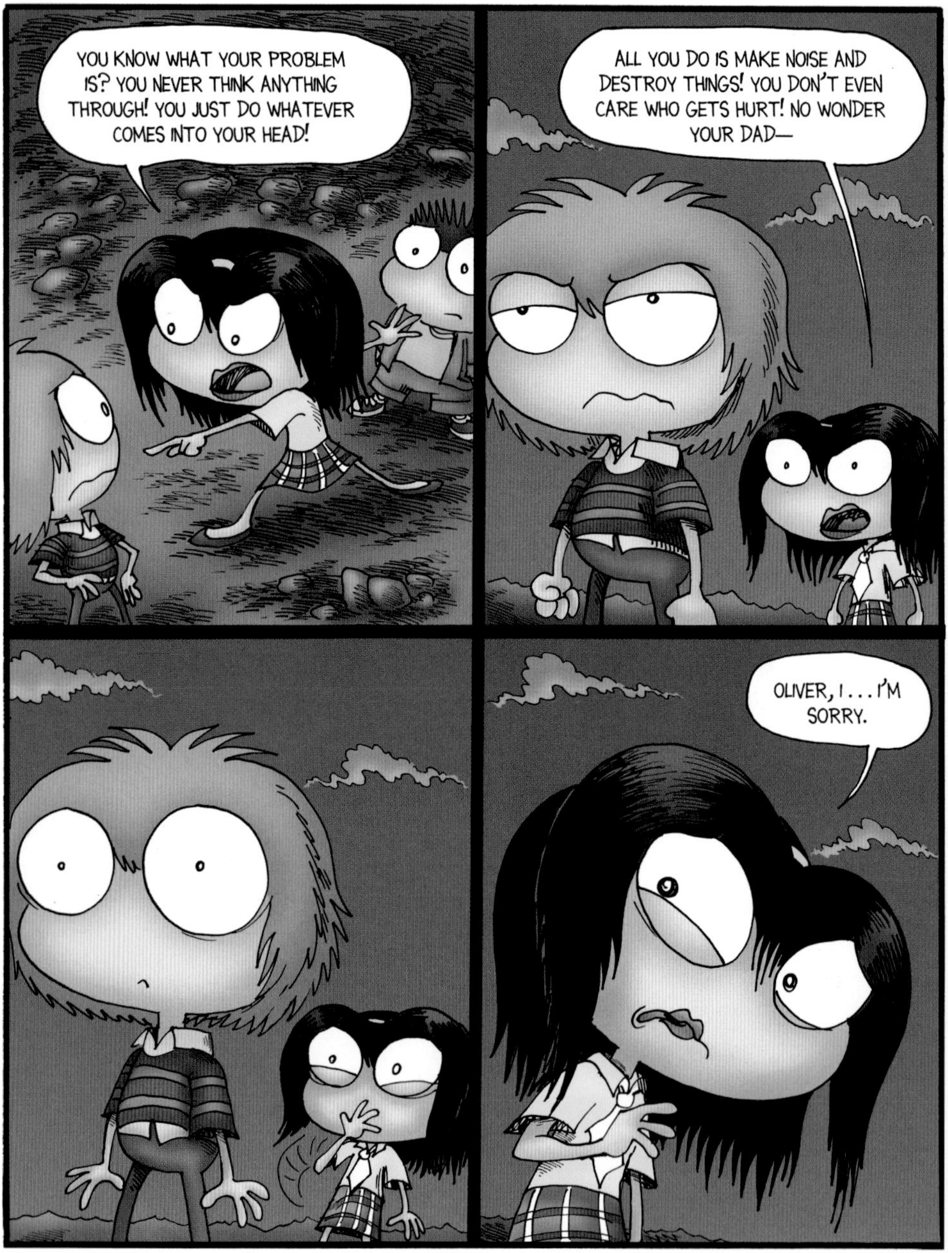
YOU KNOW WHAT YOUR PROBLEM IS? YOU NEVER THINK ANYTHING THROUGH! YOU JUST DO WHATEVER COMES INTO YOUR HEAD!
ALL YOU DO IS MAKE NOISE AND DESTROY THINGS! YOU DON'T EVEN CARE WHO GETS HURT! NO WONDER YOUR DAD—
OLIVER, I . . . I'M SORRY.

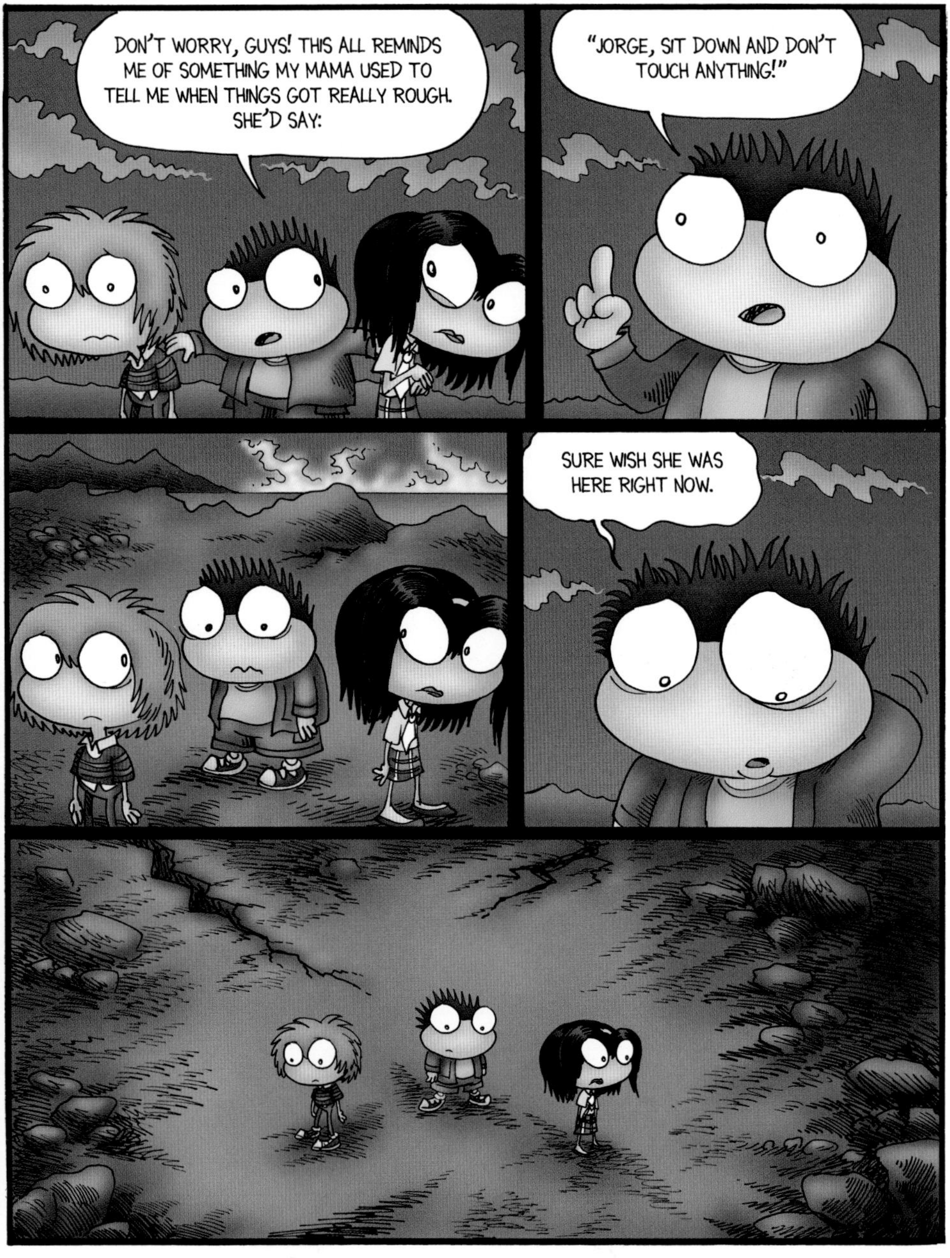
DON'T WORRY, GUYS! THIS ALL REMINDS ME OF SOMETHING MY MAMA USED TO TELL ME WHEN THINGS GOT REALLY ROUGH. SHE'D SAY:
"JORGE, SIT DOWN AND DON'T TOUCH ANYTHING!"
SURE WISH SHE WAS HERE RIGHT NOW.

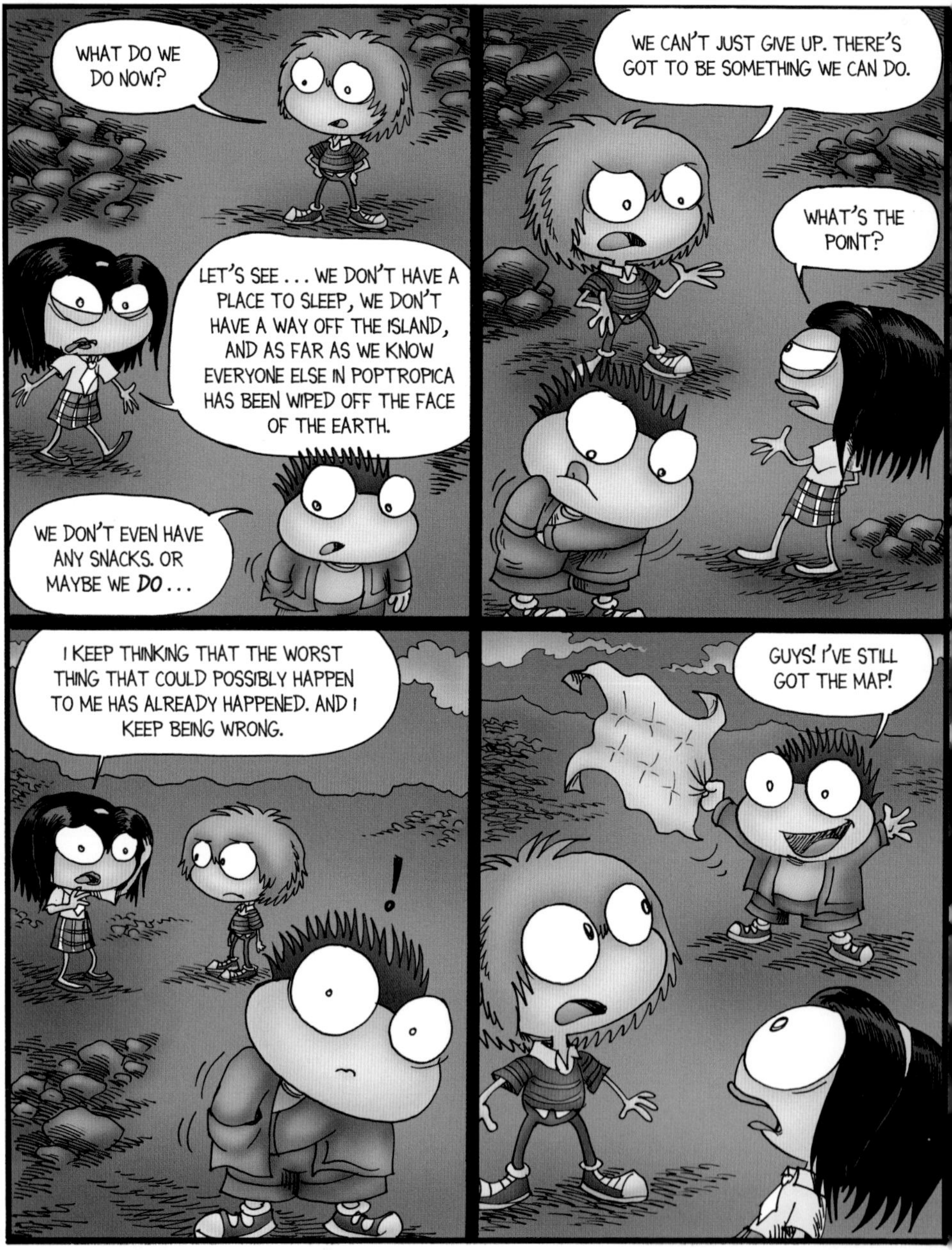
WHAT DO WE DO NOW?
LET'S SEE . . . WE DON'T HAVE A PLACE TO SLEEP, WE DON'T HAVE A WAY OFF THE ISLAND, AND AS FAR AS WE KNOW EVERYONE ELSE IN POPTROPICA HAS BEEN WIPED OFF THE FACE OF THE EARTH.
WE DON'T EVEN HAVE ANY SNACKS. OR MAYBE WE *DO* . . .
WE CAN'T JUST GIVE UP. THERE'S GOT TO BE SOMETHING WE CAN DO.
WHAT'S THE POINT?
I KEEP THINKING THAT THE WORST THING THAT COULD POSSIBLY HAPPEN TO ME HAS ALREADY HAPPENED. AND I KEEP BEING WRONG.
!
GUYS! I'VE STILL GOT THE MAP!

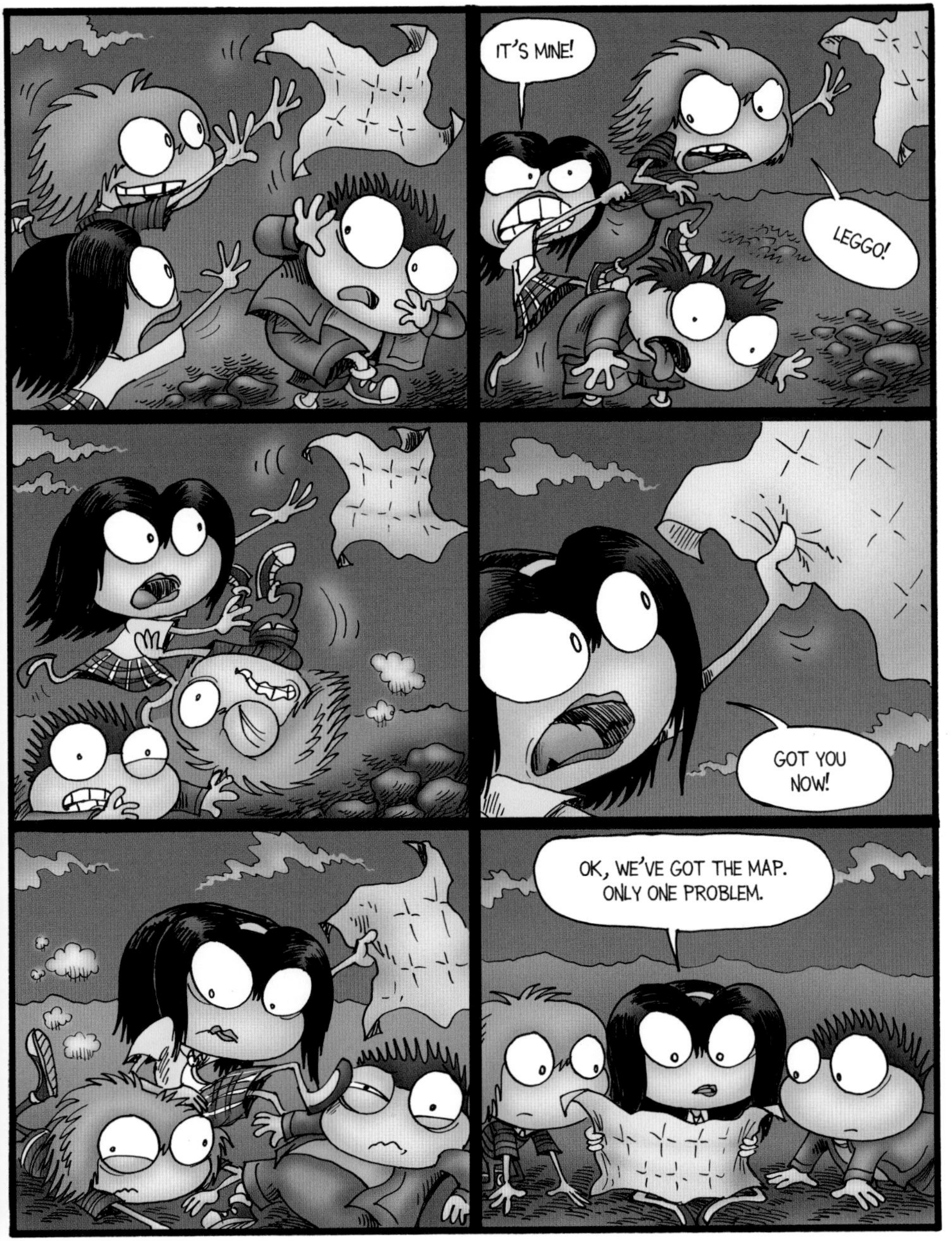
IT'S MINE!
LEGGO!
GOT YOU NOW!
OK, WE'VE GOT THE MAP. ONLY ONE PROBLEM.

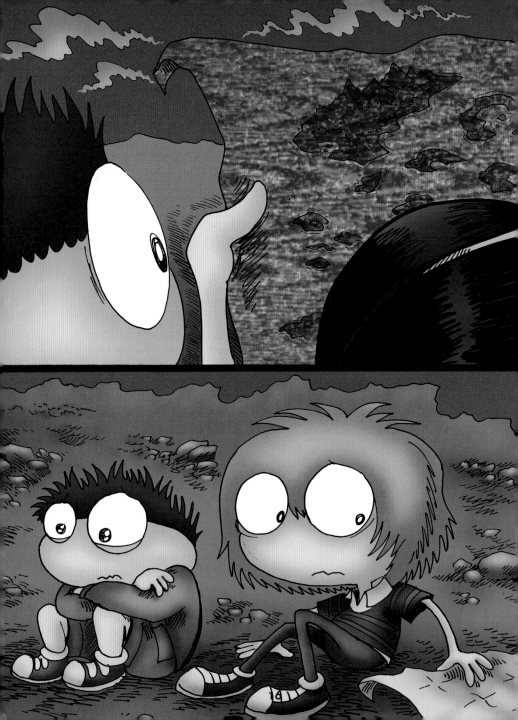

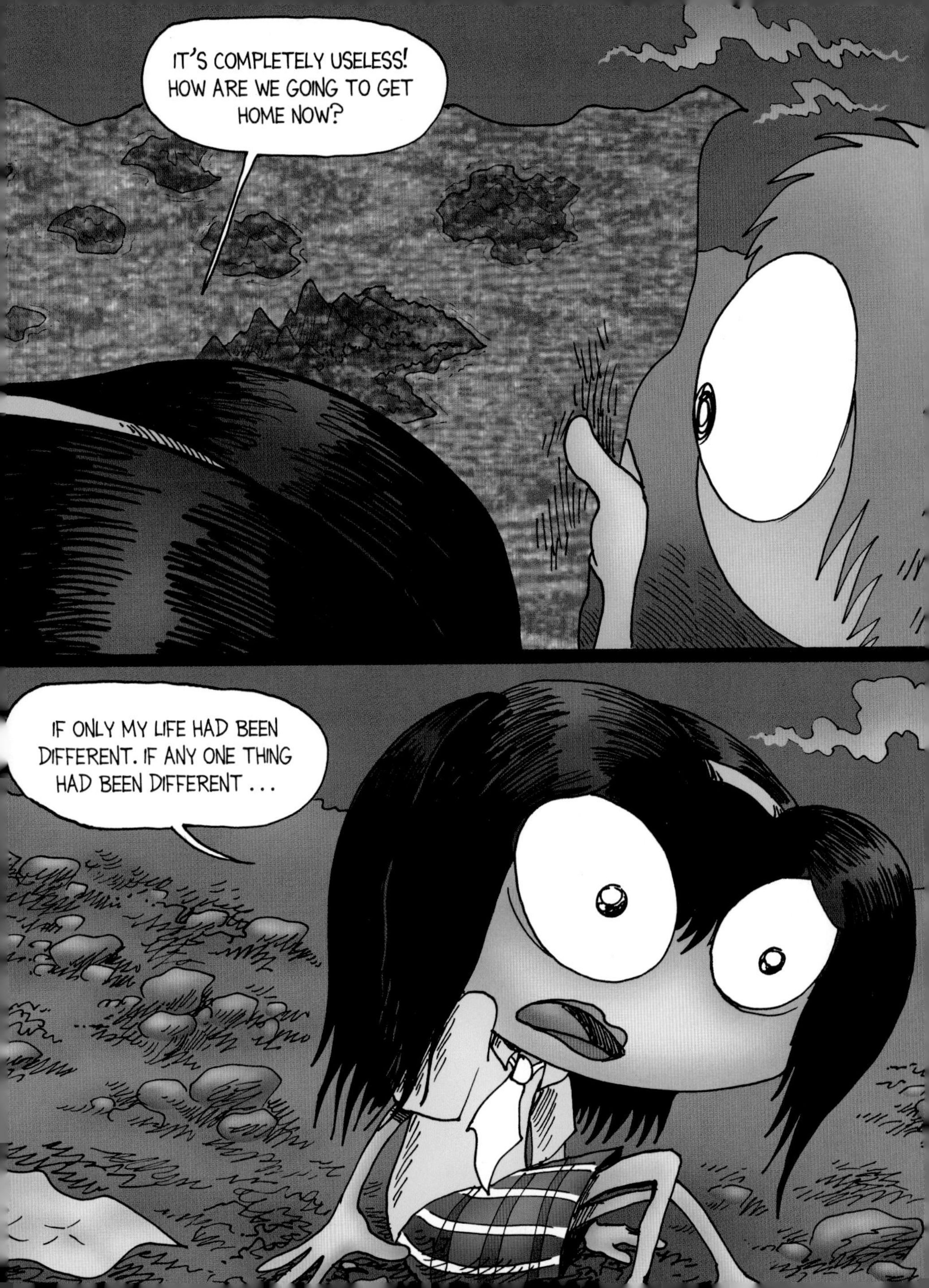
IT'S COMPLETELY USELESS! HOW ARE WE GOING TO GET HOME NOW?
IF ONLY MY LIFE HAD BEEN DIFFERENT. IF ANY ONE THING HAD BEEN DIFFERENT . . .

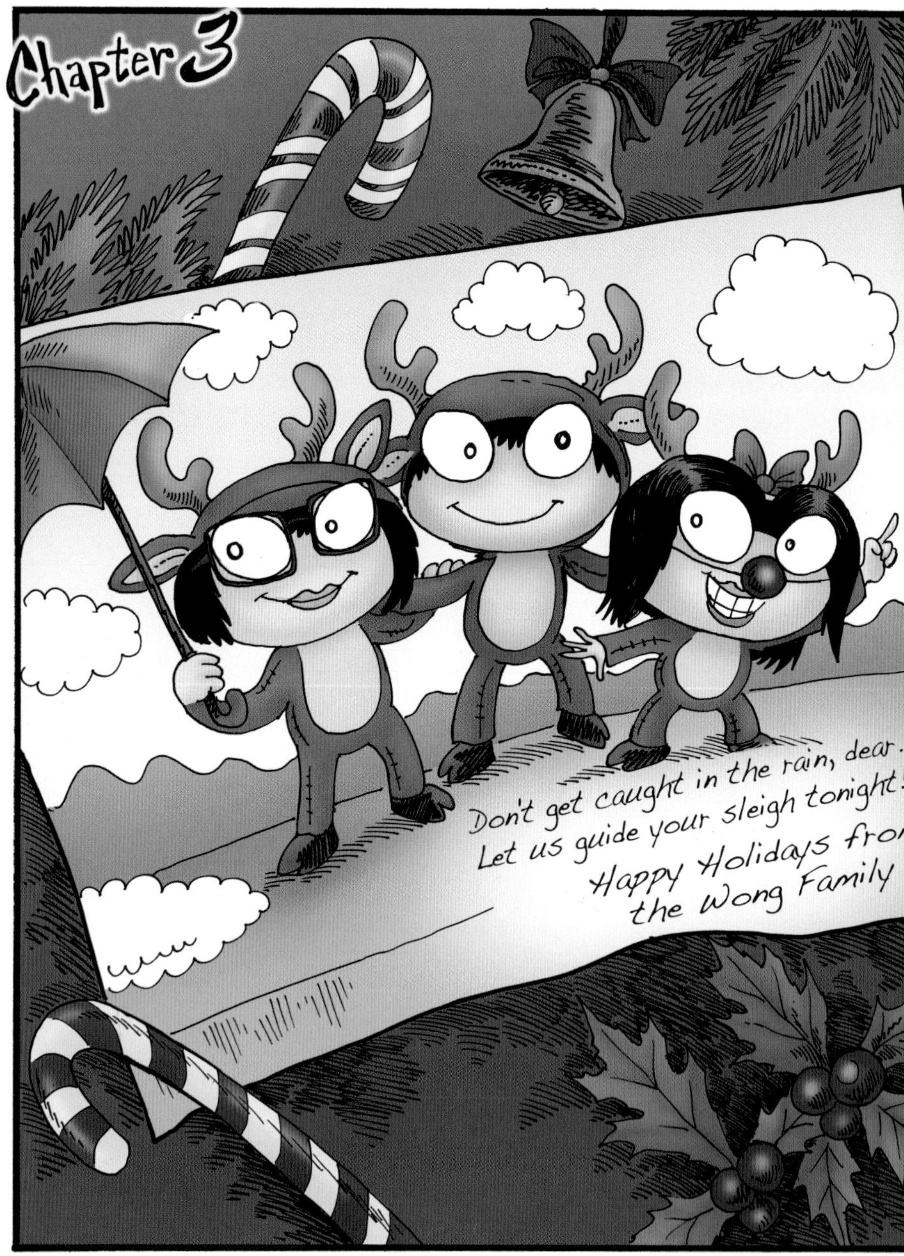
Chapter 3
Don't get caught in the rain, dear.
Let us guide your sleigh tonight!
Happy Holidays from
the Wong Family

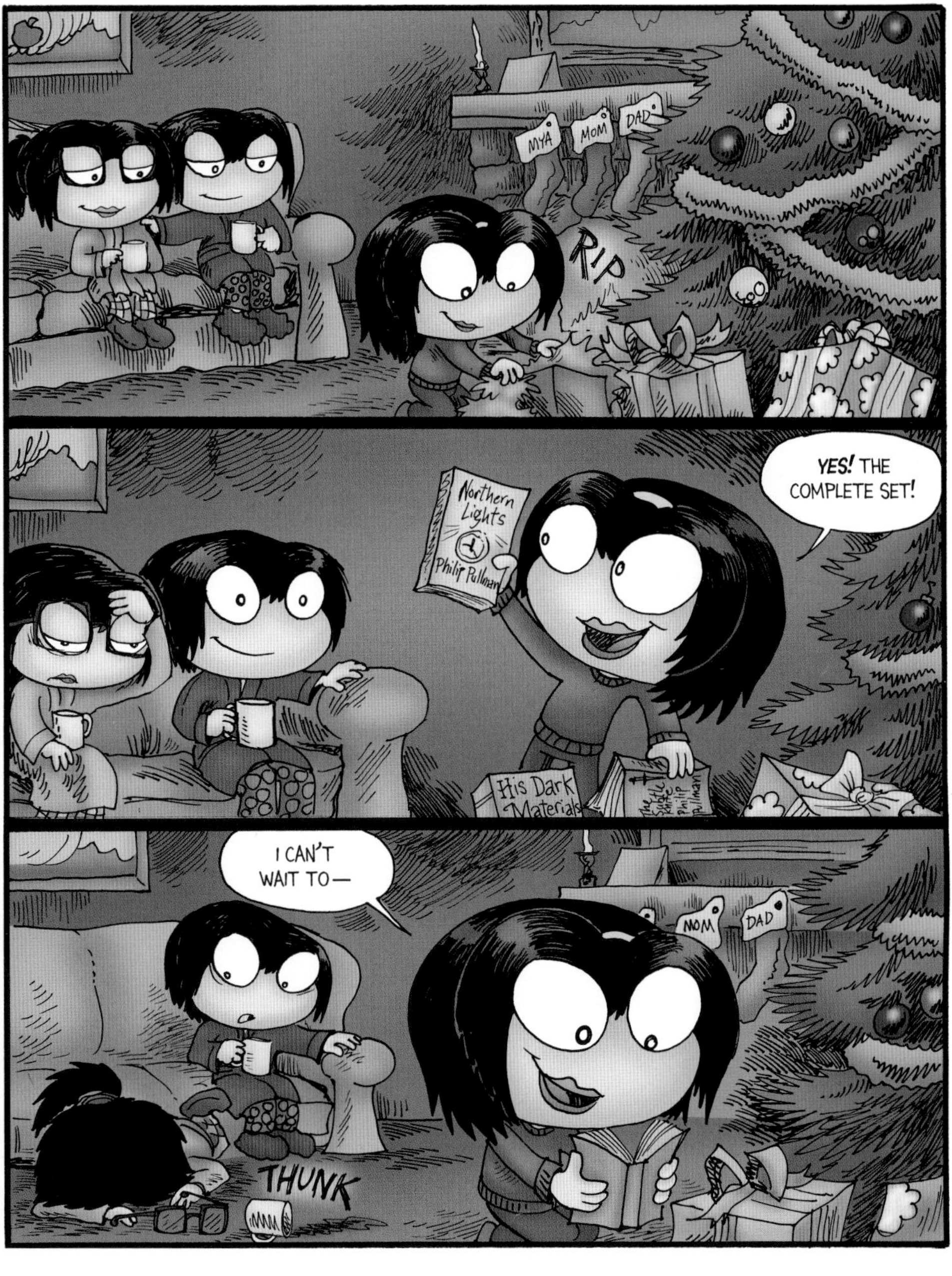
MYA
MOM
DAD
RIP
Northern Lights
Philip Pullman
YES! THE COMPLETE SET!
His Dark Materials
The Subtle Knife
Philip Pullman
I CAN'T WAIT TO—
MOM
DAD
THUNK

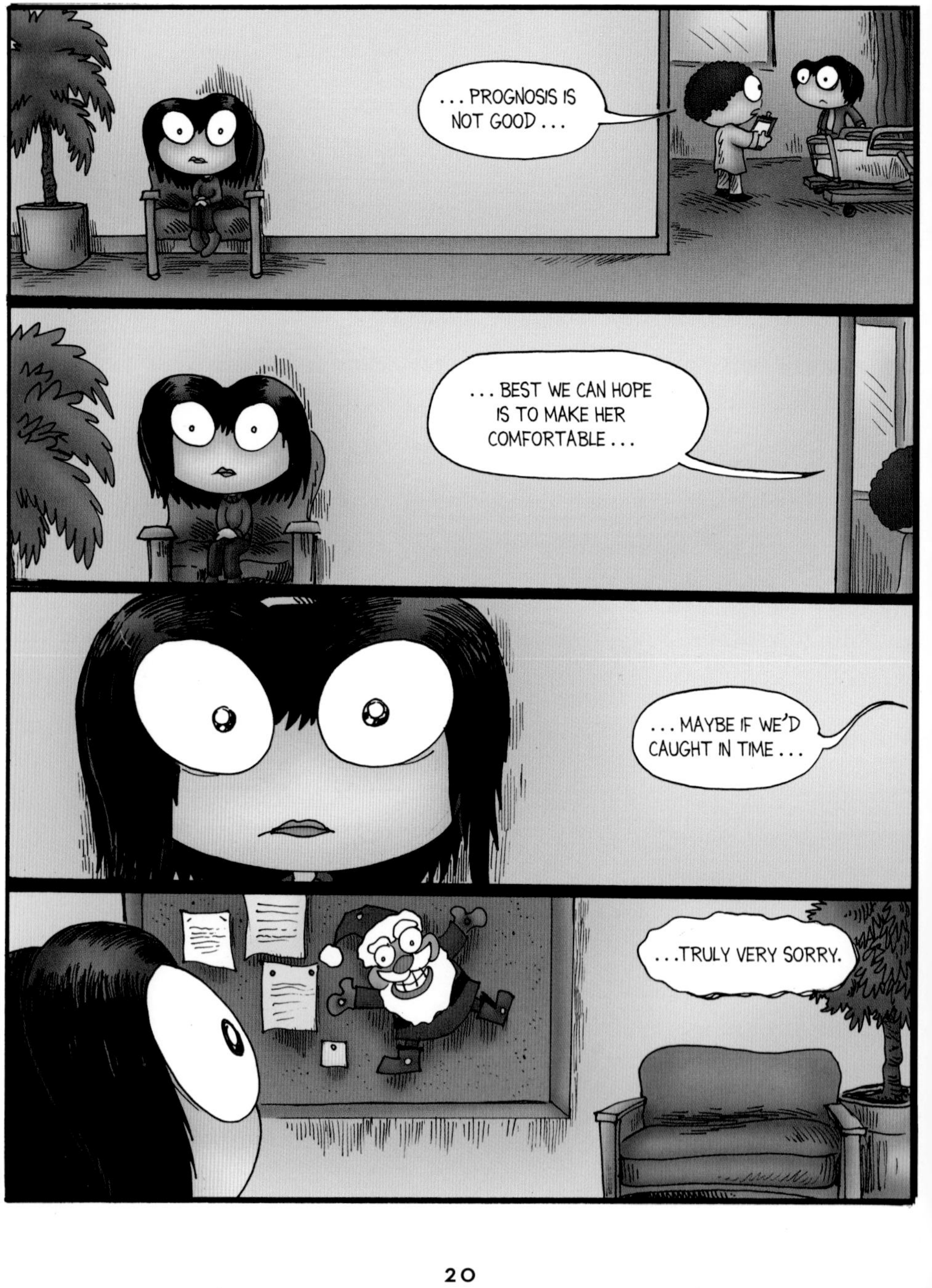
. . . PROGNOSIS IS NOT GOOD . . .
. . . BEST WE CAN HOPE IS TO MAKE HER COMFORTABLE . . .
. . . MAYBE IF WE'D CAUGHT IN TIME . . .
. . .TRULY VERY SORRY.

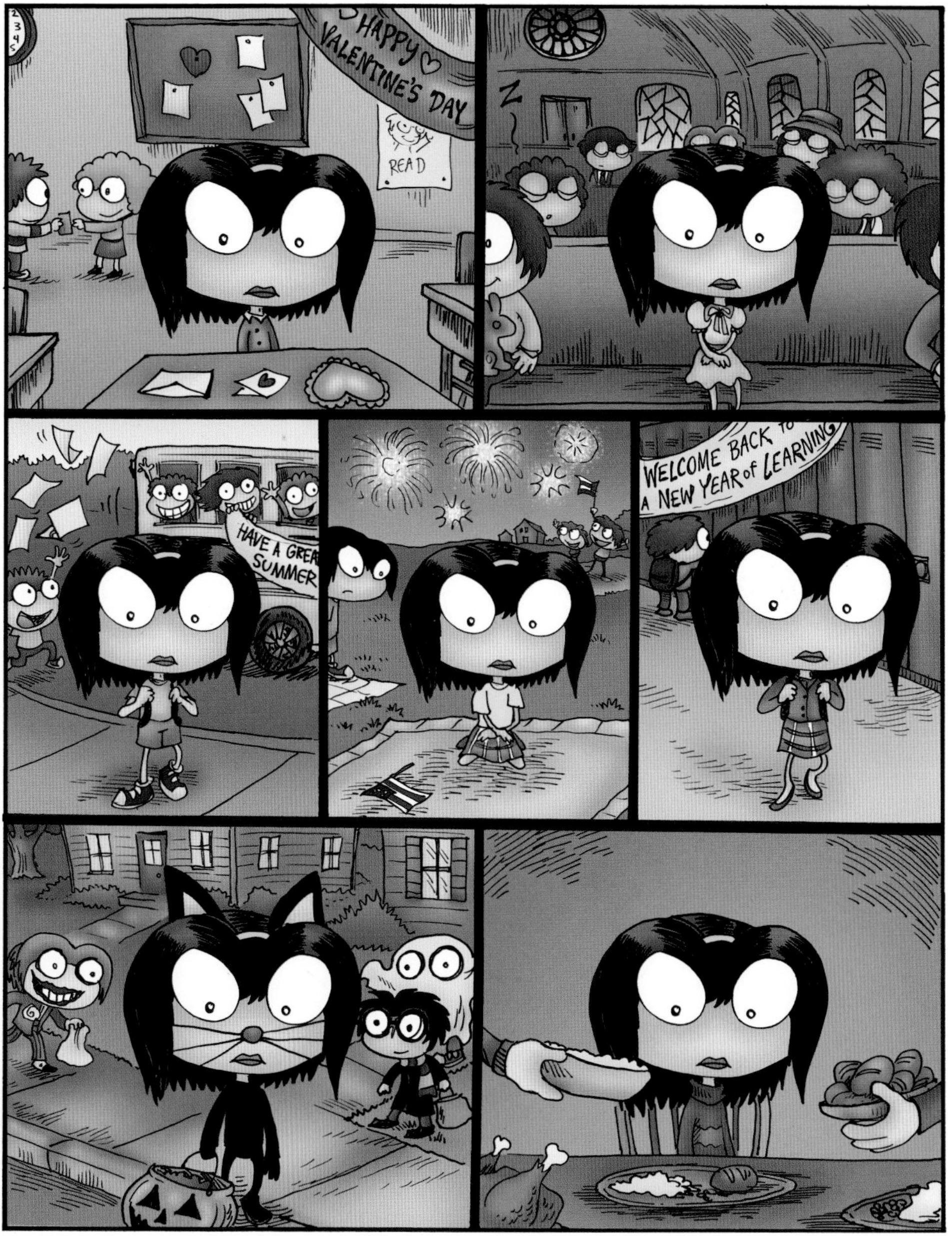
HAPPY VALENTINE'S DAY
READ
Z
HAVE A GREA
SUMMER
WELCOME BACK TO
A NEW YEAR of LEARNING

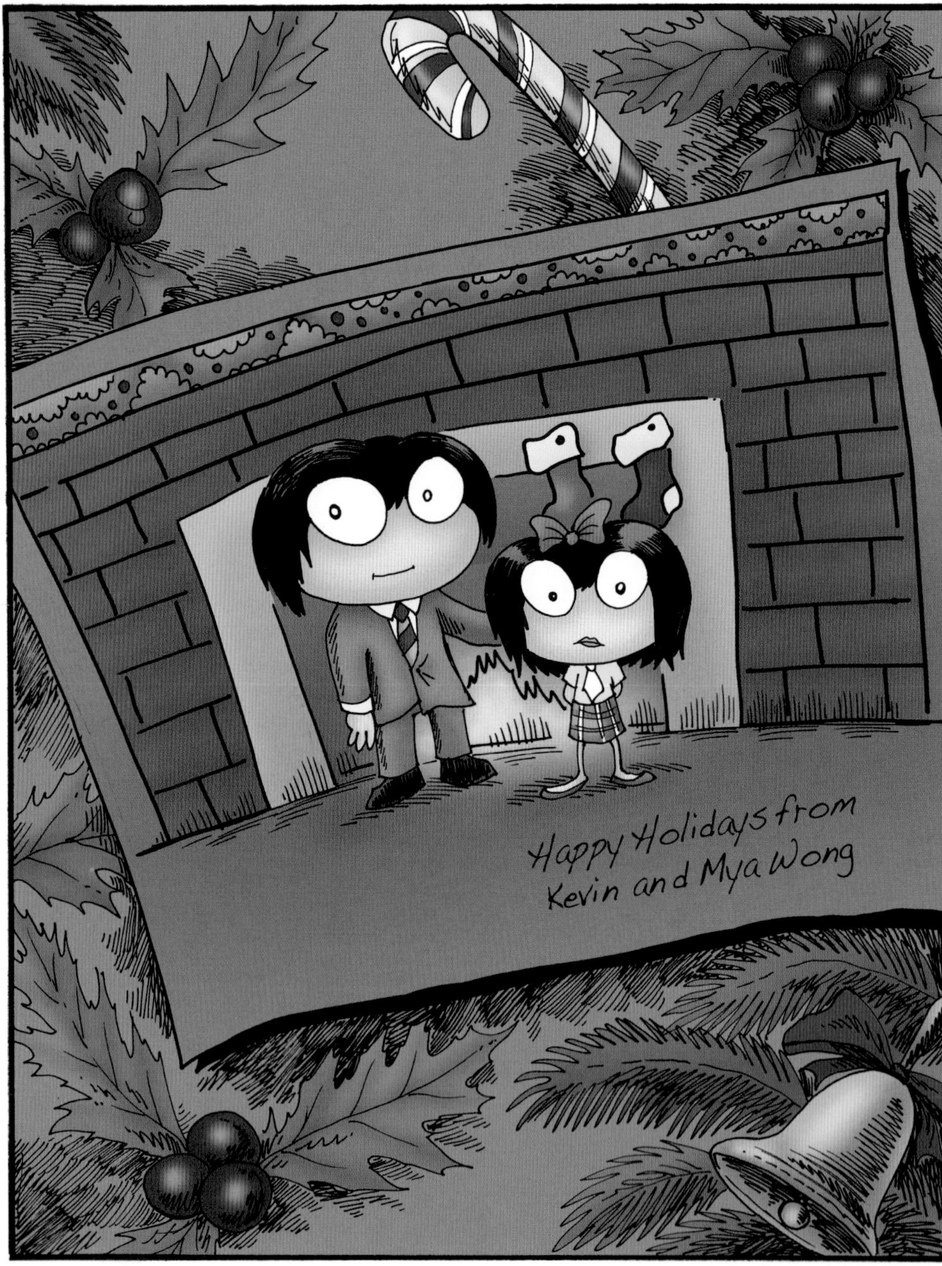
Happy Holidays from
Kevin and Mya Wong

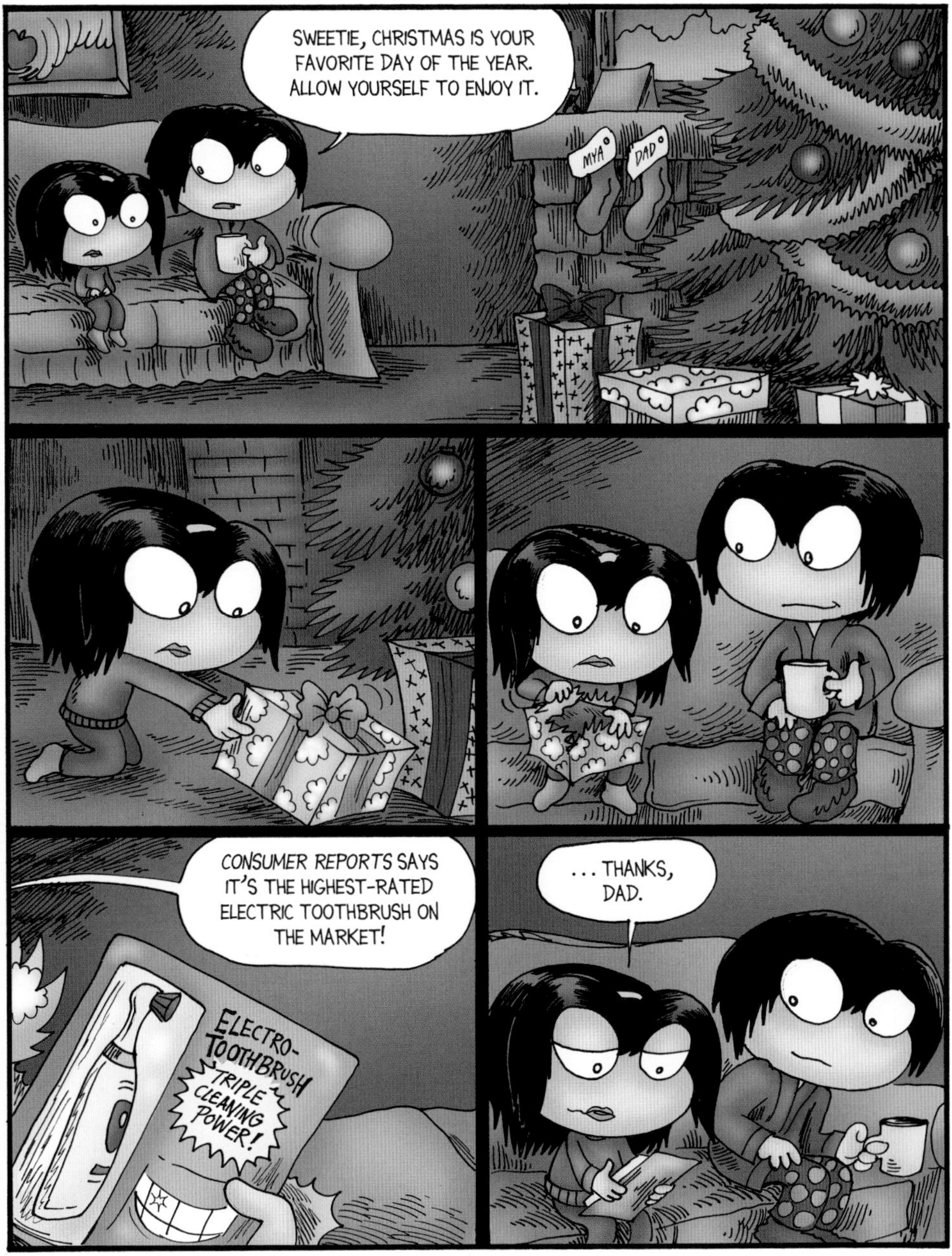
SWEETIE, CHRISTMAS IS YOUR FAVORITE DAY OF THE YEAR. ALLOW YOURSELF TO ENJOY IT.
MYA
DAD
CONSUMER REPORTS SAYS IT'S THE HIGHEST-RATED ELECTRIC TOOTHBRUSH ON THE MARKET!
ELECTRO-TOOTHBRUSH
TRIPLE CLEANING POWER!
... THANKS, DAD.

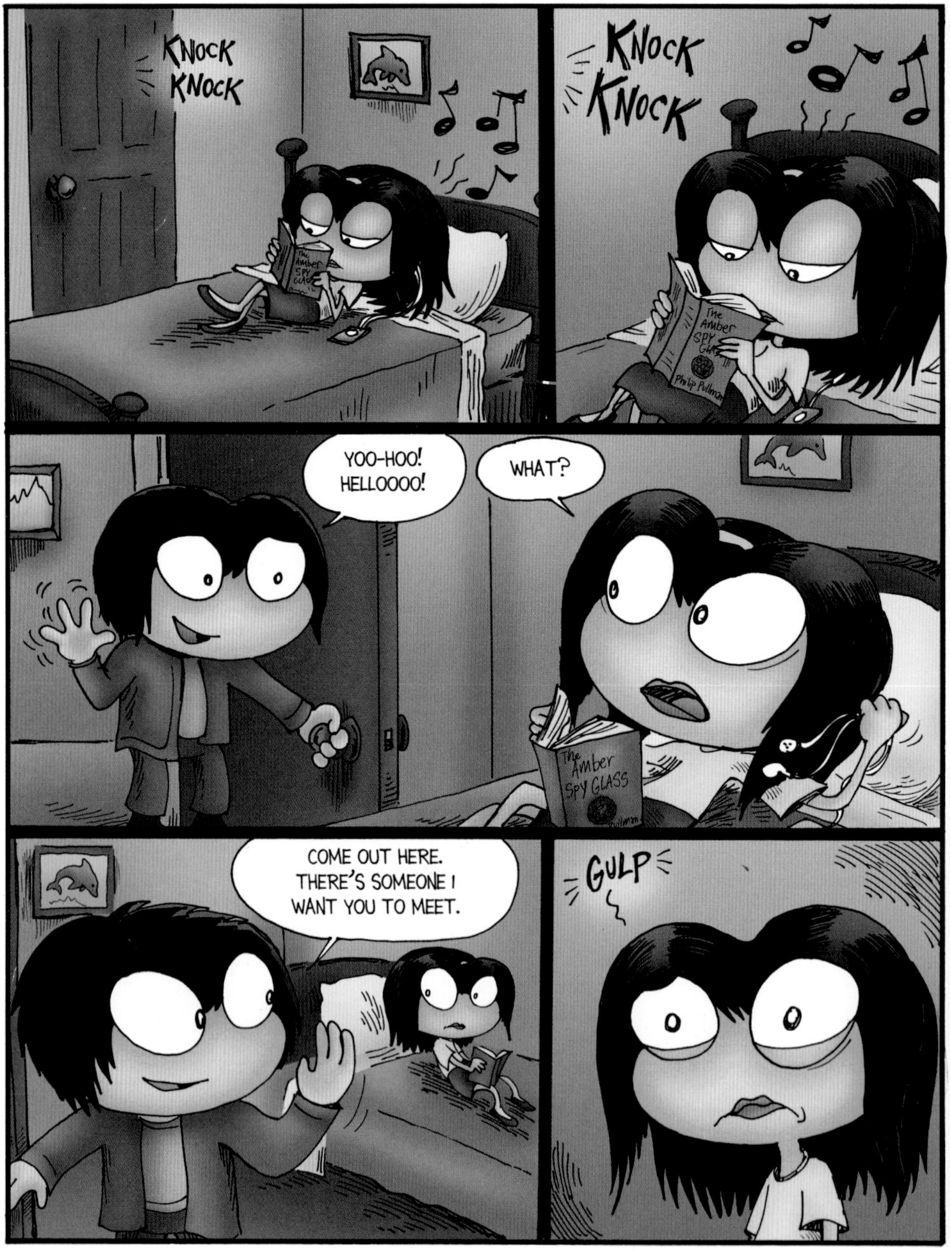
KNOCK KNOCK
KNOCK KNOCK
YOO-HOO! HELLOOOO!
WHAT?
COME OUT HERE. THERE'S SOMEONE I WANT YOU TO MEET.
GULP

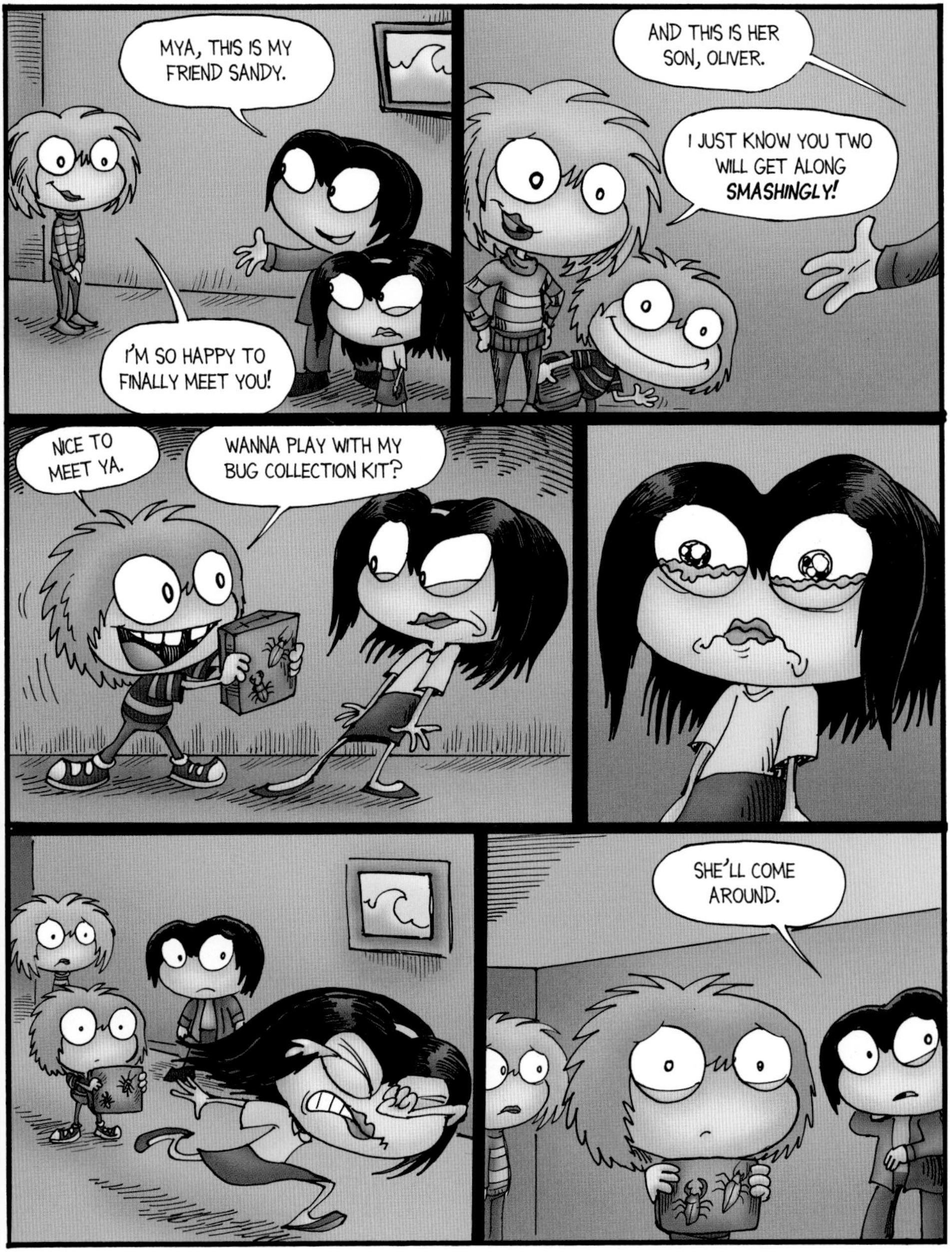
MYA, THIS IS MY FRIEND SANDY.
I'M SO HAPPY TO FINALLY MEET YOU!
AND THIS IS HER SON, OLIVER.
I JUST KNOW YOU TWO WILL GET ALONG **SMASHINGLY!**
NICE TO MEET YA.
WANNA PLAY WITH MY BUG COLLECTION KIT?
SHE'LL COME AROUND.

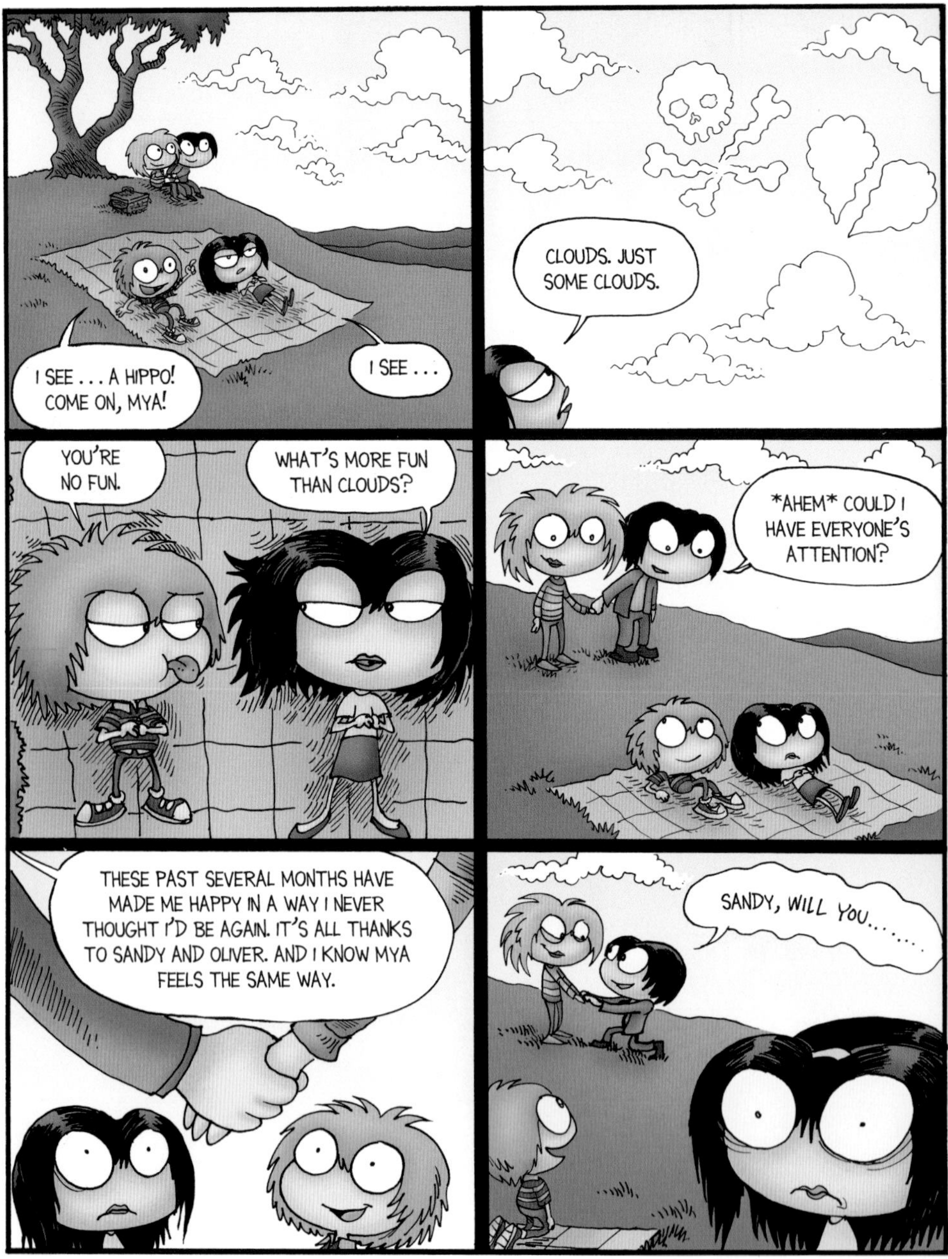
I SEE . . . A HIPPO! COME ON, MYA!
I SEE . . .
CLOUDS. JUST SOME CLOUDS.
YOU'RE NO FUN.
WHAT'S MORE FUN THAN CLOUDS?
AHEM COULD I HAVE EVERYONE'S ATTENTION?
THESE PAST SEVERAL MONTHS HAVE MADE ME HAPPY IN A WAY I NEVER THOUGHT I'D BE AGAIN. IT'S ALL THANKS TO SANDY AND OLIVER. AND I KNOW MYA FEELS THE SAME WAY.
SANDY, WILL YOU. . . . . . .

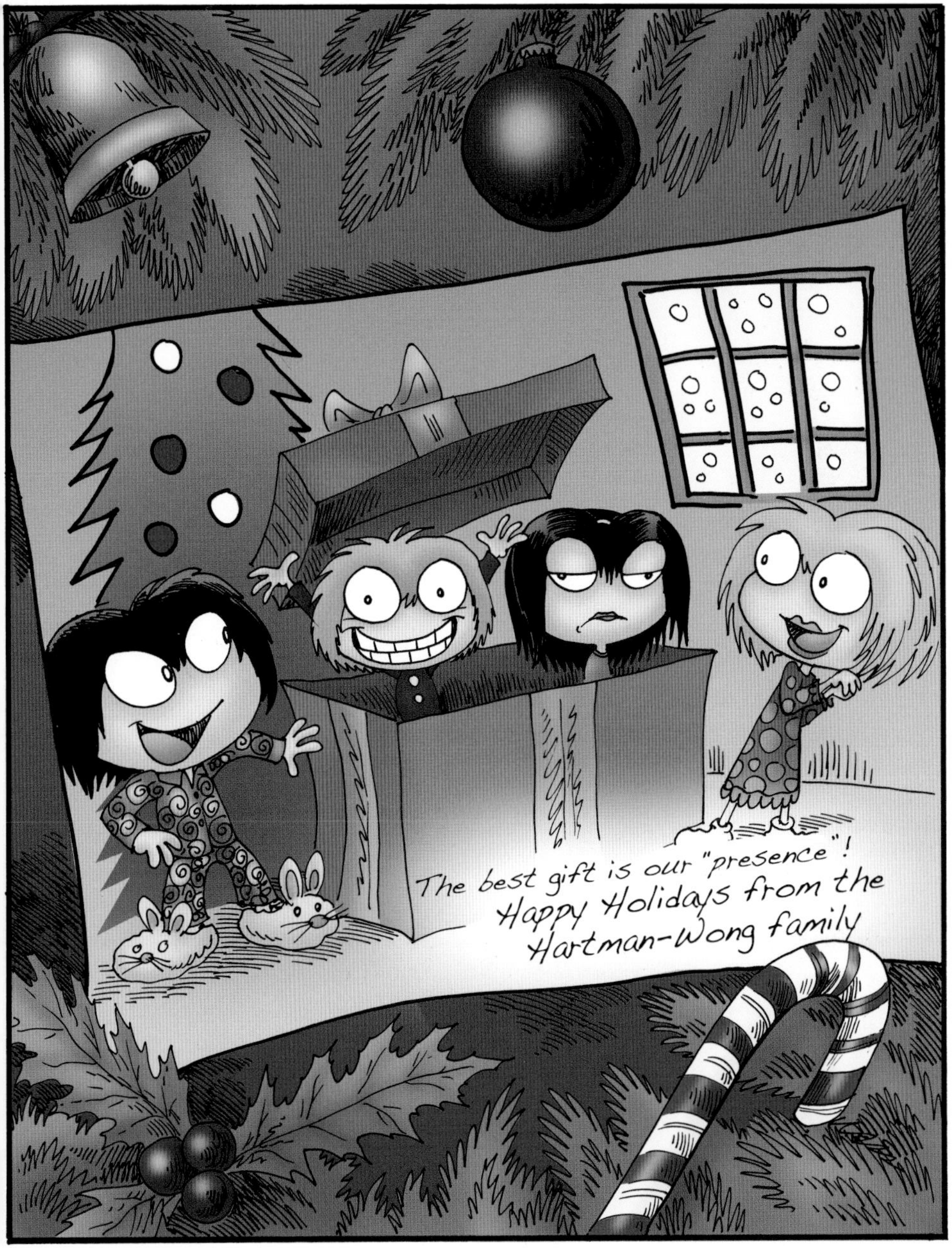
The best gift is our "presence"!
Happy Holidays from the
Hartman-Wong family

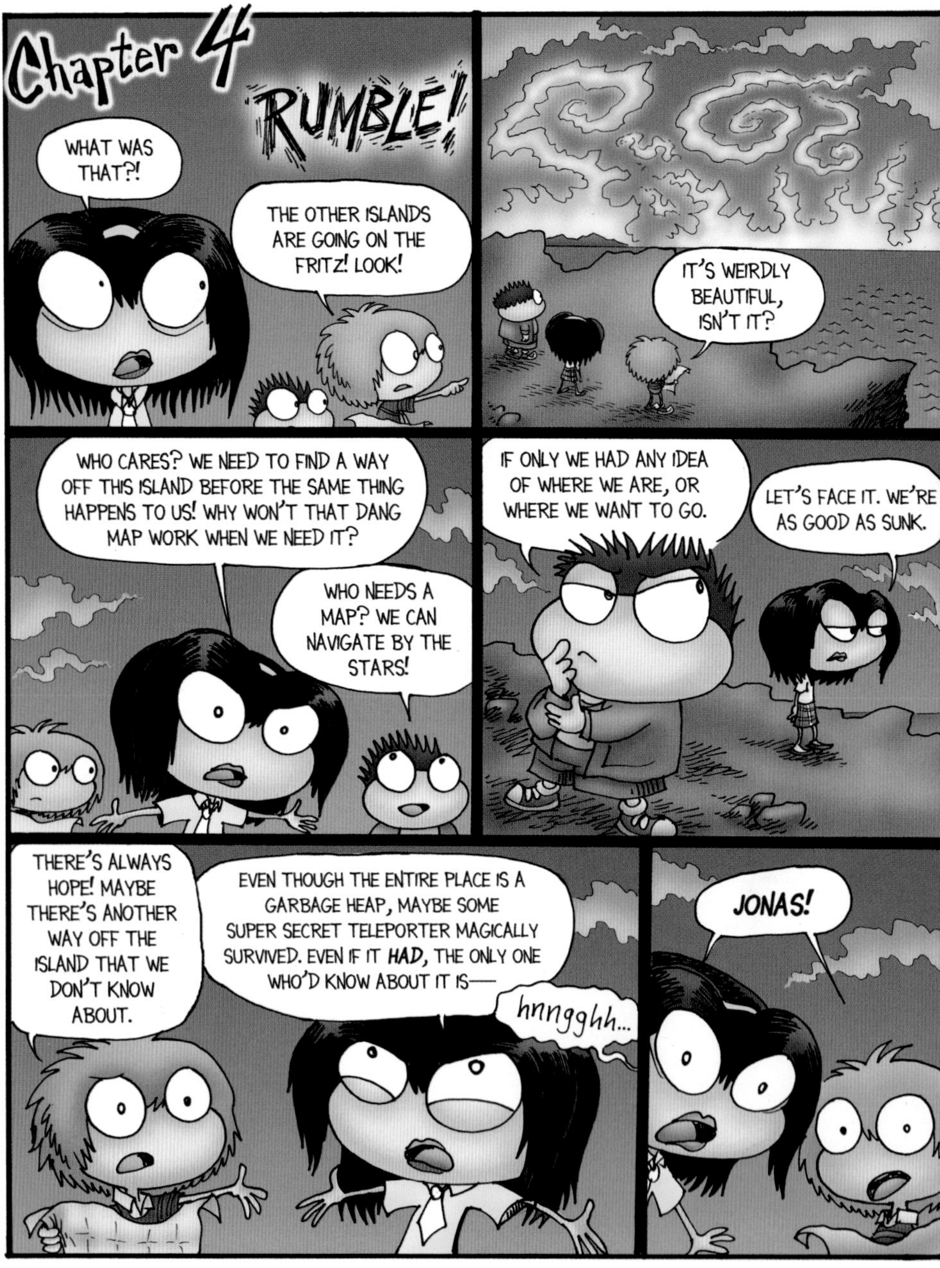

Chapter 4
RUMBLE!
WHAT WAS THAT?!
THE OTHER ISLANDS ARE GOING ON THE FRITZ! LOOK!
IT'S WEIRDLY BEAUTIFUL, ISN'T IT?
WHO CARES? WE NEED TO FIND A WAY OFF THIS ISLAND BEFORE THE SAME THING HAPPENS TO US! WHY WON'T THAT DANG MAP WORK WHEN WE NEED IT?
WHO NEEDS A MAP? WE CAN NAVIGATE BY THE STARS!
IF ONLY WE HAD ANY IDEA OF WHERE WE ARE, OR WHERE WE WANT TO GO.
LET'S FACE IT. WE'RE AS GOOD AS SUNK.
THERE'S ALWAYS HOPE! MAYBE THERE'S ANOTHER WAY OFF THE ISLAND THAT WE DON'T KNOW ABOUT.
EVEN THOUGH THE ENTIRE PLACE IS A GARBAGE HEAP, MAYBE SOME SUPER SECRET TELEPORTER MAGICALLY SURVIVED. EVEN IF IT **HAD**, THE ONLY ONE WHO'D KNOW ABOUT IT IS—
hnngghh...
JONAS!

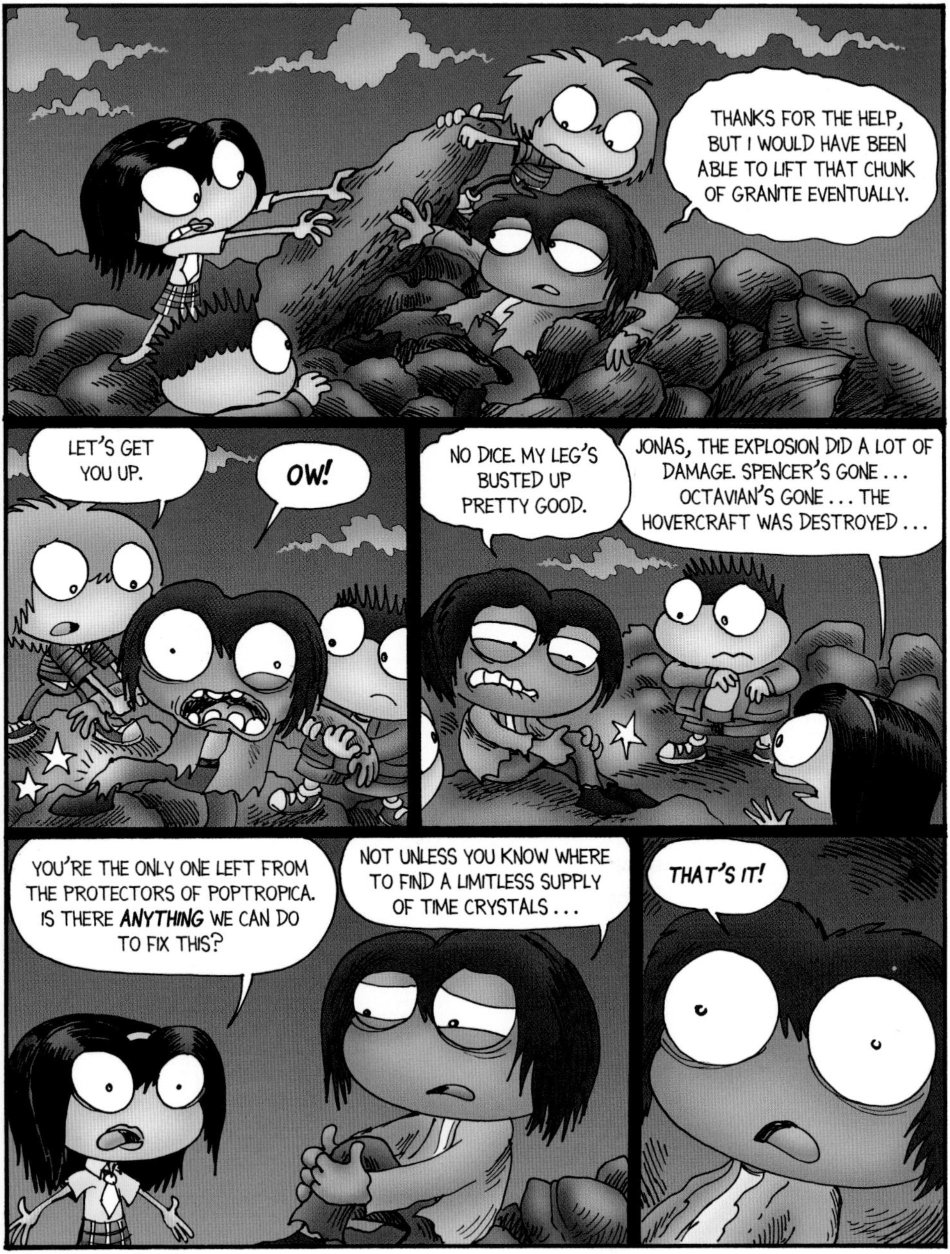
THANKS FOR THE HELP, BUT I WOULD HAVE BEEN ABLE TO LIFT THAT CHUNK OF GRANITE EVENTUALLY.
LET'S GET YOU UP.
OW!
NO DICE. MY LEG'S BUSTED UP PRETTY GOOD.
JONAS, THE EXPLOSION DID A LOT OF DAMAGE. SPENCER'S GONE . . . OCTAVIAN'S GONE . . . THE HOVERCRAFT WAS DESTROYED . . .
YOU'RE THE ONLY ONE LEFT FROM THE PROTECTORS OF POPTROPICA. IS THERE ***ANYTHING*** WE CAN DO TO FIX THIS?
NOT UNLESS YOU KNOW WHERE TO FIND A LIMITLESS SUPPLY OF TIME CRYSTALS . . .
THAT'S IT!

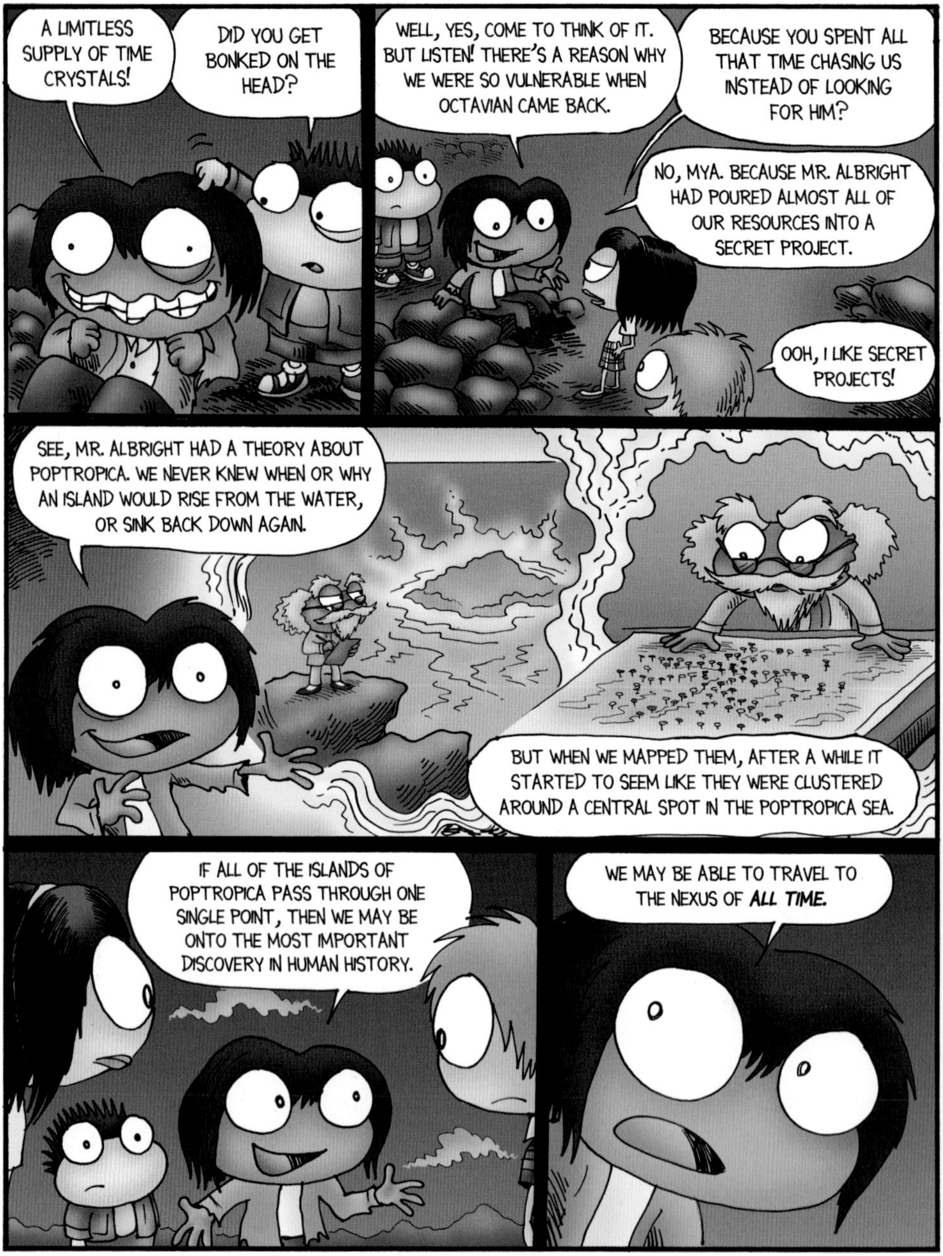

A LIMITLESS SUPPLY OF TIME CRYSTALS!
DID YOU GET BONKED ON THE HEAD?
WELL, YES, COME TO THINK OF IT. BUT LISTEN! THERE'S A REASON WHY WE WERE SO VULNERABLE WHEN OCTAVIAN CAME BACK.
BECAUSE YOU SPENT ALL THAT TIME CHASING US INSTEAD OF LOOKING FOR HIM?
NO, MYA. BECAUSE MR. ALBRIGHT HAD POURED ALMOST ALL OF OUR RESOURCES INTO A SECRET PROJECT.
OOH, I LIKE SECRET PROJECTS!
SEE, MR. ALBRIGHT HAD A THEORY ABOUT POPTROPICA. WE NEVER KNEW WHEN OR WHY AN ISLAND WOULD RISE FROM THE WATER, OR SINK BACK DOWN AGAIN.
BUT WHEN WE MAPPED THEM, AFTER A WHILE IT STARTED TO SEEM LIKE THEY WERE CLUSTERED AROUND A CENTRAL SPOT IN THE POPTROPICA SEA.
IF ALL OF THE ISLANDS OF POPTROPICA PASS THROUGH ONE SINGLE POINT, THEN WE MAY BE ONTO THE MOST IMPORTANT DISCOVERY IN HUMAN HISTORY.
WE MAY BE ABLE TO TRAVEL TO THE NEXUS OF ALL TIME.

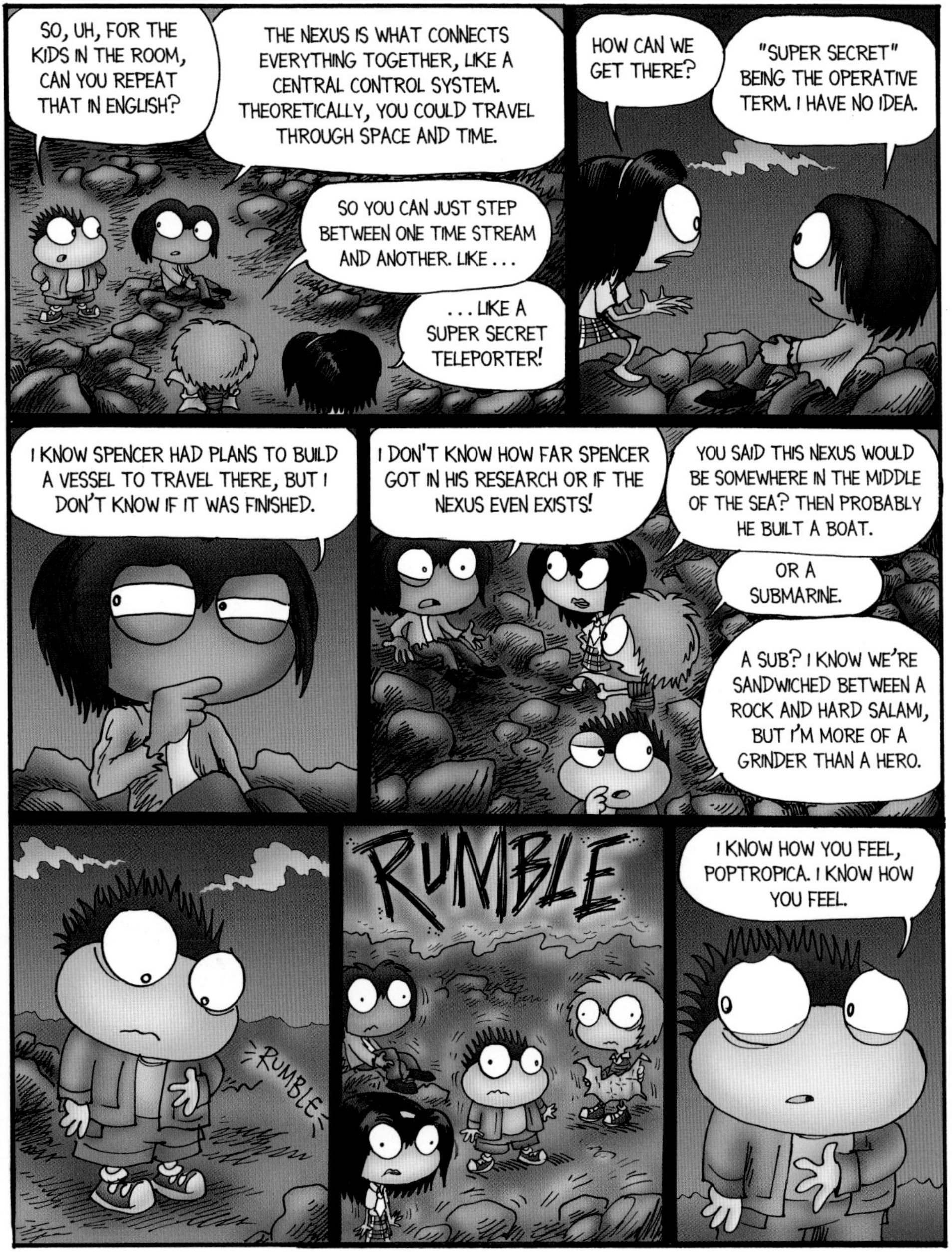
SO, UH, FOR THE KIDS IN THE ROOM, CAN YOU REPEAT THAT IN ENGLISH?
THE NEXUS IS WHAT CONNECTS EVERYTHING TOGETHER, LIKE A CENTRAL CONTROL SYSTEM. THEORETICALLY, YOU COULD TRAVEL THROUGH SPACE AND TIME.
SO YOU CAN JUST STEP BETWEEN ONE TIME STREAM AND ANOTHER. LIKE . . .
. . . LIKE A SUPER SECRET TELEPORTER!
HOW CAN WE GET THERE?
"SUPER SECRET" BEING THE OPERATIVE TERM. I HAVE NO IDEA.
I KNOW SPENCER HAD PLANS TO BUILD A VESSEL TO TRAVEL THERE, BUT I DON'T KNOW IF IT WAS FINISHED.
I DON'T KNOW HOW FAR SPENCER GOT IN HIS RESEARCH OR IF THE NEXUS EVEN EXISTS!
YOU SAID THIS NEXUS WOULD BE SOMEWHERE IN THE MIDDLE OF THE SEA? THEN PROBABLY HE BUILT A BOAT.
OR A SUBMARINE.
A SUB? I KNOW WE'RE SANDWICHED BETWEEN A ROCK AND HARD SALAMI, BUT I'M MORE OF A GRINDER THAN A HERO.
RUMBLE
RUMBLE
I KNOW HOW YOU FEEL, POPTROPICA. I KNOW HOW YOU FEEL.

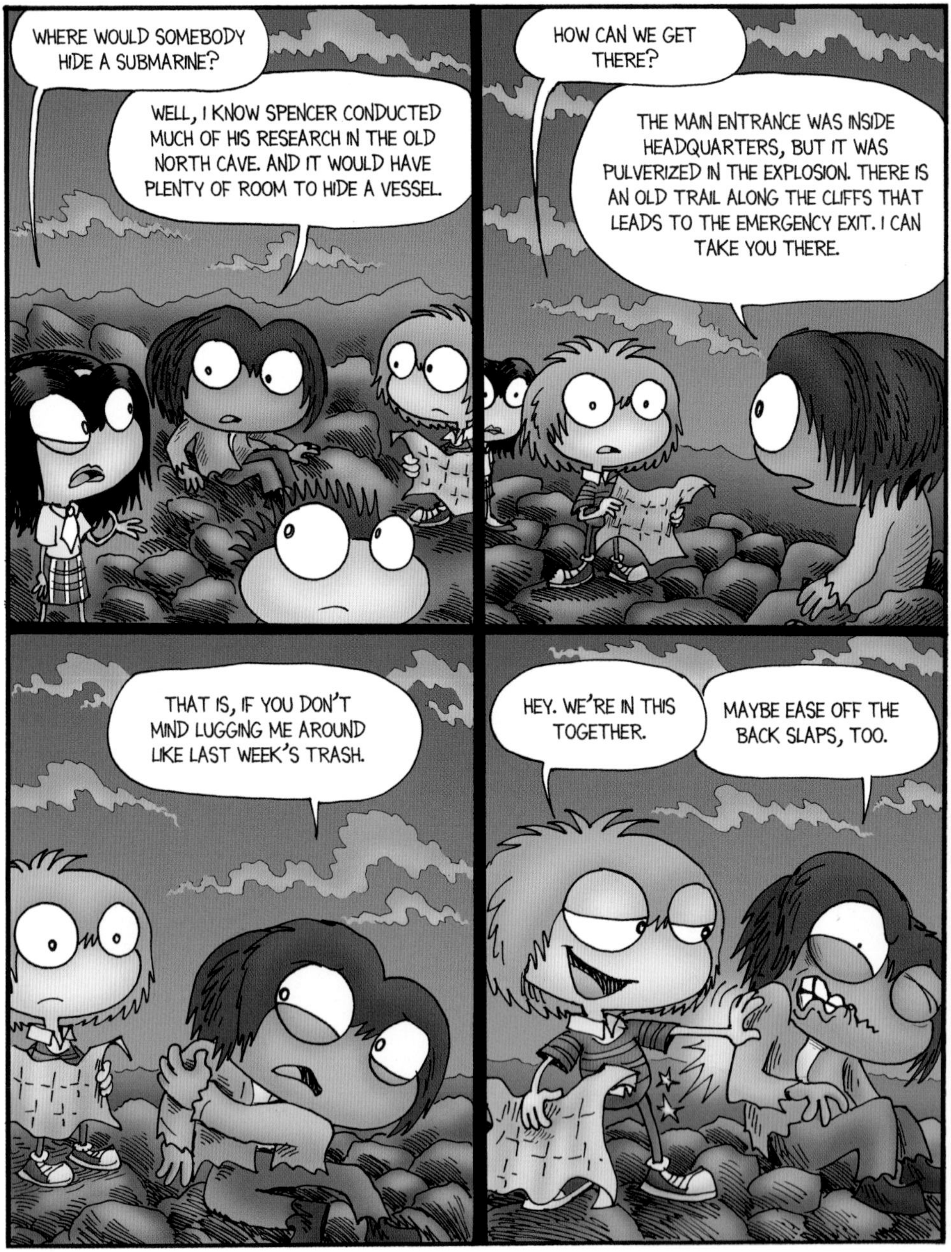
WHERE WOULD SOMEBODY HIDE A SUBMARINE?
WELL, I KNOW SPENCER CONDUCTED MUCH OF HIS RESEARCH IN THE OLD NORTH CAVE. AND IT WOULD HAVE PLENTY OF ROOM TO HIDE A VESSEL.
HOW CAN WE GET THERE?
THE MAIN ENTRANCE WAS INSIDE HEADQUARTERS, BUT IT WAS PULVERIZED IN THE EXPLOSION. THERE IS AN OLD TRAIL ALONG THE CLIFFS THAT LEADS TO THE EMERGENCY EXIT. I CAN TAKE YOU THERE.
THAT IS, IF YOU DON'T MIND LUGGING ME AROUND LIKE LAST WEEK'S TRASH.
HEY. WE'RE IN THIS TOGETHER.
MAYBE EASE OFF THE BACK SLAPS, TOO.

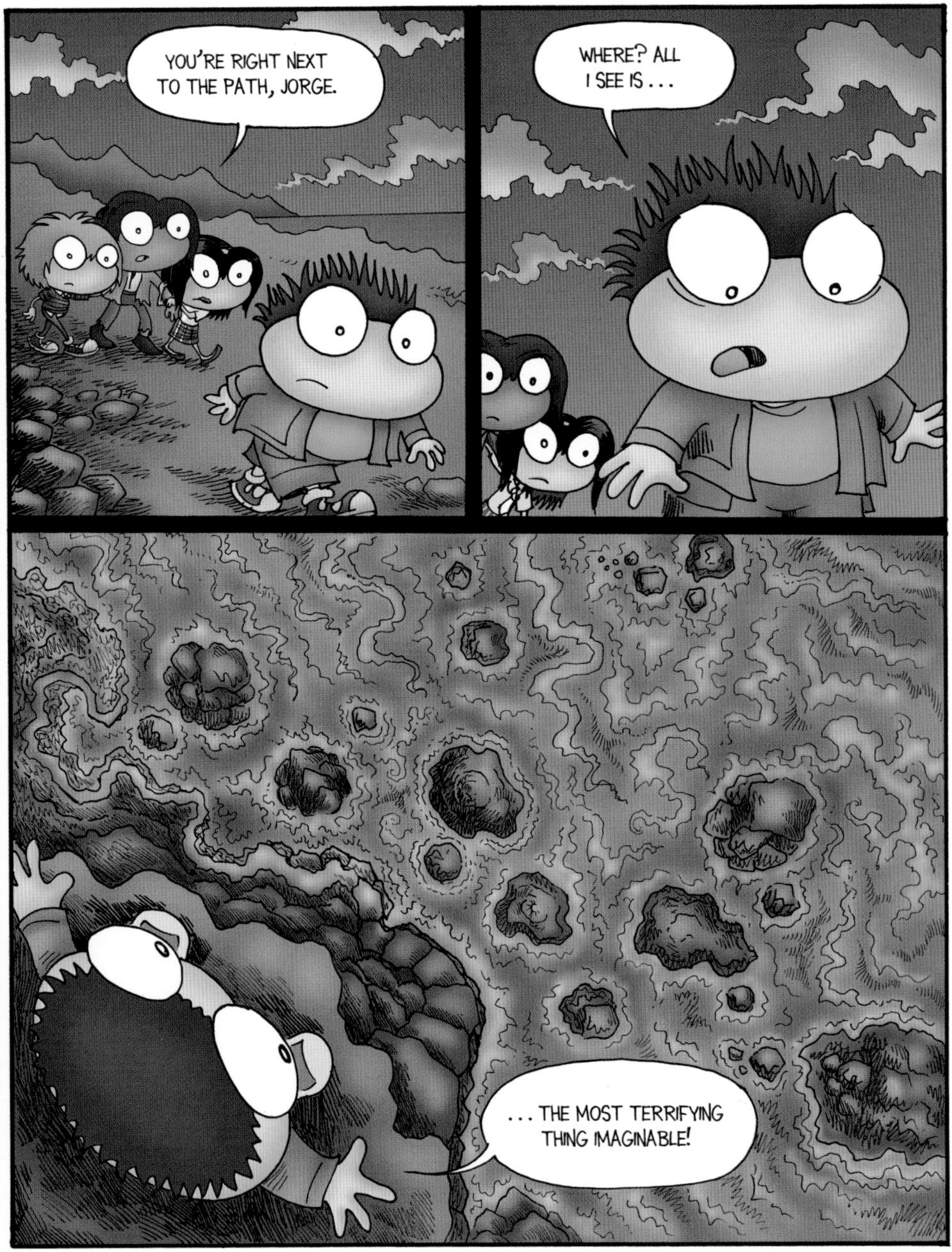
YOU'RE RIGHT NEXT TO THE PATH, JORGE.
WHERE? ALL I SEE IS . . .
. . . THE MOST TERRIFYING THING IMAGINABLE!

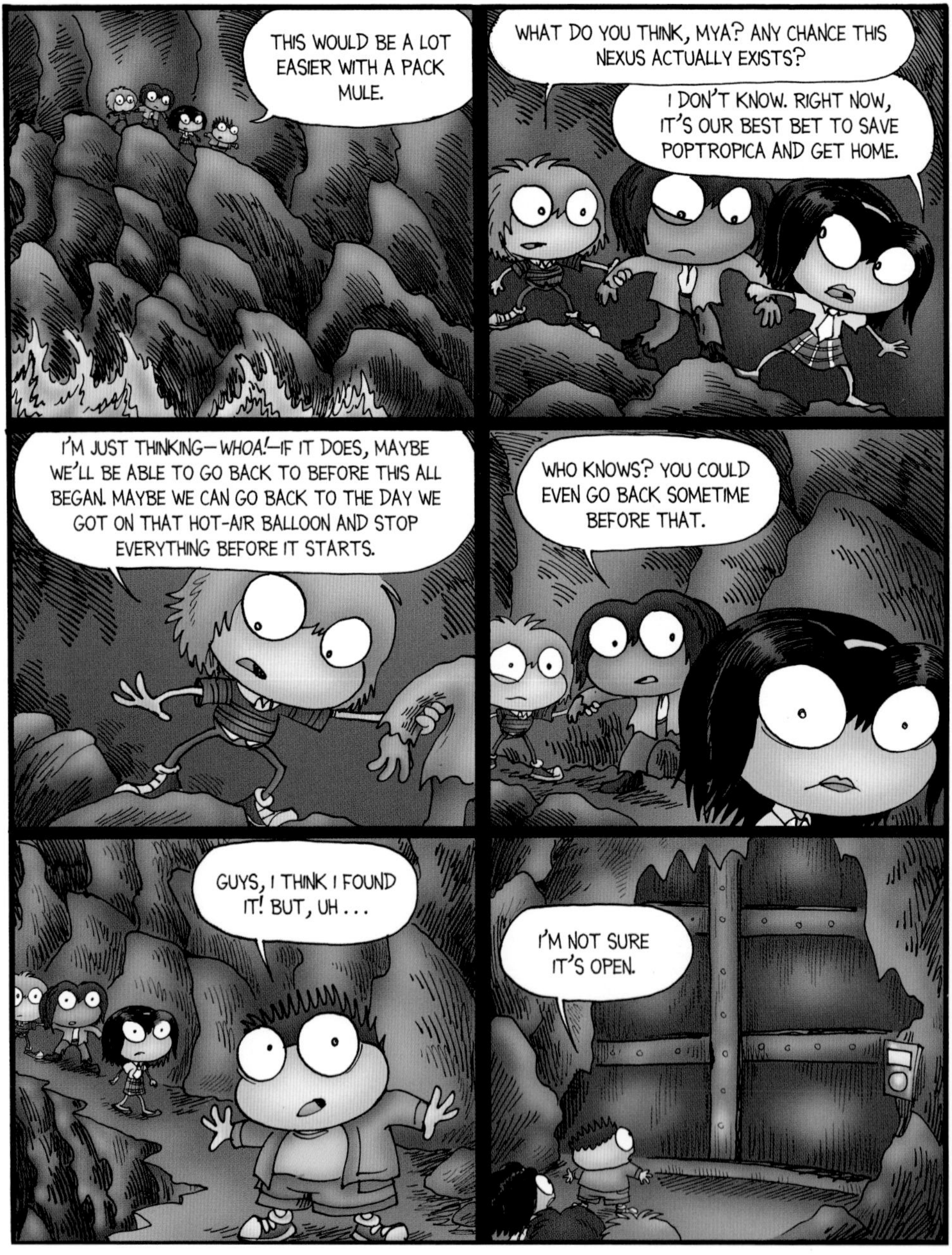
THIS WOULD BE A LOT EASIER WITH A PACK MULE.
WHAT DO YOU THINK, MYA? ANY CHANCE THIS NEXUS ACTUALLY EXISTS?
I DON'T KNOW. RIGHT NOW, IT'S OUR BEST BET TO SAVE POPTROPICA AND GET HOME.
I'M JUST THINKING—*WHOA!*—IF IT DOES, MAYBE WE'LL BE ABLE TO GO BACK TO BEFORE THIS ALL BEGAN. MAYBE WE CAN GO BACK TO THE DAY WE GOT ON THAT HOT-AIR BALLOON AND STOP EVERYTHING BEFORE IT STARTS.
WHO KNOWS? YOU COULD EVEN GO BACK SOMETIME BEFORE THAT.
GUYS, I THINK I FOUND IT! BUT, UH . . .
I'M NOT SURE IT'S OPEN.

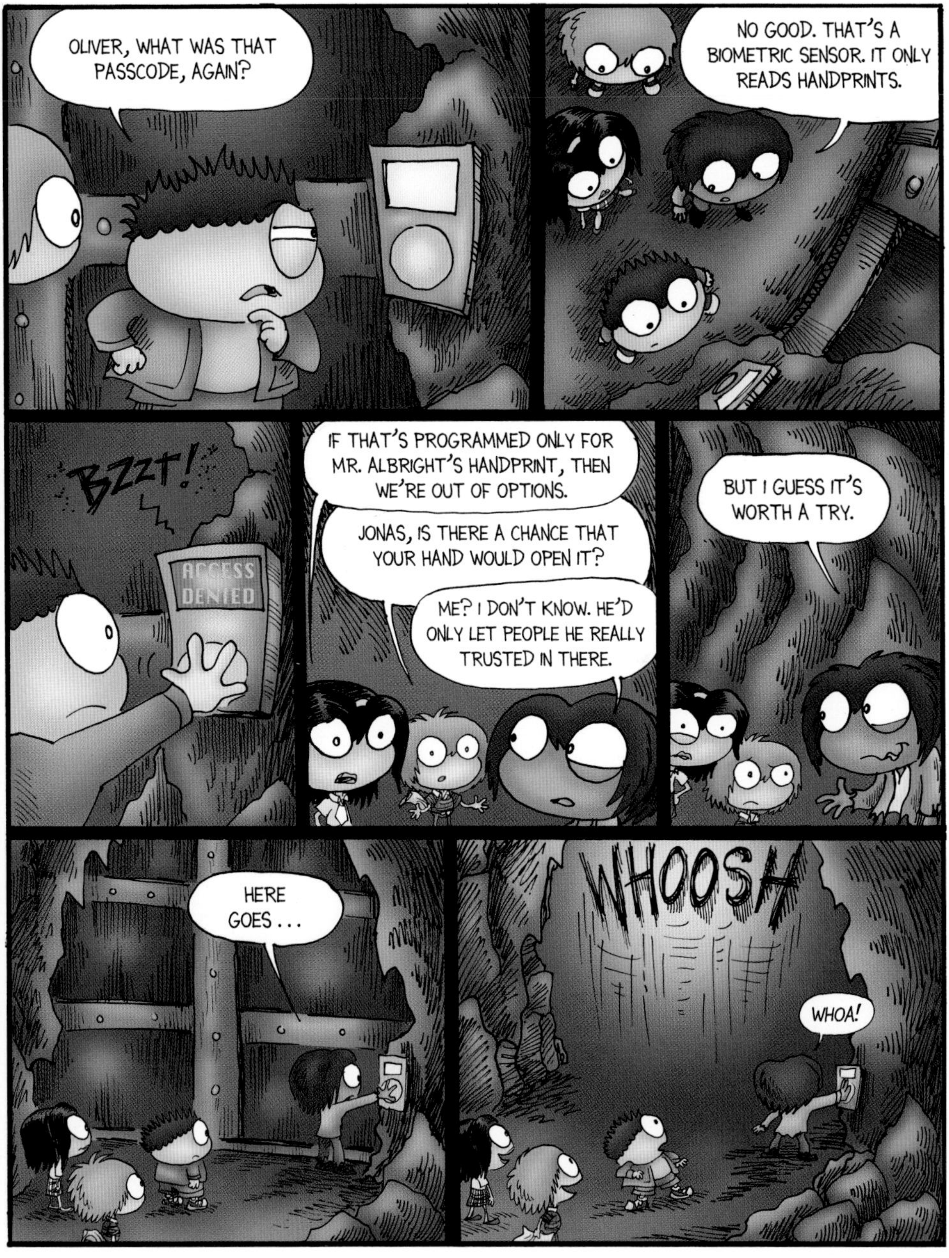

OLIVER, WHAT WAS THAT PASSCODE, AGAIN?
NO GOOD. THAT'S A BIOMETRIC SENSOR. IT ONLY READS HANDPRINTS.
BZZT!
ACCESS DENIED
IF THAT'S PROGRAMMED ONLY FOR MR. ALBRIGHT'S HANDPRINT, THEN WE'RE OUT OF OPTIONS.
JONAS, IS THERE A CHANCE THAT YOUR HAND WOULD OPEN IT?
ME? I DON'T KNOW. HE'D ONLY LET PEOPLE HE REALLY TRUSTED IN THERE.
BUT I GUESS IT'S WORTH A TRY.
HERE GOES . . .
WHOOSH
WHOA!

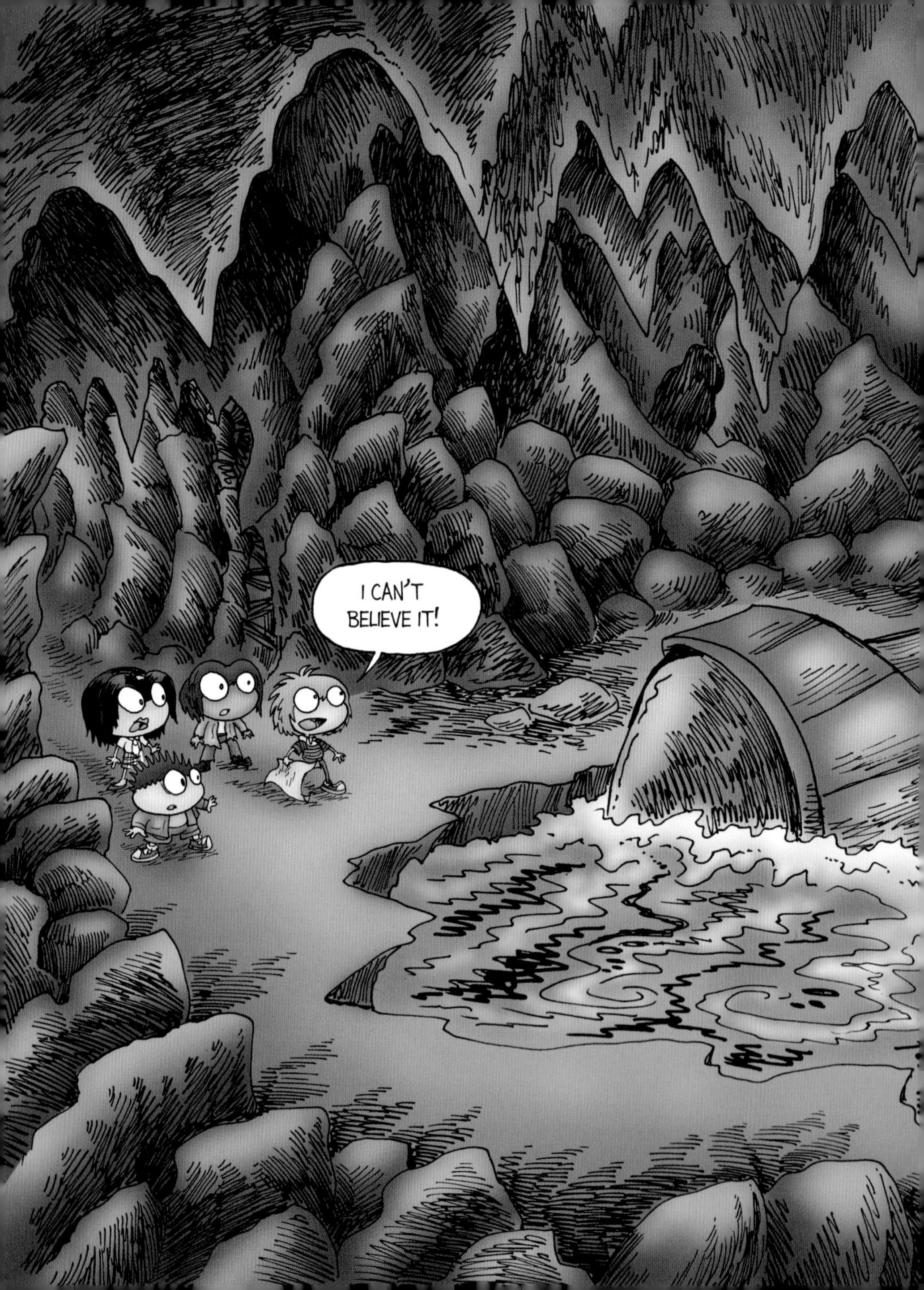
I CAN'T BELIEVE IT!

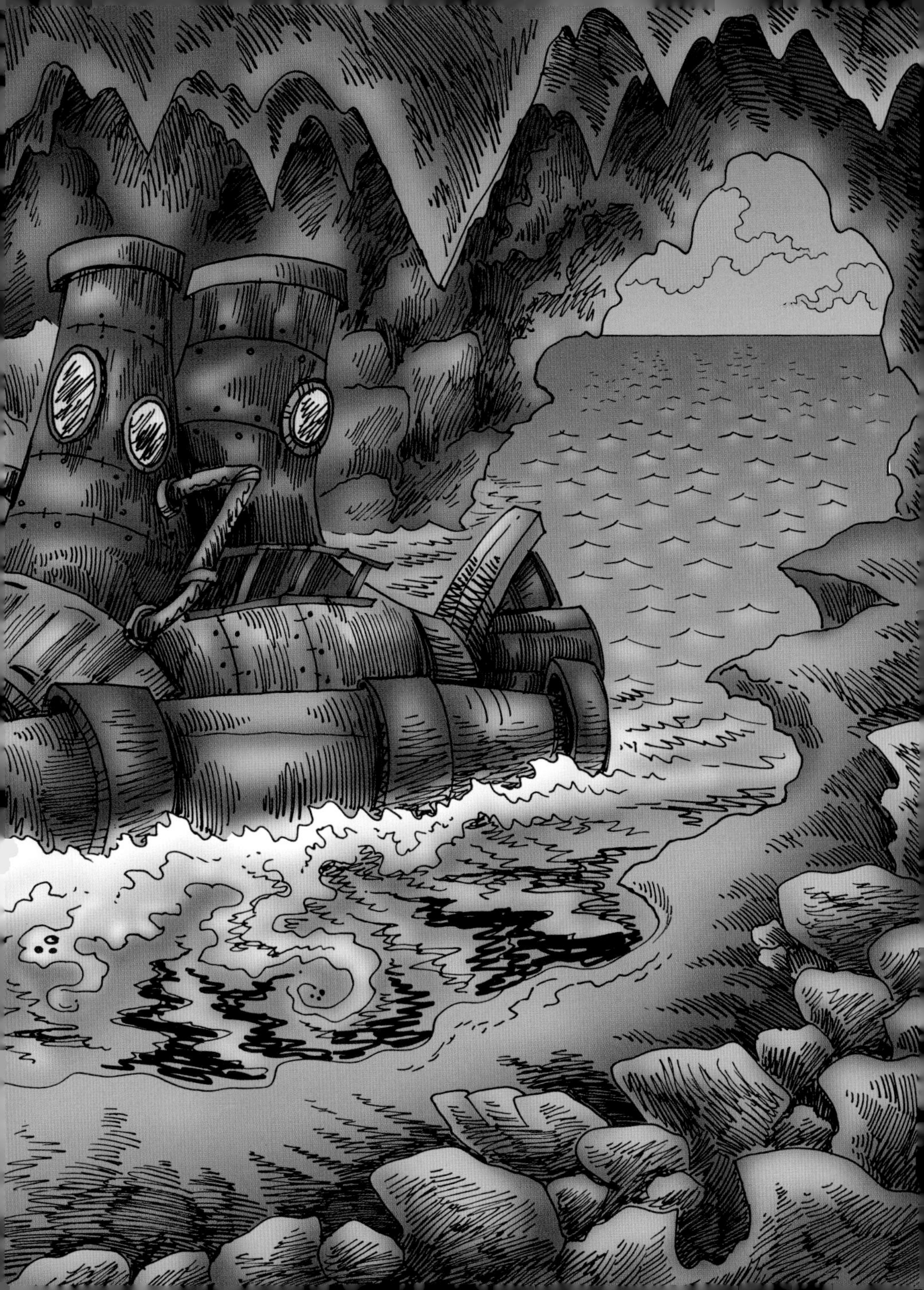

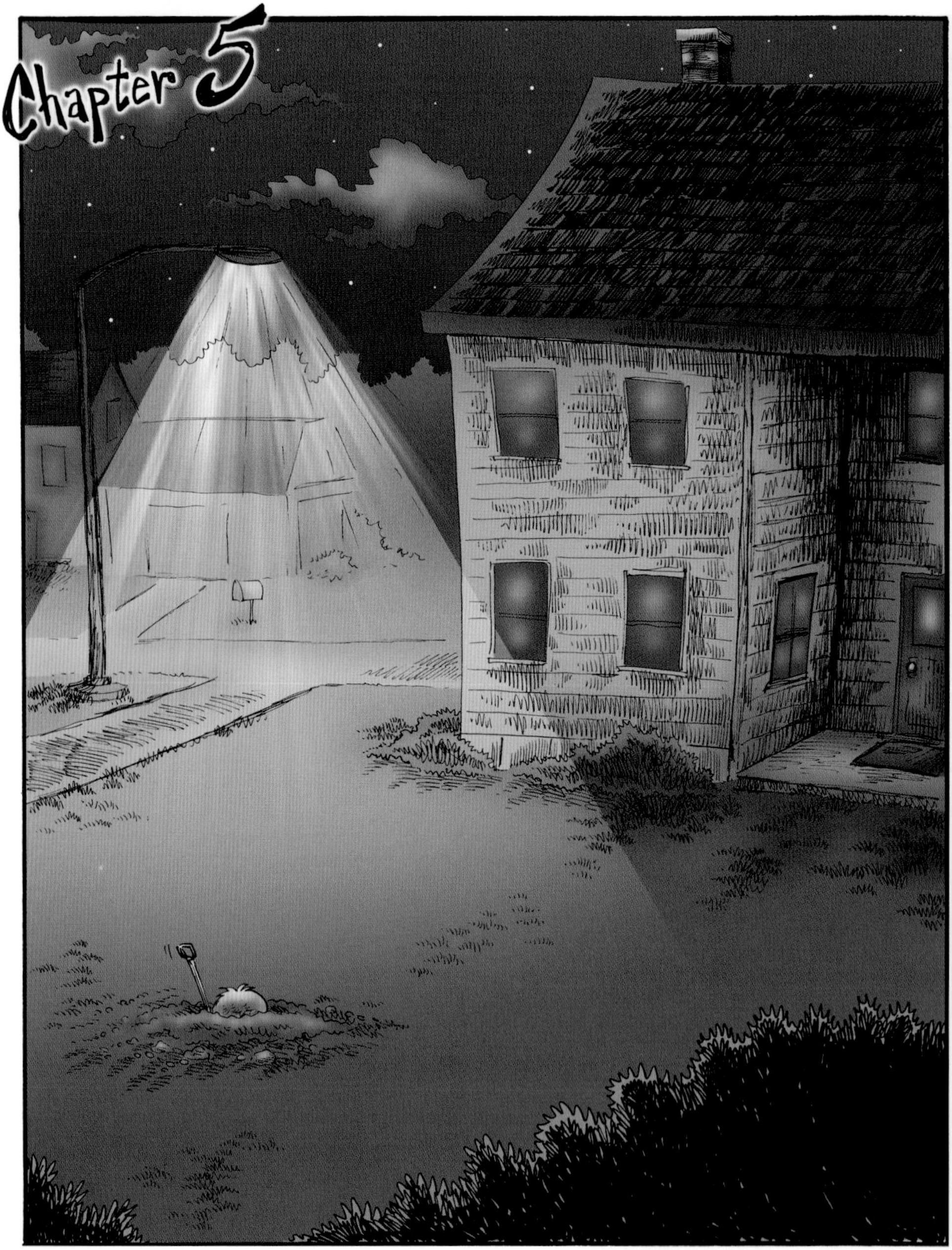
Chapter 5

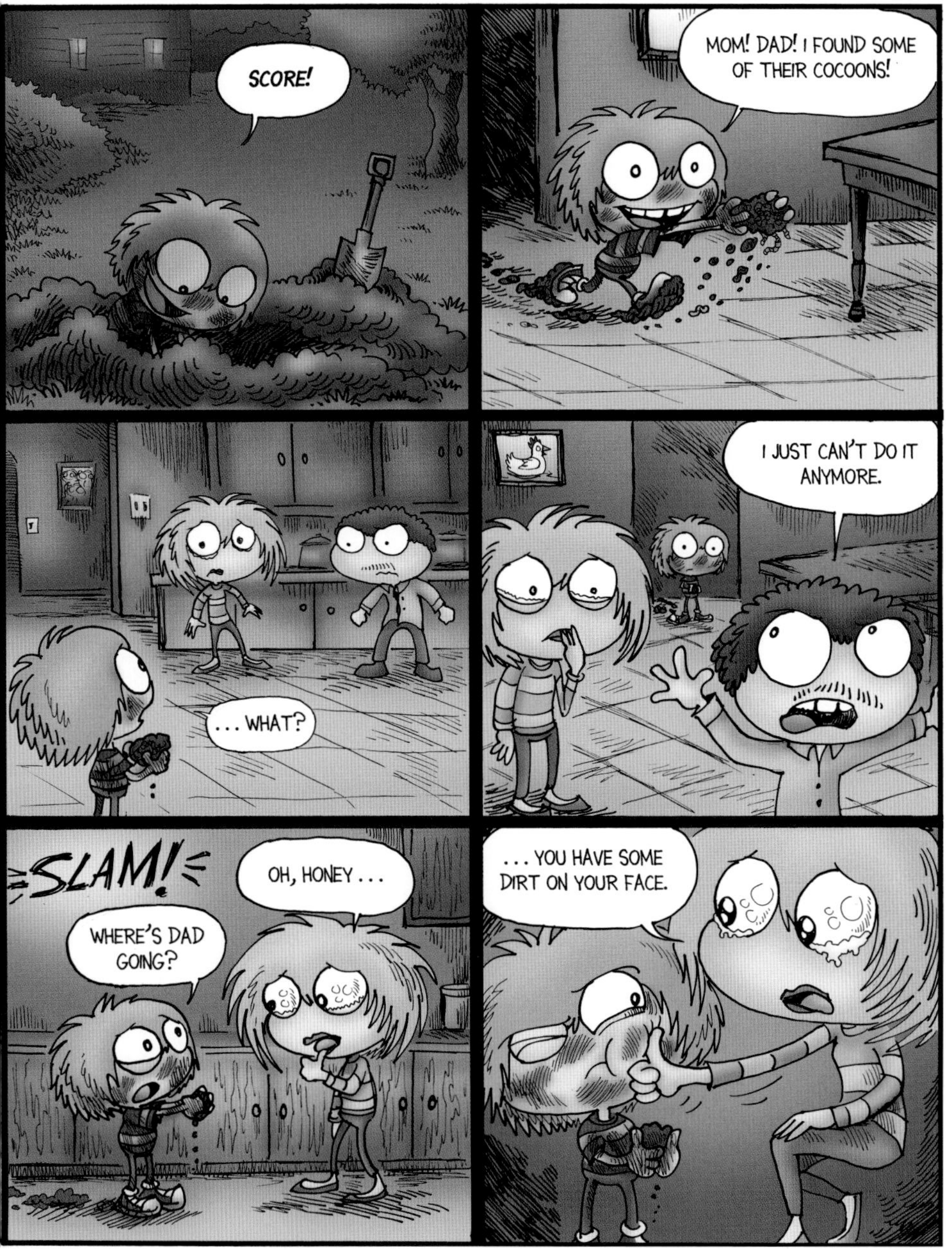
SCORE!
MOM! DAD! I FOUND SOME OF THEIR COCOONS!
... WHAT?
I JUST CAN'T DO IT ANYMORE.
SLAM!
WHERE'S DAD GOING?
OH, HONEY ...
... YOU HAVE SOME DIRT ON YOUR FACE.

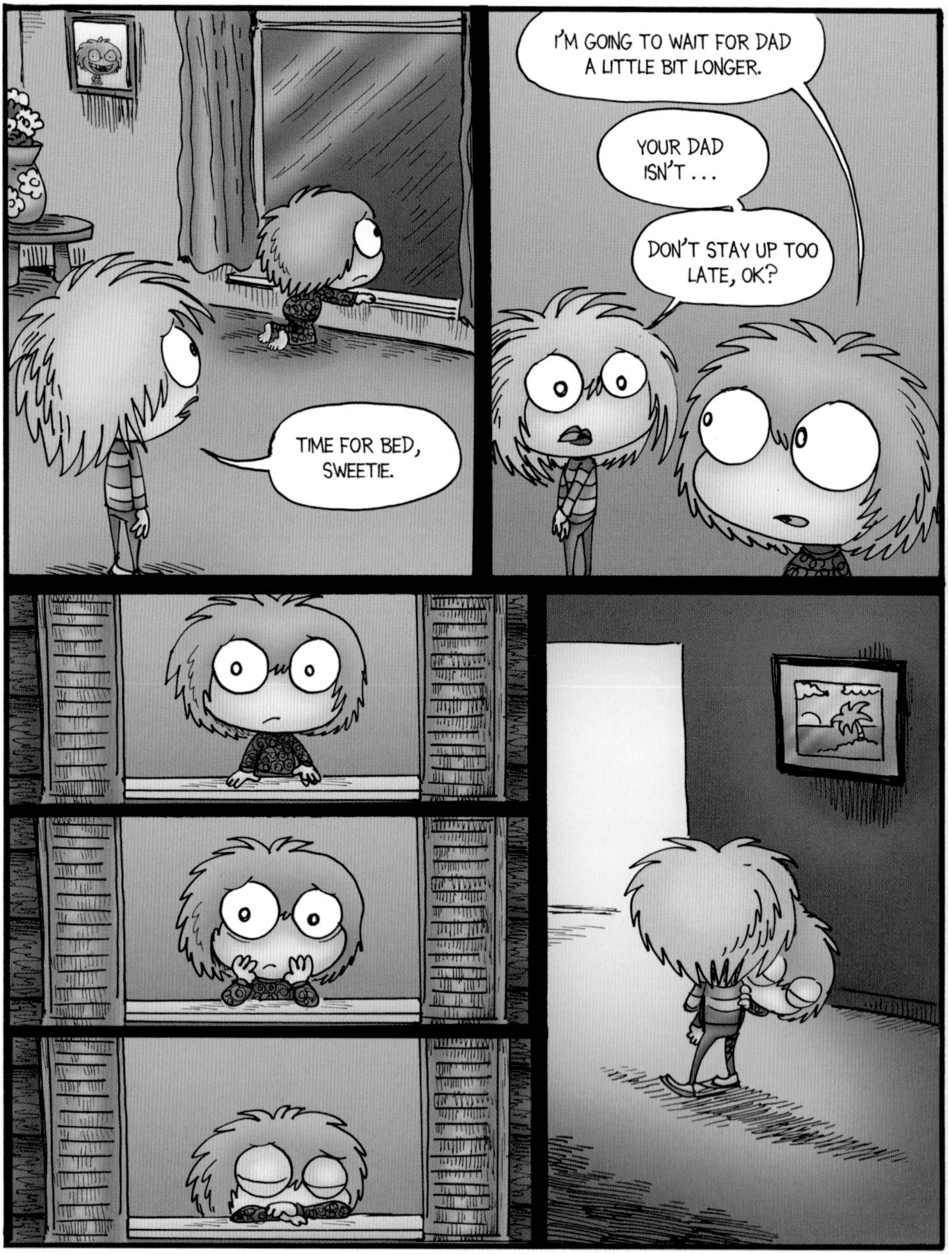

TIME FOR BED, SWEETIE.
I'M GOING TO WAIT FOR DAD A LITTLE BIT LONGER.
YOUR DAD ISN'T . . .
DON'T STAY UP TOO LATE, OK?

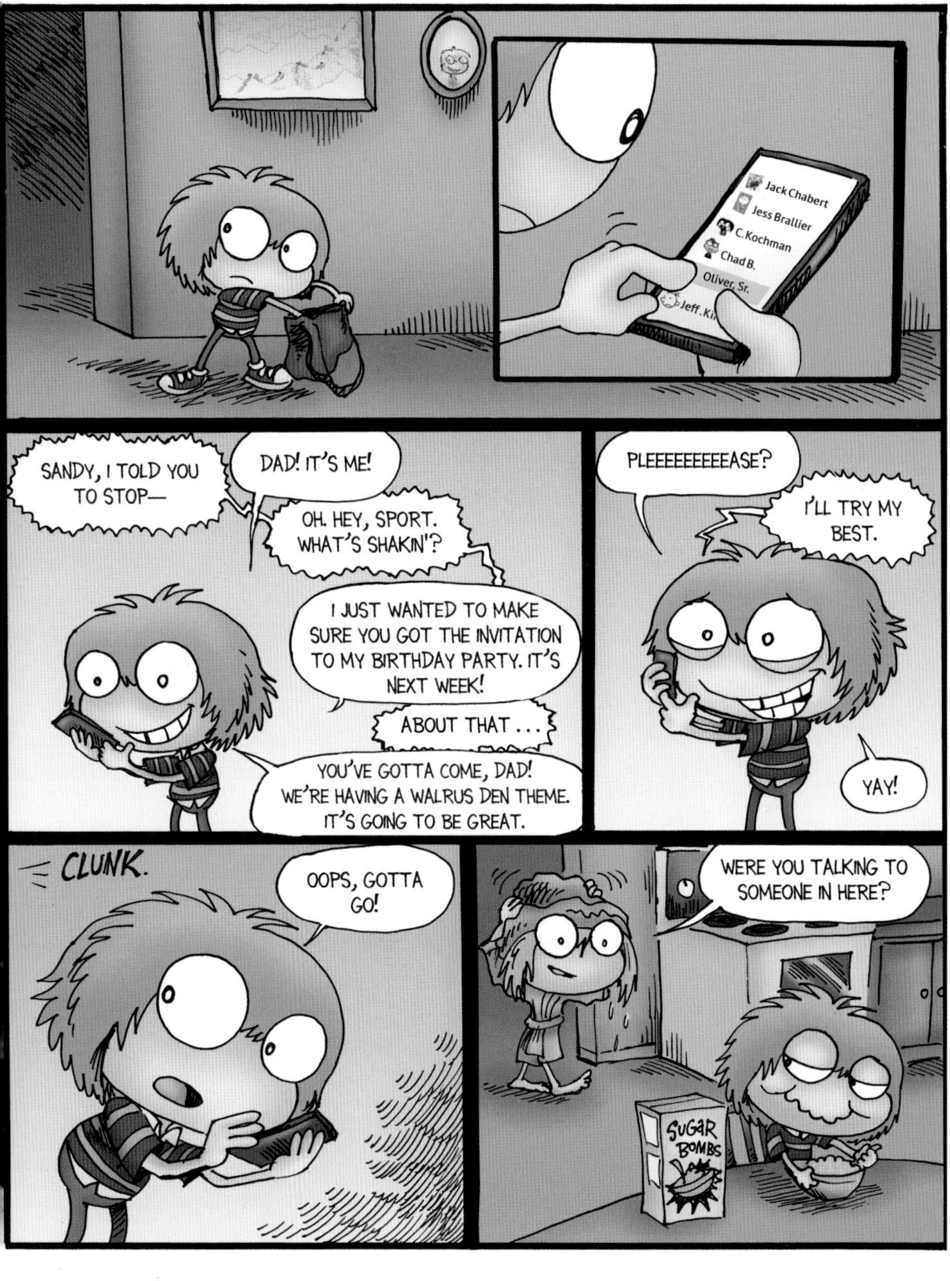
Jack Chabert
Jess Brallier
C. Kochman
Chad B.
Oliver, Sr.
SANDY, I TOLD YOU TO STOP—
DAD! IT'S ME!
OH. HEY, SPORT. WHAT'S SHAKIN'?
I JUST WANTED TO MAKE SURE YOU GOT THE INVITATION TO MY BIRTHDAY PARTY. IT'S NEXT WEEK!
ABOUT THAT . . .
YOU'VE GOTTA COME, DAD! WE'RE HAVING A WALRUS DEN THEME. IT'S GOING TO BE GREAT.
PLEEEEEEEEEEASE?
I'LL TRY MY BEST.
YAY!
CLUNK.
OOPS, GOTTA GO!
WERE YOU TALKING TO SOMEONE IN HERE?
SUGAR BOMBS

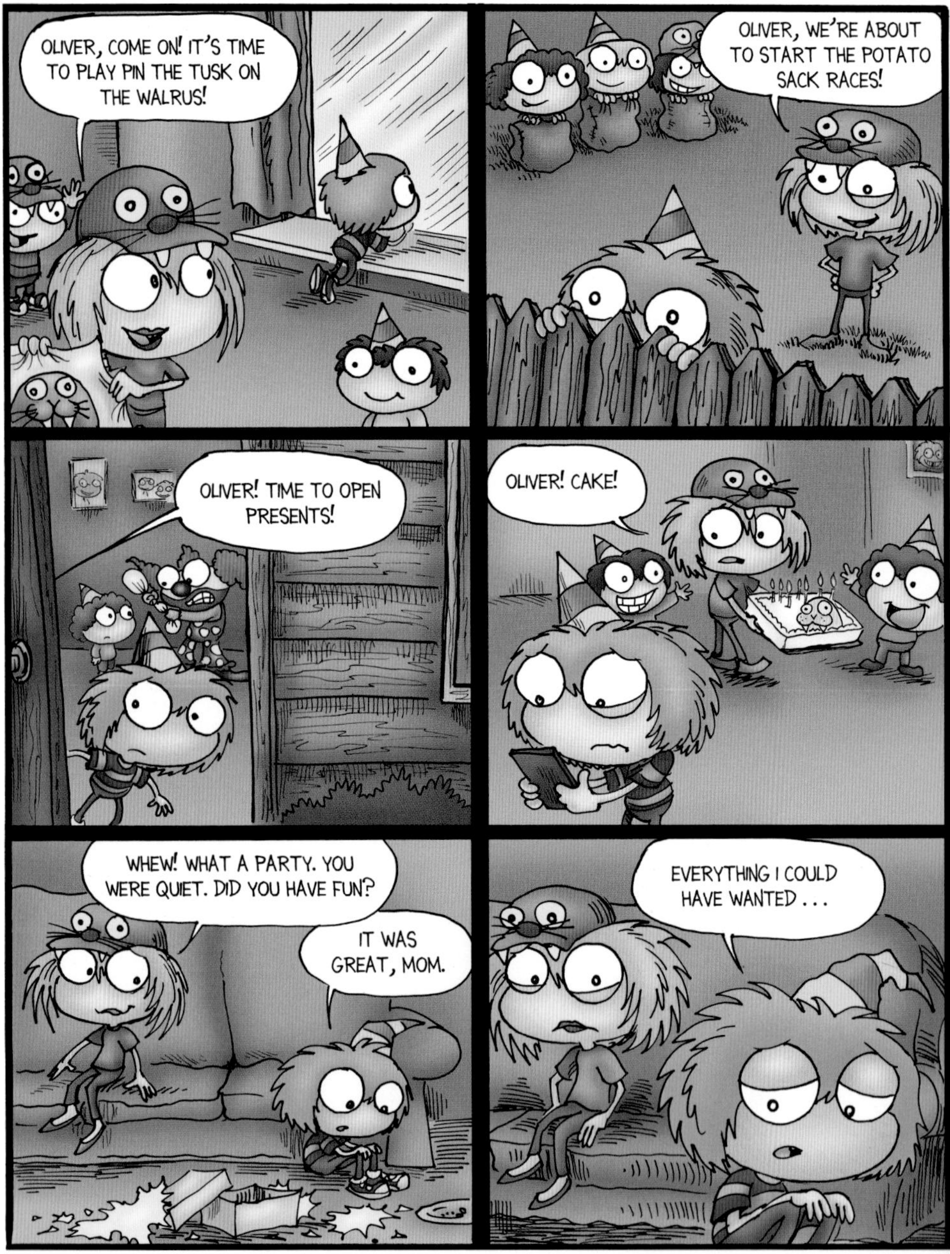
OLIVER, COME ON! IT'S TIME TO PLAY PIN THE TUSK ON THE WALRUS!
OLIVER, WE'RE ABOUT TO START THE POTATO SACK RACES!
OLIVER! TIME TO OPEN PRESENTS!
OLIVER! CAKE!
WHEW! WHAT A PARTY. YOU WERE QUIET. DID YOU HAVE FUN?
IT WAS GREAT, MOM.
EVERYTHING I COULD HAVE WANTED . . .

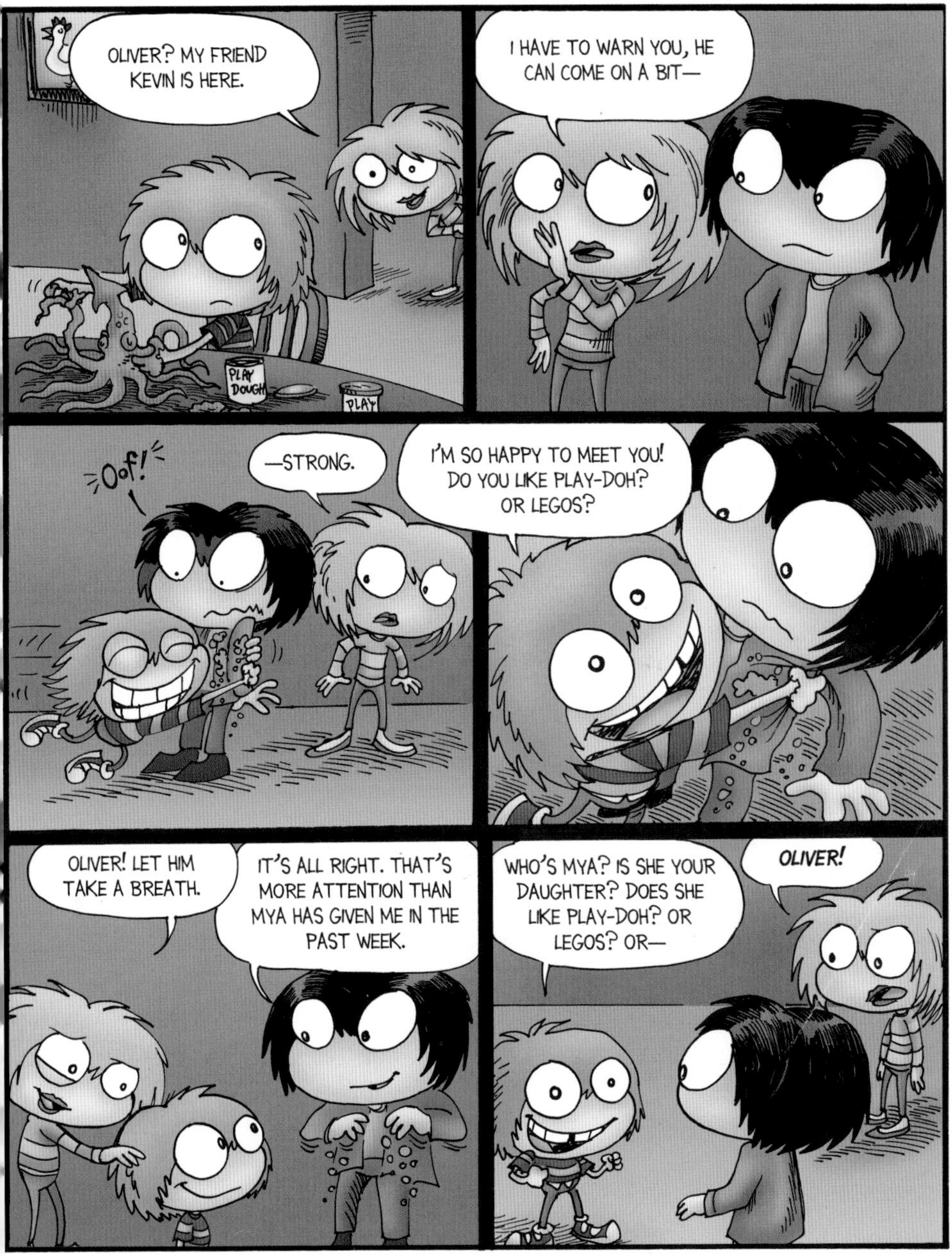
OLIVER? MY FRIEND KEVIN IS HERE.
PLAY DOUGH
PLAY
I HAVE TO WARN YOU, HE CAN COME ON A BIT—
OOF!
—STRONG.
I'M SO HAPPY TO MEET YOU! DO YOU LIKE PLAY-DOH? OR LEGOS?
OLIVER! LET HIM TAKE A BREATH.
IT'S ALL RIGHT. THAT'S MORE ATTENTION THAN MYA HAS GIVEN ME IN THE PAST WEEK.
WHO'S MYA? IS SHE YOUR DAUGHTER? DOES SHE LIKE PLAY-DOH? OR LEGOS? OR—
OLIVER!

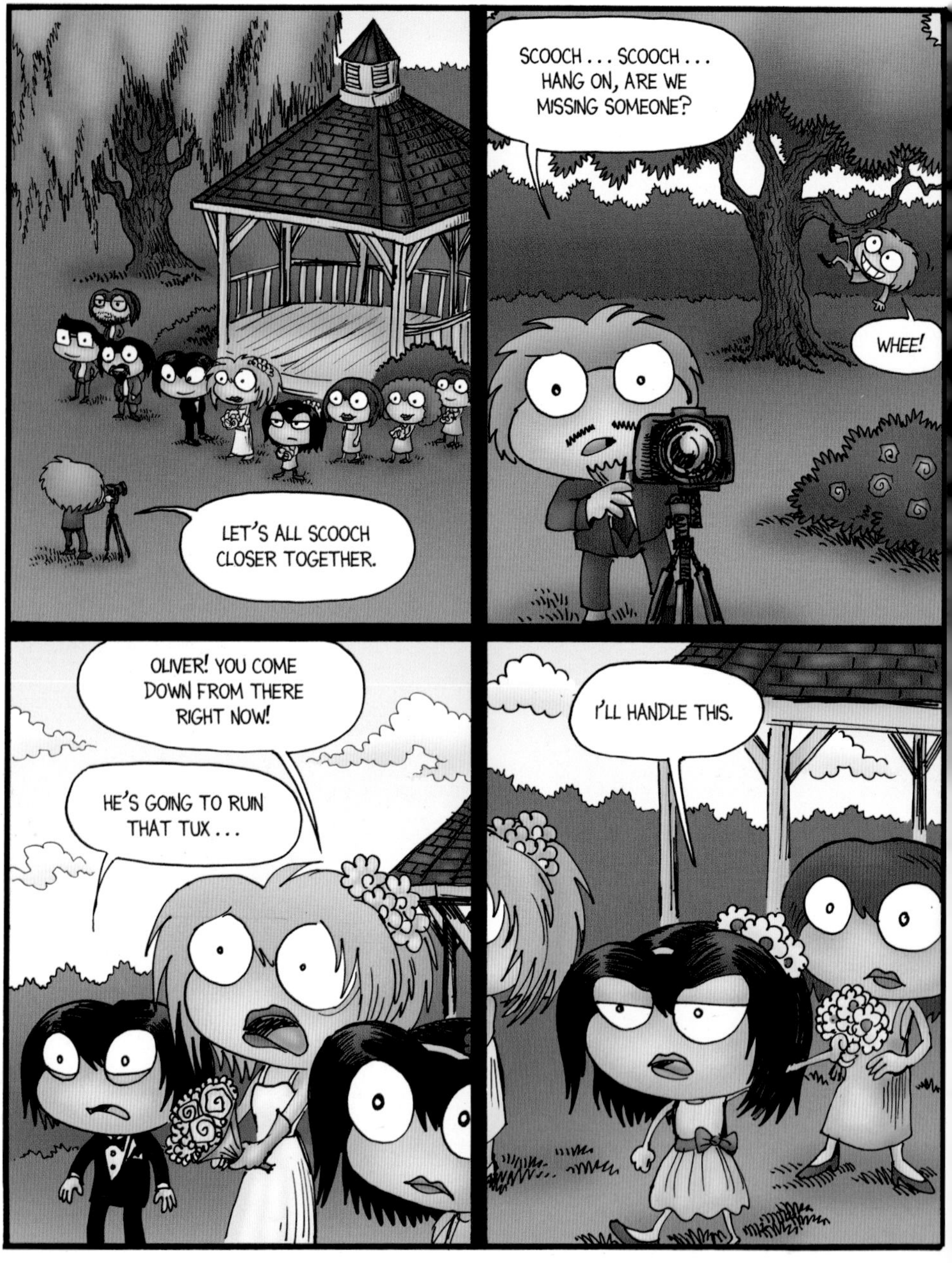
LET'S ALL SCOOCH CLOSER TOGETHER.
SCOOCH . . . SCOOCH . . . HANG ON, ARE WE MISSING SOMEONE?
WHEE!
OLIVER! YOU COME DOWN FROM THERE RIGHT NOW!
HE'S GOING TO RUIN THAT TUX . . .
I'LL HANDLE THIS.

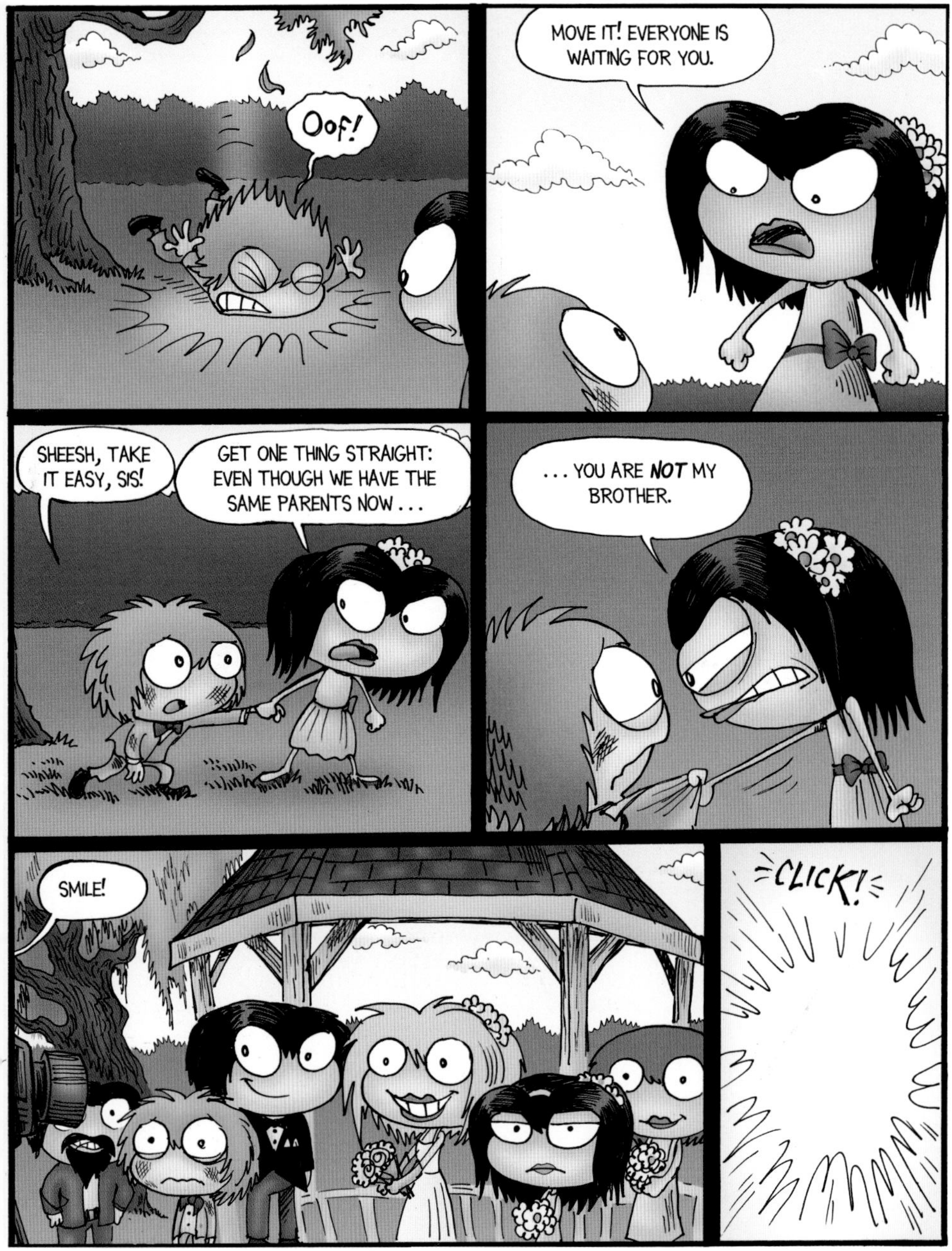
Oof!
MOVE IT! EVERYONE IS WAITING FOR YOU.
SHEESH, TAKE IT EASY, SIS!
GET ONE THING STRAIGHT: EVEN THOUGH WE HAVE THE SAME PARENTS NOW . . .
. . . YOU ARE **NOT** MY BROTHER.
SMILE!
CLICK!

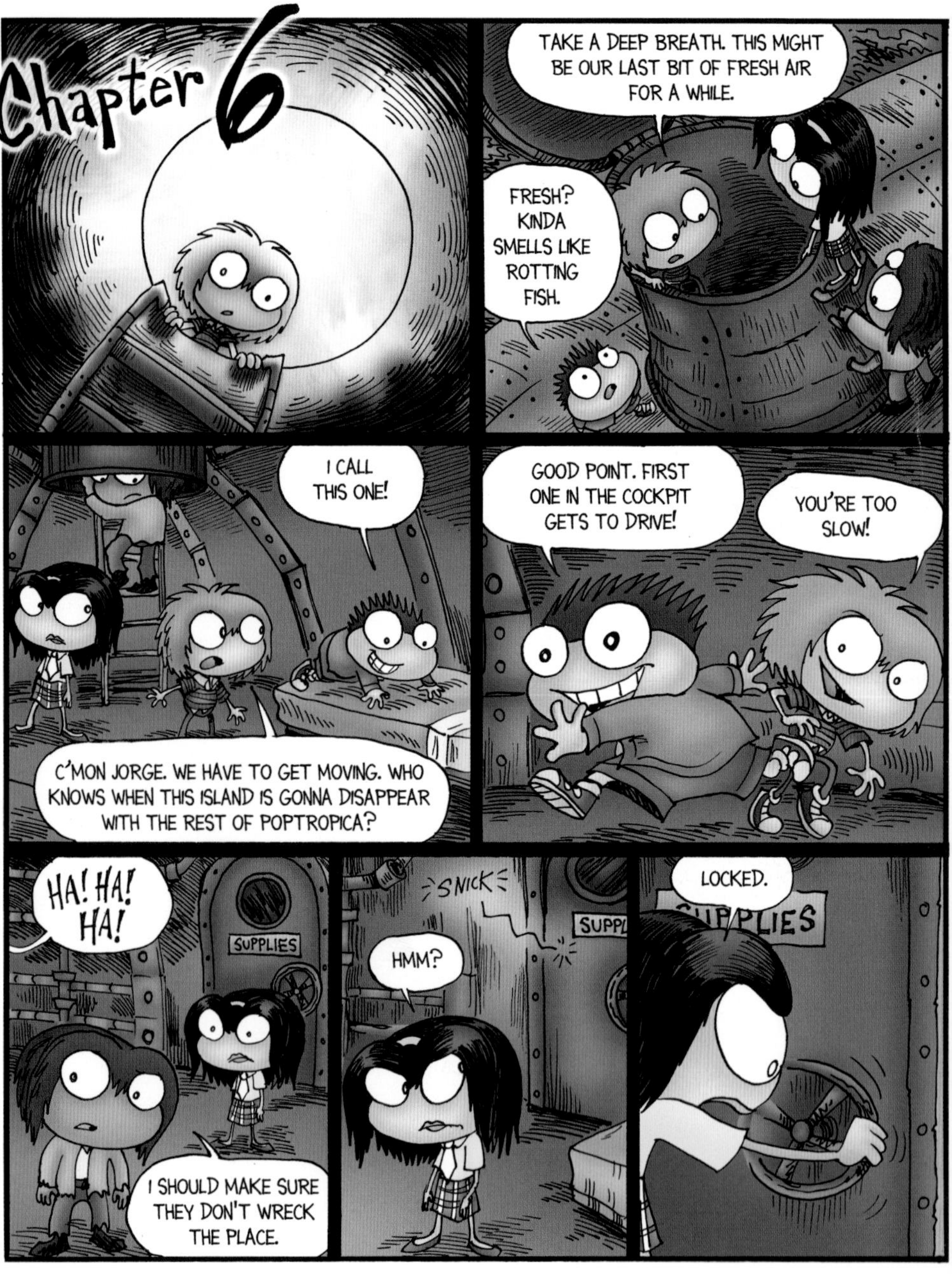
Chapter 6
TAKE A DEEP BREATH. THIS MIGHT BE OUR LAST BIT OF FRESH AIR FOR A WHILE.
FRESH? KINDA SMELLS LIKE ROTTING FISH.
I CALL THIS ONE!
C'MON JORGE. WE HAVE TO GET MOVING. WHO KNOWS WHEN THIS ISLAND IS GONNA DISAPPEAR WITH THE REST OF POPTROPICA?
GOOD POINT. FIRST ONE IN THE COCKPIT GETS TO DRIVE!
YOU'RE TOO SLOW!
HA! HA! HA!
SUPPLIES
I SHOULD MAKE SURE THEY DON'T WRECK THE PLACE.
SNICK
HMM?
LOCKED.
SUPPLIES

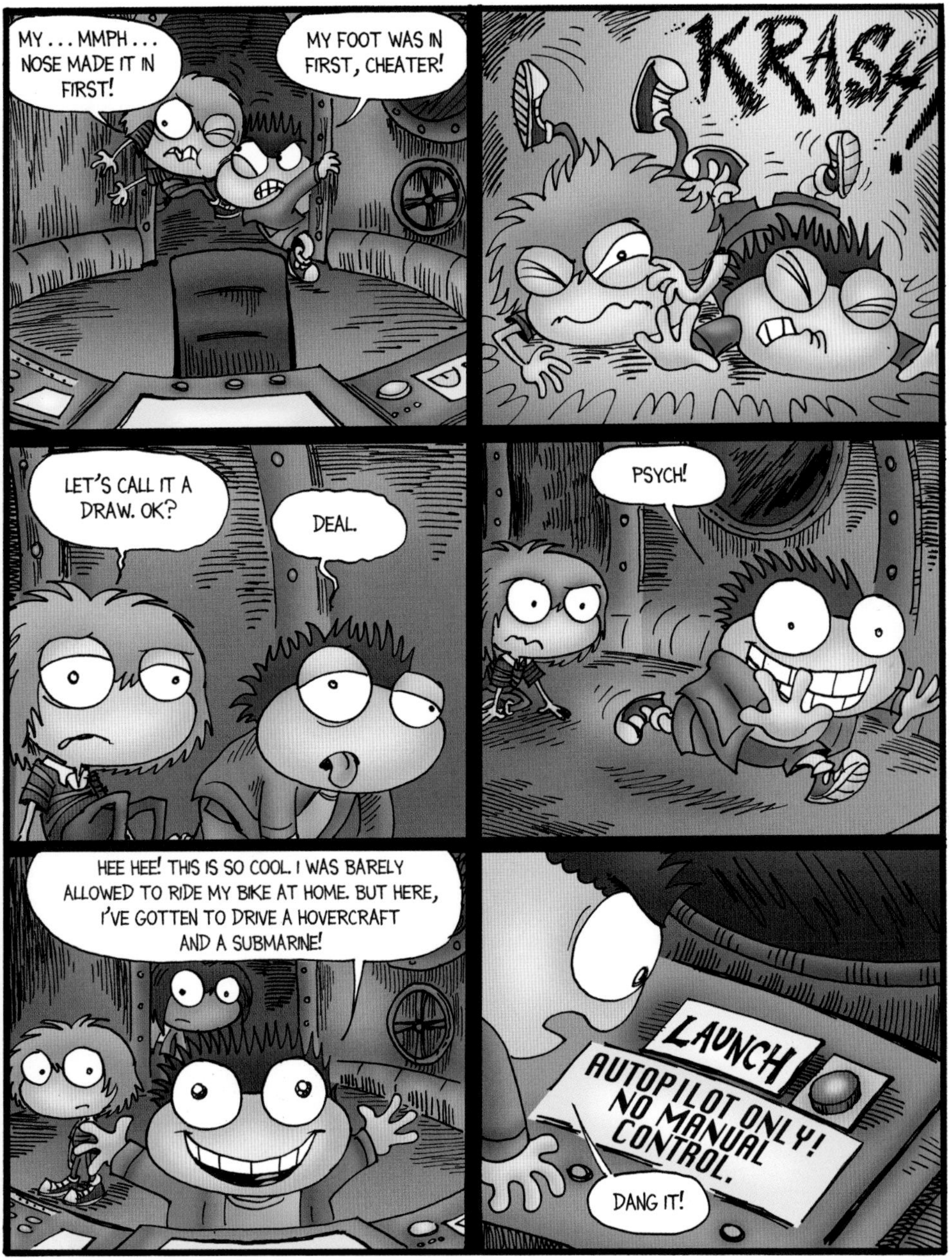
MY . . . MMPH . . . NOSE MADE IT IN FIRST!
MY FOOT WAS IN FIRST, CHEATER!
KRASH!
LET'S CALL IT A DRAW. OK?
DEAL.
PSYCH!
HEE HEE! THIS IS SO COOL. I WAS BARELY ALLOWED TO RIDE MY BIKE AT HOME. BUT HERE, I'VE GOTTEN TO DRIVE A HOVERCRAFT AND A SUBMARINE!
LAUNCH
AUTOPILOT ONLY! NO MANUAL CONTROL.
DANG IT!

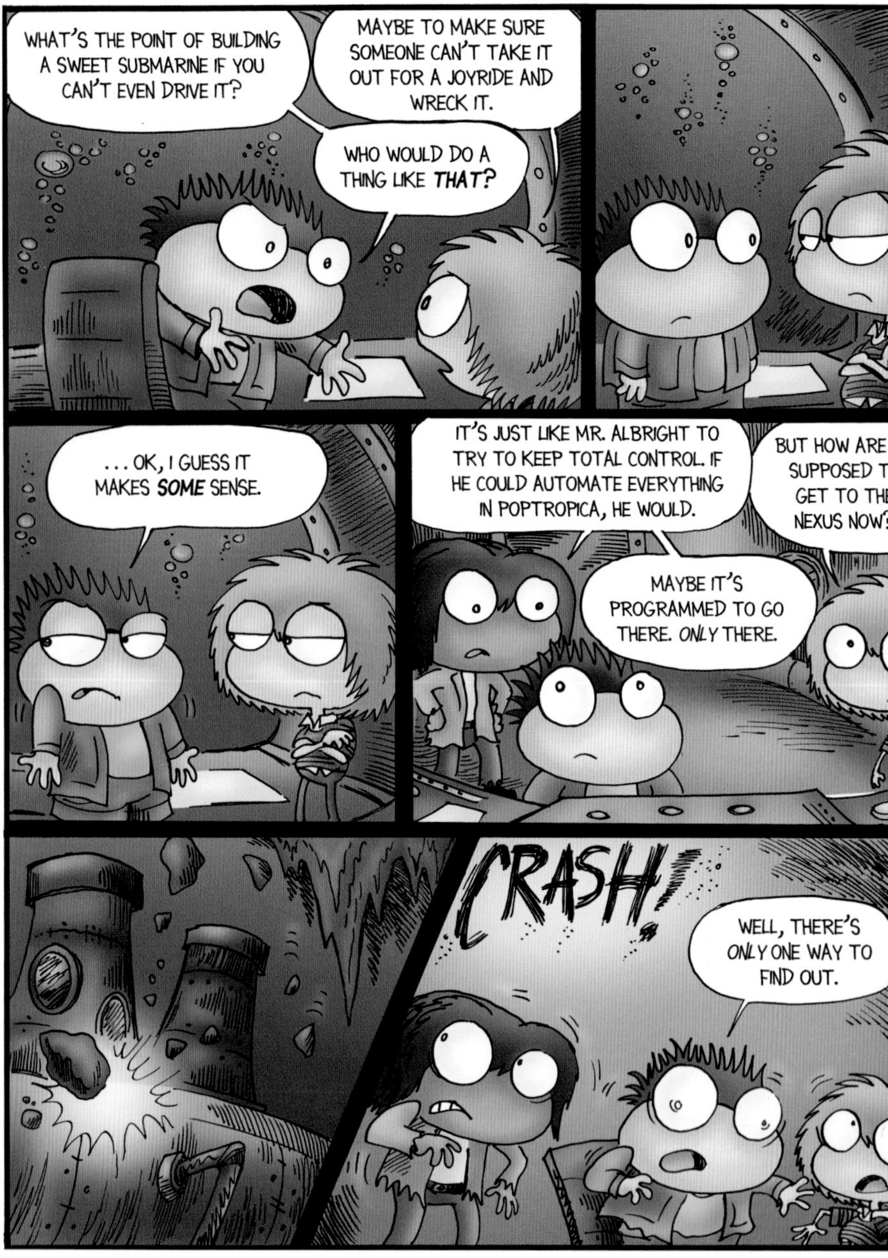
WHAT'S THE POINT OF BUILDING A SWEET SUBMARINE IF YOU CAN'T EVEN DRIVE IT?
MAYBE TO MAKE SURE SOMEONE CAN'T TAKE IT OUT FOR A JOYRIDE AND WRECK IT.
WHO WOULD DO A THING LIKE **THAT?**
. . . OK, I GUESS IT MAKES **SOME** SENSE.
IT'S JUST LIKE MR. ALBRIGHT TO TRY TO KEEP TOTAL CONTROL. IF HE COULD AUTOMATE EVERYTHING IN POPTROPICA, HE WOULD.
BUT HOW ARE WE SUPPOSED TO GET TO THE NEXUS NOW?
MAYBE IT'S PROGRAMMED TO GO THERE. *ONLY* THERE.
CRASH!
WELL, THERE'S *ONLY* ONE WAY TO FIND OUT.

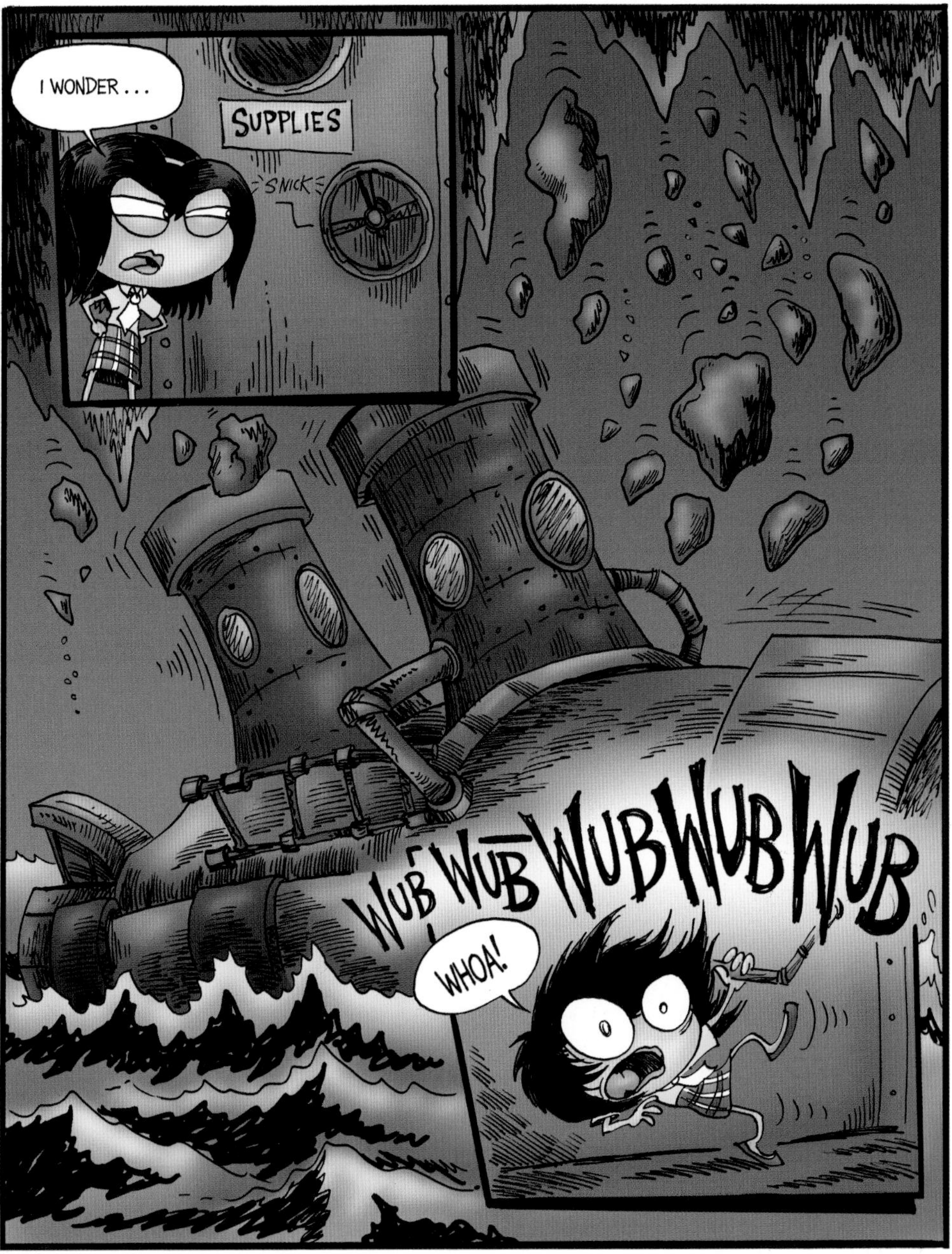
I WONDER . . .
SUPPLIES
SNICK
WUB WUB WUB WUB WUB
WHOA!

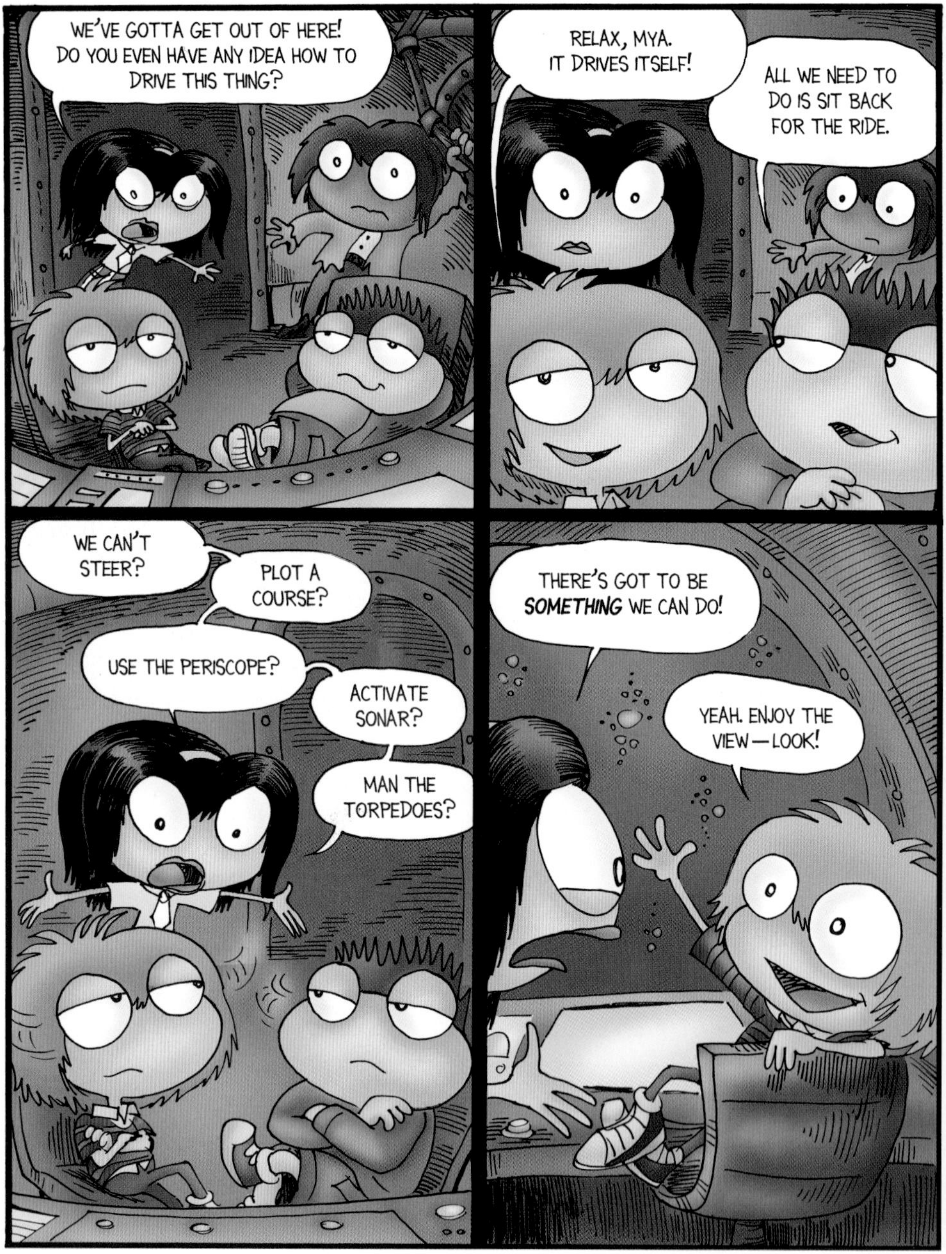
WE'VE GOTTA GET OUT OF HERE! DO YOU EVEN HAVE ANY IDEA HOW TO DRIVE THIS THING?
RELAX, MYA. IT DRIVES ITSELF!
ALL WE NEED TO DO IS SIT BACK FOR THE RIDE.
WE CAN'T STEER?
PLOT A COURSE?
USE THE PERISCOPE?
ACTIVATE SONAR?
MAN THE TORPEDOES?
THERE'S GOT TO BE **SOMETHING** WE CAN DO!
YEAH. ENJOY THE VIEW—LOOK!

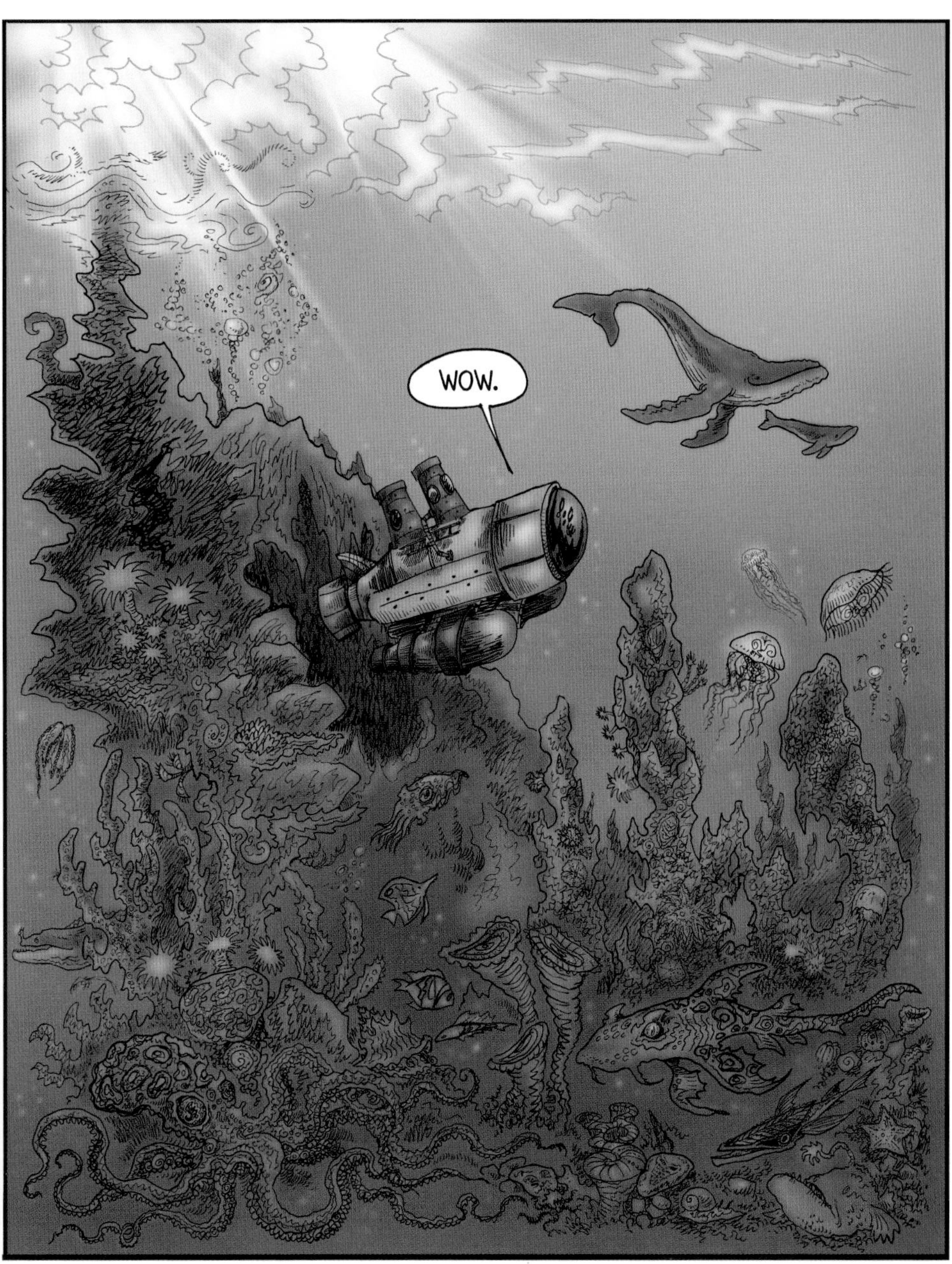
WOW.

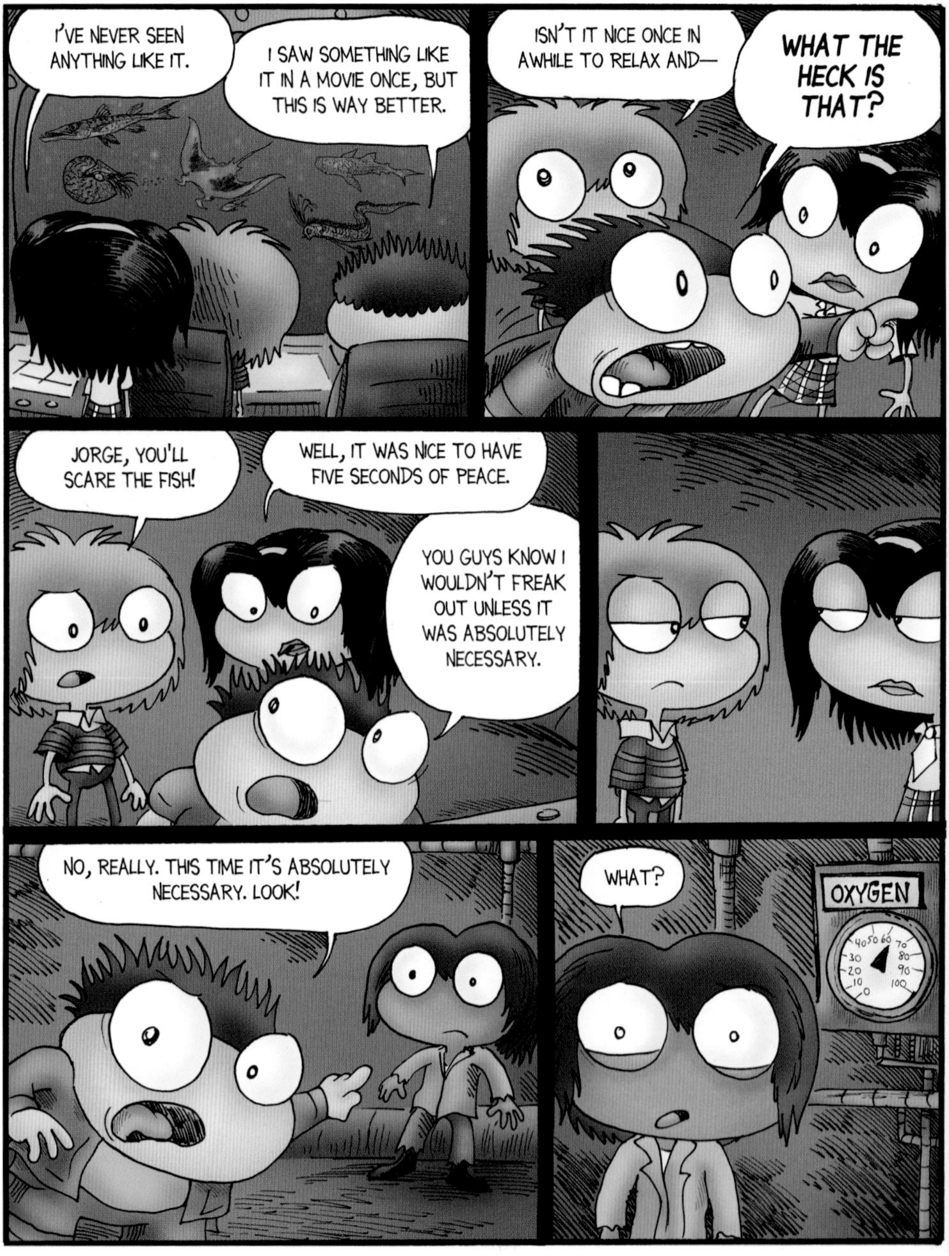
I'VE NEVER SEEN ANYTHING LIKE IT.
I SAW SOMETHING LIKE IT IN A MOVIE ONCE, BUT THIS IS WAY BETTER.
ISN'T IT NICE ONCE IN AWHILE TO RELAX AND—
WHAT THE HECK IS THAT?
JORGE, YOU'LL SCARE THE FISH!
WELL, IT WAS NICE TO HAVE FIVE SECONDS OF PEACE.
YOU GUYS KNOW I WOULDN'T FREAK OUT UNLESS IT WAS ABSOLUTELY NECESSARY.
NO, REALLY. THIS TIME IT'S ABSOLUTELY NECESSARY. LOOK!
WHAT?
OXYGEN

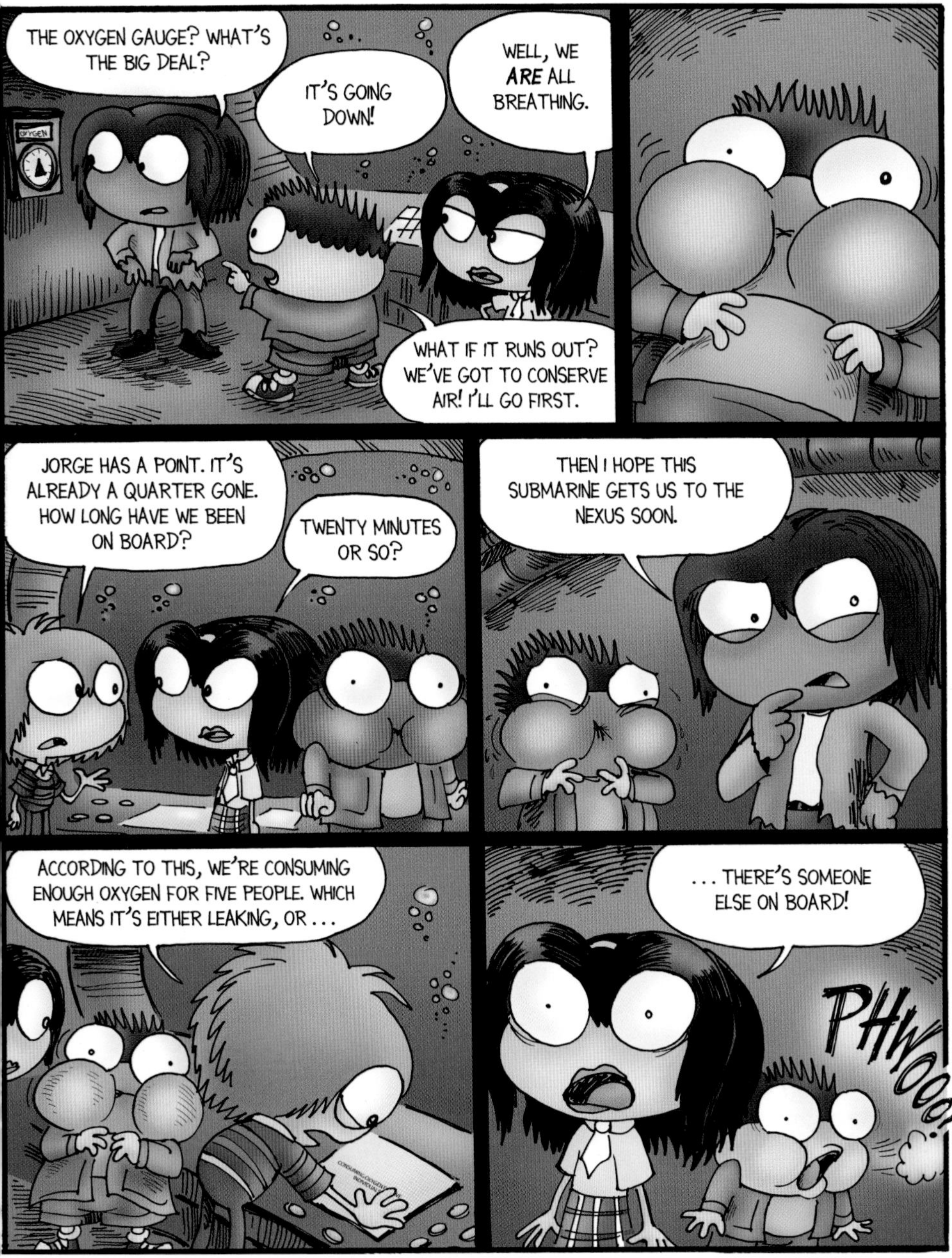
THE OXYGEN GAUGE? WHAT'S THE BIG DEAL?
OXYGEN
IT'S GOING DOWN!
WELL, WE ARE ALL BREATHING.
WHAT IF IT RUNS OUT? WE'VE GOT TO CONSERVE AIR! I'LL GO FIRST.
JORGE HAS A POINT. IT'S ALREADY A QUARTER GONE. HOW LONG HAVE WE BEEN ON BOARD?
TWENTY MINUTES OR SO?
THEN I HOPE THIS SUBMARINE GETS US TO THE NEXUS SOON.
ACCORDING TO THIS, WE'RE CONSUMING ENOUGH OXYGEN FOR FIVE PEOPLE. WHICH MEANS IT'S EITHER LEAKING, OR . . .
. . . THERE'S SOMEONE ELSE ON BOARD!
PHWOOO!

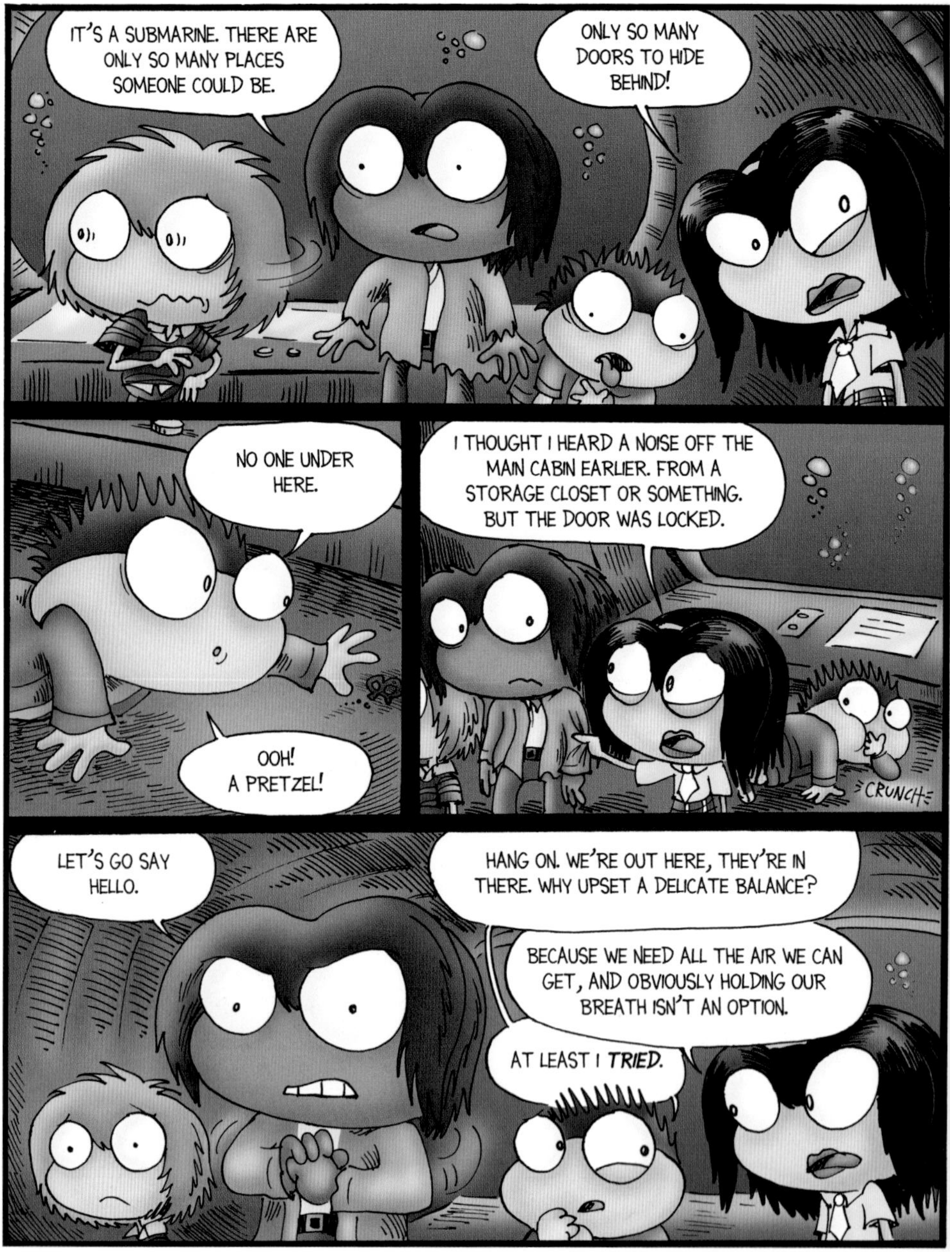
IT'S A SUBMARINE. THERE ARE ONLY SO MANY PLACES SOMEONE COULD BE.
ONLY SO MANY DOORS TO HIDE BEHIND!
NO ONE UNDER HERE.
OOH! A PRETZEL!
I THOUGHT I HEARD A NOISE OFF THE MAIN CABIN EARLIER. FROM A STORAGE CLOSET OR SOMETHING. BUT THE DOOR WAS LOCKED.
CRUNCH
LET'S GO SAY HELLO.
HANG ON. WE'RE OUT HERE, THEY'RE IN THERE. WHY UPSET A DELICATE BALANCE?
BECAUSE WE NEED ALL THE AIR WE CAN GET, AND OBVIOUSLY HOLDING OUR BREATH ISN'T AN OPTION.
AT LEAST I TRIED.

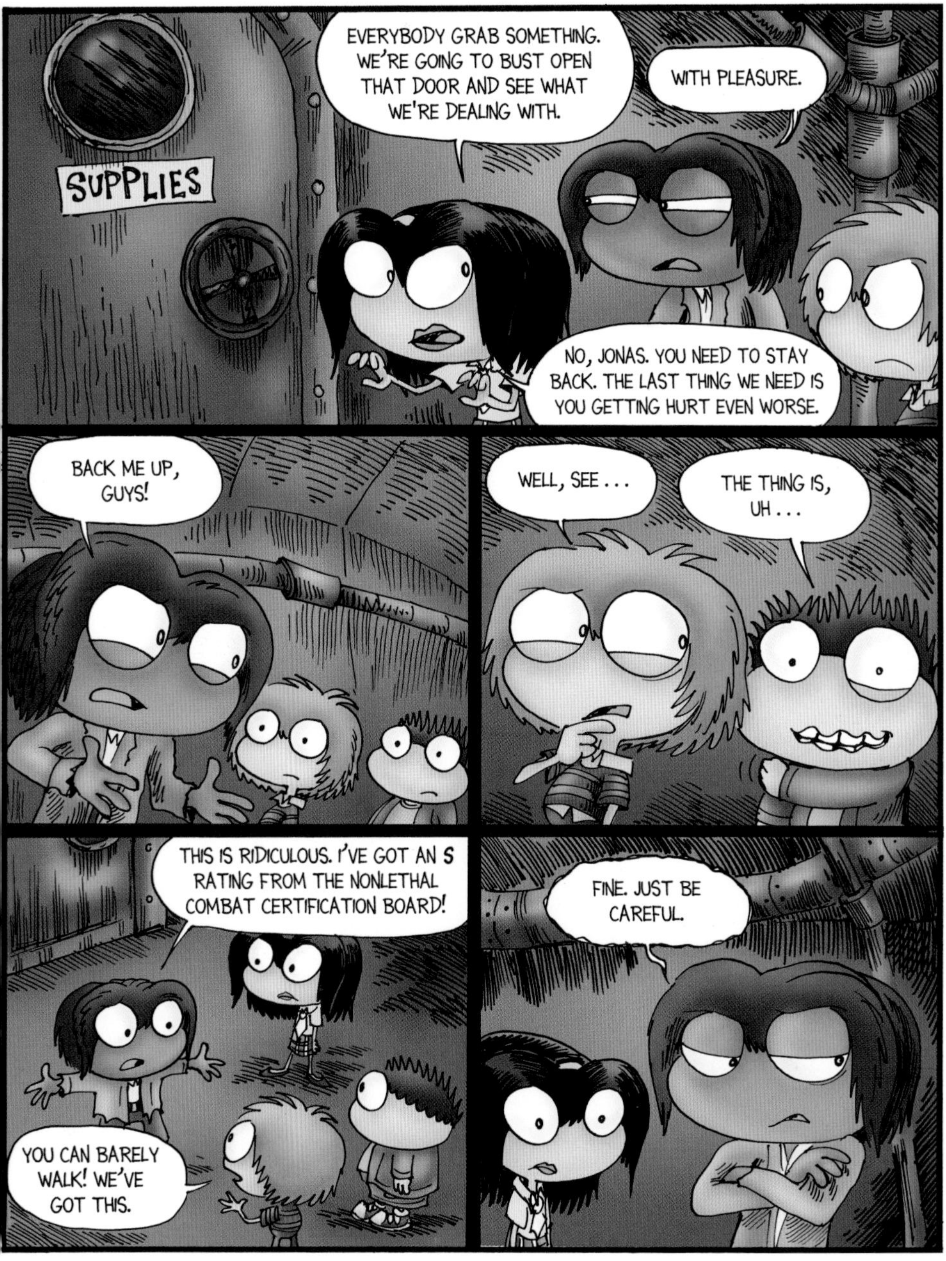
SUPPLIES
EVERYBODY GRAB SOMETHING. WE'RE GOING TO BUST OPEN THAT DOOR AND SEE WHAT WE'RE DEALING WITH.
WITH PLEASURE.
NO, JONAS. YOU NEED TO STAY BACK. THE LAST THING WE NEED IS YOU GETTING HURT EVEN WORSE.
BACK ME UP, GUYS!
WELL, SEE . . .
THE THING IS, UH . . .
THIS IS RIDICULOUS. I'VE GOT AN S RATING FROM THE NONLETHAL COMBAT CERTIFICATION BOARD!
YOU CAN BARELY WALK! WE'VE GOT THIS.
FINE. JUST BE CAREFUL.

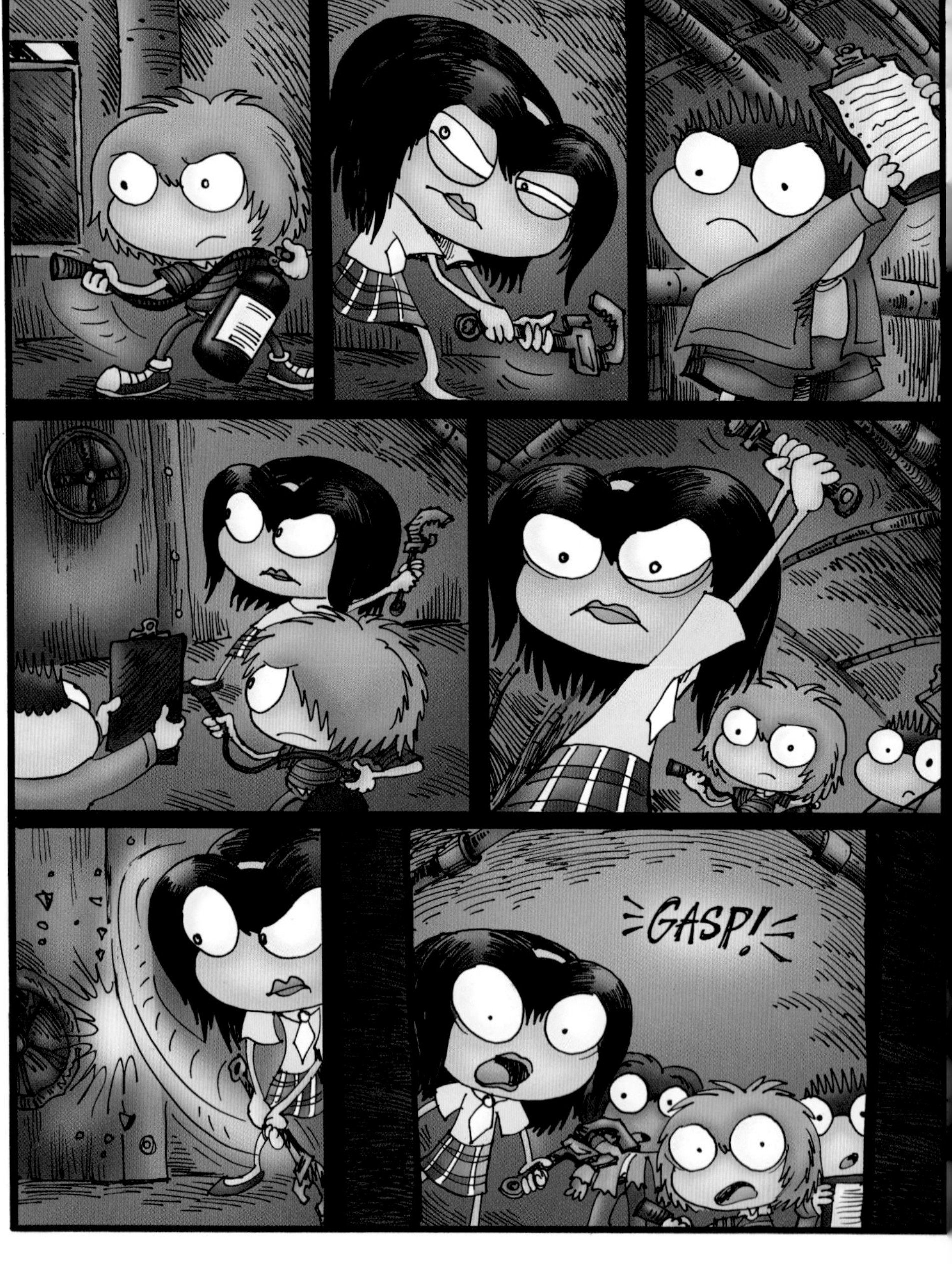
GASP!

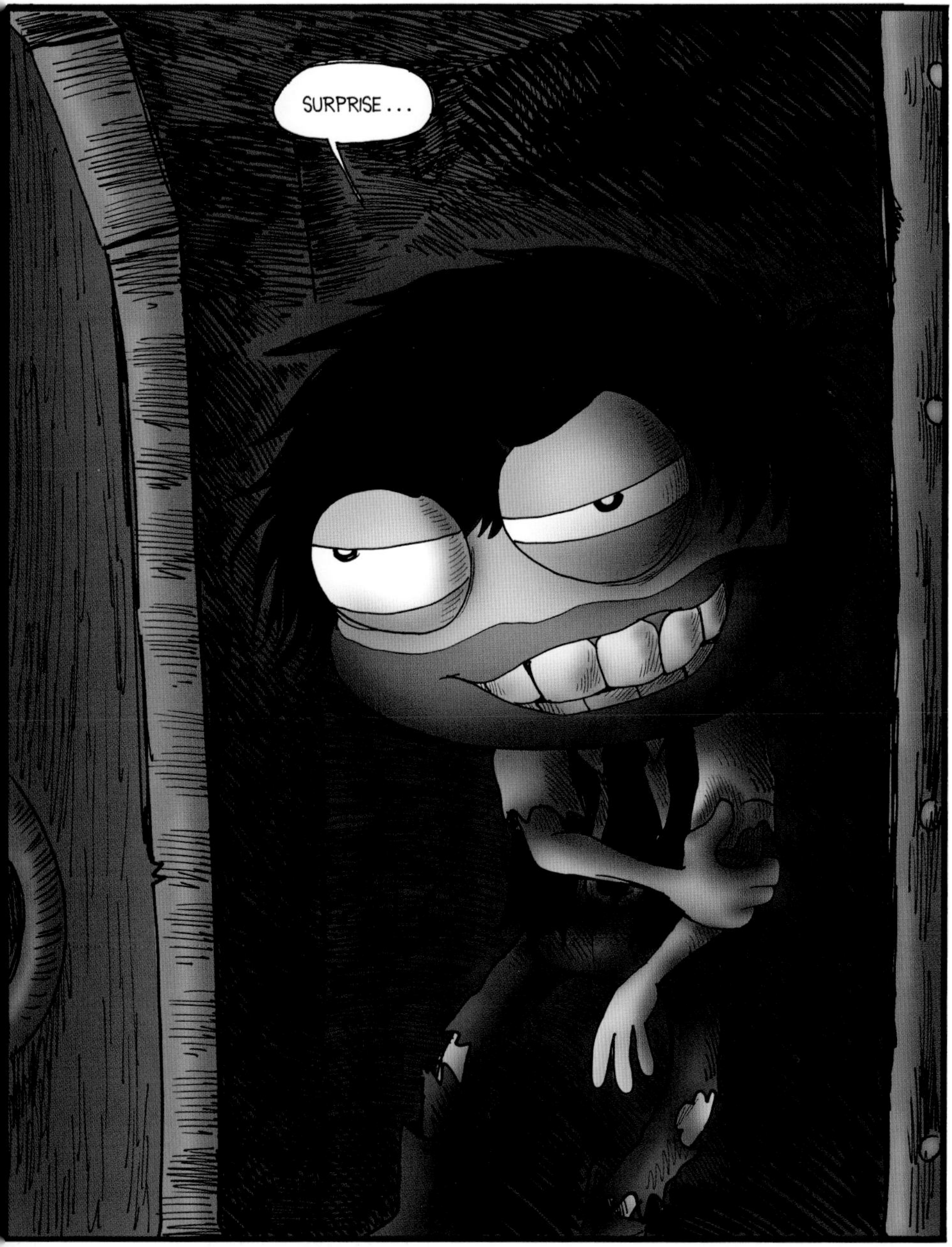
SURPRISE . . .

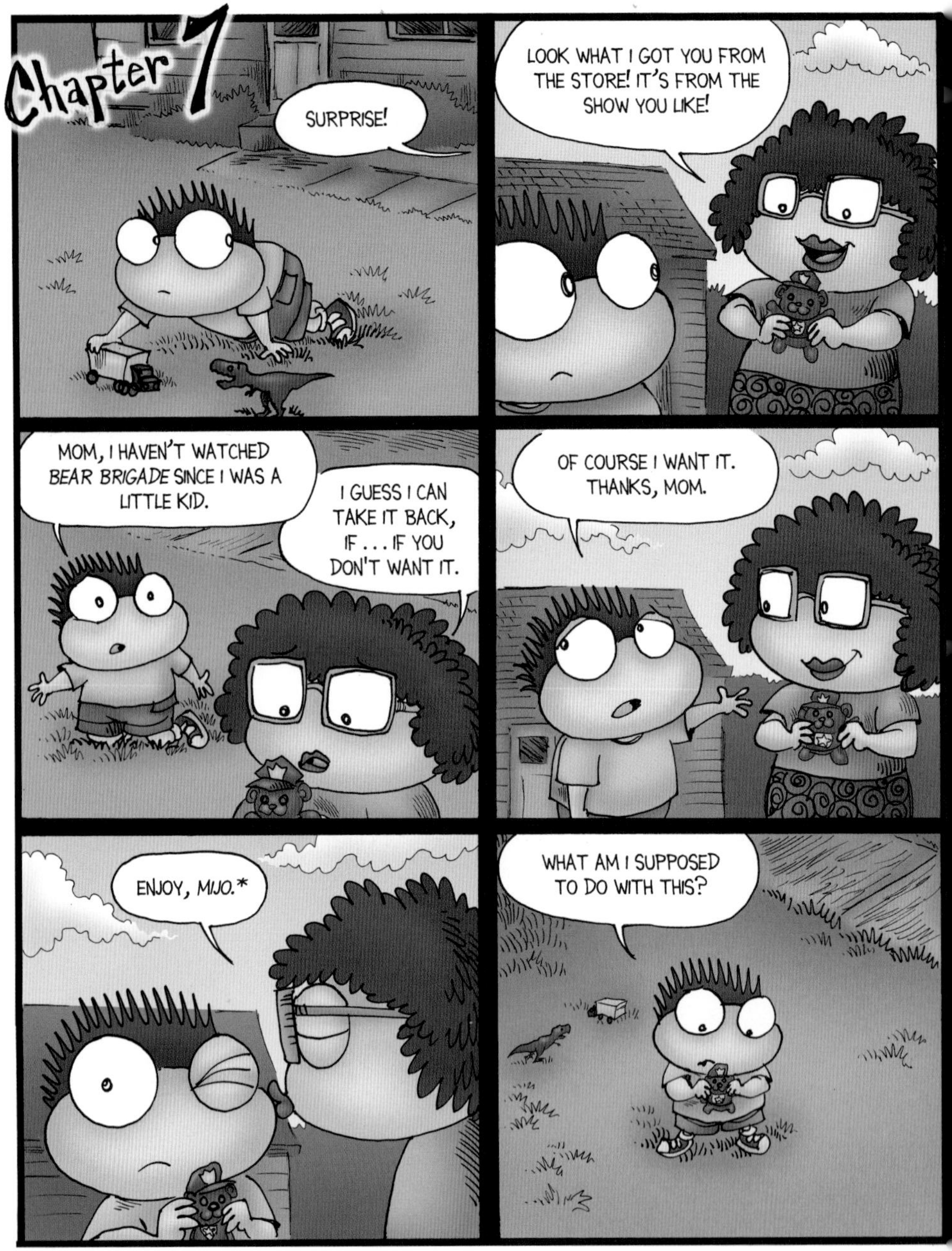
Chapter 7
SURPRISE!
LOOK WHAT I GOT YOU FROM THE STORE! IT'S FROM THE SHOW YOU LIKE!
MOM, I HAVEN'T WATCHED *BEAR BRIGADE* SINCE I WAS A LITTLE KID.
I GUESS I CAN TAKE IT BACK, IF . . . IF YOU DON'T WANT IT.
OF COURSE I WANT IT. THANKS, MOM.
ENJOY, MIJO.*
WHAT AM I SUPPOSED TO DO WITH THIS?

*DEAR

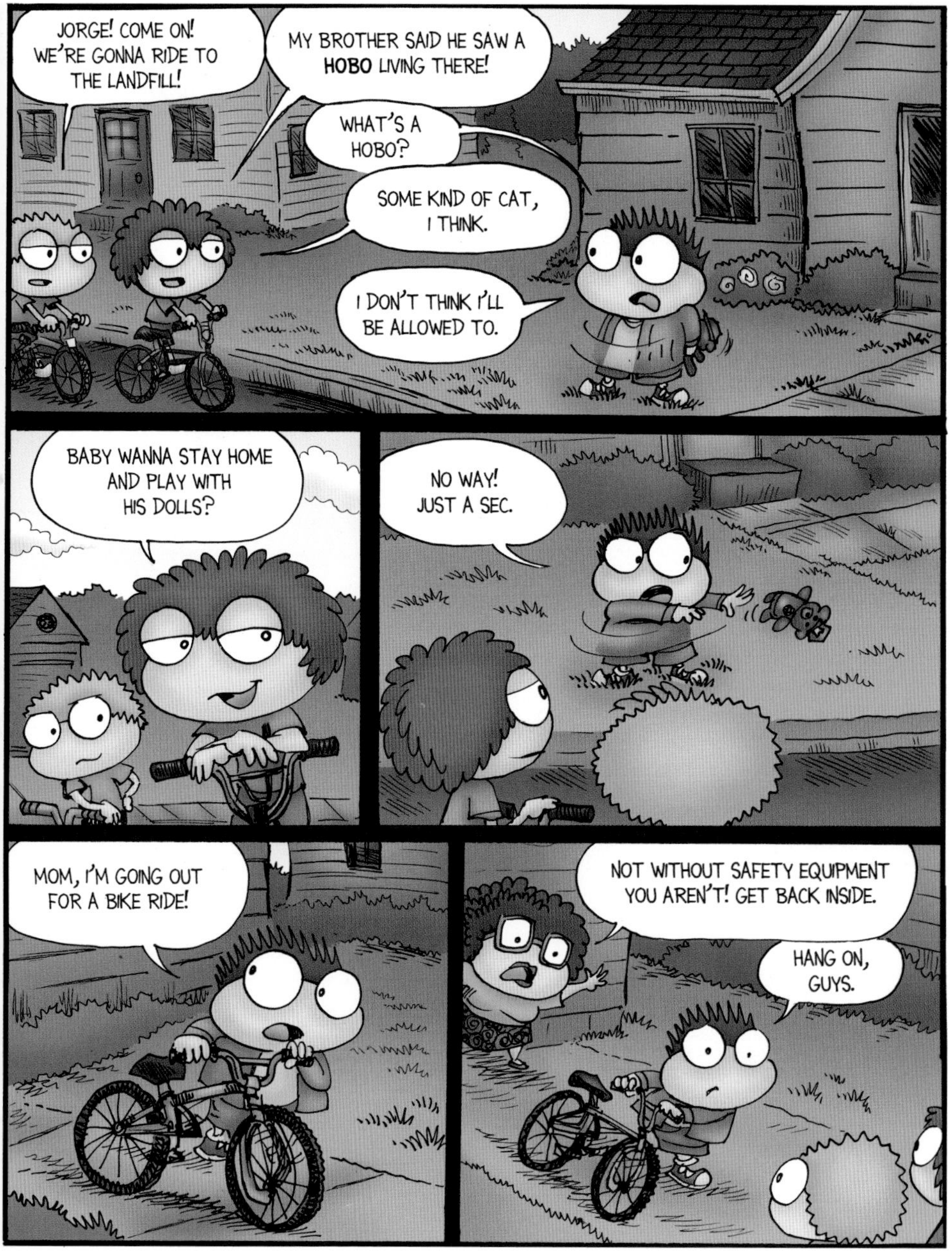
JORGE! COME ON! WE'RE GONNA RIDE TO THE LANDFILL!
MY BROTHER SAID HE SAW A **HOBO** LIVING THERE!
WHAT'S A HOBO?
SOME KIND OF CAT, I THINK.
I DON'T THINK I'LL BE ALLOWED TO.
BABY WANNA STAY HOME AND PLAY WITH HIS DOLLS?
NO WAY! JUST A SEC.
MOM, I'M GOING OUT FOR A BIKE RIDE!
NOT WITHOUT SAFETY EQUIPMENT YOU AREN'T! GET BACK INSIDE.
HANG ON, GUYS.

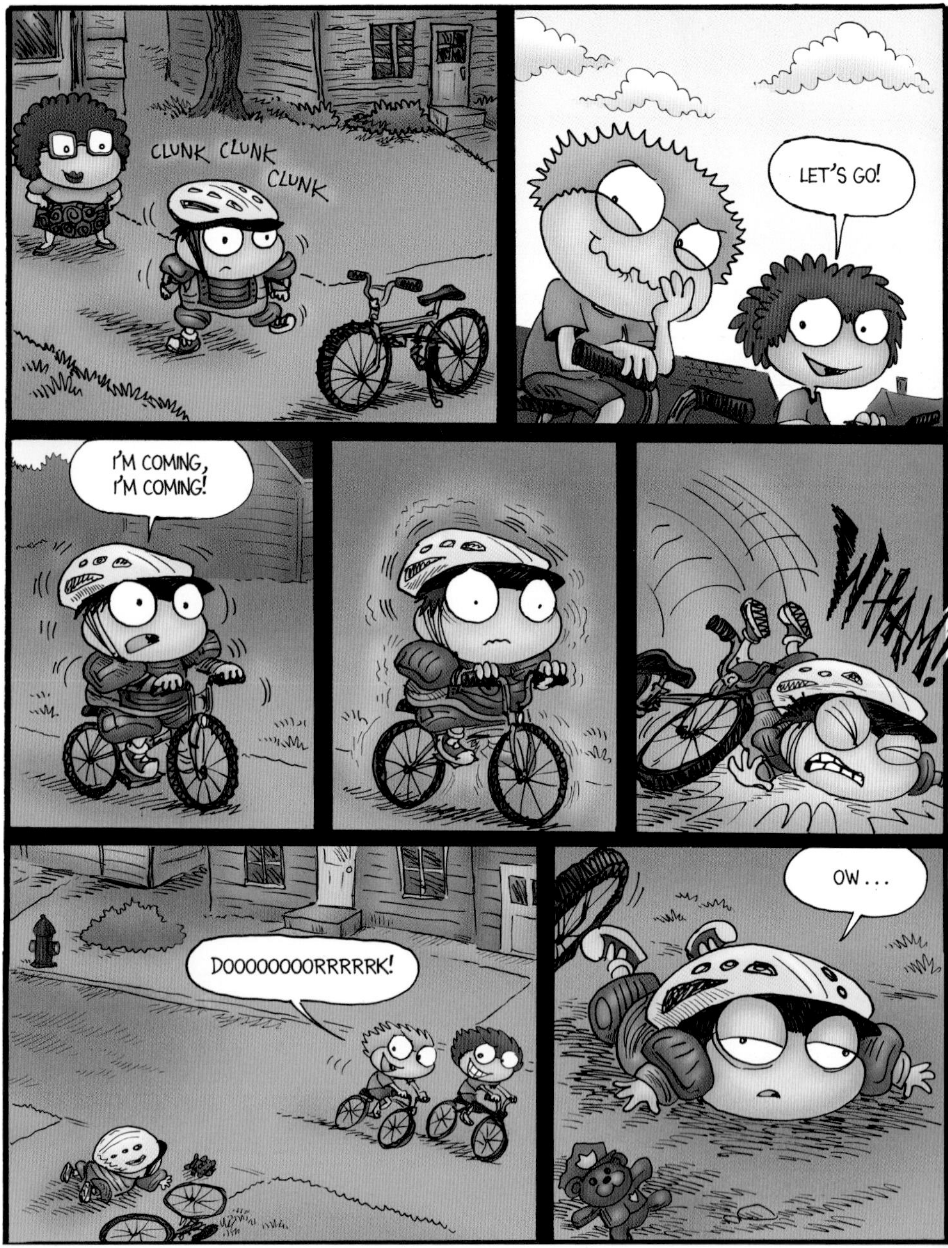
CLUNK CLUNK
CLUNK
LET'S GO!
I'M COMING,
I'M COMING!
WHAM!
DOOOOOOOORRRRRK!
OW...

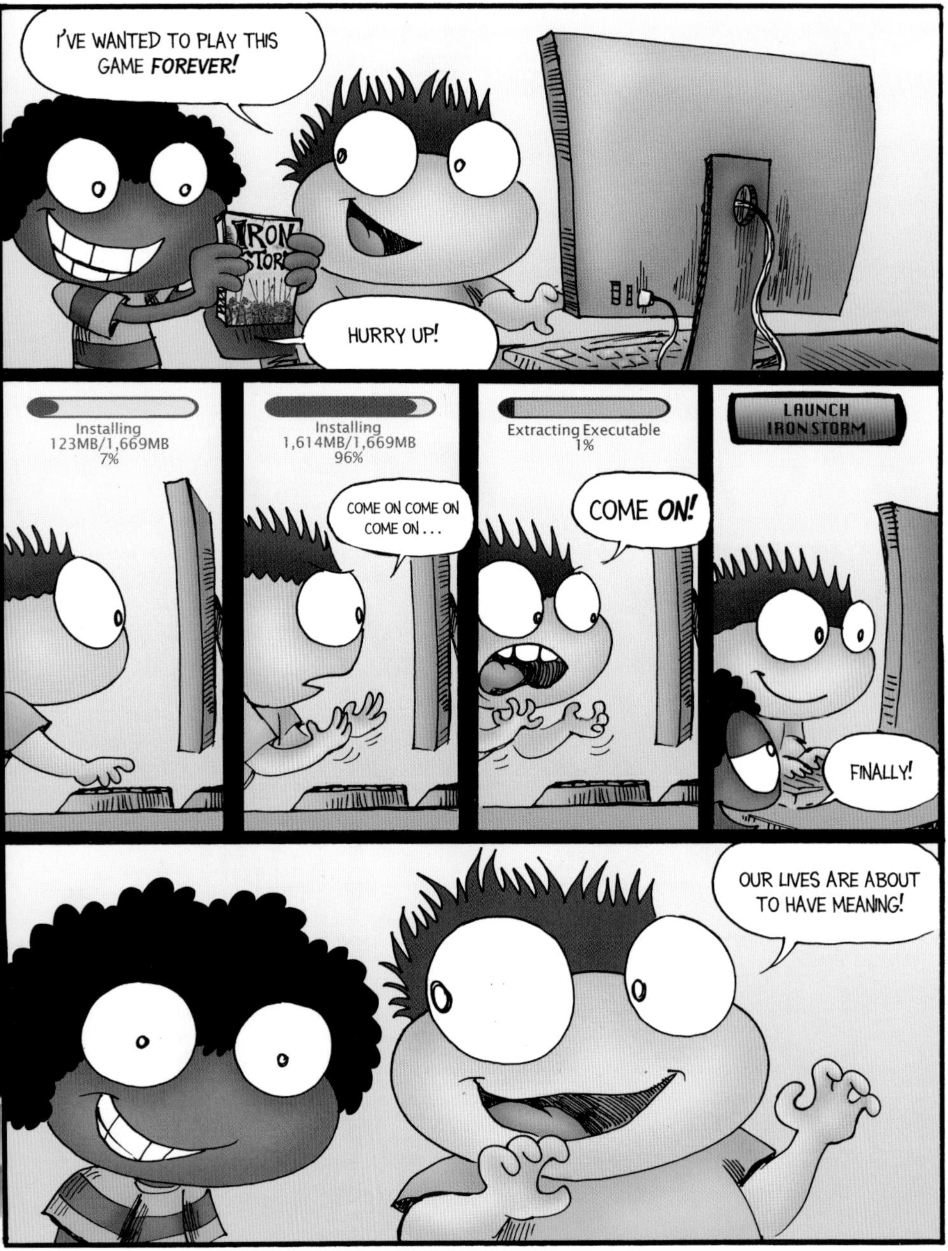
I'VE WANTED TO PLAY THIS GAME FOREVER!
HURRY UP!
Installing
123MB/1,669MB
7%
Installing
1,614MB/1,669MB
96%
COME ON COME ON COME ON . . .
Extracting Executable
1%
COME ON!
LAUNCH IRONSTORM
FINALLY!
OUR LIVES ARE ABOUT TO HAVE MEANING!

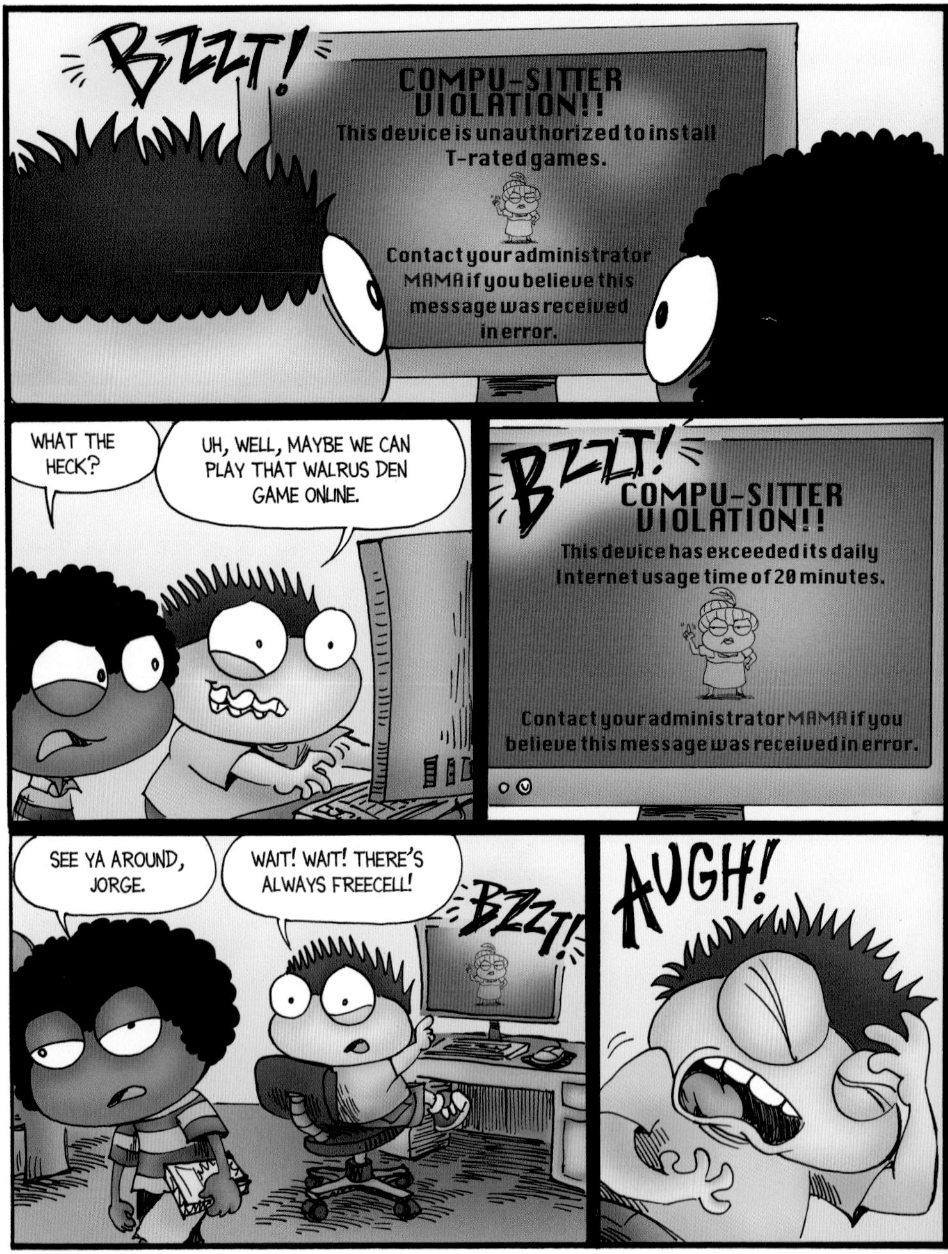

BZZT!
COMPU-SITTER VIOLATION!!
This device is unauthorized to install T-rated games.
Contact your administrator MAMA if you believe this message was received in error.
WHAT THE HECK?
UH, WELL, MAYBE WE CAN PLAY THAT WALRUS DEN GAME ONLINE.
BZZT!
COMPU-SITTER VIOLATION!!
This device has exceeded its daily Internet usage time of 20 minutes.
Contact your administrator MAMA if you believe this message was received in error.
SEE YA AROUND, JORGE.
WAIT! WAIT! THERE'S ALWAYS FREECELL!
BZZT!
AUGH!

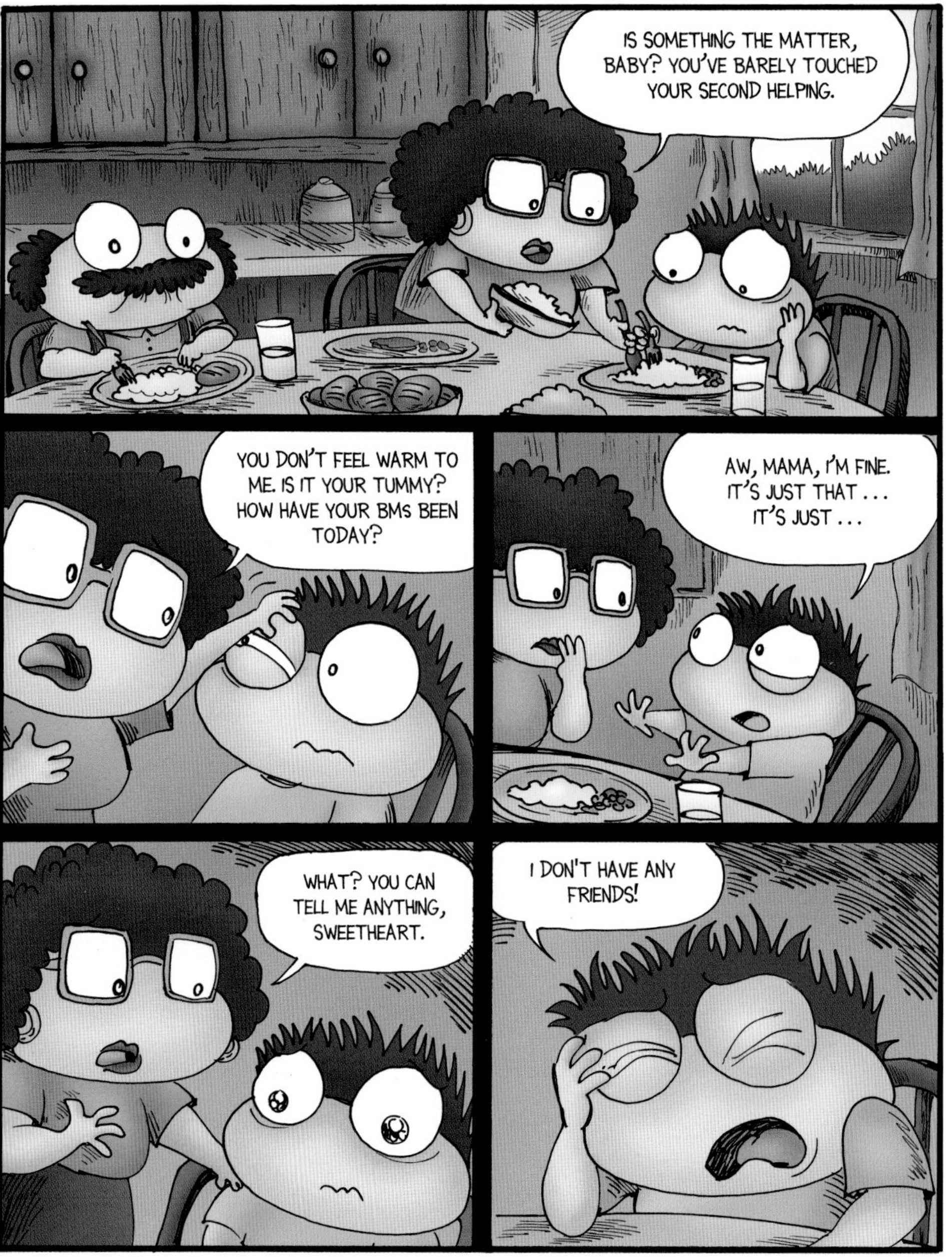
IS SOMETHING THE MATTER, BABY? YOU'VE BARELY TOUCHED YOUR SECOND HELPING.
YOU DON'T FEEL WARM TO ME. IS IT YOUR TUMMY? HOW HAVE YOUR BMs BEEN TODAY?
AW, MAMA, I'M FINE. IT'S JUST THAT . . . IT'S JUST . . .
WHAT? YOU CAN TELL ME ANYTHING, SWEETHEART.
I DON'T HAVE ANY FRIENDS!

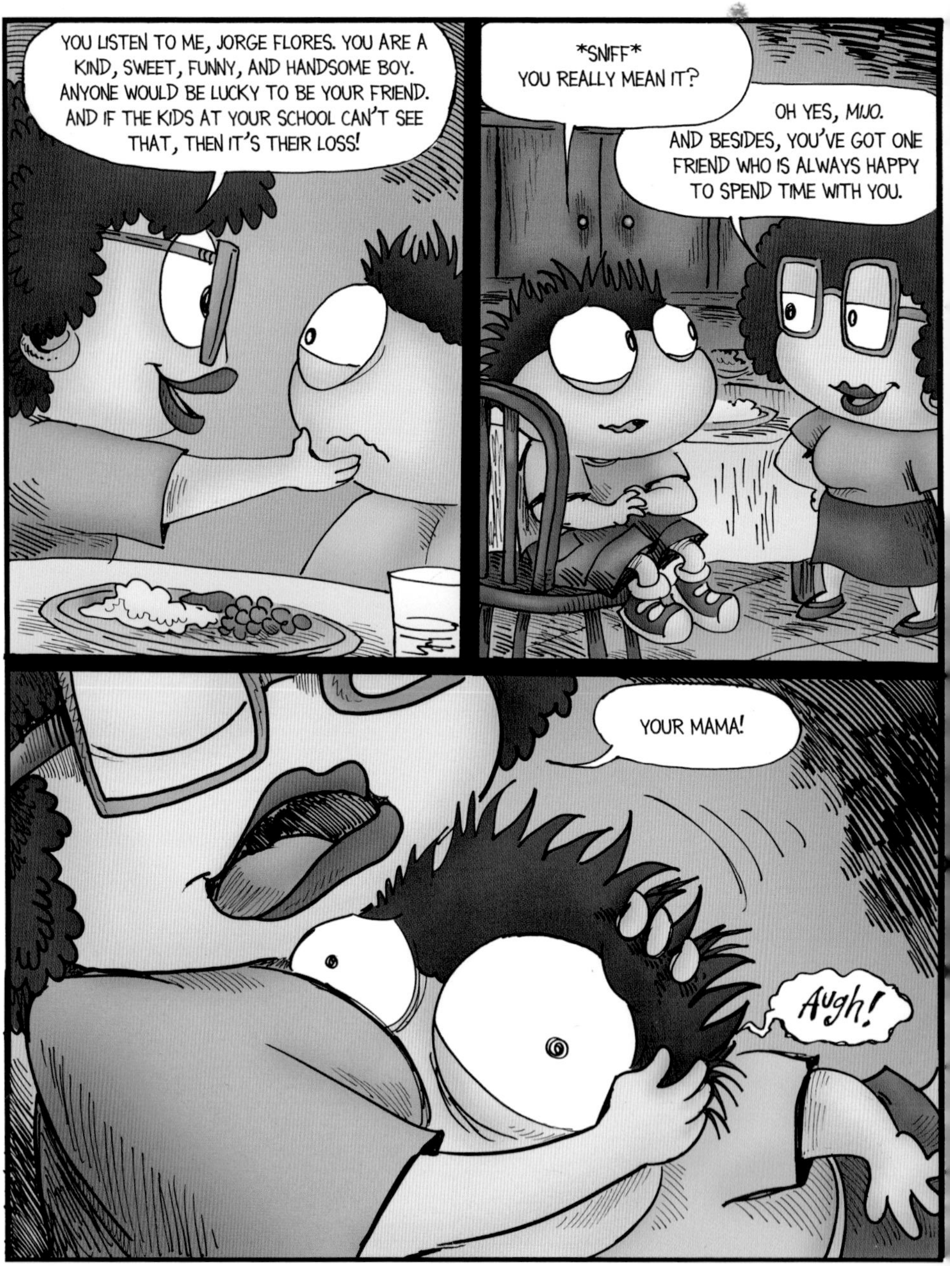
YOU LISTEN TO ME, JORGE FLORES. YOU ARE A KIND, SWEET, FUNNY, AND HANDSOME BOY. ANYONE WOULD BE LUCKY TO BE YOUR FRIEND. AND IF THE KIDS AT YOUR SCHOOL CAN'T SEE THAT, THEN IT'S THEIR LOSS!
SNIFF YOU REALLY MEAN IT?
OH YES, MIJO. AND BESIDES, YOU'VE GOT ONE FRIEND WHO IS ALWAYS HAPPY TO SPEND TIME WITH YOU.
YOUR MAMA!
Augh!

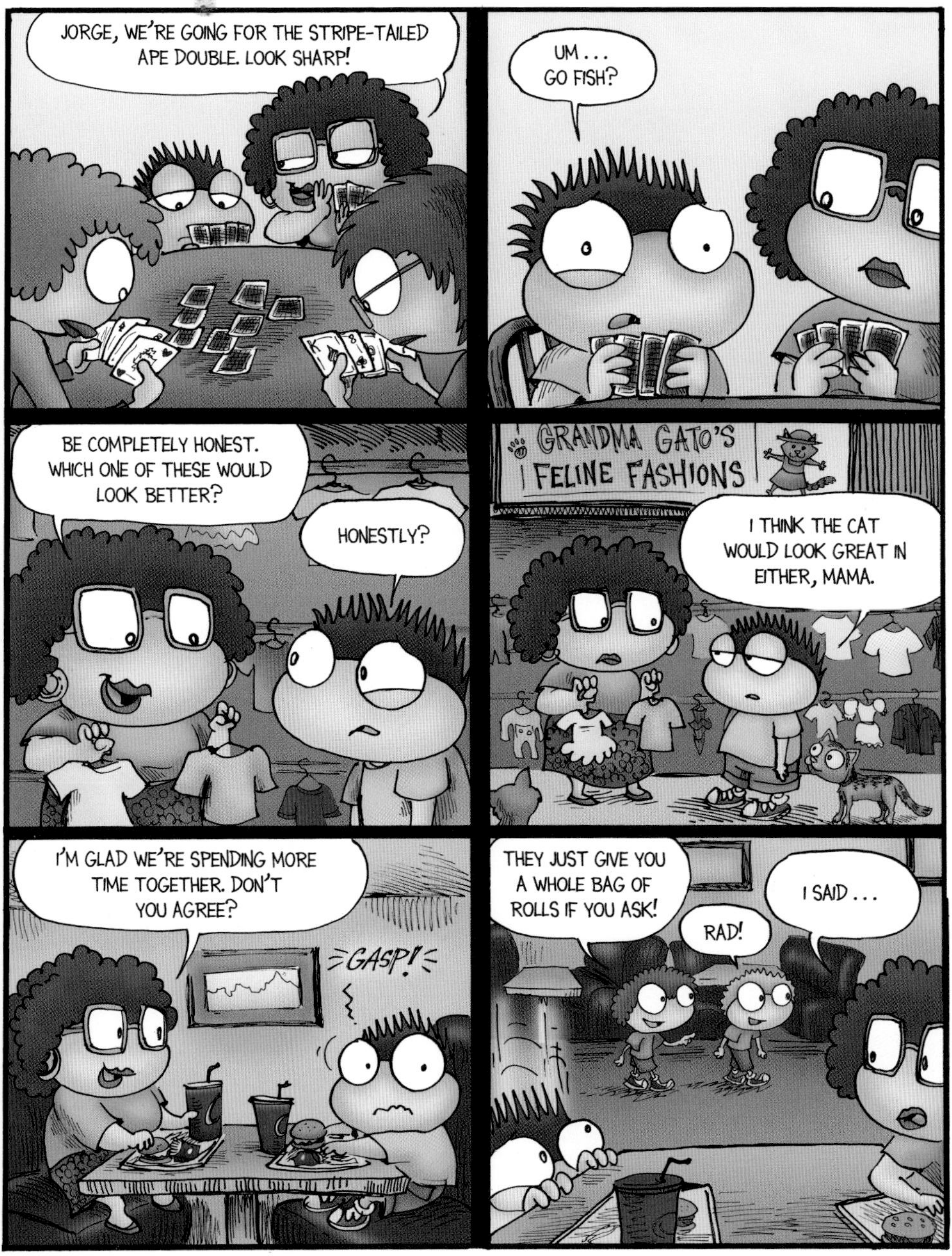
JORGE, WE'RE GOING FOR THE STRIPE-TAILED APE DOUBLE. LOOK SHARP!
UM . . . GO FISH?
BE COMPLETELY HONEST. WHICH ONE OF THESE WOULD LOOK BETTER?
HONESTLY?
GRANDMA GATO'S FELINE FASHIONS
I THINK THE CAT WOULD LOOK GREAT IN EITHER, MAMA.
I'M GLAD WE'RE SPENDING MORE TIME TOGETHER. DON'T YOU AGREE?
GASP!
THEY JUST GIVE YOU A WHOLE BAG OF ROLLS IF YOU ASK!
RAD!
I SAID . . .

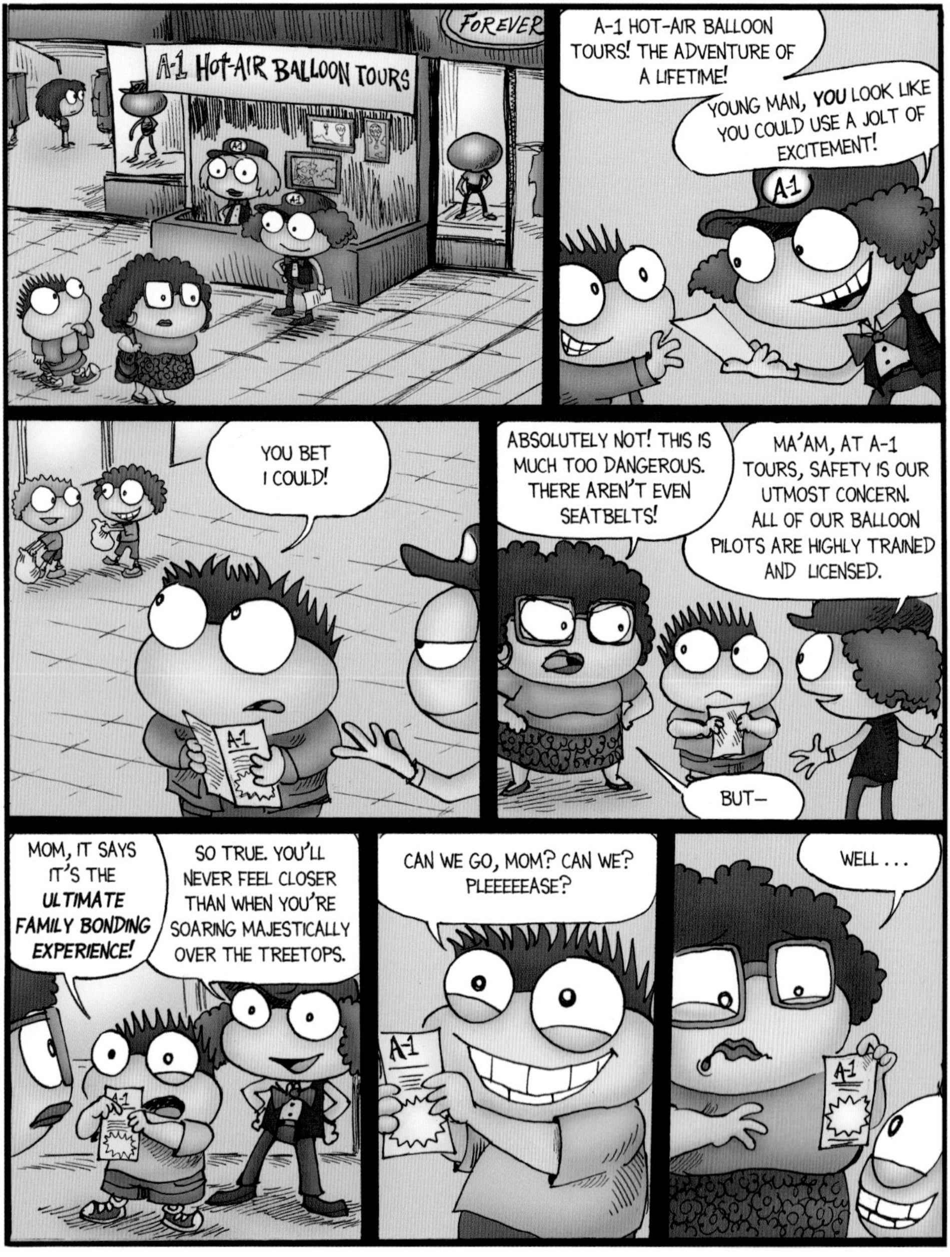
A-1 HOT-AIR BALLOON TOURS
FOREVER
A-1 HOT-AIR BALLOON TOURS! THE ADVENTURE OF A LIFETIME!
YOUNG MAN, **YOU** LOOK LIKE YOU COULD USE A JOLT OF EXCITEMENT!
YOU BET I COULD!
ABSOLUTELY NOT! THIS IS MUCH TOO DANGEROUS. THERE AREN'T EVEN SEATBELTS!
MA'AM, AT A-1 TOURS, SAFETY IS OUR UTMOST CONCERN. ALL OF OUR BALLOON PILOTS ARE HIGHLY TRAINED AND LICENSED.
BUT—
MOM, IT SAYS IT'S THE ***ULTIMATE FAMILY BONDING EXPERIENCE!***
SO TRUE. YOU'LL NEVER FEEL CLOSER THAN WHEN YOU'RE SOARING MAJESTICALLY OVER THE TREETOPS.
CAN WE GO, MOM? CAN WE? PLEEEEEASE?
WELL . . .

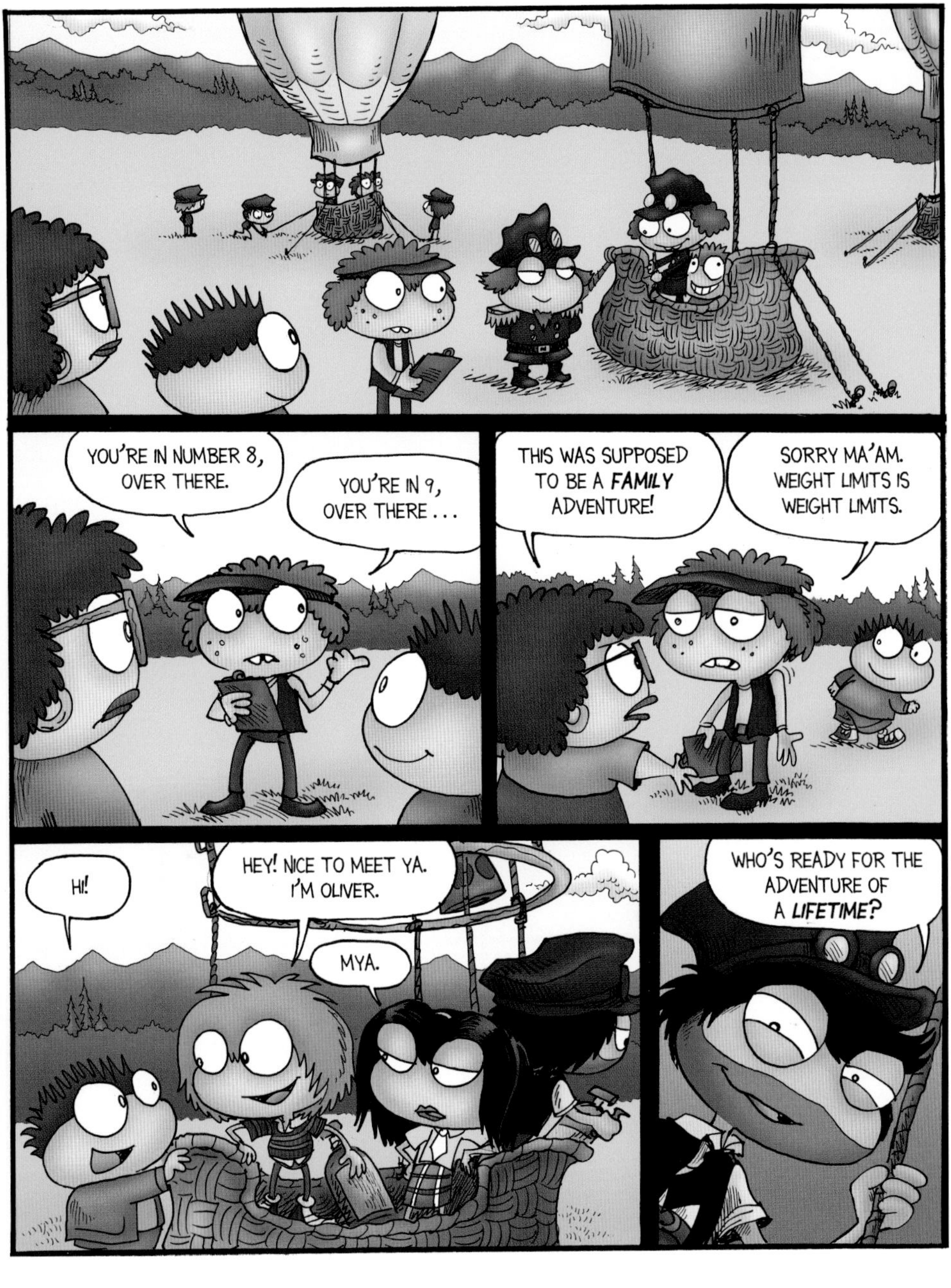
YOU'RE IN NUMBER 8,
OVER THERE.
YOU'RE IN 9,
OVER THERE . . .
THIS WAS SUPPOSED
TO BE A **FAMILY**
ADVENTURE!
SORRY MA'AM.
WEIGHT LIMITS IS
WEIGHT LIMITS.
HI!
HEY! NICE TO MEET YA.
I'M OLIVER.
MYA.
WHO'S READY FOR THE
ADVENTURE OF
A ***LIFETIME?***

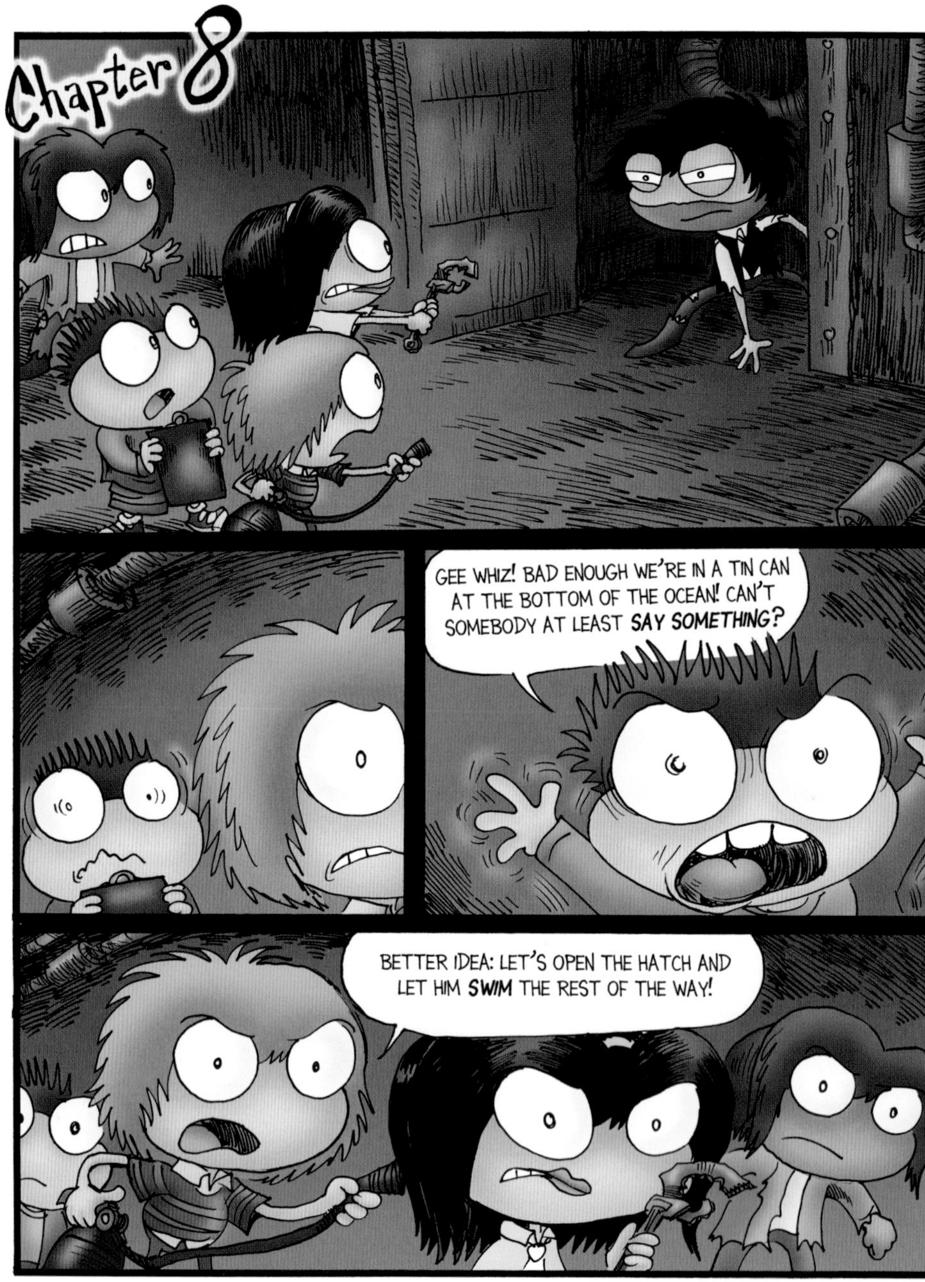
Chapter 8
GEE WHIZ! BAD ENOUGH WE'RE IN A TIN CAN AT THE BOTTOM OF THE OCEAN! CAN'T SOMEBODY AT LEAST SAY SOMETHING?
BETTER IDEA: LET'S OPEN THE HATCH AND LET HIM SWIM THE REST OF THE WAY!

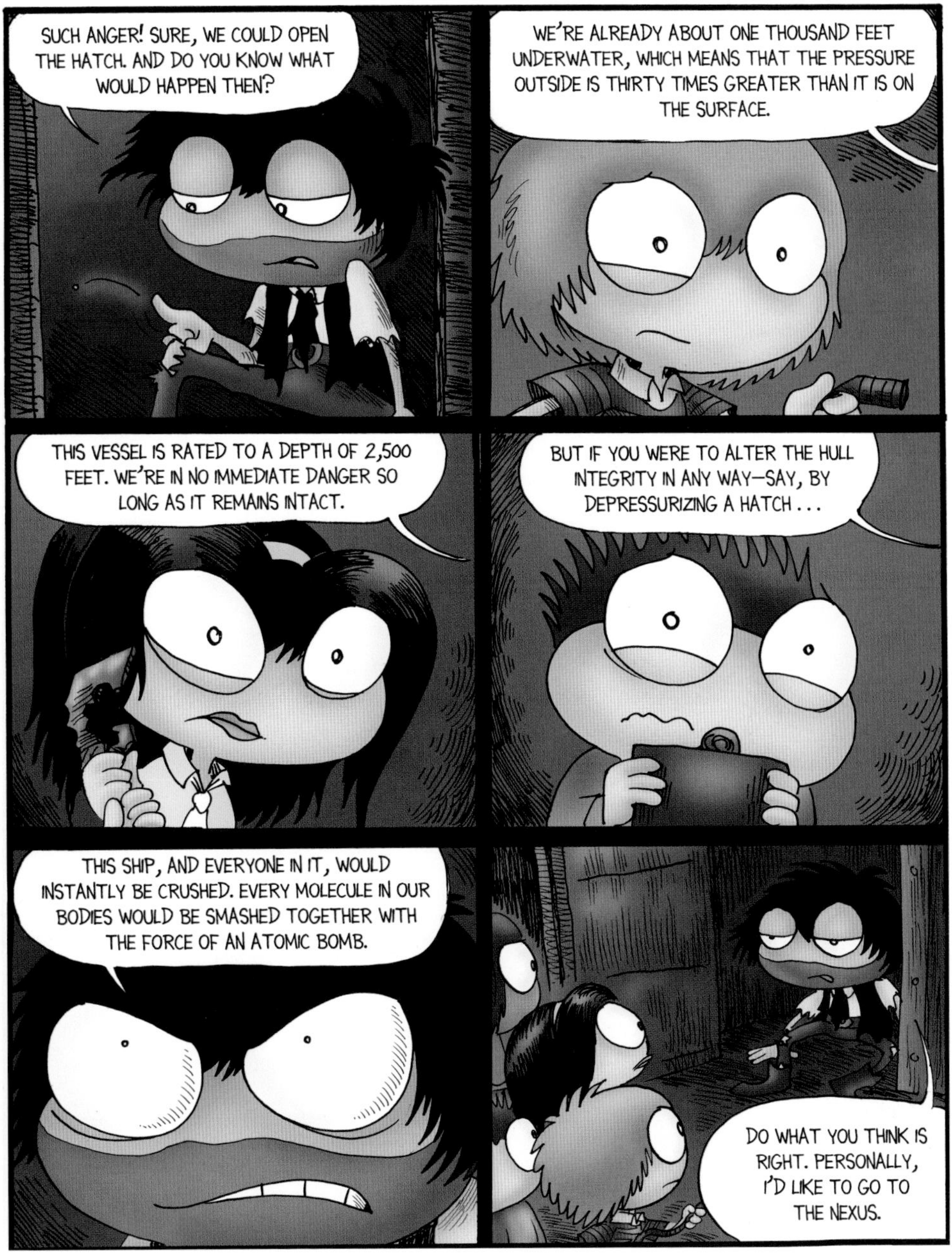
SUCH ANGER! SURE, WE COULD OPEN THE HATCH. AND DO YOU KNOW WHAT WOULD HAPPEN THEN?
WE'RE ALREADY ABOUT ONE THOUSAND FEET UNDERWATER, WHICH MEANS THAT THE PRESSURE OUTSIDE IS THIRTY TIMES GREATER THAN IT IS ON THE SURFACE.
THIS VESSEL IS RATED TO A DEPTH OF 2,500 FEET. WE'RE IN NO IMMEDIATE DANGER SO LONG AS IT REMAINS INTACT.
BUT IF YOU WERE TO ALTER THE HULL INTEGRITY IN ANY WAY—SAY, BY DEPRESSURIZING A HATCH . . .
THIS SHIP, AND EVERYONE IN IT, WOULD INSTANTLY BE CRUSHED. EVERY MOLECULE IN OUR BODIES WOULD BE SMASHED TOGETHER WITH THE FORCE OF AN ATOMIC BOMB.
DO WHAT YOU THINK IS RIGHT. PERSONALLY, I'D LIKE TO GO TO THE NEXUS.

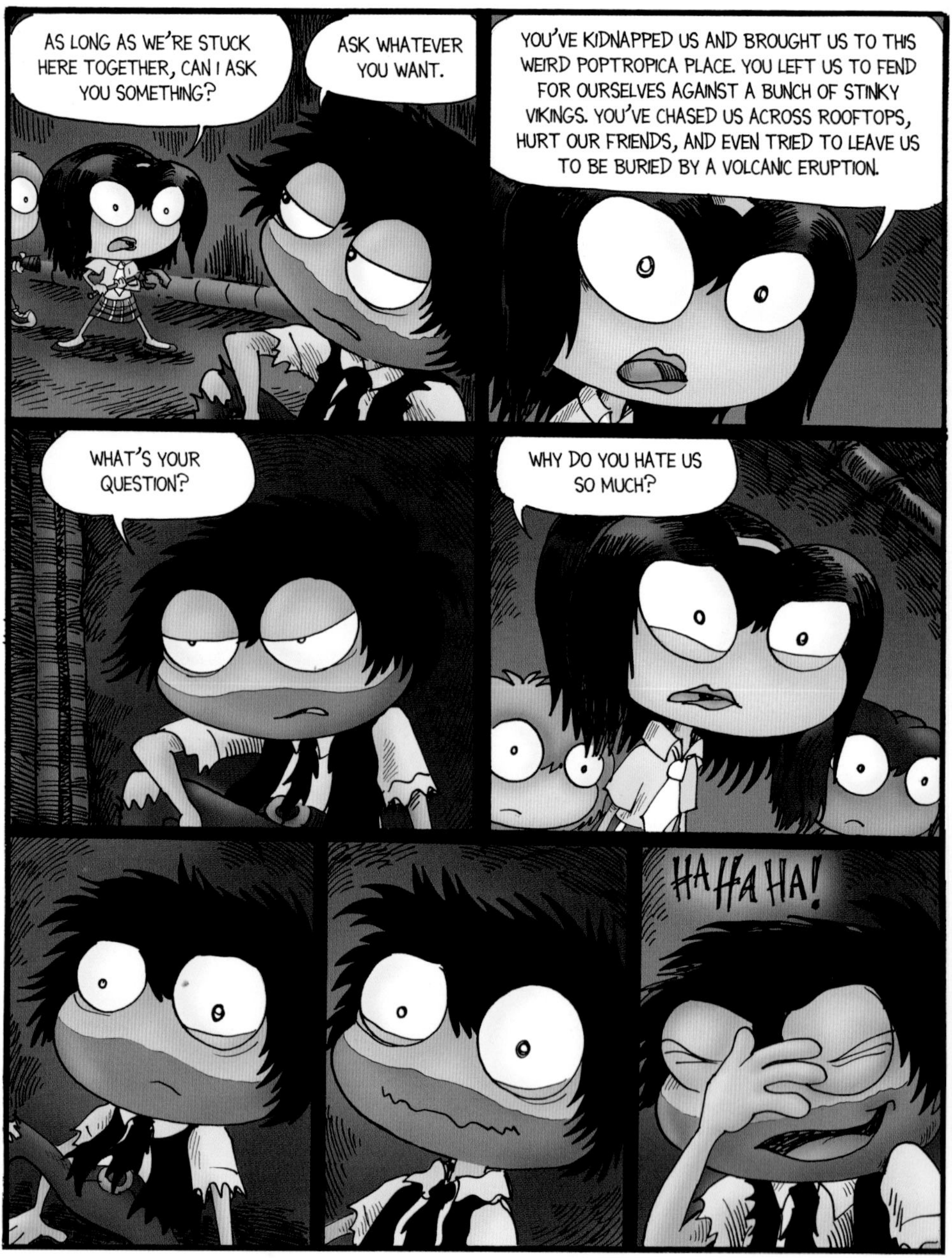
AS LONG AS WE'RE STUCK HERE TOGETHER, CAN I ASK YOU SOMETHING?
ASK WHATEVER YOU WANT.
YOU'VE KIDNAPPED US AND BROUGHT US TO THIS WEIRD POPTROPICA PLACE. YOU LEFT US TO FEND FOR OURSELVES AGAINST A BUNCH OF STINKY VIKINGS. YOU'VE CHASED US ACROSS ROOFTOPS, HURT OUR FRIENDS, AND EVEN TRIED TO LEAVE US TO BE BURIED BY A VOLCANIC ERUPTION.
WHAT'S YOUR QUESTION?
WHY DO YOU HATE US SO MUCH?
HA HA HA HA!

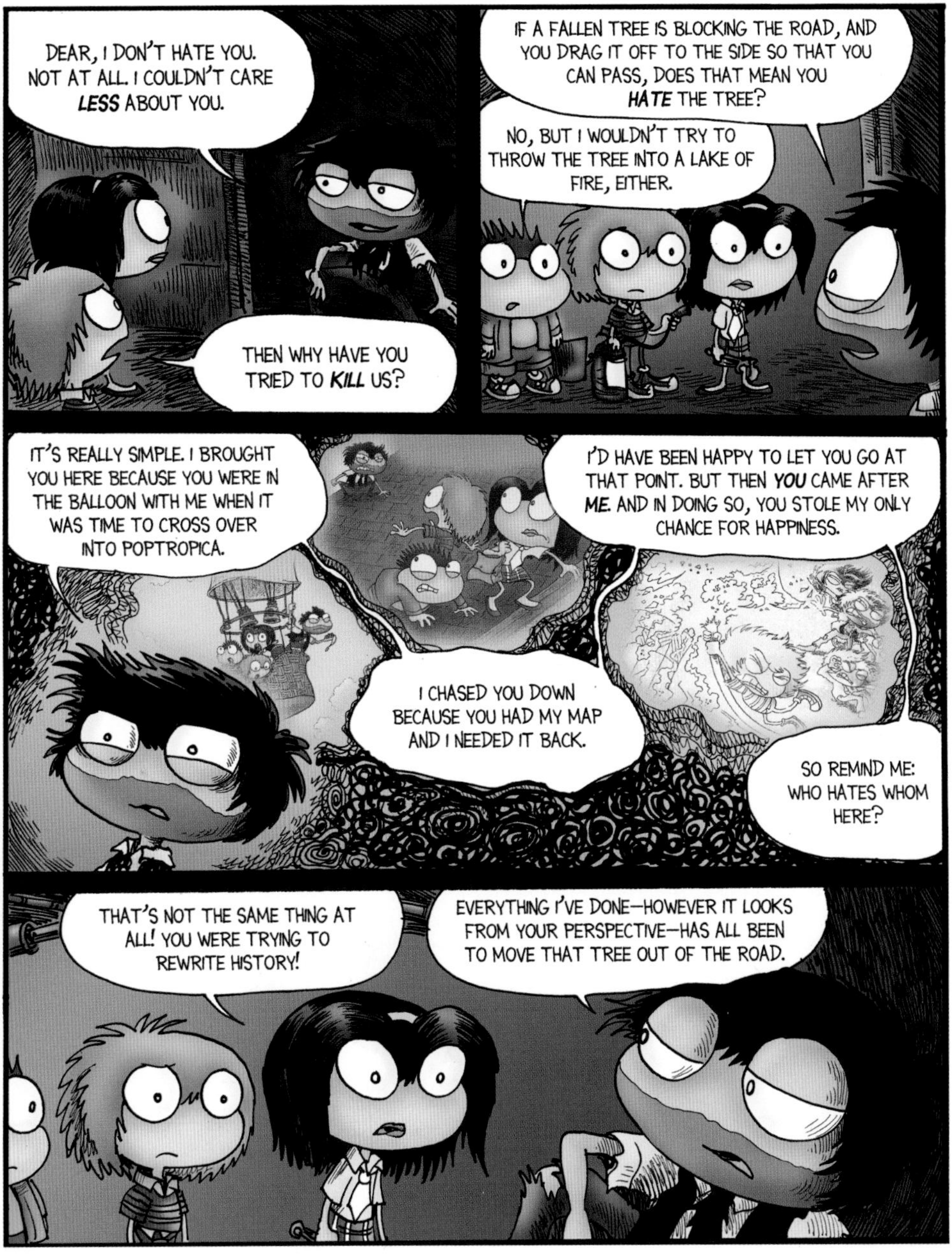
DEAR, I DON'T HATE YOU. NOT AT ALL. I COULDN'T CARE LESS ABOUT YOU.
THEN WHY HAVE YOU TRIED TO KILL US?
IF A FALLEN TREE IS BLOCKING THE ROAD, AND YOU DRAG IT OFF TO THE SIDE SO THAT YOU CAN PASS, DOES THAT MEAN YOU HATE THE TREE?
NO, BUT I WOULDN'T TRY TO THROW THE TREE INTO A LAKE OF FIRE, EITHER.
IT'S REALLY SIMPLE. I BROUGHT YOU HERE BECAUSE YOU WERE IN THE BALLOON WITH ME WHEN IT WAS TIME TO CROSS OVER INTO POPTROPICA.
I CHASED YOU DOWN BECAUSE YOU HAD MY MAP AND I NEEDED IT BACK.
I'D HAVE BEEN HAPPY TO LET YOU GO AT THAT POINT. BUT THEN YOU CAME AFTER ME. AND IN DOING SO, YOU STOLE MY ONLY CHANCE FOR HAPPINESS.
SO REMIND ME: WHO HATES WHOM HERE?
THAT'S NOT THE SAME THING AT ALL! YOU WERE TRYING TO REWRITE HISTORY!
EVERYTHING I'VE DONE—HOWEVER IT LOOKS FROM YOUR PERSPECTIVE—HAS ALL BEEN TO MOVE THAT TREE OUT OF THE ROAD.

WHEN I STUDIED UNDER SPENCER ALBRIGHT, I BOUGHT HIS STORY. I THOUGHT MY JOB WAS TO PREVENT ANYTHING FROM CHANGING HISTORY AS WE'VE LEARNED IT. BUT THEN I MET *HER.*

PAULLA WAS A PEASANT GIRL IN POMPEII. THE WARMEST, SWEETEST, MOST BEAUTIFUL SOUL I'D EVER MET—IN ANY ERA. I WAS SUPPOSED TO BE UNDERCOVER, BUT AFTER WE FELL IN LOVE, I COULDN'T LIVE A LIE ANYMORE.

I KNEW WHAT AWAITED HER IF SHE STAYED IN POMPEII.

I TRIED TO GET HER OUT, BUT SPENCER AND HIS GOONS STOPPED ME. HE SAID RESCUING HER WOULD ALTER HISTORY, AND THE FIRST RULE OF THE PROTECTORS IS TO PRESERVE HISTORY AT ALL COSTS.

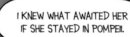

BUT WHAT ABOUT **MY** HISTORY? WHAT ABOUT THE TIME THAT PAULLA AND I SHARED? DID THAT COUNT FOR NOTHING?

AS FIRE RAINED FROM THE SKY, I REALIZED THAT I HAD A CHOICE—NO MATTER WHAT SPENCER ALBRIGHT SAID. I COULD HAVE SAVED HER. I *SHOULD* HAVE SAVED HER.

EVEN IF IT MEANS STARTING EVERYTHING OVER FROM THE BEGINNING, *SO BE IT.* I SWORE THAT I WOULD DO ANYTHING TO BE WITH PAULLA AGAIN.

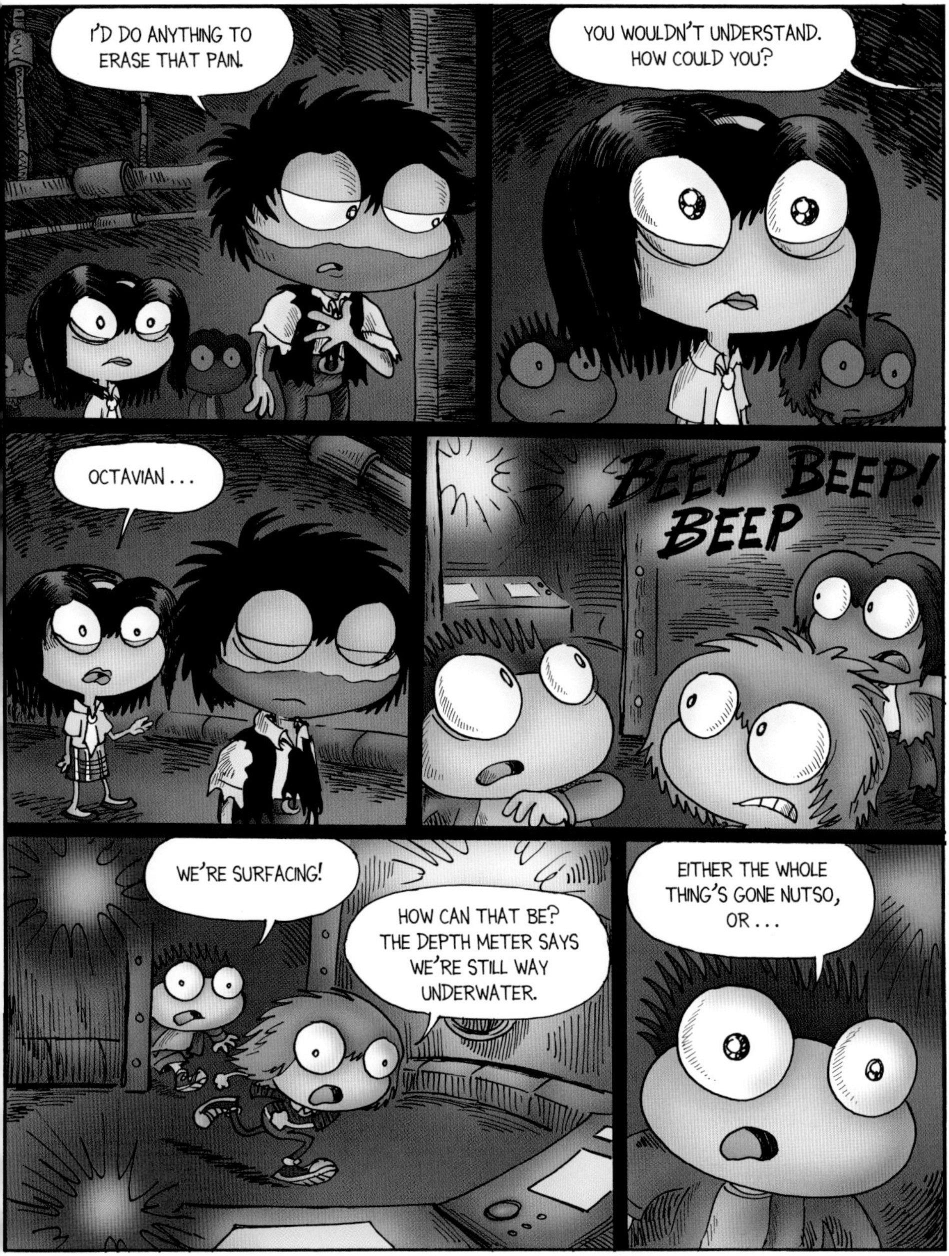
I'D DO ANYTHING TO ERASE THAT PAIN.
YOU WOULDN'T UNDERSTAND. HOW COULD YOU?
OCTAVIAN . . .
BEEP BEEP! BEEP
WE'RE SURFACING!
HOW CAN THAT BE? THE DEPTH METER SAYS WE'RE STILL WAY UNDERWATER.
EITHER THE WHOLE THING'S GONE NUTSO, OR . . .

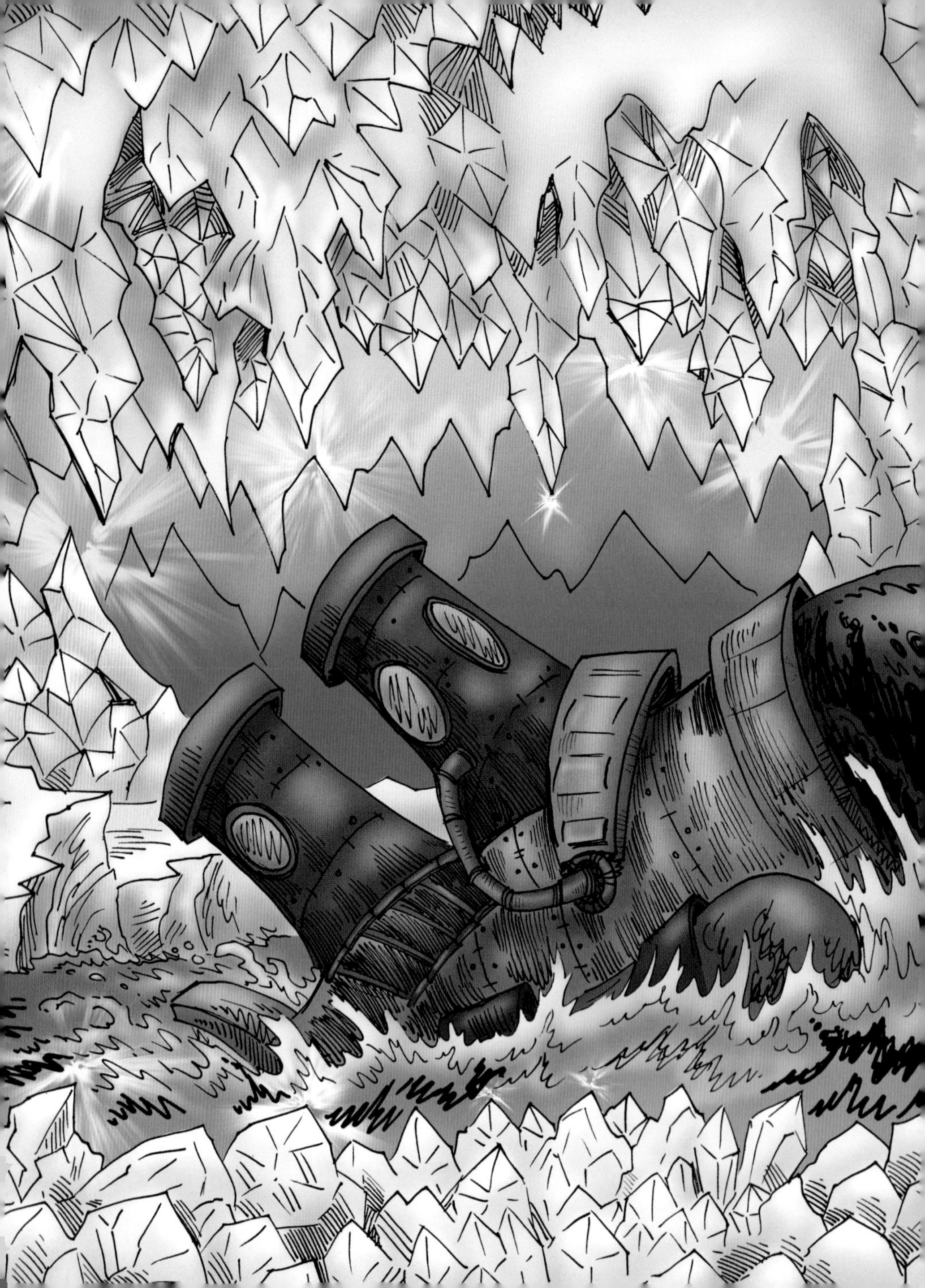

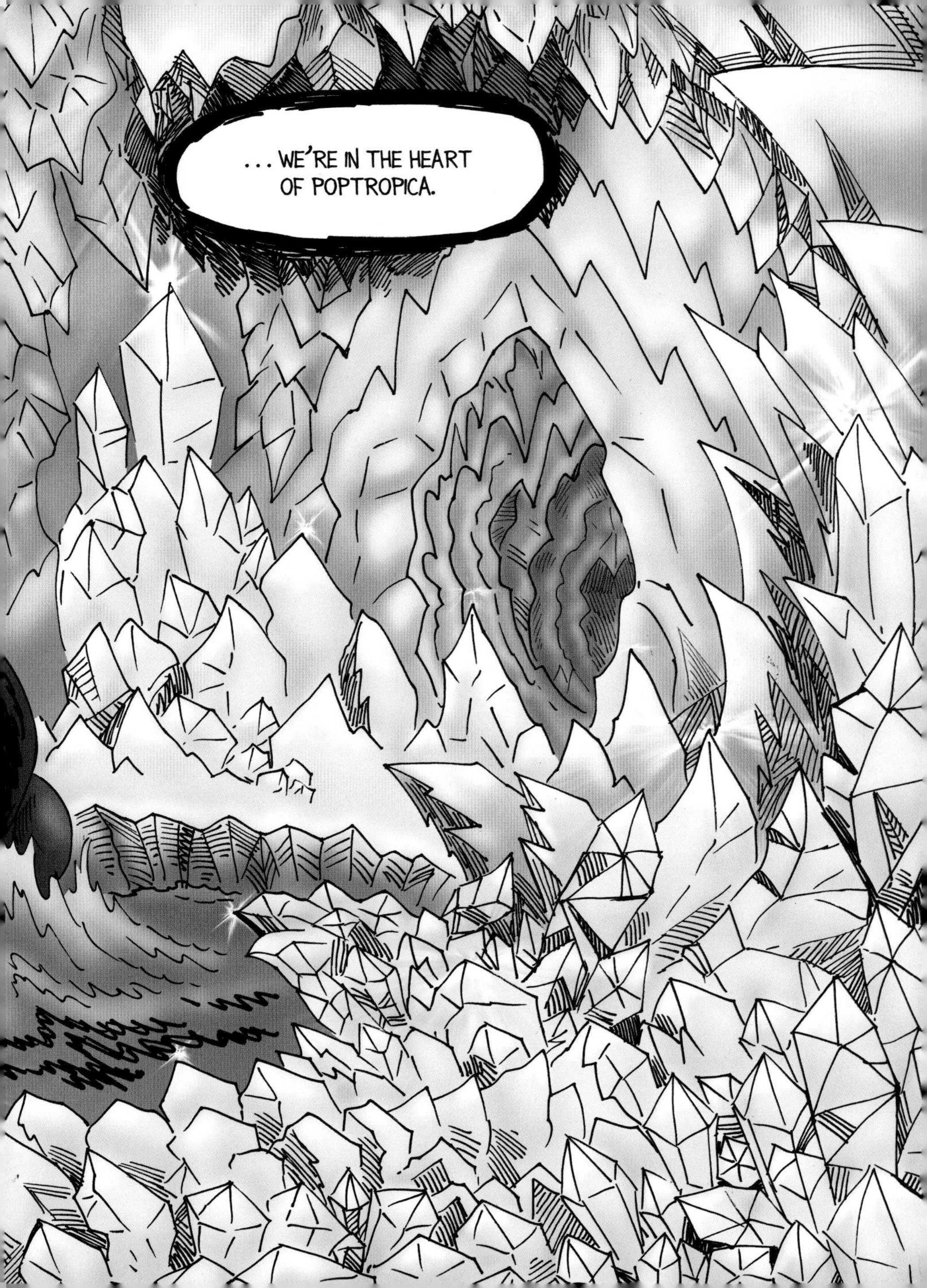
. . . WE'RE IN THE HEART OF POPTROPICA.

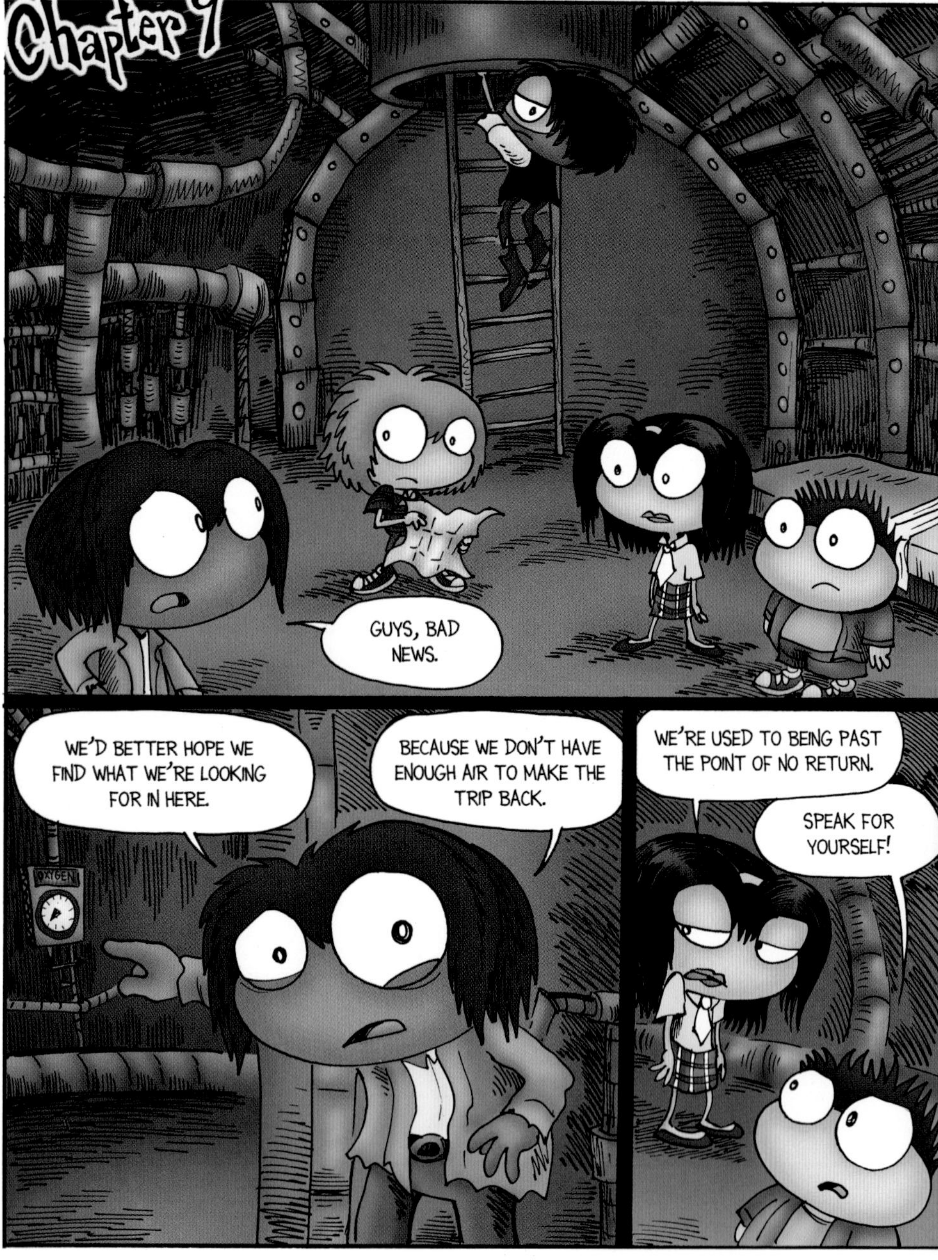
Chapter 9
GUYS, BAD NEWS.
WE'D BETTER HOPE WE FIND WHAT WE'RE LOOKING FOR IN HERE.
BECAUSE WE DON'T HAVE ENOUGH AIR TO MAKE THE TRIP BACK.
OXYGEN
WE'RE USED TO BEING PAST THE POINT OF NO RETURN.
SPEAK FOR YOURSELF!

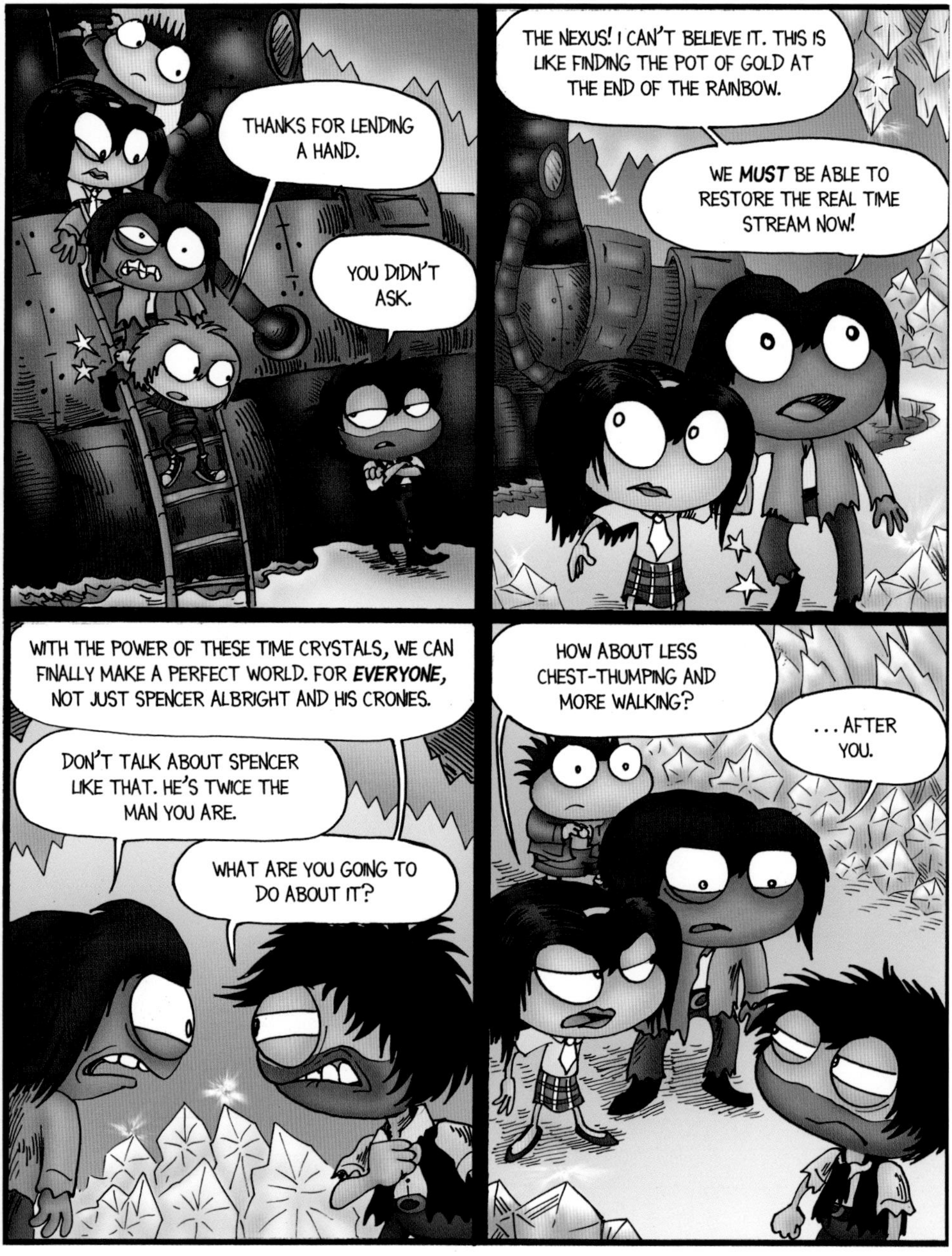
THANKS FOR LENDING A HAND.
YOU DIDN'T ASK.
THE NEXUS! I CAN'T BELIEVE IT. THIS IS LIKE FINDING THE POT OF GOLD AT THE END OF THE RAINBOW.
WE **MUST** BE ABLE TO RESTORE THE REAL TIME STREAM NOW!
WITH THE POWER OF THESE TIME CRYSTALS, WE CAN FINALLY MAKE A PERFECT WORLD. FOR **EVERYONE,** NOT JUST SPENCER ALBRIGHT AND HIS CRONIES.
DON'T TALK ABOUT SPENCER LIKE THAT. HE'S TWICE THE MAN YOU ARE.
WHAT ARE YOU GOING TO DO ABOUT IT?
HOW ABOUT LESS CHEST-THUMPING AND MORE WALKING?
. . . AFTER YOU.

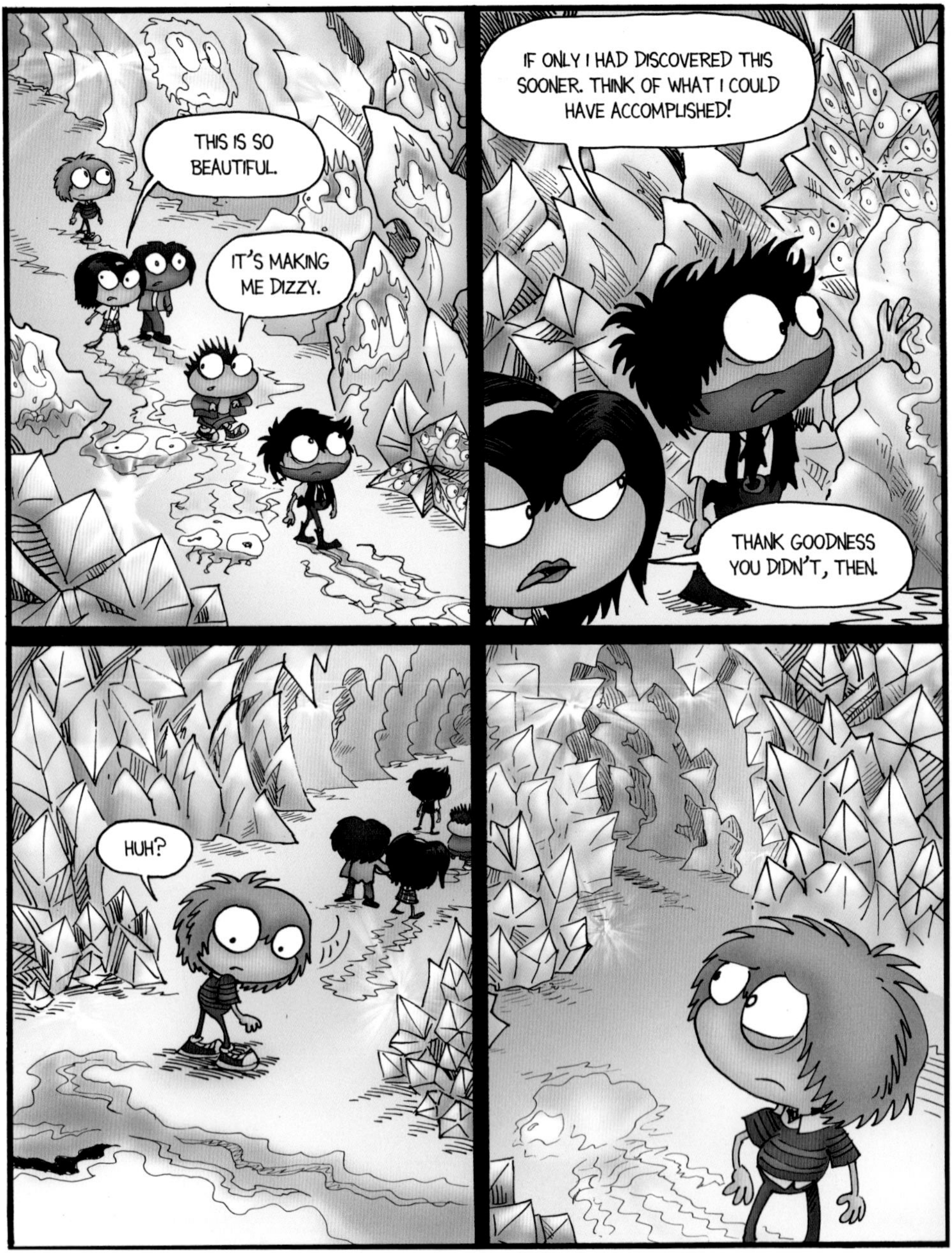
THIS IS SO BEAUTIFUL.
IT'S MAKING ME DIZZY.
IF ONLY I HAD DISCOVERED THIS SOONER. THINK OF WHAT I COULD HAVE ACCOMPLISHED!
THANK GOODNESS YOU DIDN'T, THEN.
HUH?

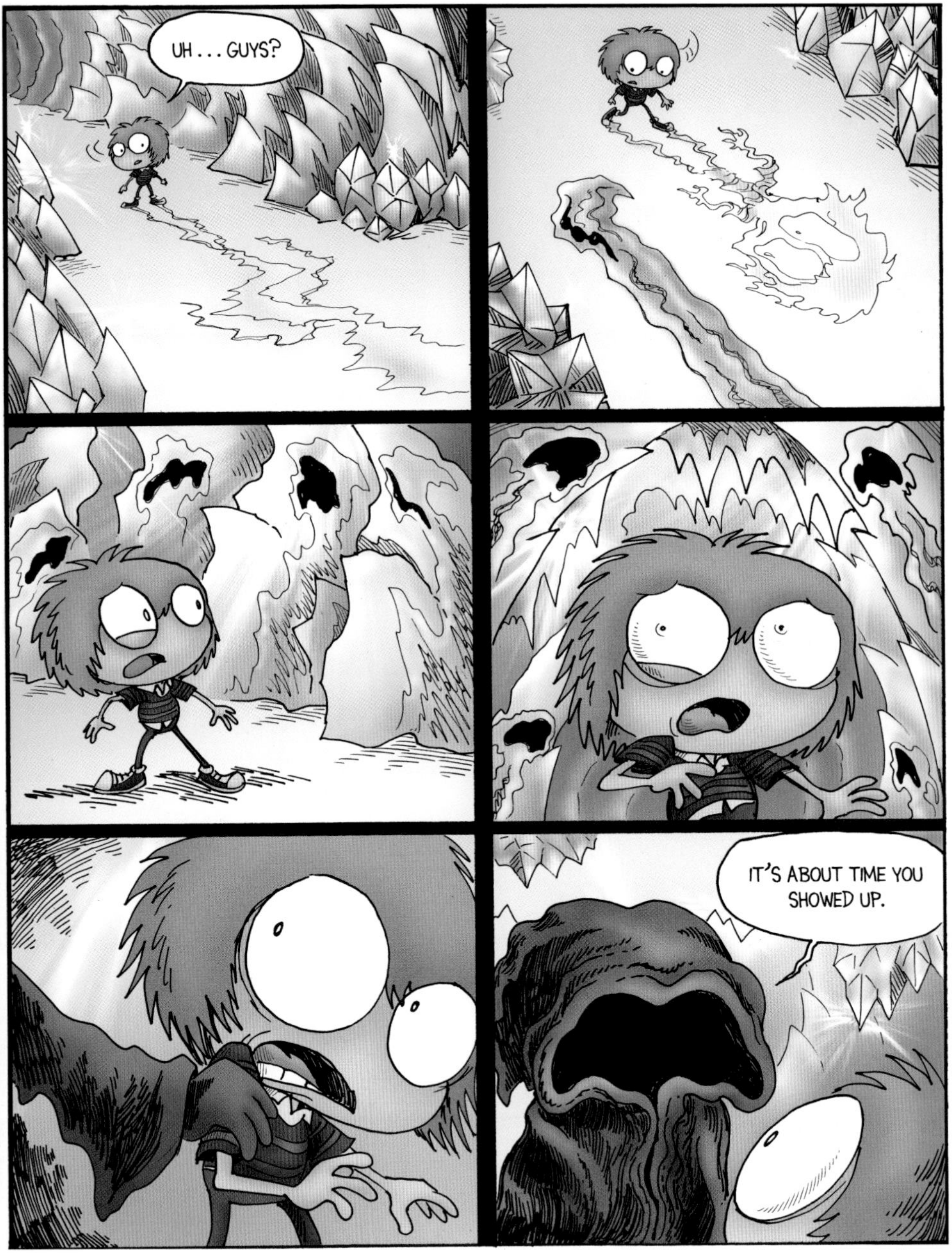
UH . . . GUYS?
IT'S ABOUT TIME YOU SHOWED UP.

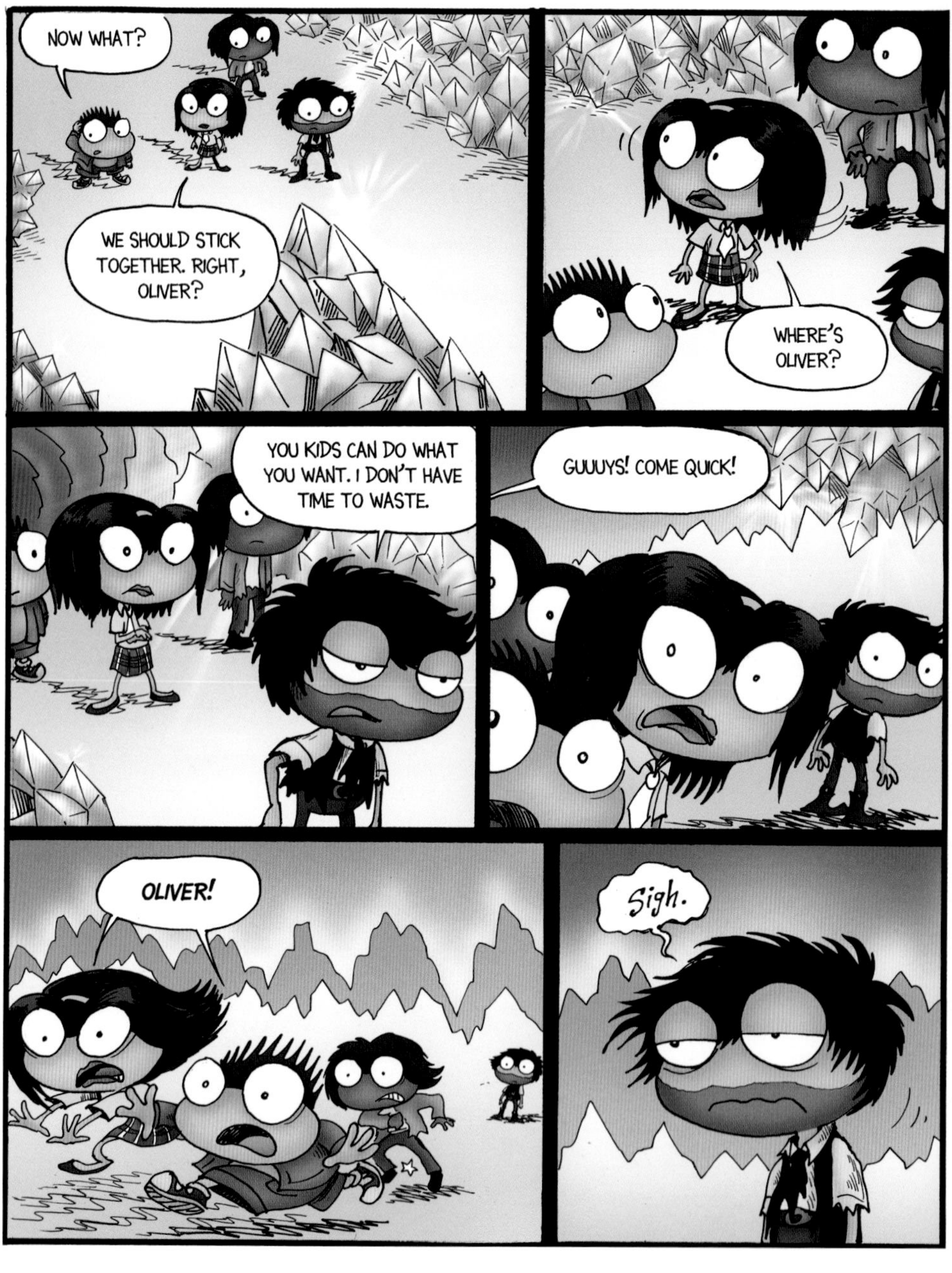
NOW WHAT?
WE SHOULD STICK TOGETHER. RIGHT, OLIVER?
WHERE'S OLIVER?
YOU KIDS CAN DO WHAT YOU WANT. I DON'T HAVE TIME TO WASTE.
GUUUYS! COME QUICK!
OLIVER!
Sigh.

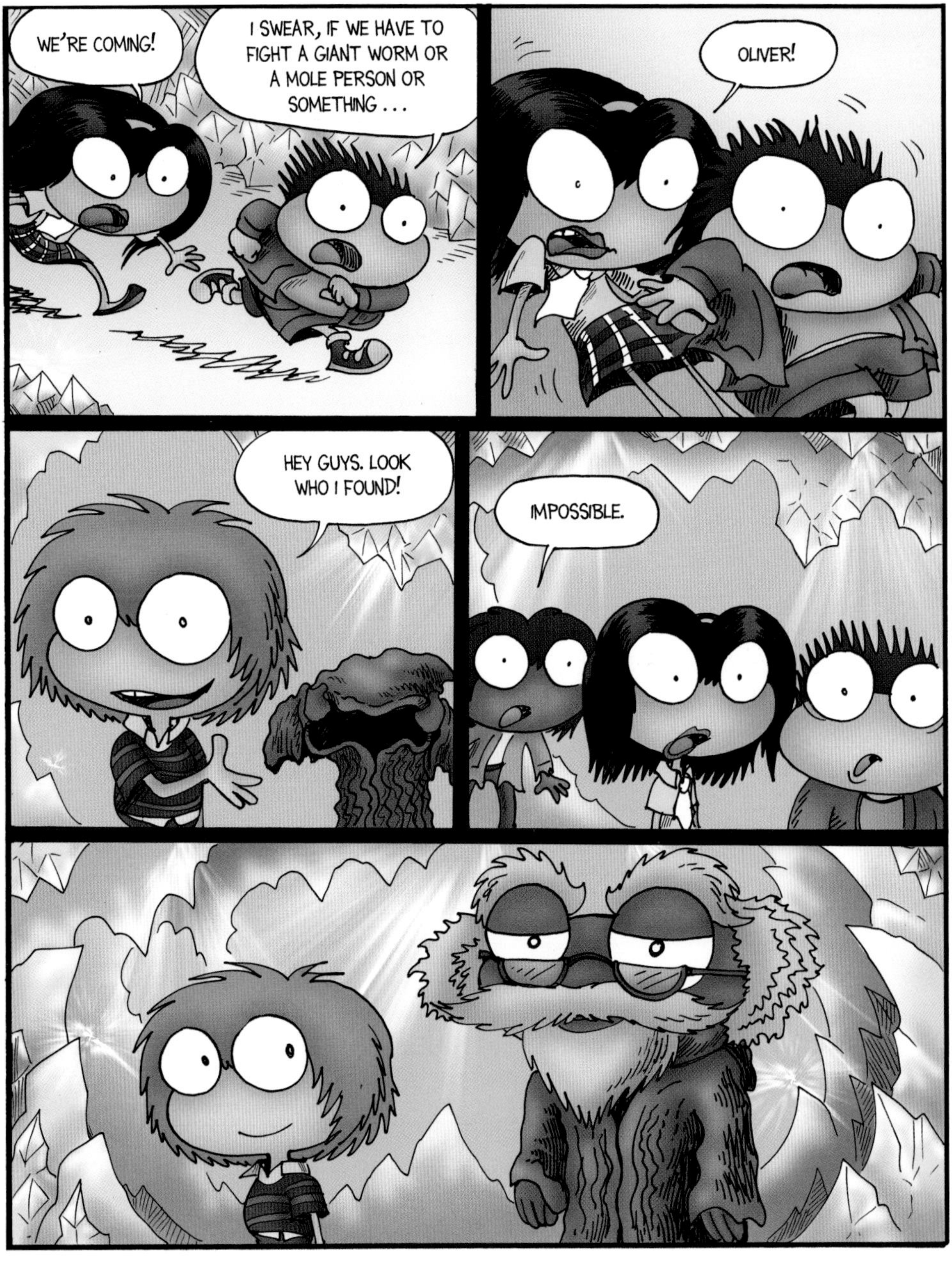
WE'RE COMING!
I SWEAR, IF WE HAVE TO FIGHT A GIANT WORM OR A MOLE PERSON OR SOMETHING . . .
OLIVER!
HEY GUYS. LOOK WHO I FOUND!
IMPOSSIBLE.

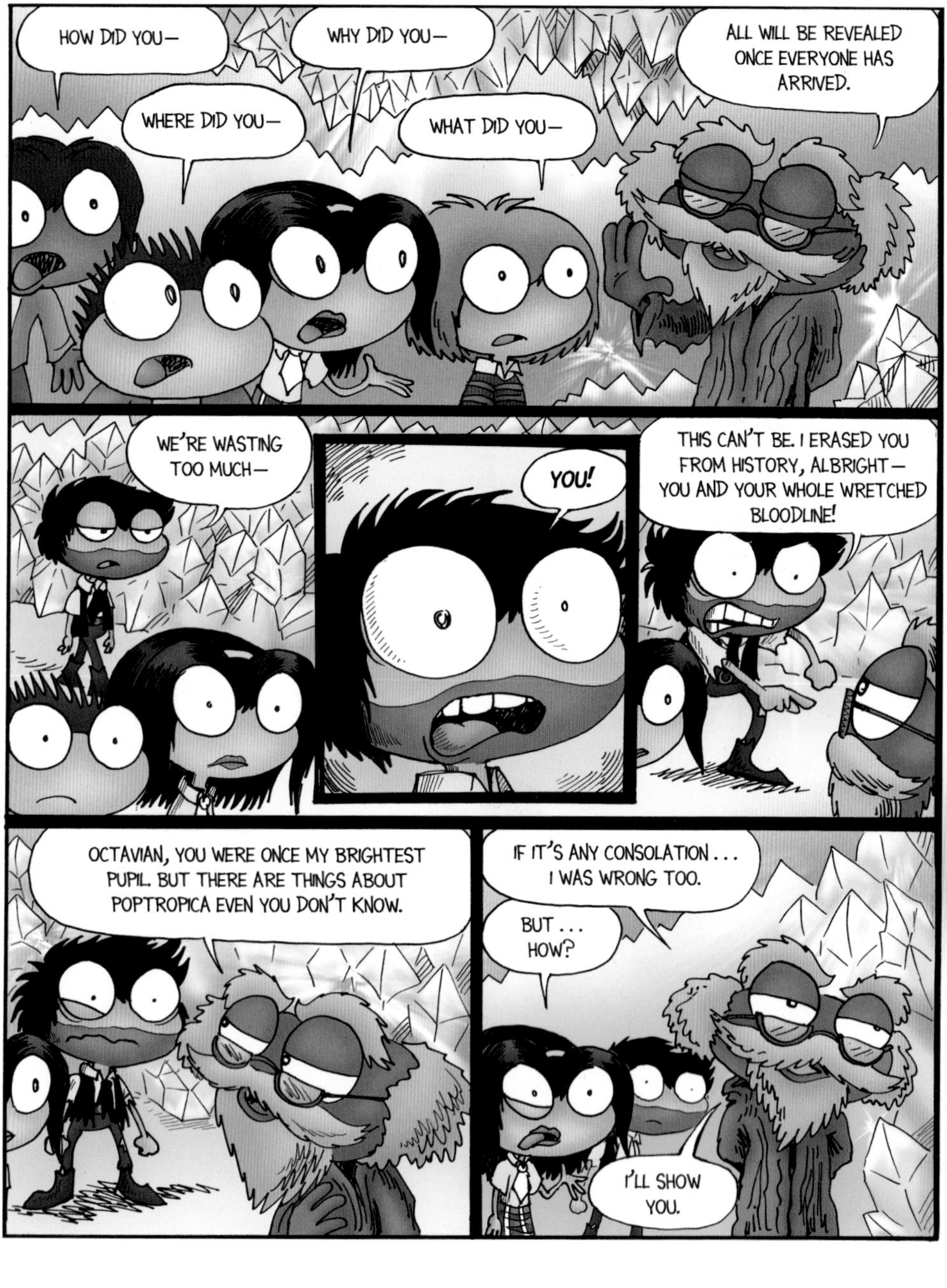
HOW DID YOU—
WHERE DID YOU—
WHY DID YOU—
WHAT DID YOU—
ALL WILL BE REVEALED ONCE EVERYONE HAS ARRIVED.
WE'RE WASTING TOO MUCH—
YOU!
THIS CAN'T BE. I ERASED YOU FROM HISTORY, ALBRIGHT— YOU AND YOUR WHOLE WRETCHED BLOODLINE!
OCTAVIAN, YOU WERE ONCE MY BRIGHTEST PUPIL. BUT THERE ARE THINGS ABOUT POPTROPICA EVEN YOU DON'T KNOW.
IF IT'S ANY CONSOLATION . . . I WAS WRONG TOO.
BUT . . . HOW?
I'LL SHOW YOU.

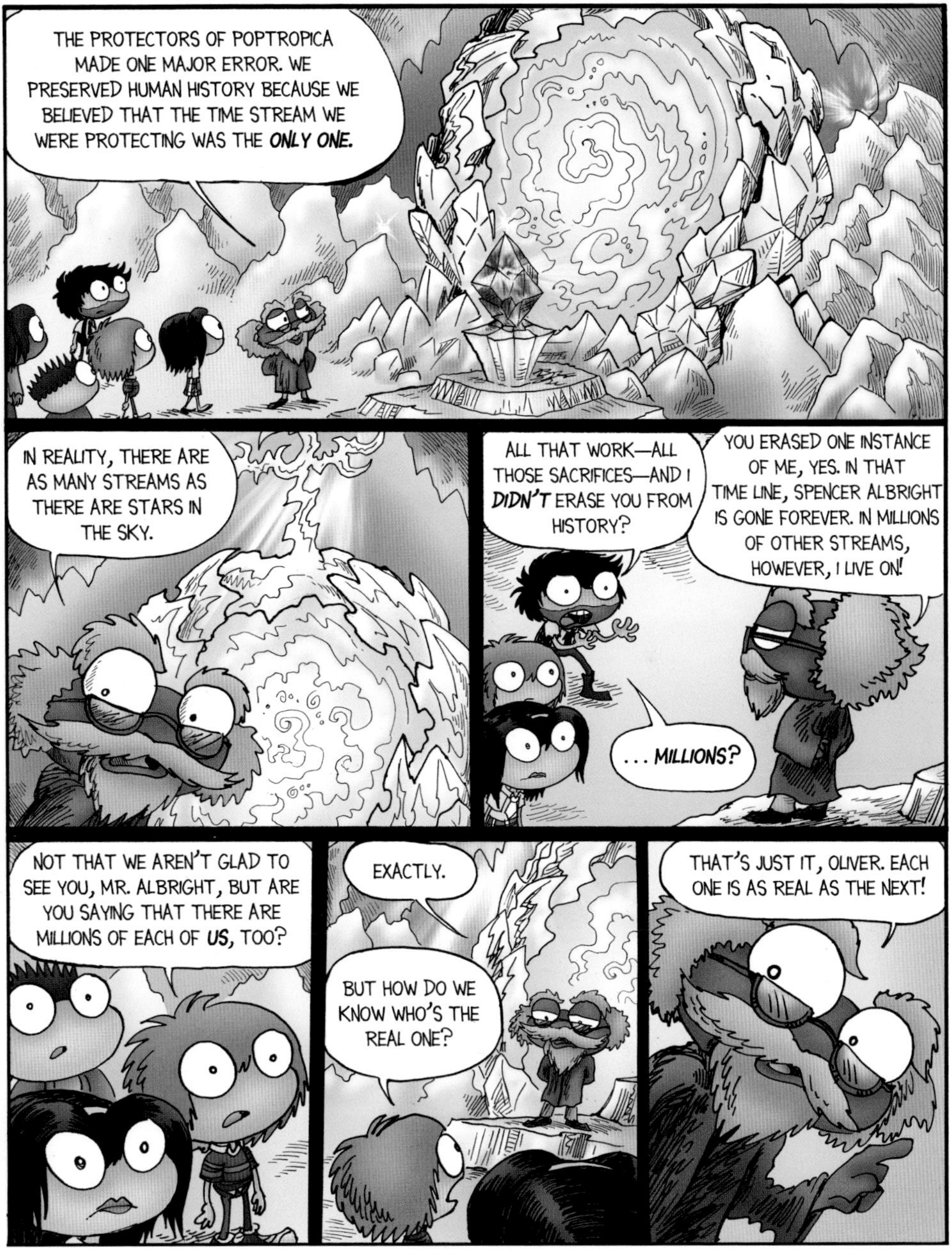
THE PROTECTORS OF POPTROPICA MADE ONE MAJOR ERROR. WE PRESERVED HUMAN HISTORY BECAUSE WE BELIEVED THAT THE TIME STREAM WE WERE PROTECTING WAS THE **ONLY ONE.**
IN REALITY, THERE ARE AS MANY STREAMS AS THERE ARE STARS IN THE SKY.
ALL THAT WORK—ALL THOSE SACRIFICES—AND I ***DIDN'T*** ERASE YOU FROM HISTORY?
YOU ERASED ONE INSTANCE OF ME, YES. IN THAT TIME LINE, SPENCER ALBRIGHT IS GONE FOREVER. IN MILLIONS OF OTHER STREAMS, HOWEVER, I LIVE ON!
. . . **MILLIONS?**
NOT THAT WE AREN'T GLAD TO SEE YOU, MR. ALBRIGHT, BUT ARE YOU SAYING THAT THERE ARE MILLIONS OF EACH OF **US**, TOO?
EXACTLY.
BUT HOW DO WE KNOW WHO'S THE REAL ONE?
THAT'S JUST IT, OLIVER. EACH ONE IS AS REAL AS THE NEXT!

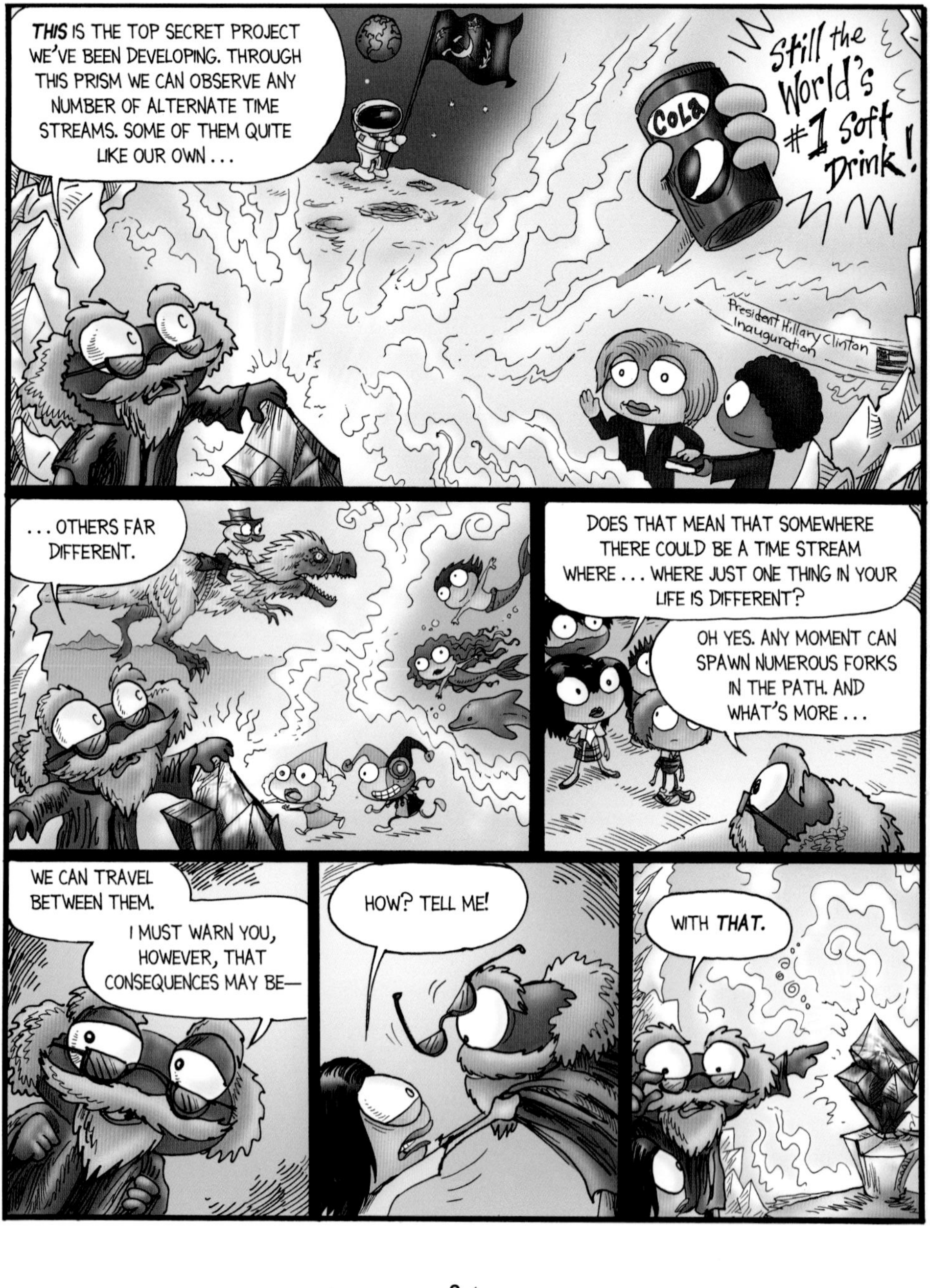
THIS IS THE TOP SECRET PROJECT WE'VE BEEN DEVELOPING. THROUGH THIS PRISM WE CAN OBSERVE ANY NUMBER OF ALTERNATE TIME STREAMS. SOME OF THEM QUITE LIKE OUR OWN . . .
COLA
Still the World's #1 Soft Drink!
President Hillary Clinton Inauguration
. . . OTHERS FAR DIFFERENT.
DOES THAT MEAN THAT SOMEWHERE THERE COULD BE A TIME STREAM WHERE . . . WHERE JUST ONE THING IN YOUR LIFE IS DIFFERENT?
OH YES. ANY MOMENT CAN SPAWN NUMEROUS FORKS IN THE PATH. AND WHAT'S MORE . . .
WE CAN TRAVEL BETWEEN THEM.
I MUST WARN YOU, HOWEVER, THAT CONSEQUENCES MAY BE—
HOW? TELL ME!
WITH THAT.

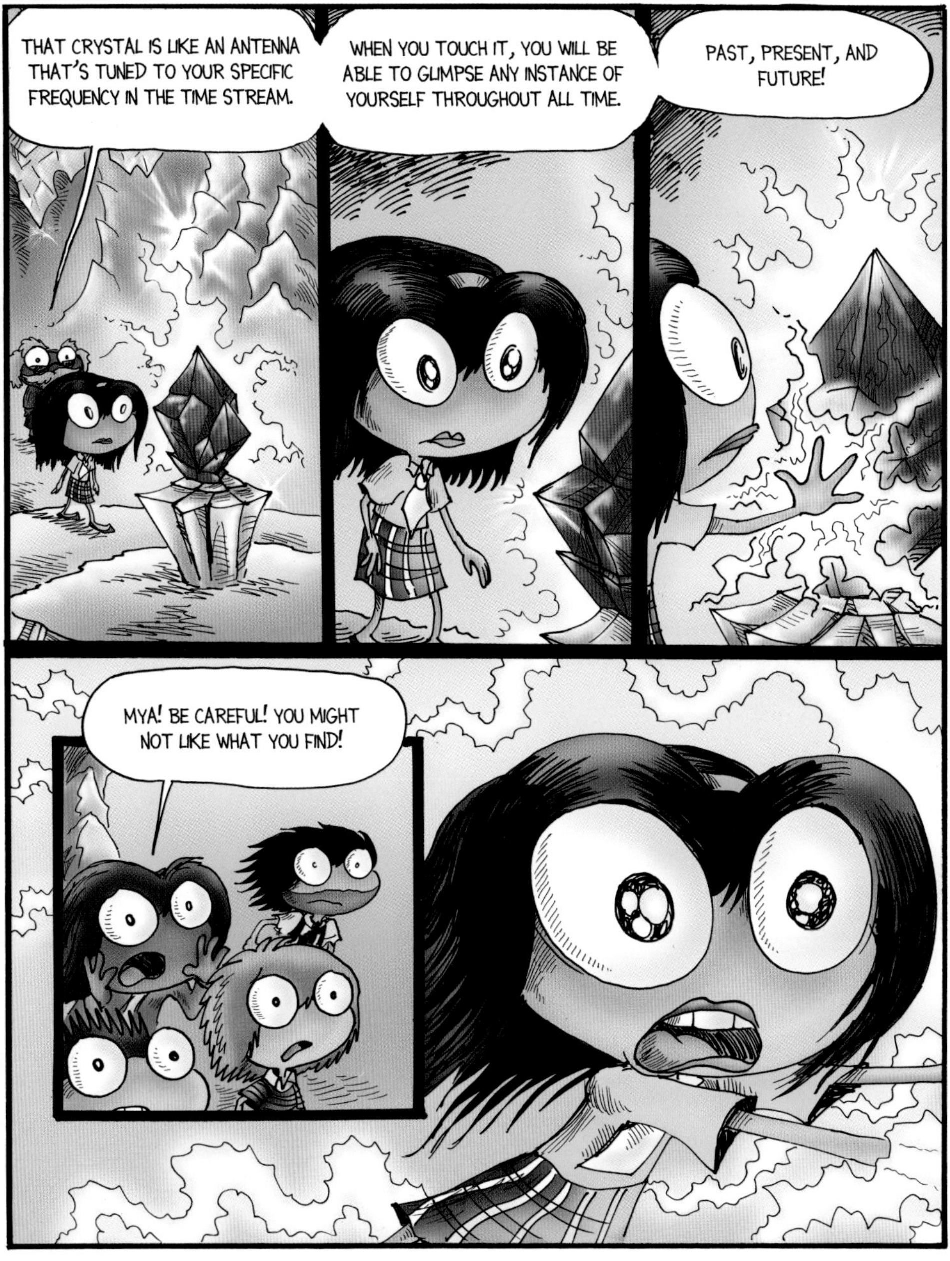
THAT CRYSTAL IS LIKE AN ANTENNA THAT'S TUNED TO YOUR SPECIFIC FREQUENCY IN THE TIME STREAM.
WHEN YOU TOUCH IT, YOU WILL BE ABLE TO GLIMPSE ANY INSTANCE OF YOURSELF THROUGHOUT ALL TIME.
PAST, PRESENT, AND FUTURE!
MYA! BE CAREFUL! YOU MIGHT NOT LIKE WHAT YOU FIND!

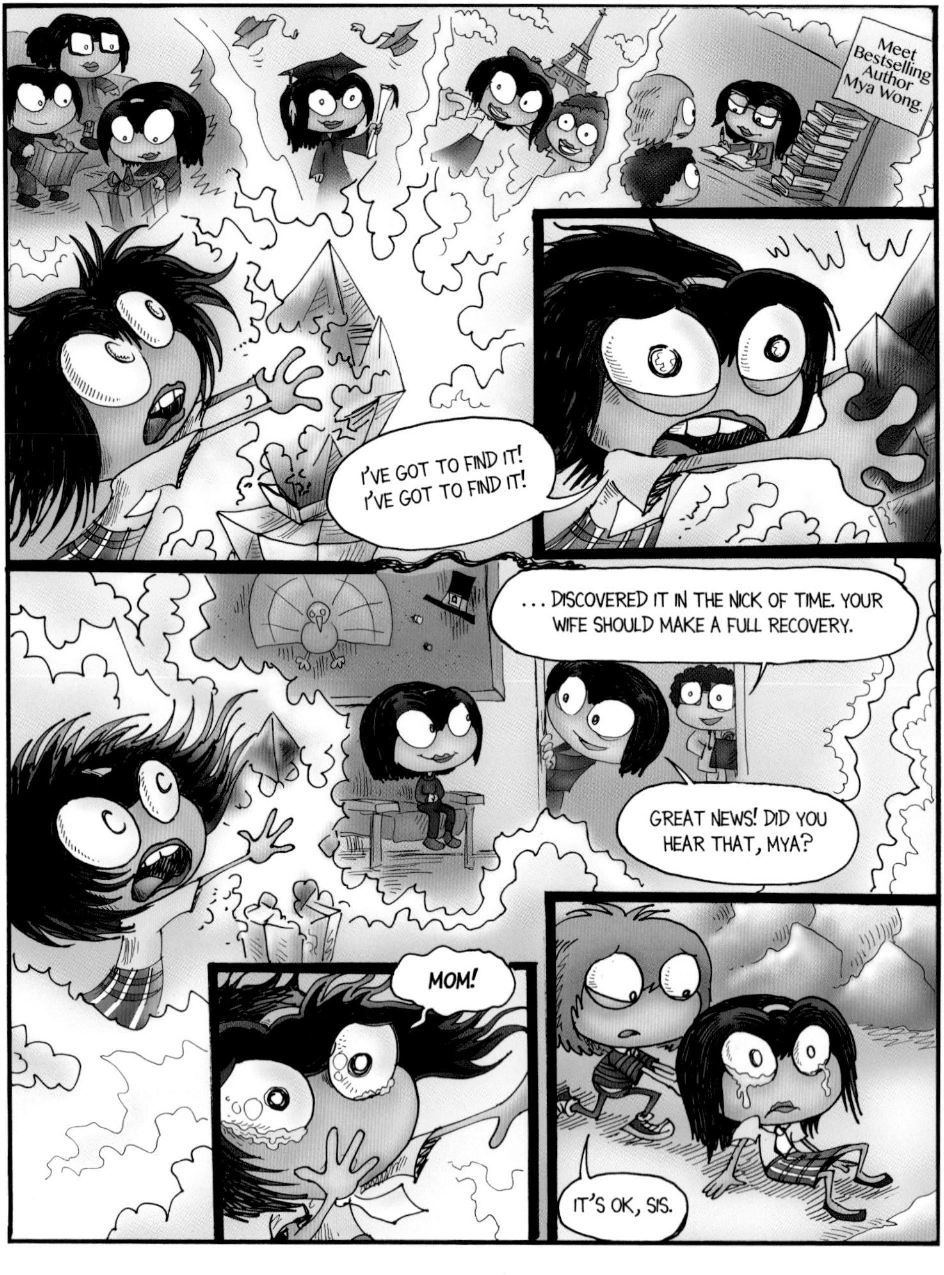
Meet Bestselling Author Mya Wong.
I'VE GOT TO FIND IT! I'VE GOT TO FIND IT!
. . . DISCOVERED IT IN THE NICK OF TIME. YOUR WIFE SHOULD MAKE A FULL RECOVERY.
GREAT NEWS! DID YOU HEAR THAT, MYA?
MOM!
IT'S OK, SIS.

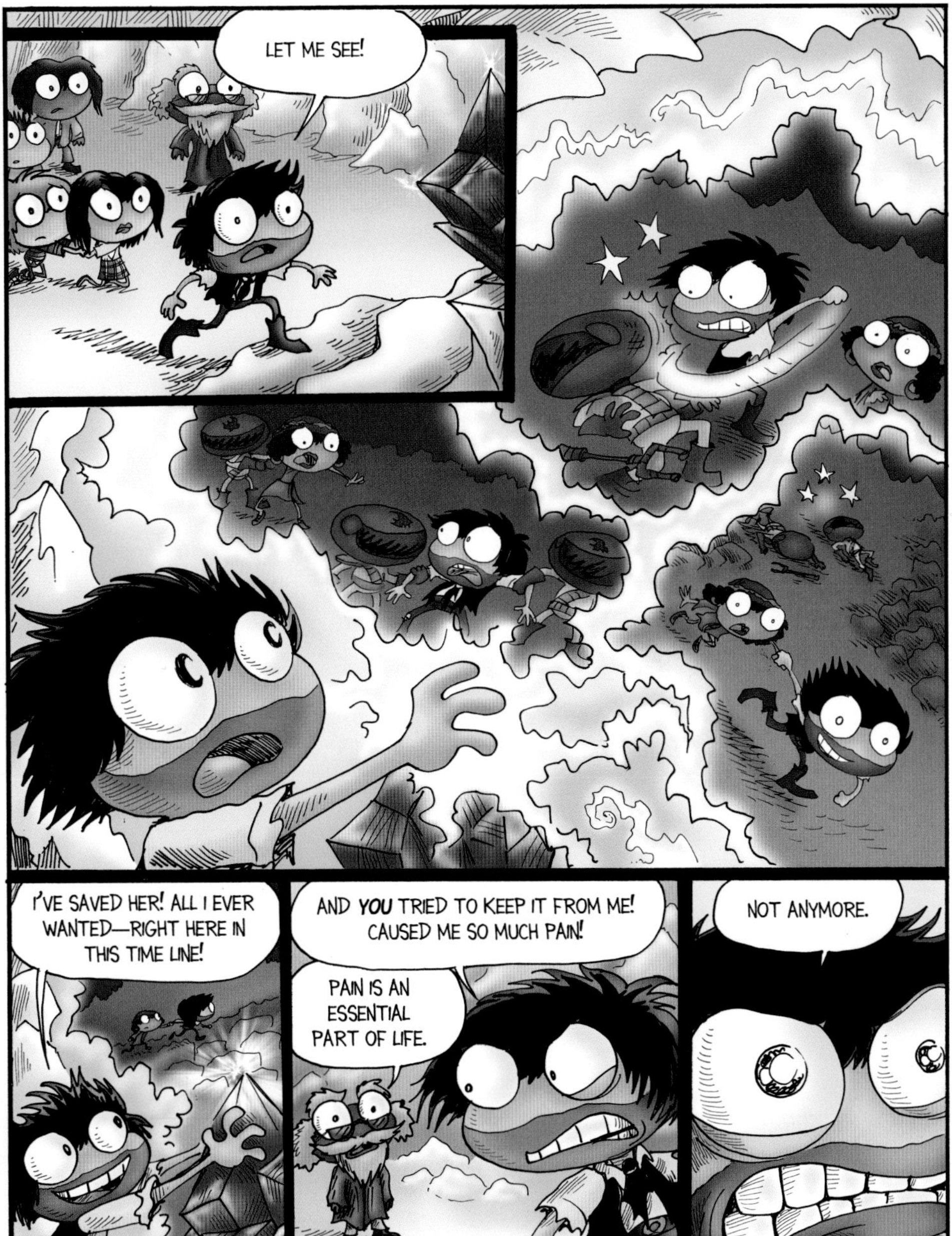
LET ME SEE!
I'VE SAVED HER! ALL I EVER WANTED—RIGHT HERE IN THIS TIME LINE!
AND *YOU* TRIED TO KEEP IT FROM ME! CAUSED ME SO MUCH PAIN!
PAIN IS AN ESSENTIAL PART OF LIFE.
NOT ANYMORE.

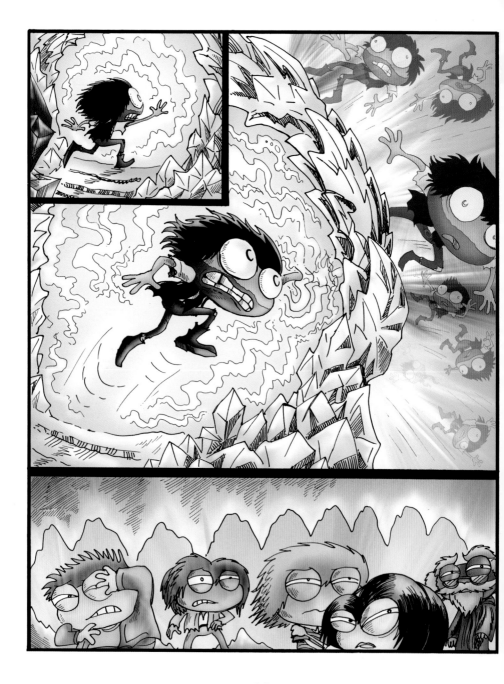

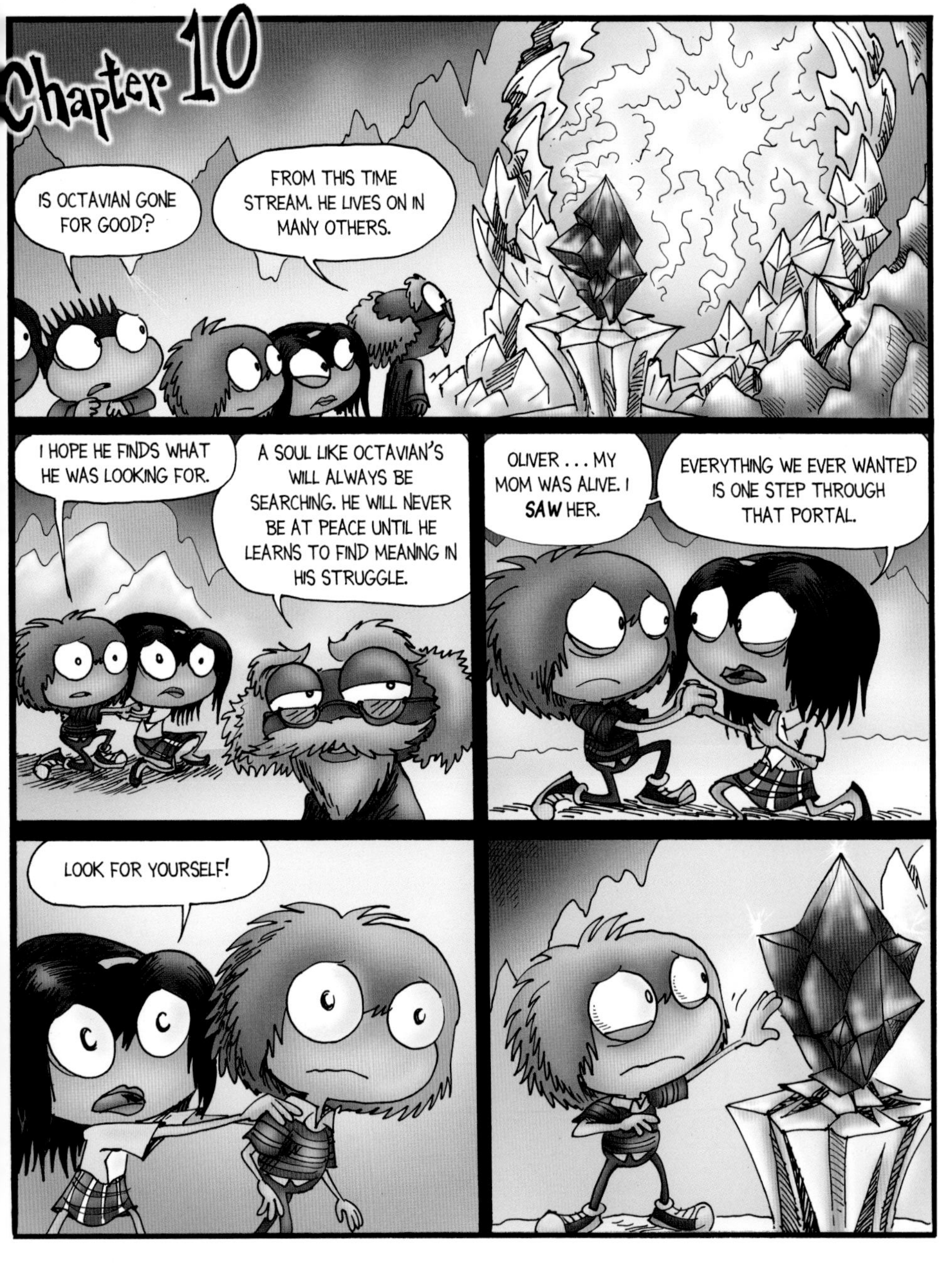
Chapter 10
IS OCTAVIAN GONE FOR GOOD?
FROM THIS TIME STREAM. HE LIVES ON IN MANY OTHERS.
I HOPE HE FINDS WHAT HE WAS LOOKING FOR.
A SOUL LIKE OCTAVIAN'S WILL ALWAYS BE SEARCHING. HE WILL NEVER BE AT PEACE UNTIL HE LEARNS TO FIND MEANING IN HIS STRUGGLE.
OLIVER . . . MY MOM WAS ALIVE. I SAW HER.
EVERYTHING WE EVER WANTED IS ONE STEP THROUGH THAT PORTAL.
LOOK FOR YOURSELF!

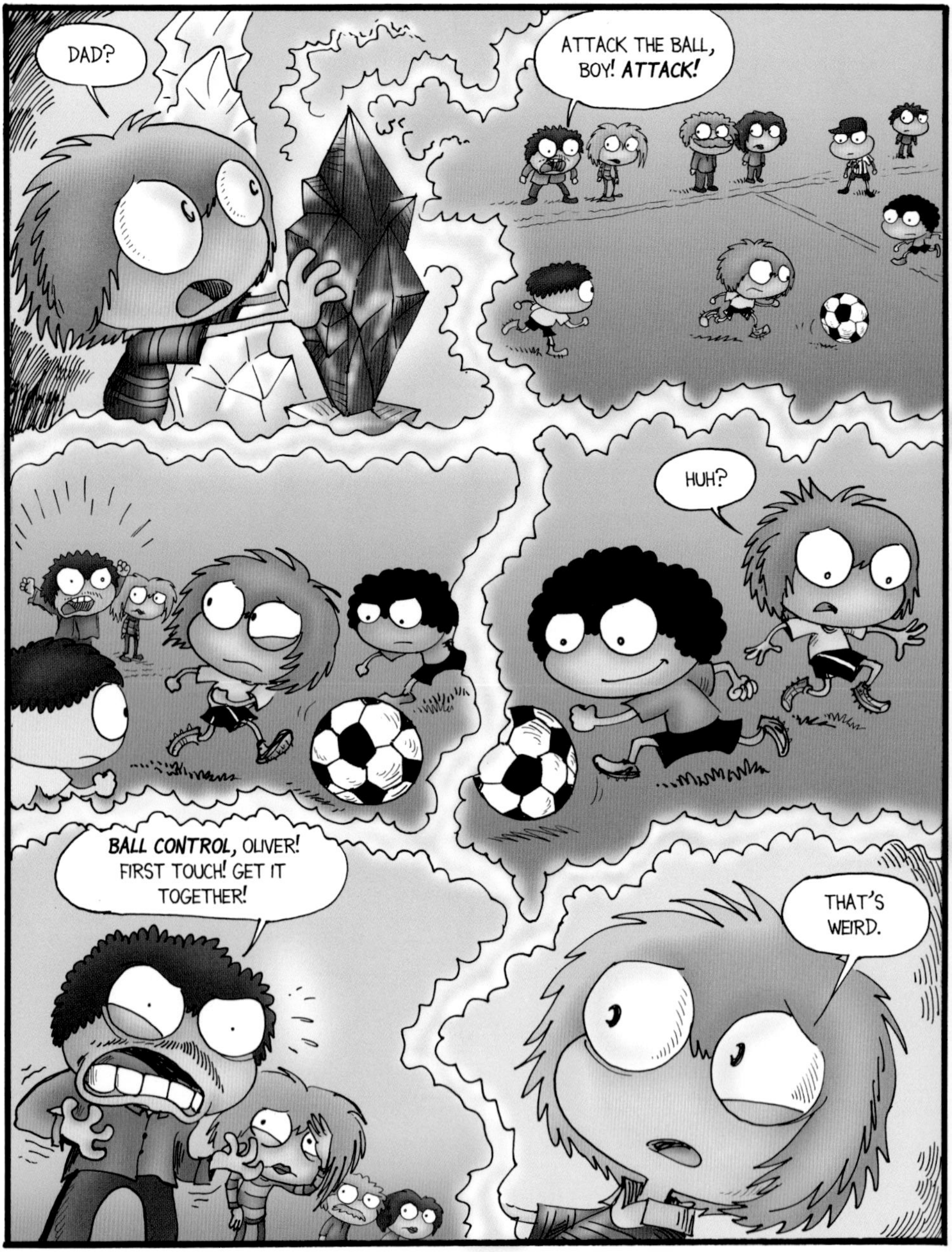
DAD?
ATTACK THE BALL, BOY! ATTACK!
HUH?
BALL CONTROL, OLIVER! FIRST TOUCH! GET IT TOGETHER!
THAT'S WEIRD.

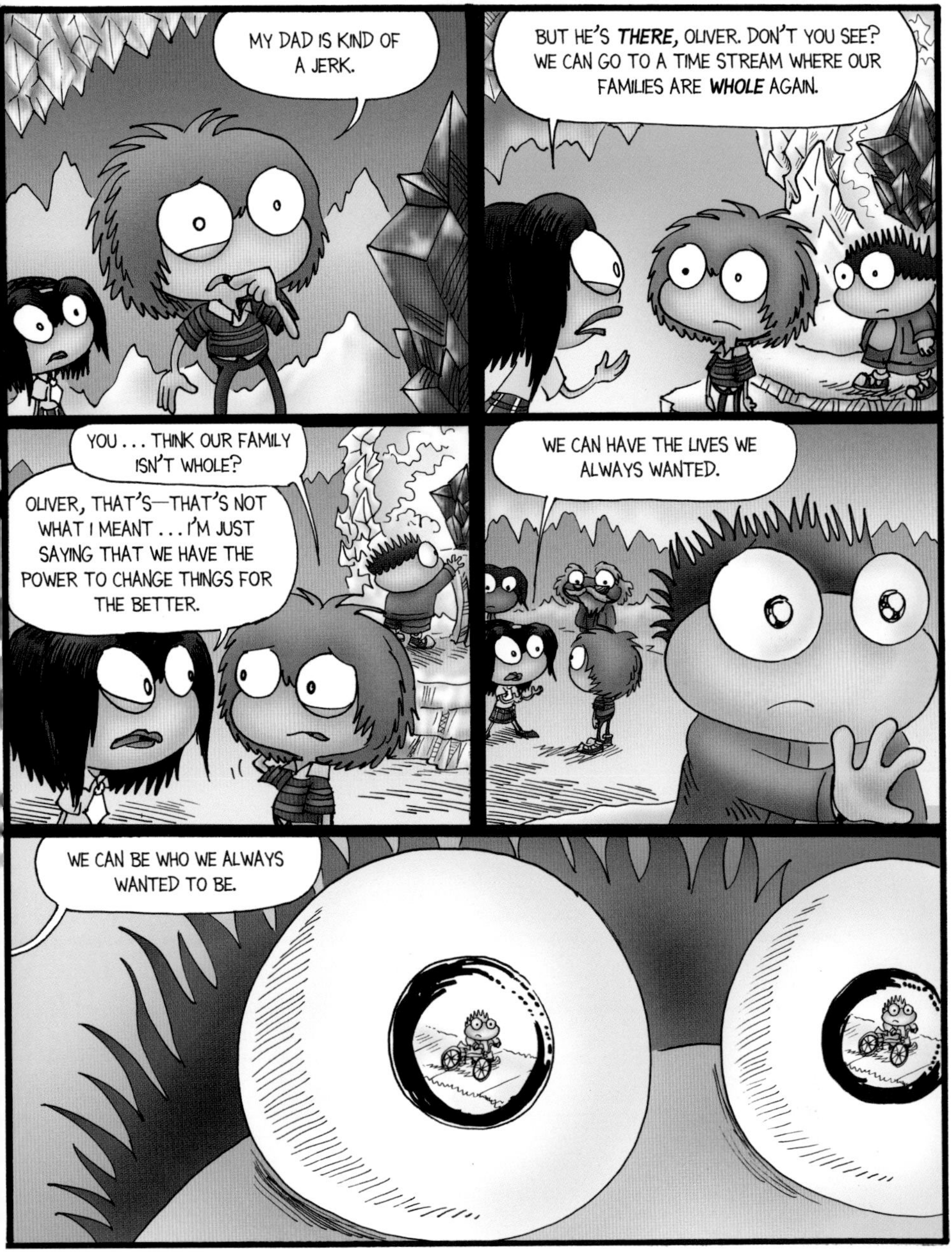
MY DAD IS KIND OF A JERK.
BUT HE'S THERE, OLIVER. DON'T YOU SEE? WE CAN GO TO A TIME STREAM WHERE OUR FAMILIES ARE WHOLE AGAIN.
YOU . . . THINK OUR FAMILY ISN'T WHOLE?
OLIVER, THAT'S—THAT'S NOT WHAT I MEANT . . . I'M JUST SAYING THAT WE HAVE THE POWER TO CHANGE THINGS FOR THE BETTER.
WE CAN HAVE THE LIVES WE ALWAYS WANTED.
WE CAN BE WHO WE ALWAYS WANTED TO BE.

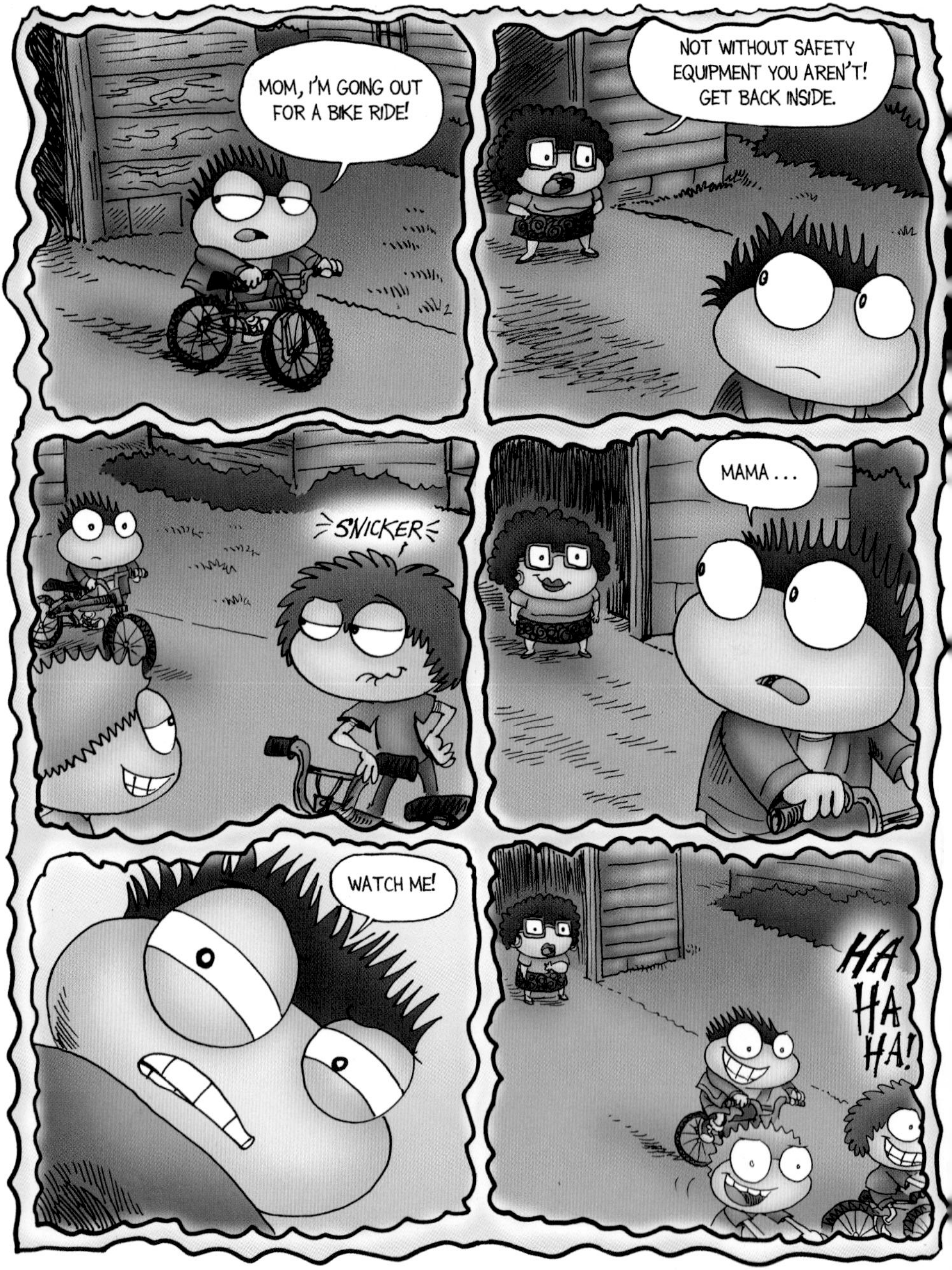
MOM, I'M GOING OUT FOR A BIKE RIDE!
NOT WITHOUT SAFETY EQUIPMENT YOU AREN'T! GET BACK INSIDE.
SNICKER
MAMA . . .
WATCH ME!
HA HA HA!

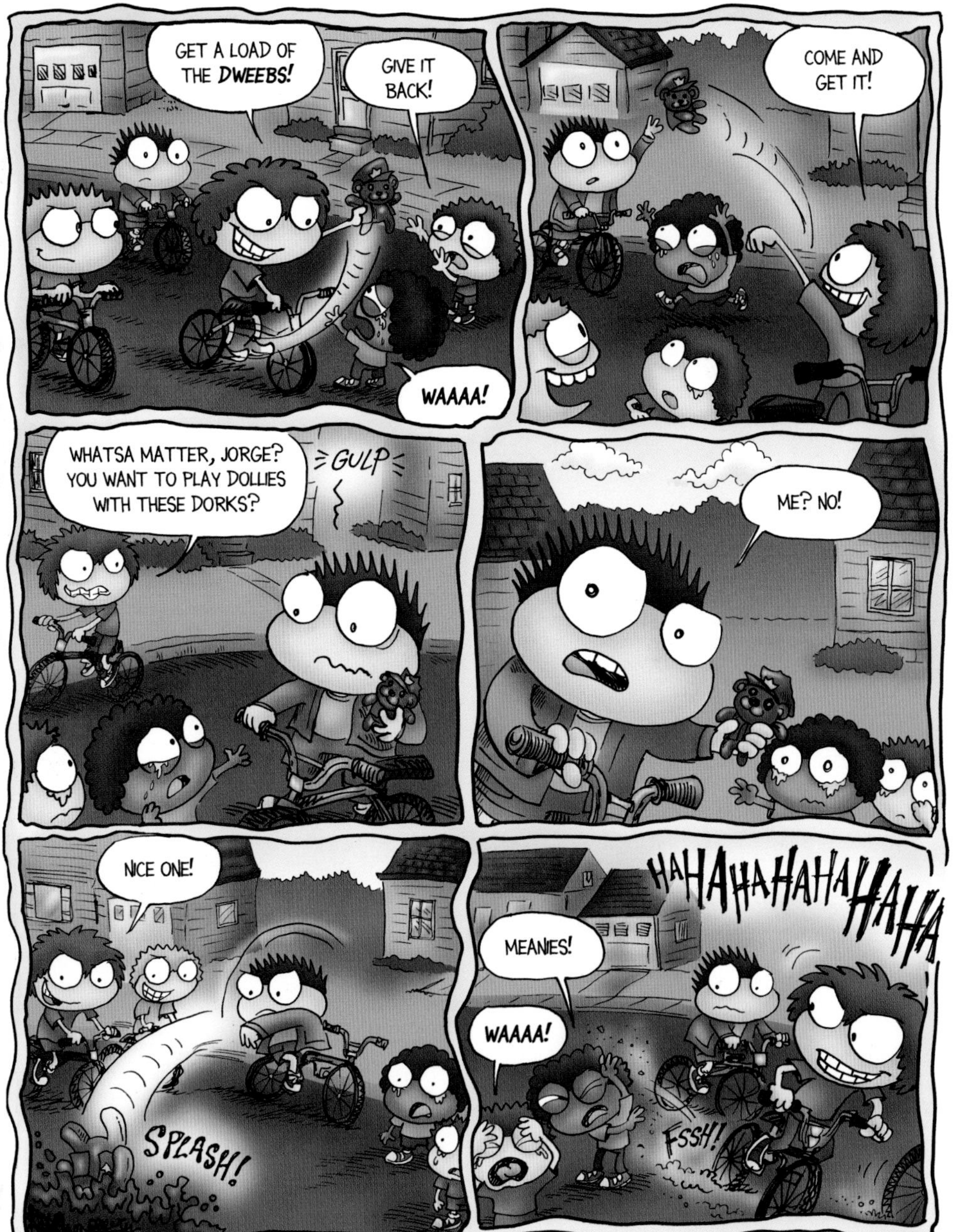
GET A LOAD OF THE DWEEBS!
GIVE IT BACK!
WAAAA!
COME AND GET IT!
WHATSA MATTER, JORGE? YOU WANT TO PLAY DOLLIES WITH THESE DORKS?
GULP
ME? NO!
NICE ONE!
SPLASH!
HAHAHAHAHAHAHAHA
MEANIES!
WAAAA!
FSSH!

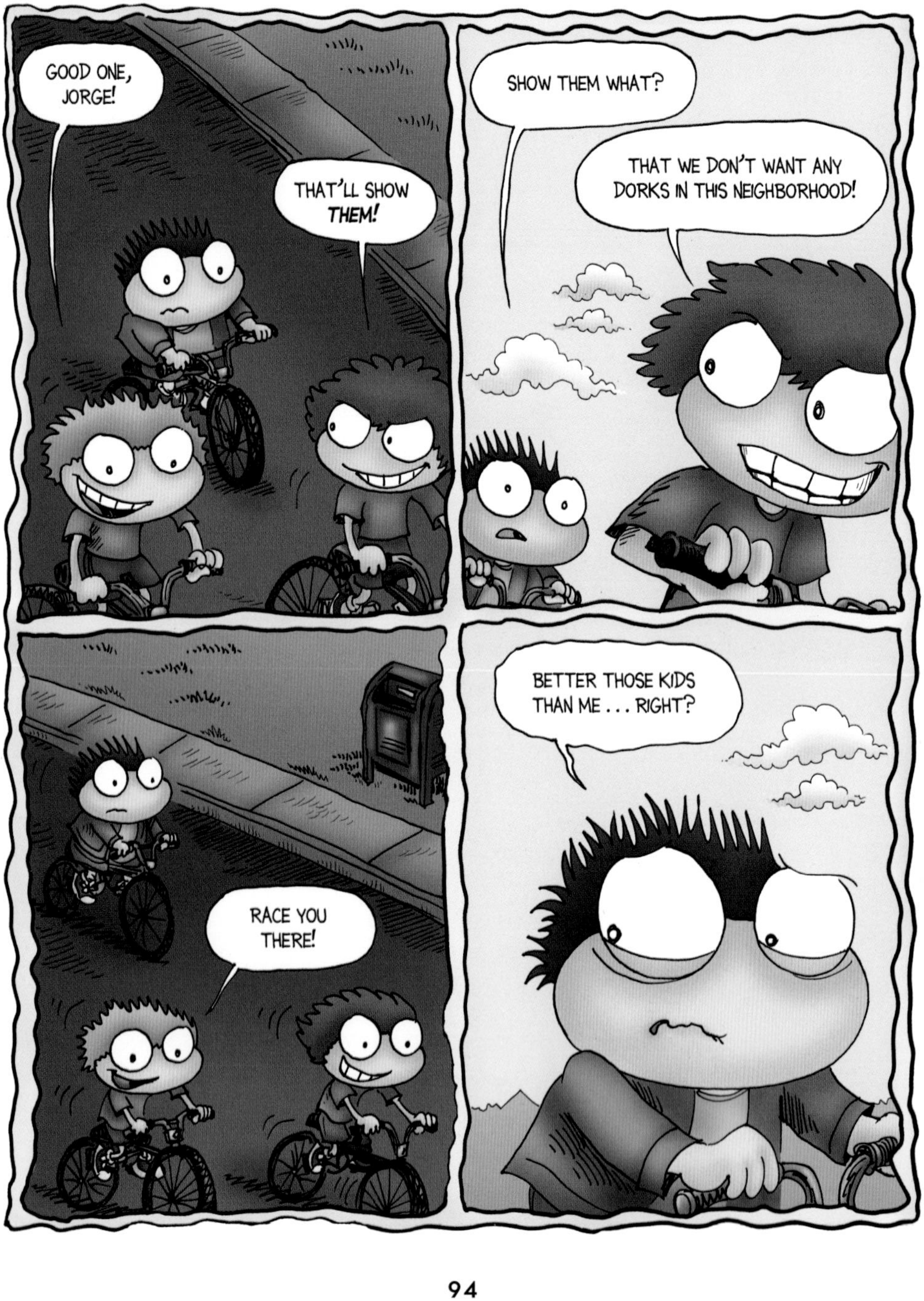
GOOD ONE, JORGE!
THAT'LL SHOW *THEM!*
SHOW THEM WHAT?
THAT WE DON'T WANT ANY DORKS IN THIS NEIGHBORHOOD!
RACE YOU THERE!
BETTER THOSE KIDS THAN ME . . . RIGHT?

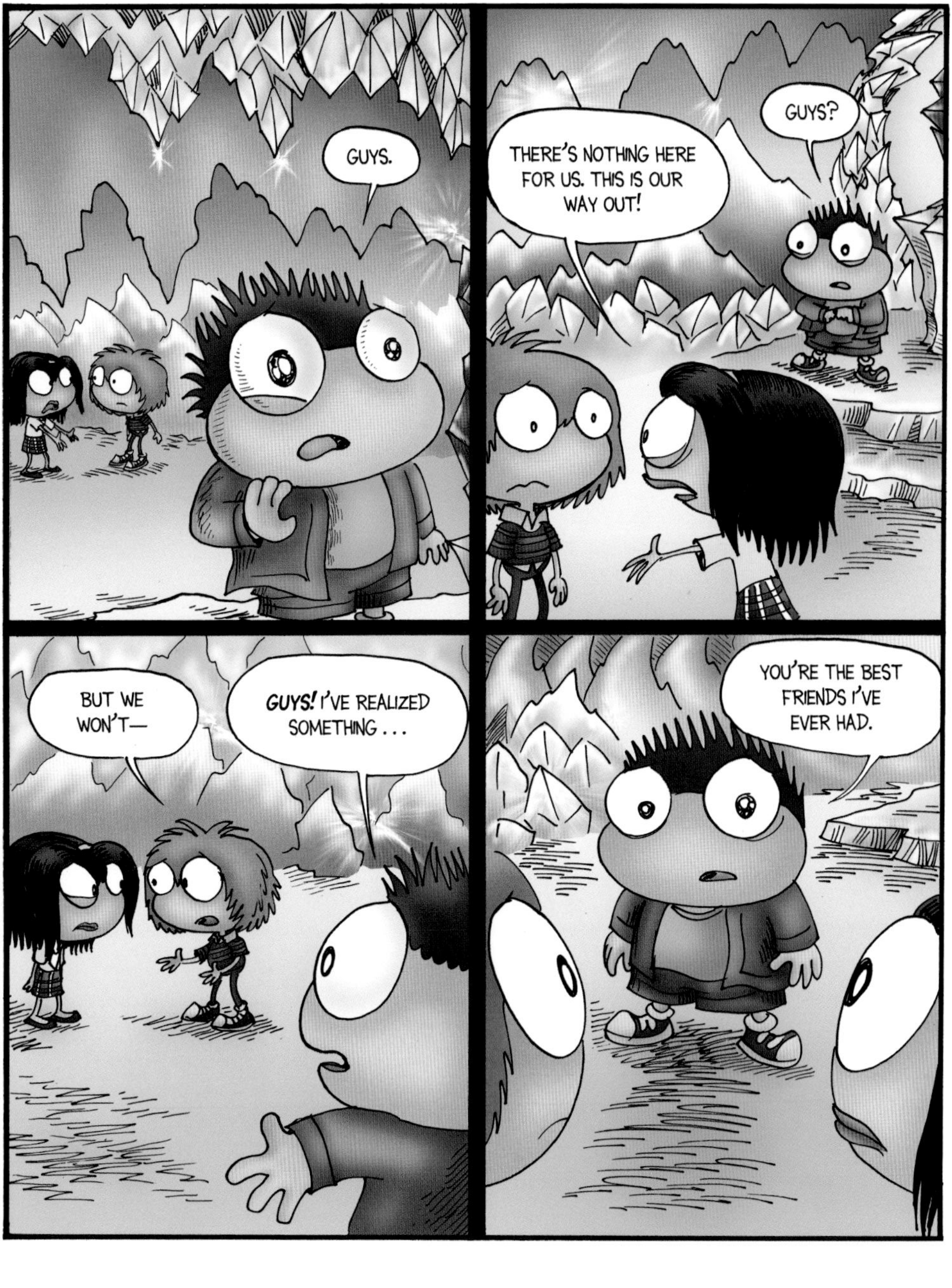

GUYS.
THERE'S NOTHING HERE FOR US. THIS IS OUR WAY OUT!
GUYS?
BUT WE WON'T—
GUYS! I'VE REALIZED SOMETHING . . .
YOU'RE THE BEST FRIENDS I'VE EVER HAD.

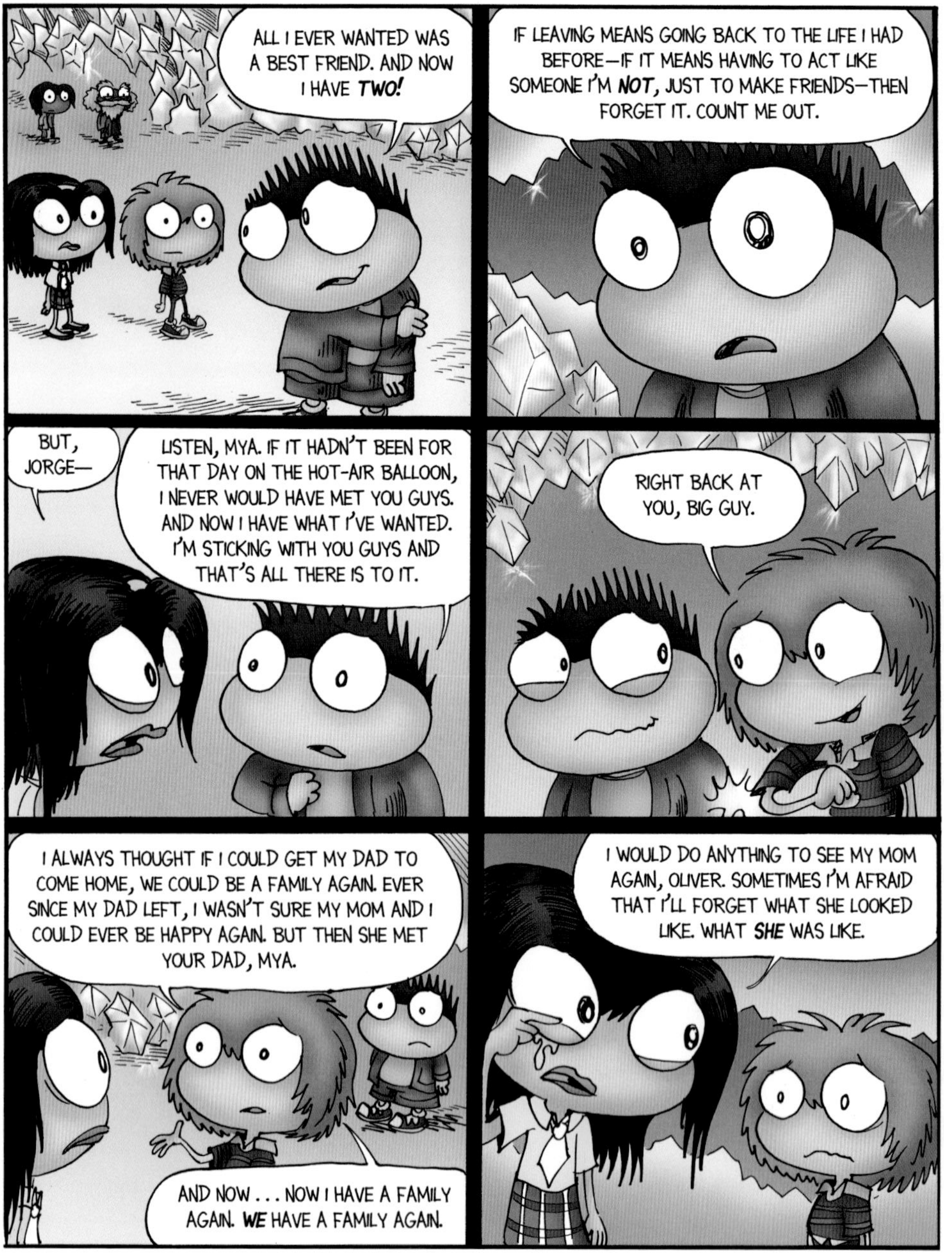
ALL I EVER WANTED WAS A BEST FRIEND. AND NOW I HAVE **TWO!**
IF LEAVING MEANS GOING BACK TO THE LIFE I HAD BEFORE—IF IT MEANS HAVING TO ACT LIKE SOMEONE I'M **NOT**, JUST TO MAKE FRIENDS—THEN FORGET IT. COUNT ME OUT.
BUT, JORGE—
LISTEN, MYA. IF IT HADN'T BEEN FOR THAT DAY ON THE HOT-AIR BALLOON, I NEVER WOULD HAVE MET YOU GUYS. AND NOW I HAVE WHAT I'VE WANTED. I'M STICKING WITH YOU GUYS AND THAT'S ALL THERE IS TO IT.
RIGHT BACK AT YOU, BIG GUY.
I ALWAYS THOUGHT IF I COULD GET MY DAD TO COME HOME, WE COULD BE A FAMILY AGAIN. EVER SINCE MY DAD LEFT, I WASN'T SURE MY MOM AND I COULD EVER BE HAPPY AGAIN. BUT THEN SHE MET YOUR DAD, MYA.
AND NOW . . . NOW I HAVE A FAMILY AGAIN. **WE** HAVE A FAMILY AGAIN.
I WOULD DO ANYTHING TO SEE MY MOM AGAIN, OLIVER. SOMETIMES I'M AFRAID THAT I'LL FORGET WHAT SHE LOOKED LIKE. WHAT **SHE** WAS LIKE.

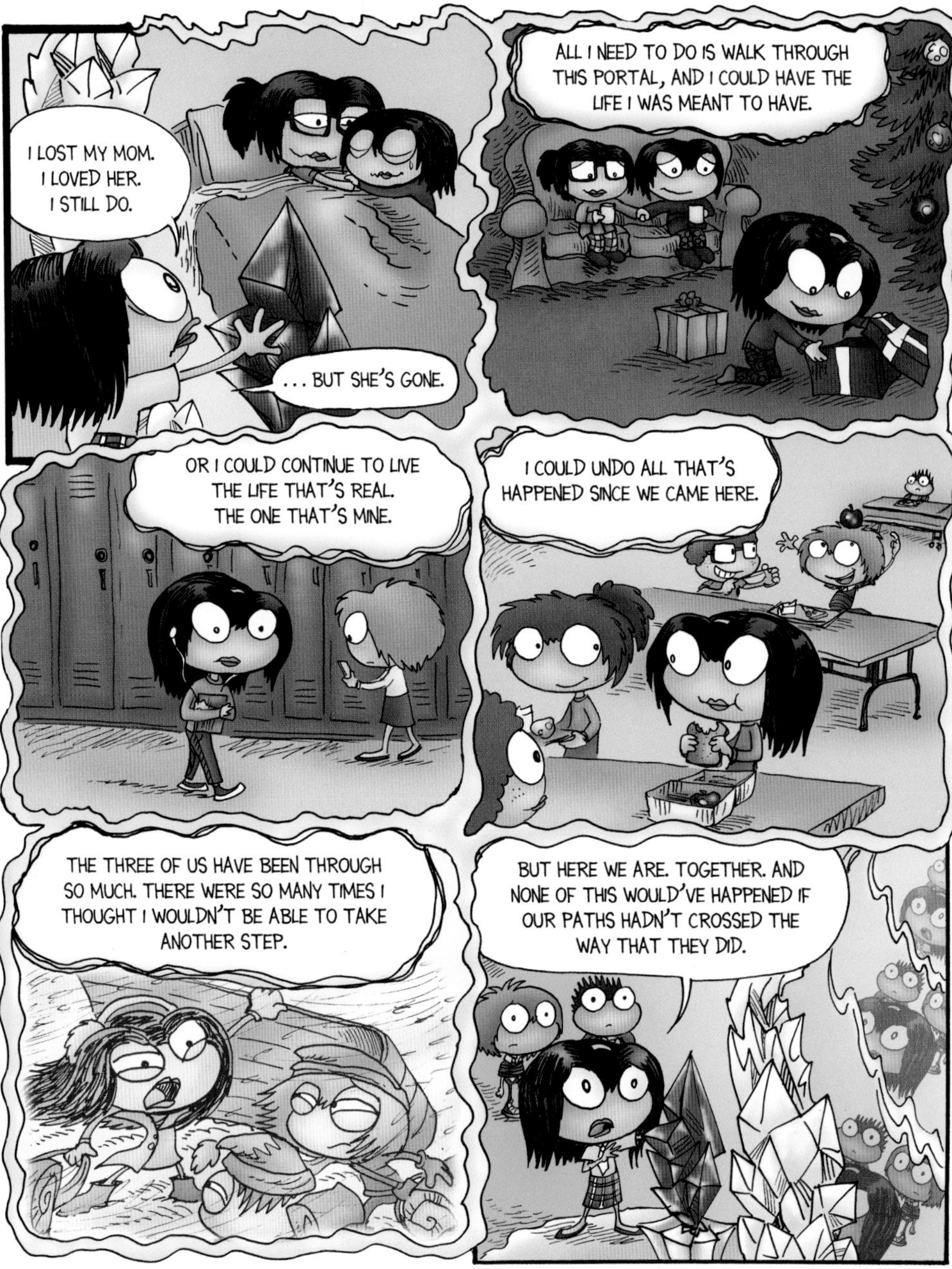
I LOST MY MOM. I LOVED HER. I STILL DO.
. . . BUT SHE'S GONE.
ALL I NEED TO DO IS WALK THROUGH THIS PORTAL, AND I COULD HAVE THE LIFE I WAS MEANT TO HAVE.
OR I COULD CONTINUE TO LIVE THE LIFE THAT'S REAL. THE ONE THAT'S MINE.
I COULD UNDO ALL THAT'S HAPPENED SINCE WE CAME HERE.
THE THREE OF US HAVE BEEN THROUGH SO MUCH. THERE WERE SO MANY TIMES I THOUGHT I WOULDN'T BE ABLE TO TAKE ANOTHER STEP.
BUT HERE WE ARE. TOGETHER. AND NONE OF THIS WOULD'VE HAPPENED IF OUR PATHS HADN'T CROSSED THE WAY THAT THEY DID.

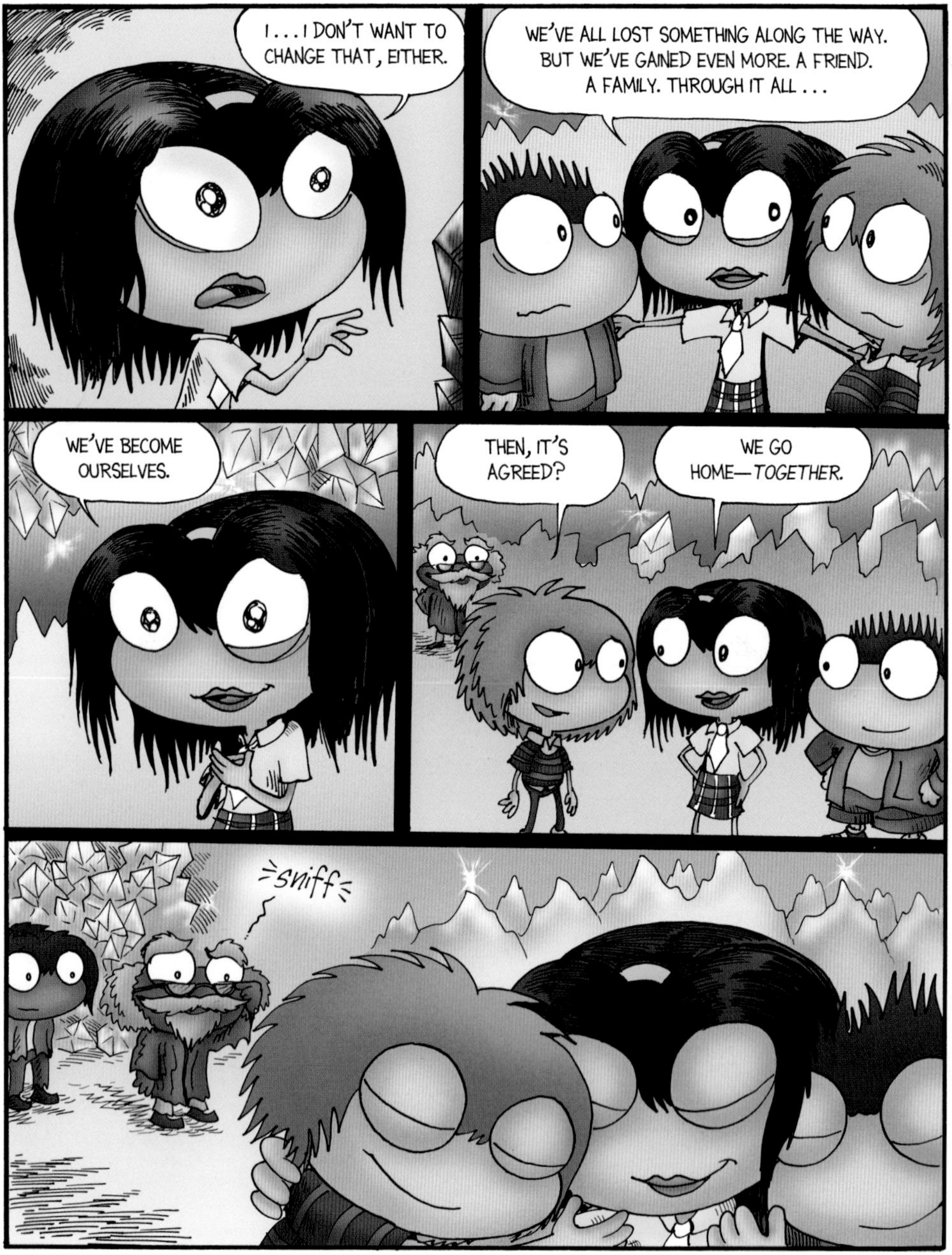
I . . . I DON'T WANT TO CHANGE THAT, EITHER.
WE'VE ALL LOST SOMETHING ALONG THE WAY. BUT WE'VE GAINED EVEN MORE. A FRIEND. A FAMILY. THROUGH IT ALL . . .
WE'VE BECOME OURSELVES.
THEN, IT'S AGREED?
WE GO HOME—*TOGETHER.*
sniff

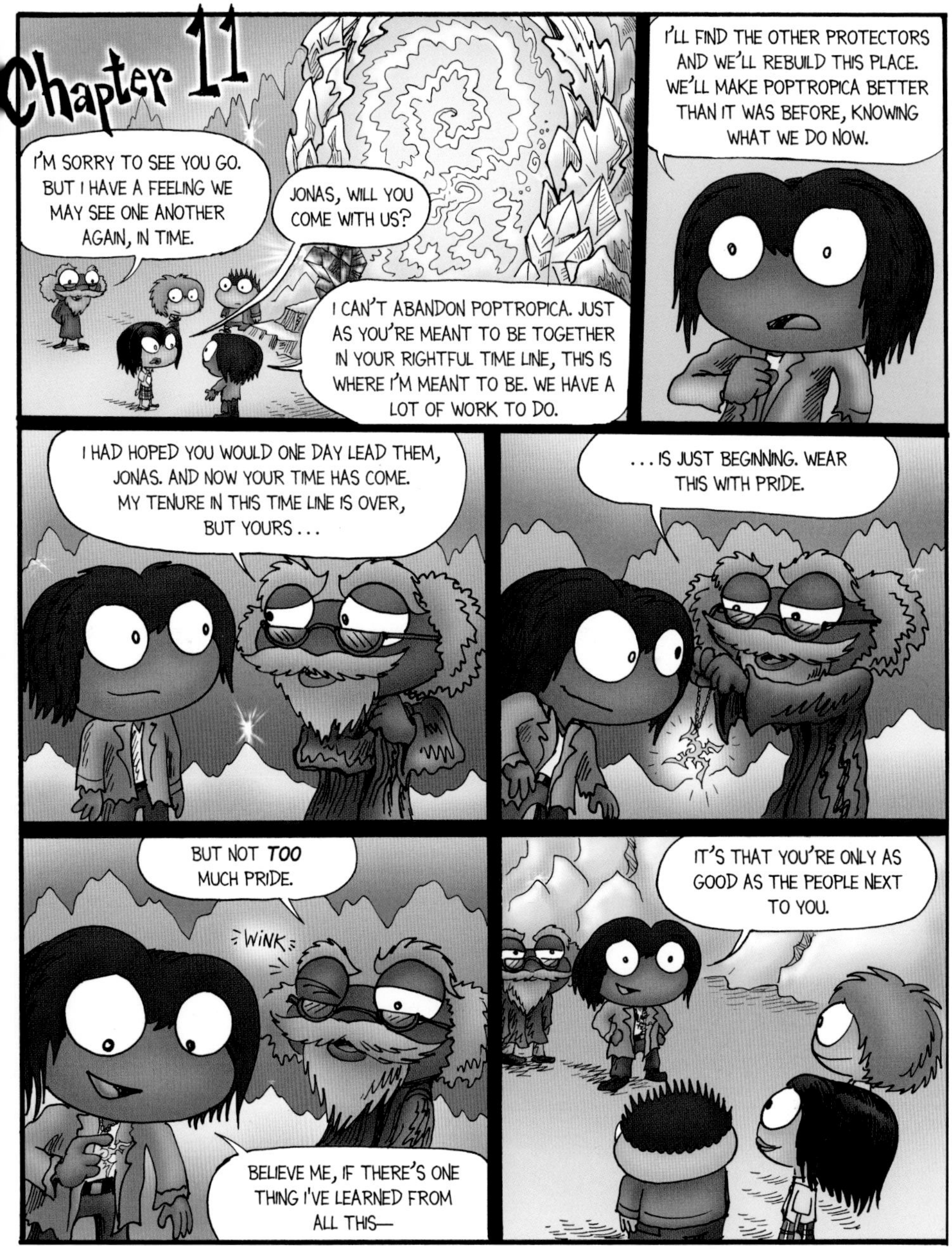
Chapter 11
I'M SORRY TO SEE YOU GO. BUT I HAVE A FEELING WE MAY SEE ONE ANOTHER AGAIN, IN TIME.
JONAS, WILL YOU COME WITH US?
I CAN'T ABANDON POPTROPICA. JUST AS YOU'RE MEANT TO BE TOGETHER IN YOUR RIGHTFUL TIME LINE, THIS IS WHERE I'M MEANT TO BE. WE HAVE A LOT OF WORK TO DO.
I'LL FIND THE OTHER PROTECTORS AND WE'LL REBUILD THIS PLACE. WE'LL MAKE POPTROPICA BETTER THAN IT WAS BEFORE, KNOWING WHAT WE DO NOW.
I HAD HOPED YOU WOULD ONE DAY LEAD THEM, JONAS. AND NOW YOUR TIME HAS COME. MY TENURE IN THIS TIME LINE IS OVER, BUT YOURS . . .
. . . IS JUST BEGINNING. WEAR THIS WITH PRIDE.
BUT NOT TOO MUCH PRIDE.
WINK
BELIEVE ME, IF THERE'S ONE THING I'VE LEARNED FROM ALL THIS—
IT'S THAT YOU'RE ONLY AS GOOD AS THE PEOPLE NEXT TO YOU.

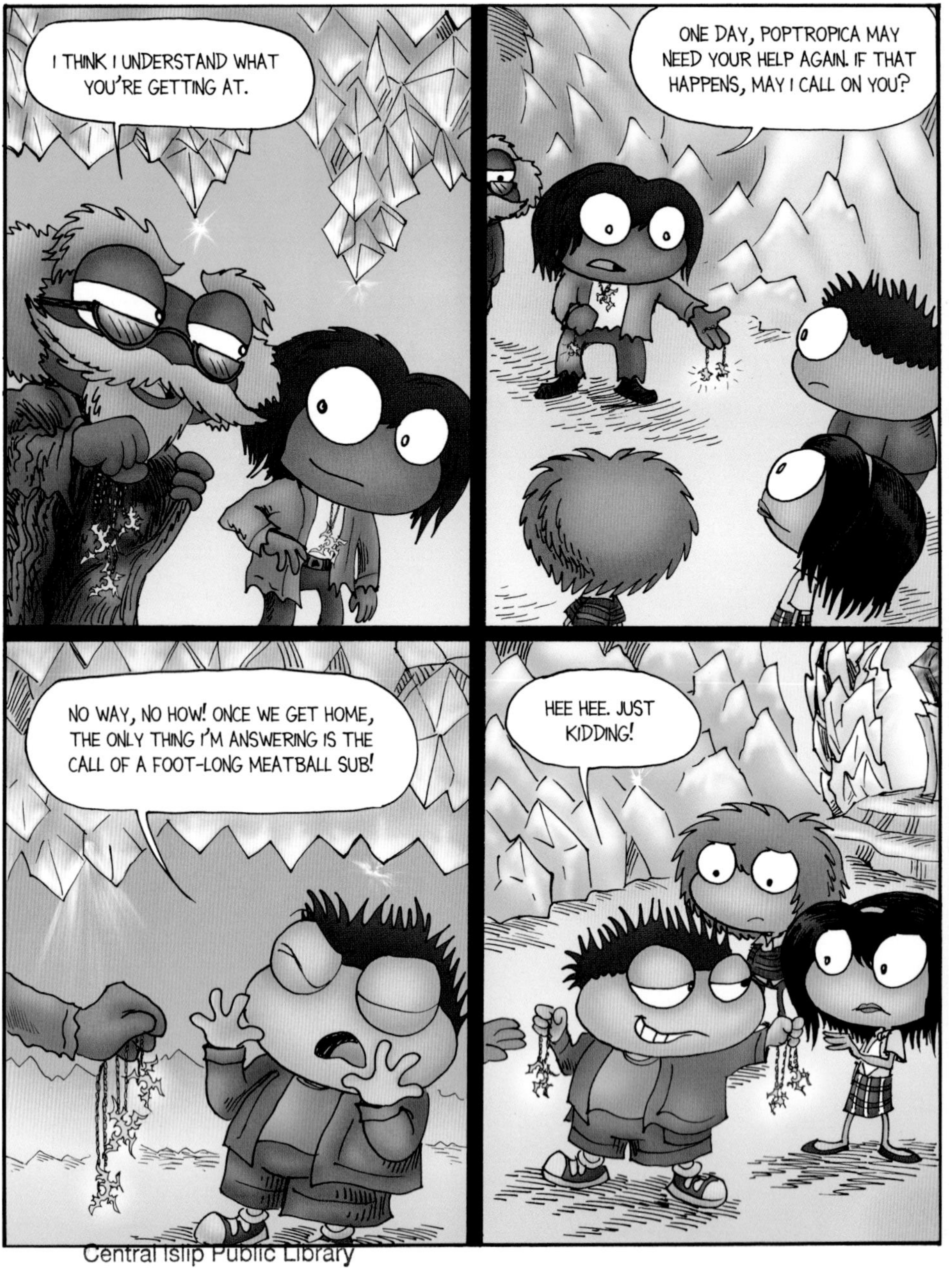
I THINK I UNDERSTAND WHAT YOU'RE GETTING AT.
ONE DAY, POPTROPICA MAY NEED YOUR HELP AGAIN. IF THAT HAPPENS, MAY I CALL ON YOU?
NO WAY, NO HOW! ONCE WE GET HOME, THE ONLY THING I'M ANSWERING IS THE CALL OF A FOOT-LONG MEATBALL SUB!
HEE HEE. JUST KIDDING!

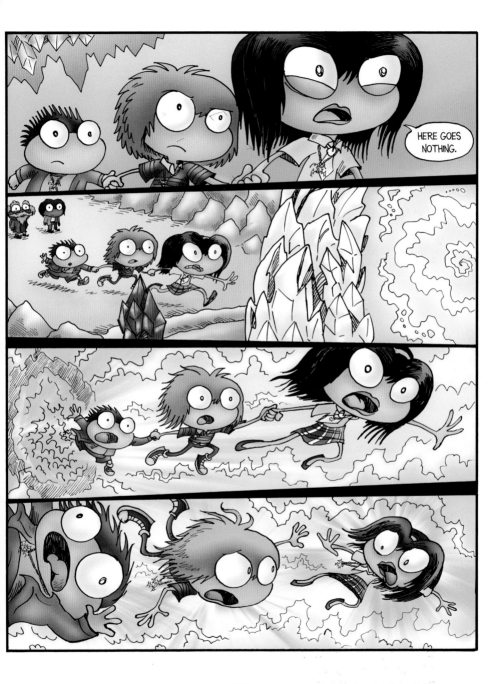

HERE GOES NOTHING.

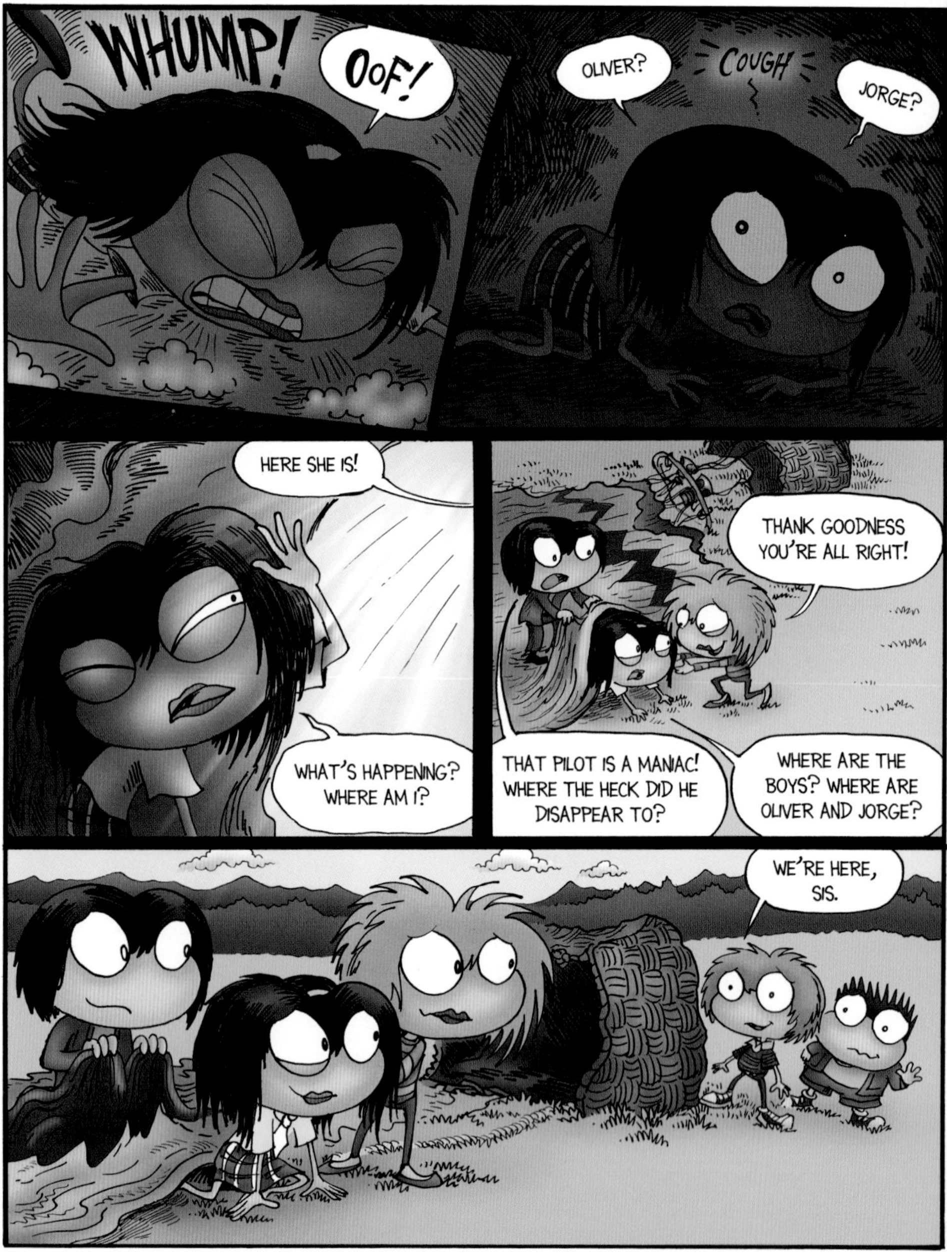
WHUMP!
OOF!
OLIVER?
COUGH
JORGE?
HERE SHE IS!
WHAT'S HAPPENING? WHERE AM I?
THANK GOODNESS YOU'RE ALL RIGHT!
THAT PILOT IS A MANIAC! WHERE THE HECK DID HE DISAPPEAR TO?
WHERE ARE THE BOYS? WHERE ARE OLIVER AND JORGE?
WE'RE HERE, SIS.

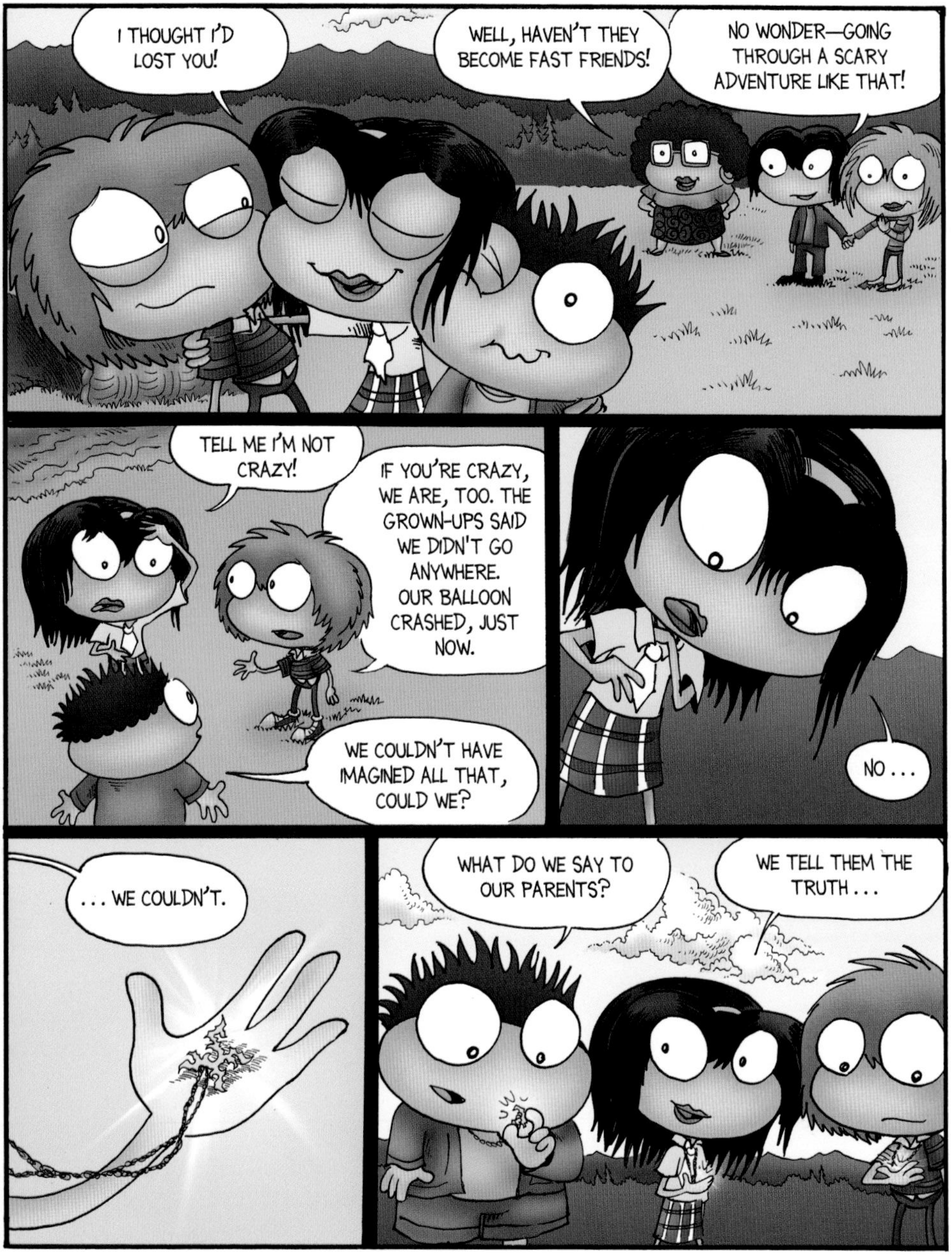
I THOUGHT I'D LOST YOU!
WELL, HAVEN'T THEY BECOME FAST FRIENDS!
NO WONDER—GOING THROUGH A SCARY ADVENTURE LIKE THAT!
TELL ME I'M NOT CRAZY!
IF YOU'RE CRAZY, WE ARE, TOO. THE GROWN-UPS SAID WE DIDN'T GO ANYWHERE. OUR BALLOON CRASHED, JUST NOW.
WE COULDN'T HAVE IMAGINED ALL THAT, COULD WE?
NO . . .
. . . WE COULDN'T.
WHAT DO WE SAY TO OUR PARENTS?
WE TELL THEM THE TRUTH . . .

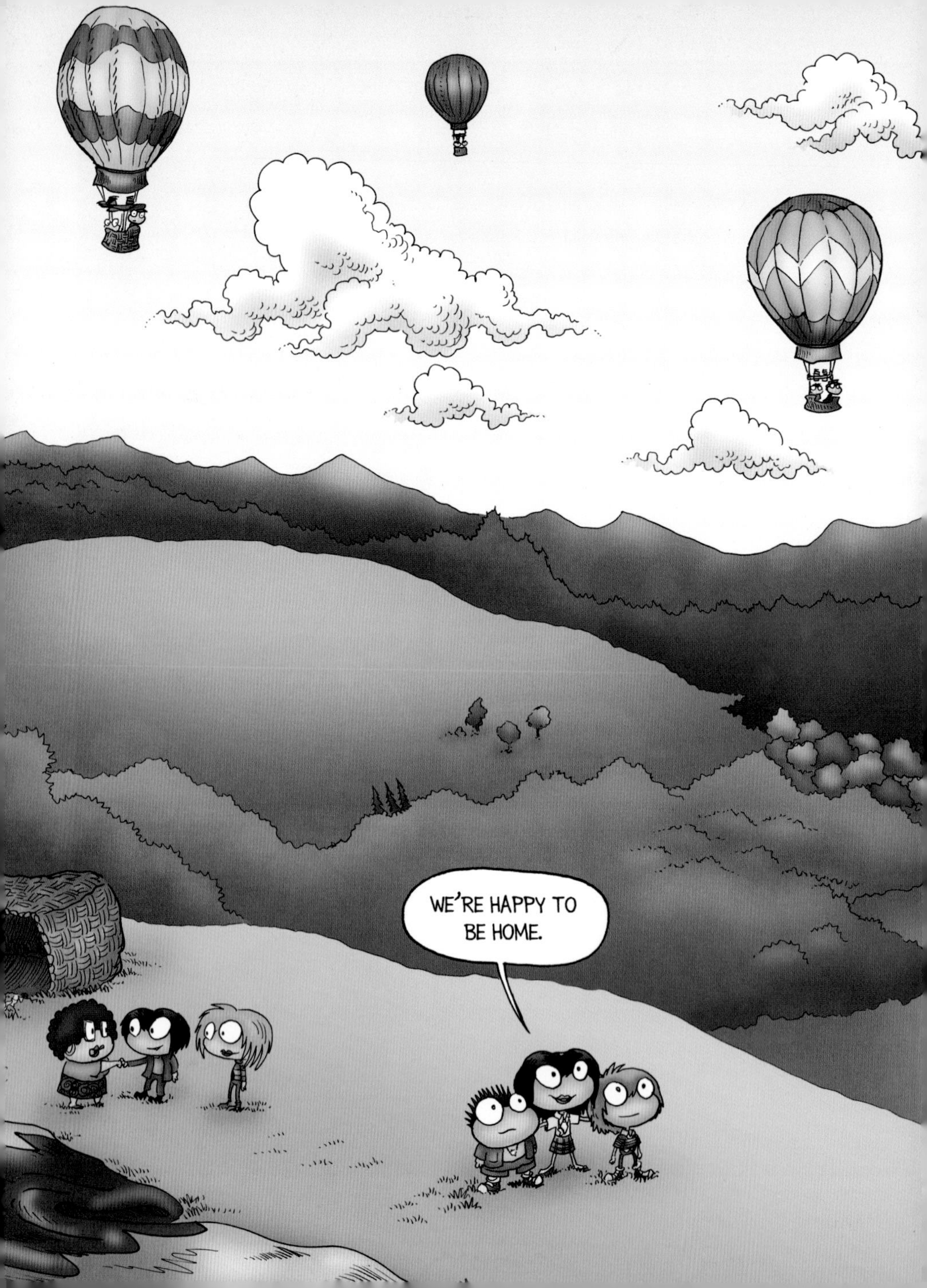
WE'RE HAPPY TO BE HOME.

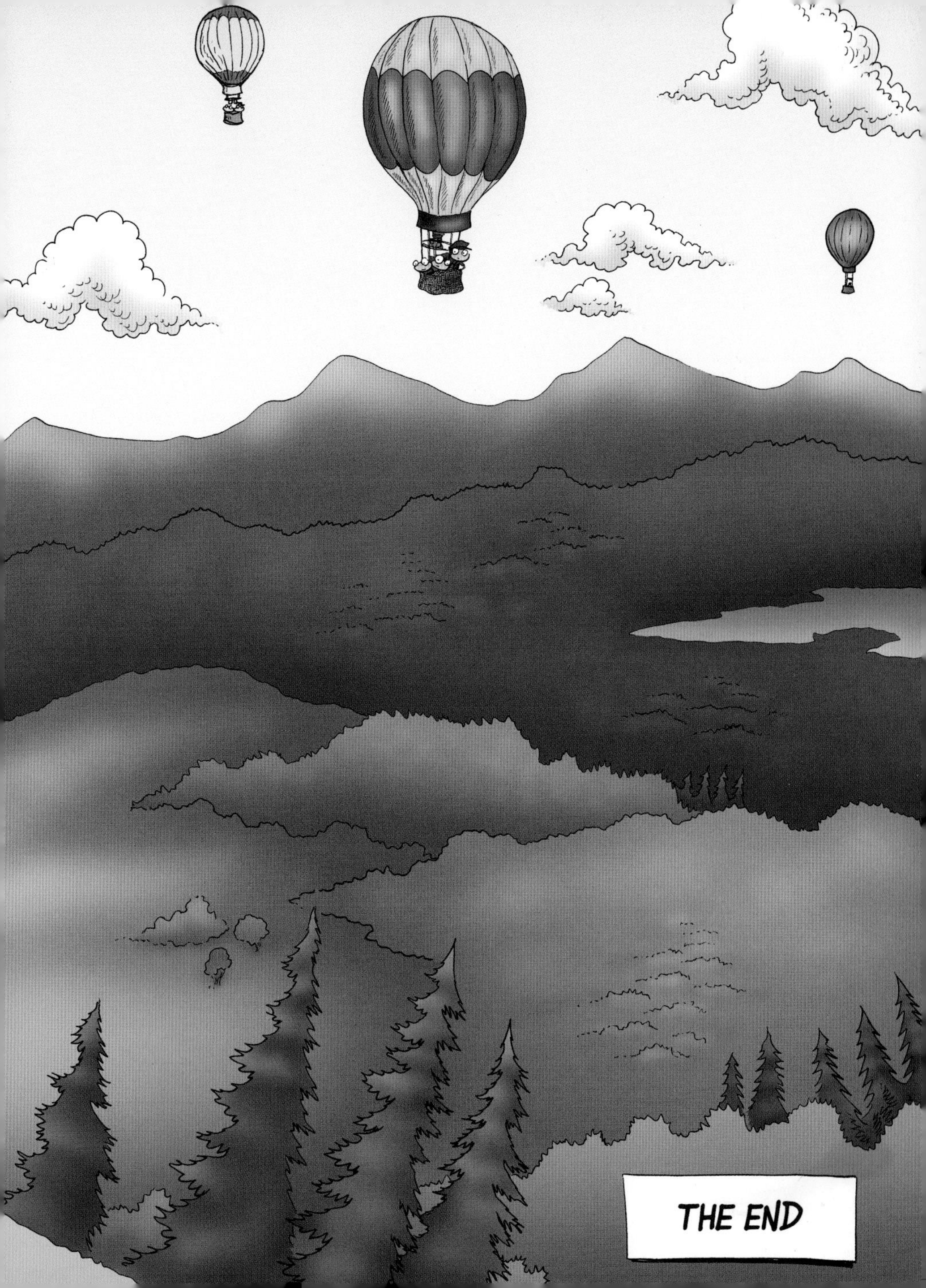
THE END

TO MOLLY, SEBASTIAN, AND LYRA
—MK

THANKS TO ORLANDO DOS REIS, CHAD W. BECKERMAN, CHARLES KOCHMAN,
SAMANTHA HOBACK, JASON WELLS, KYLE MOORE, NICOLE SCHAEFER, DAN
LAZAR, JEFF KINNEY, AND JESS BRALLIER FOR MAKING THIS BOOK HAPPEN.
—KM

ABOUT THE AUTHORS

POPTROPICA is best known for its website, in which stories are shared via gaming literac
Every month, millions of kids from around the world are entertained and informed by Poptropica's engagin
quests, including those featuring Diary of a Wimpy Kid, Big Nate, Peanuts, Galactic Hot Dogs, Timmy Failur
Magic Tree House, and Charlie and the Chocolate Factory.

MITCH KRPATA is a writer and producer for the Poptropica website, and the author of *The Lost Expeditic*
and *The Secret Society*. Krpata lives in Massachusetts with his family.

KORY MERRITT is the co-creator of Poptropica comics. He is the illustrator of *Mystery of the Map* an
the writer/artist of *The Dreadful Fate of Jonathan York*.

Cataloging-in-Publication Data has been applied for and
may be obtained from the Library of Congress.

ISBN 978-7-4197-2557-9

Copyright © 2017 Sandbox Networks, Inc. All rights reserved.

Font designed by David Ohman and Kory Merritt
Color by Nate Merritt
Book design by Chad W. Beckerman

Printed and bound in China
10 9 8 7 6 5 4 3 2 1

ABRAMS The Art of Books
West 18th Street, New York, NY 10011
abramsbooks.com